COLORADO STORM ONE

Seal THE Deal

HAILEY RODGER

Book cover design: Caravelle Creates

Editing: Gabby D'Aloia at GCD Editorial

ISBN: 978-1-06705-270-6

1st Edition 2025

Published by Atlas and Oak Digital LTD

TRIGGERS AND CONTENT WARNING

Triggers

This book features references to emotional abuse, including manipulation and controlling behavior by a former spouse. It also contains mentions of past infidelity, custody threats, depictions of anxiety and panic attacks, and a brief scene involving a lost child. If you are triggered by these situations, please consider whether this book is right for you.

Content Warning

This book contains profane language and explicit sexual content, including consensual breath play, elements of dominance, and praise.

For anyone who's ever felt like they're too much and not enough all at once,
or felt they need to prove they're worthy of love.
You aren't. You don't.
I'm glad you exist.

PROLOGUE

---·✦·---

I'M GLAD YOU EXIST

Jake - 12 Years Ago

"Shit," I yelp, stumbling over a rock.

The night is warm, the kind of summer heat that lingers long after the sun sets. Crickets chirp and the faint hum of laughter drifts up the hill from the camp below.

I glance over at Charlotte walking ahead of me, her laugh mingling with the others as we climb. The last of the setting sun casts a soft glow over her, reflecting a fiery halo around her auburn hair. I've been drawn to her all summer, and tonight's no different.

We've spent the last ten weeks as camp leaders, wrangling kids, organizing games, and pretending not to notice how close we're getting. With only a few hours left before we all go our separate ways, there's this tension in the air that I can't shake. A sense that time's slipping through my fingers.

At the top of the hill, someone cracks open some beers and passes them around as we all settle in. Our chatter is easy and light after so many weeks together, but my eyes keep drifting back to Charlie. The way she throws her head back when she laughs, the crinkle at the corners of her eyes. I know I'll be replaying this sight of her for a long time.

As the night wears on, one by one the others start heading back down to their cabins. I should go, too—my flight's early, and I've got to pack. But I don't move. Neither does she.

Eventually it's just the two of us, lying side by side on the grass, staring up at the stars. The sky stretches above us, a deep, endless ceiling of glowing pinpricks. It's quietly intimate now. Like the whole world's shrunk down to just us.

"You ever wonder what it'd be like to live somewhere with no light pollution?" Charlie's voice breaks the silence. "Where the stars are so bright, you can see every constellation without trying?"

I turn my head, catching the soft outline of her profile bathed in moonlight. She's staring up at the sky with that faraway look she gets sometimes, the one that makes me wonder what she's thinking.

"Yeah," I admit. "The stars make everything else feel smaller... less important."

She nods, and we lapse into silence again, the night wrapping around us. After a while, the conversation shifts, becoming more personal.

She talks about her parents: still together, still in love in that easy, uncomplicated way I've never known. I tell her about my mom, who struggles to get out of bed most days, and my dad, who cares more about his job than me.

"It's like he wishes I didn't exist." The words slip out before I can stop them. I've never said that out loud to anyone before, but with Charlie it feels different. Safe, somehow, like she can handle them without shrinking away.

She turns to me, her eyes soft. "Jake, that's not your fault."

I shrug, looking away. "Maybe. But it doesn't change anything." My voice comes out harsher than I intend, like I'm still trying to swallow down the feeling of being invisible, of wishing just once he'd look at me like I mattered.

She's quiet for a moment, turning back to stare at the stars. Then, as if there's no doubt in her mind, she says, "Well, I'm glad you exist."

The words are simple. Ordinary. But they wash over me, slipping into all the places that usually feel dark and hollow. *She's glad I exist.* I can't remember anyone ever saying that to me, and the weight of it is more than I know what to do with. I'm caught somewhere between gratitude and disbelief, wondering how she makes something so simple feel like the most profound thing I've ever heard.

Warmth slowly spreads through my chest, a quiet burn I'm afraid will go out if I move. For once, the bitterness fades, leaving something softer in its place.

I glance at her, taking in the way she looks up at the stars, her expression calm like giving me this moment doesn't cost her anything. She doesn't pity me. She never has. She just gets it—sees me in a way that feels honest, notices the parts I keep locked up without making it feel heavy.

We fall back into silence, but her words linger, shifting something inside me I didn't know could move. All summer, I've watched her. Admired the quiet confidence she carries, the way she believes in people like doubt doesn't exist.

"You ever think about what's next?" I break the silence because I want to hear her thoughts. Every dream, every fear.

She turns back to me, her eyes bright even in the dark. "All the time. It's kind of terrifying, isn't it? Leaving all this behind. Being an adult, whatever that means."

"Yeah, it is," I admit, feeling the twist in my gut. The draft is coming soon. "What do you wanna do?"

She smiles. A small, wistful thing. "I want to create. Doesn't matter what—art, food, stories. I just want to make things that make people *feel* something."

I nod, understanding more than she realizes. "You will. You're gonna do great things, Charlie."

Her eyes crinkle, and she hesitates only for a moment before turning on her side to extend her pinky finger. A shy smile tugs at her lips. "Only if you promise to do the same."

"A pinky promise?"

Green eyes sparkle at me as her grin widens. "Yeah. But it's not just any pinky promise. It's special. You have to do it right."

I chuckle. "Oh yeah? What makes it special?"

"Here." She scoots closer and lifts my hand. "First, you hook pinkies like this," she says, her teacher-like tone making me smile. "Then you press your thumbs together, like this."

I follow her lead, our thumbs now touching, and she leans in closer. "Now, to seal the deal, you lean in and kiss your thumb."

I'm still grinning as I lean in, our faces close enough that I can feel her breath, see the light in her eyes. "Like this?"

She nods, her expression serious but playful. I lean in further and kiss my thumb, our hands still linked together.

"Promise," I say softly.

Her eyes meet mine, and my pulse thunders. "Promise," she whispers.

For a moment, it's just us. Lying under the stars, sealing a promise that feels bigger than words. I consider closing the distance between us, but I stop myself. Something about this moment feels perfect as it is. No need to complicate it.

Instead, I squeeze her hand gently before letting go, feeling the weight of our promise settle between us.

With her, everything feels balanced, like the world is exactly as it should be. But as the night wears on, the reality of our separate lives looms closer.

In a few hours, I'll be on a plane, heading back to an NHL draft that could change everything. And she'll go back to New Zealand. The thought punches me in the gut, a hollowness opening inside me I'm not ready to face. I don't want this night to end. I don't want to say goodbye.

I sneak another glance at her, the urge to kiss her nearly overwhelming. I've wanted to kiss her all summer. It'd be so easy to just lean in...

But I hold back. Kissing her would only make leaving harder, and I can't afford to get attached—not when we're about to be a world apart. Still, the pull is there, creating a constant ache in my chest.

I swallow the impulse and force myself to smile. "You know, if you ever come back to the States, look me up."

She smiles, but there's a sadness in it. "Same goes for you with New Zealand."

"Deal," I say, even though we both know the chances are slim.

We stay there, talking about everything and nothing until dawn breaks the horizon. I can't remember ever feeling this connected to someone, or this peaceful. But too soon, the moment passes and it's time to go.

As we walk back down the hill, I keep sneaking glances at her, memorizing every detail. The color of her hair and how it curls at the ends, the curve of her neck, the way she smiles. This is probably the last time I'll see her, and the thought leaves a bitter taste in my mouth.

At the edge of the camp, we stop. She faces me, her expression unreadable. Our cabins are in different directions, and we're on separate buses first thing.

"Take care of yourself, okay?"

"You too."

Before I can talk myself out of it, I lean in and press a quick kiss to her cheek. It's not what I want, but it's all I can give her. When I pull back, she smiles softly, and it takes everything in me not to pull her back again.

"Bye, Jake."

"See ya, Charlie."

She turns and walks away, and I stand there watching her go. My heart's in my throat, a goodbye I'm not ready for lodged there, too.

CHAPTER ONE

REASSESS THIS, YOU PRICK

––––––––––––––––––––✦––––––––––––––––––––

Charlie - Present Day

The plane hits a pocket of turbulence, jolting me awake from a half sleep. I blink groggily, trying to orient myself, the steady hum of the engines a reminder we're still in the air.

I glance at the kids, still fast asleep. Meadow's face is smushed against her unicorn pillow, and Noah is sprawled out, mouth slightly open. Their peacefulness makes me smile—so blissfully unaware of the weight of this moment. I envy that innocence, but mostly feel lucky they can rest.

We're really doing this. We're really here.

As the plane starts its descent, I can see unfamiliar terrain appearing out the window. A pang of anxiety creeps in, questioning if I've made the right choice. Uprooting the kids, moving to a country where we know practically no one, leaving behind the safety net of family and friends. It's terrifying.

But staying would have been terrifying, too. Staying meant living with constant reminders of a life I'd already left behind, of a marriage that had slowly eroded my confidence.

I think back to that final conversation with my ex-husband, Alex. The way his smirk barely masked his contempt. He'd scoffed, looking at me like I was a child with a fleeting whim. "Go ahead, Lottie. If you think you can make it work, fine. But when you can't..." He paused, letting the words linger, his tone dripping with disdain. "You bring the kids back, and we reassess."

Reassess. As if our lives were just another asset to measure and manage. He'd always made me feel inadequate, like I'd crumble without him. He never believed I could do this on my own. Never thought I was capable of making a life without him.

And that's exactly why I had to leave. To prove to myself that I can. That I don't need his approval or permission to build a life worth living.

But the doubts linger, gnawing at my resolve. Doubts I know were cultivated by years of Alex's voice, the way he'd chip away at my confidence, convincing me I was barely capable of standing on my own.

What if he's right? What if I fail? What if I can't give Noah and Meadow the life they deserve here?

I close my eyes and try to dispel the what-ifs. It's too late for second-guessing. We're in this, and I have to make it work. For all of us.

As the plane begins its final approach, my thoughts drift to the job that brought us here. It still feels surreal, being headhunted by one of the most prestigious marketing agencies in Denver: *Pulse Creative.*

I wasn't looking for a new job. I wasn't looking for anything, really. I was just trying to survive, to keep my head above water in the wake of my crumbling marriage. And then this opportunity landed in my lap. It felt like the universe was nudging me forward to a new life, where I could finally leave behind the disappointment and doubt, and build something meaningful.

I'm damn good at what I do. Marketing feels like second nature—the creativity, the strategy, the thrill of piecing together a campaign that just clicks. But sometimes I wonder if it's all a bit hollow, to create desire from thin air and fuel endless consumerism.

Still, there are days when it feels powerful, like I'm creating something that matters, something that can make people *feel*. Those are the days I live for: flexing my creative muscles, working with amazing teams, sitting in rooms where big decisions are made. Being part of something bigger. That's what keeps me going.

Pulse Creative isn't an entirely new world, either. It's the sister company to the agency I worked for in New Zealand. I met Zoe, who is based here in Denver, through our joint projects and business trips between the two agencies.

Our professional relationship quickly became a friendship, and when she found out about my situation, she pushed for me to come here. She vouched for me, sang my praises to the higher-ups, made the transition seamless. Zoe's been in my corner through it all.

The plane touches down with a slight jolt, pulling me out of my thoughts. Meadow stirs, blinking awake and rubbing her eyes, while Noah yawns and stretches in his seat.

"Are we here, Mama?" Meadow mumbles, her voice thick with sleep.

"We're here, honey bee." I smooth her hair and kiss the top of her head. "Welcome to Denver."

As we make our way off the plane, the reality of our new life sinks in. The airport is a bustling hive of activity, a sharp contrast to the quieter life we left behind.

Meadow clings to me with her small arms wrapped tightly around my neck, while Noah holds my hand, his eyes wide with wonder. "Wow, it's huge here!" he exclaims. "Where's the snow?"

"Soon, buddy," I chuckle. "We'll see plenty of snow soon."

After a grueling stretch through immigration and security with two tired kids in tow, we finally reach the arrivals hall, where I quickly spot a familiar figure waving animatedly from across the room.

Zoe.

It's one thing to have a friendly face greet you in a new city; it's another when that person has been your biggest cheerleader through thick and thin.

My heart lifts at the sight of her, the first real wave of relief I've felt since we left New Zealand. She's holding up a sign that reads, 'WELCOME TO DENVER, KIWI & KIDDOS!' complete with doodles of planes and mountains. It's so effortlessly Zoe.

"There she is!" Zoe's grin stretches wide as she rushes over, bouncing with excitement.

She's tall, with silky dark hair cascading down her back and a natural tan that is testament to both her Arapaho heritage and love for the outdoors. Athletic and effortlessly beautiful, Zoe's the type who could hike a mountain one day and run a marathon the next without breaking a sweat. She's stunning. Even in the chaos of the airport, she turns heads.

Emotion rushes through me as she pulls me into a quick hug, careful not to squish Meadow, who's still wrapped around me like a koala.

"God, they're even cuter in person!" Zoe coos, running a perfectly manicured hand through Meadow's strawberry-blonde hair. "And who might you be, little miss?

Meadow blinks at her, half-shy, half-intrigued, slowly recognizing Zoe from all the video calls we've shared. "I'm Meadow," she says, clutching me tighter.

"Well, it's lovely to meet you in person, Meadow. And you must be Noah!" Zoe holds out her hand for a high-five, which Noah eagerly returns. "You guys ready to see your new home?"

Their excitement gives me the calm I've been searching for, the reassurance I need. This is going to work. It has to.

Ever the planner, Zoe has thought of everything. "The car's just outside, and I stocked your fridge with basics, so you don't have to worry about anything tonight. Just relax, settle in, and breathe."

I feel a rush of gratitude. Zoe has been a lifesaver, not just with the move but in the months leading up to it. We've known each other for a while through work, but our relationship deepened when she started helping me prepare for this relocation.

I'd confided in her during those late-night business trips, fueled by too much wine and the safety of being far from home. She knows more about my life than most people, and hates Alex with a fiery passion.

"You're a godsend, Zoe. I don't know how I would've done this without you." Emotion wells up, and I blink it back.

"Hey, that's what friends are for." She gives my arm a gentle squeeze then grabs two of our suitcases. "And don't worry, Denver's amazing. We'll make sure you fall in love with it, babe."

As we step outside, the crisp air hits us. It's the start of fall here—a stark contrast to the New Zealand spring we left behind. The mountains rise silently in the distance, their presence as steady as ever.

I take a deep breath, letting the newness of it all sink in, though I'd be lying if I said there wasn't something hauntingly familiar about it, too. The last time I was in Colorado was a lifetime ago. Late nights under the stars, a boy with hazel eyes, and a summer that still lingers in the corners of my mind. But I shake it off. There's no time for old memories now, not when we're here to make new ones.

This is it. Our new beginning.

***

Jake

The sound of skates slicing through ice has always been my favorite kind of music. The cold air, the adrenaline—it's everything. Out here, it's just me and the game, like it's always been.

Coach is running us through some new drills, mixing things up to keep us sharp. We're a couple of weeks into the pre-season, and the pressure is already mounting.

Even though I've been at this for over a decade, every practice counts. Every moment on the ice is a chance to prove I'm still the guy they can count on, even with younger, hungrier rookies vying for the same spotlight. At 31, I'm technically one of the veterans setting the example. Funny how things change.

Back when I was first drafted, it was all about proving myself, showing everyone that I belonged here. Now it's about keeping up, staying sharp, making sure I'm still the guy they can count on in the clutch moments.

But as much as I hate to admit it, I've started thinking more about what comes next. Hockey has been my life for as long as I can remember, but I know it won't last forever. I've seen guys struggle with the transition, not knowing who they are without the game. And I've always told myself that when the time comes, I'll be ready. That I won't be one of those guys clinging to the last threads of their career.

But what if I am? What if there's nothing else I want as much as this?

The thought feels like a bruise that won't heal, one I keep pressing on, even when I try to ignore it.

That's not a problem for today, though. Today is about the upcoming home opener, about keeping my focus, and about pushing for a shot at the playoffs.

As practice winds down, I catch sight of Zoe Carlson by the boards with her camera out, capturing footage for the team's social media. She's been working with the Colorado Storm for years now, contracted through her marketing agency.

With each season, she's become a solid friend—the kind who knows when to dish out tough advice or throw in a quick-witted comment to break the tension. She's sharp, clever, and never lets anyone take themselves too seriously, least of all me.

"Nice hustle today, Brooks," she calls out.

"Thanks, Carlson," I say, skating over. "You here for the whole practice?"

"Nah, just the first half. Then I'm off to meet my bestie, she's just landed here from New Zealand. Pulse poached her for some of their big accounts."

"New Zealand, huh? Big move." My words are casual, but hearing that country's name throws me off guard.

"Right? She's a rockstar, though she's been through a lot." She glances at her watch. "Pulse is so lucky to have nabbed her. I'm excited to have her here too, for more selfish reasons obviously."

I nod, making a small sound of acknowledgment, but my thoughts drift.

New Zealand.

It's been a while since I thought about that place, or more specifically, a person I knew from there. Charlie. The summer I spent with her at that camp felt like another life, but the connection we shared was rare. Unfinished. We were just kids, but she was unforgettable.

"Sounds like a good fit," I say, my mind already shifting back to the ice and the game plan for our next match.

Zoe gives me a quick wave from the stands before hurrying off, and I skate a few more laps to cool down, thinking about what Zoe's friend must be like. It takes guts to start over somewhere new, to throw yourself into something unfamiliar. That kind of leap feels miles away from the life I've poured everything into.

Even as I think that, there's a restless ache I can't shake. Most days, I'm satisfied. I love the game, the team, the rush of it all. But lately, it feels like something's missing. Like I've been skating in circles, chasing a future I thought I wanted but can't quite see anymore.

And sometimes when I least expect it, that ache sharpens into something more. A memory. A question. A fleeting thought about the one thing I never chased. The one thing I let go of.

I shake it off and push harder, burning the edge of the rink like speed alone could drown out the hum of my thoughts. But no matter how fast I go, it always catches up eventually. The nagging sense that the ice, the crowd, the victories—they're not enough anymore.

The scariest part is, I'm not sure I'm enough for whatever comes next.

As I head off the ice and start peeling off my gear in the locker room, the usual post-practice banter is already in full swing.

Chase Walton is in the middle of recounting some wild night, his grin wide as he exaggerates every detail. "And then, just when I thought it couldn't get any crazier, she pulls out this—"

"Spare us the details, Walton," Elijah cuts in, shoving Chase's shoulder as he passes by. "Some of us don't need to live vicariously through your escapades."

Chase just laughs, unfazed. "Not all of us are as boring as you, Eli."

"Boring is what wins games, remember that," Elijah replies as he drops onto his bench and starts unlacing his skates.

Ryan, our captain, chuckles from his spot by the lockers. "We should let Walton lead the next strategy meeting. See how far his *interesting ideas* get us."

"I'm full of brilliant ideas," Chase says, puffing up in mock pride. "For one, we should definitely be doing more fan events. Preferably in Vegas."

"You just want another excuse to see that stripper," I say, tossing gear into my locker.

"And your point is?" he counters. "Come on Brooks, you could use a little fun. You're too serious these days."

I shrug. "Serious is what gets us to the playoffs."

Coach walks in, clapping his hands to get our attention. "Alright, listen up. Good work today, but we've got a lot of ground to cover. Stay sharp. We've got a tough schedule, but if we keep this up, we'll have a real shot at the playoffs."

A murmur of agreement sweeps through the room. We've got a strong team this year, a mix of seasoned veterans and hungry rookies, and something big feels just within reach.

Coach nods, satisfied, and turns to me. "Brooks, keep leading by example. The rookies look up to you."

I nod, feeling a familiar mix of pride and pressure. "Will do, Coach."

As Coach leaves, the conversation shifts to lighter topics: weekend plans, league gossip, and Chase's endless string of women. The guys are loud and full of energy, like they always are after a solid practice, and I should be right there with them. Instead, I feel a hollow place beneath all the noise, like I'm circling something I can't quite figure out.

"Brooks, you spacing out?" Chase drops onto the bench beside me with a grin. "You thinking about that sick deke today, or are you just planning your retirement?"

I roll my eyes, chucking my gloves into my locker. "Don't get your hopes up, Walton. I'm not going anywhere."

"Good," Ryan calls over. "We need you out there, old man."

"Don't worry, I'm not in my grave just yet." As if in response, my shoulder twinges, a reminder that my body's not as forgiving as it used to be.

Turning towards the showers, I catch one of the rookies, Logan, watching me with that wide-eyed look of someone who's still getting used to being here.

"Nice hustle out there today, Pooks," I say, clapping him on the shoulder.

He's just a kid, barely out of high school, and the team immediately dubbed him 'Pookie' because of his baby face. He grins tentatively, and it reminds me of that feeling of trying to prove myself. Hell, maybe that's all I've ever done. Prove I belong. Show that I'm enough.

Stepping into the scalding hot shower, Zoe's words resurface in my mind about her colleague from New Zealand. Just the name of that country thrusts me back into my memories. I try not to dwell on the past much, but a part of me has always held onto my summer at camp. Held onto my memory of Charlie.

Maybe it's because she was the first person who saw me beyond hockey, who made me feel like I mattered just as I was. But it's pointless to think about it now. We haven't seen each other since then, and she probably has a life a thousand miles away from anything to do with me.

I try to shake the memories away. The season has just started, and there's no room for distractions. For now, it's about the game, the team, and proving that I still belong. Still, as I head out of the locker room, the feeling lingers like a whisper in the back of my mind.

Maybe this season isn't just going to be about hockey. Maybe there's something else in store, something I'm not quite ready to face yet.

CHAPTER TWO

DARK AND BITTER, LIKE MY SOUL

———————✦———————

Charlie

M *waaaarp, mwaaaarp.*

God, it's already 6:30am. I swing my hand out to grab my phone and turn off the most annoying alarm sound ever to exist, chosen specifically by me last night to ensure I wouldn't sleep through it.

Jet lag's a bitch, even after a full week here. In fact, it feels like it's getting worse instead of better. But I've got no time to dwell on that right now.

This is day one of a new chapter, a fresh start for me and the kids. But instead of the excitement I expected, there's an uneasy knot in my chest, tightening with every passing minute. I sit up in bed, kicking off the swathes of cloudy bedding and linen and take a deep breath.

I glance at the clock, realizing I've got just enough time to get myself and the kids ready before Zoe arrives. Rolling out of bed, I tiptoe into the hallway and head toward the kids' rooms.

Meadow is still fast asleep in her room, her little face peaceful with all her covers bunched up on one side of the bed. In the next room, I peek through the door to see Noah sprawled out with one arm hanging off his bed. They look so small in this big, new house.

This *house*. It's still so surreal being here, in a home to call our own, where we can finally breathe. Zoe found us a rental that's somehow both cozy and airy. It's a

15

Craftsman-style with warm wood accents, loads of natural light, and a sprawling porch with a swing for watching the kids play in the yard.

The kitchen is a dream. Spacious, with a large island perfect for the kids to sit at to have breakfast. Or for me to bake at. Zoe even stocked the pantry with some essentials, knowing how much I love to stress bake.

I quietly make my way downstairs to start the coffee. The house is still, the only sounds coming from the gentle hum of the refrigerator and the birds chirping outside. I savor the calm, knowing it won't last long. Today is going to be a whirlwind, and I need to be ready.

As I sip my coffee, familiar doubts creep in. The agency back home was smaller, more personal. But here, Pulse Creative is a different level altogether. It's bigger, faster-paced, more corporate. They headhunted me, and they expect big things. And as much as I remind myself I've earned this, Alex's voice echoes in the back of my mind.

You can't make a career out of words and pictures, Lottie. That's not a real job. Running away from your problems won't fix them. Zoe must have had to pull a decent favor to land you this job.

His tone and that dismissive scoff prickles over my skin, dragging up memories I wish I'd left behind.

My grip tightens on the mug. Even miles away, his words have a way of creeping in, clawing through my confidence. But that's why I'm here. To silence his voice for good, to prove that I'm more than he ever believed.

I shake my head, pushing his words aside.

I'm here, and I've got this.

"Mum?" Noah's voice pulls me out of my thoughts. I turn to see him standing at the top of the stairs in his pajamas, rubbing his eyes.

"Morning, buddy." I force a smile. "You ready for your first day with your sitter?"

He nods, though I can see the uncertainty in his eyes. "Is Jade nice?"

I chuckle, remembering how Zoe described her cousin that has offered to babysit today—young, energetic, and eager to help out. "She's very nice. You'll like her, I promise."

16

"Okay," he says, though he doesn't look entirely convinced. "What about school? When do I start?"

I walk over and ruffle his hair as he walks down the stairs, jumping off the final step. "Soon, big guy. We're giving you a little time to settle in first. But don't worry, you're going to make lots of new friends."

He nods again but the uncertainty doesn't leave his face. His expression mirrors my own worries, and I pull him into a hug, wishing I could take away all his fears as easily as I wipe crumbs off his face.

After I get the kids sorted with breakfast, I head back to my room to get ready. I catch a glimpse of myself in the mirror. Freckle-speckled skin, dark auburn hair in need of taming, green eyes that can't hide the strain of the past few years. I'll need every bit of my concealer and coffee arsenal today.

I get to work, choosing an outfit that feels corporate but creative—essential in this industry—and fussing with my hair, determined to look professional. Zoe would scold me for overthinking this, but she doesn't have a decade of Alex's voice under her skin.

The kids are clearly done with breakfast, their laughter echoing from the living room as they bounce around with an energy that only seems to exist in the under-six crowd. I head back downstairs, ready to meet the chaos as the doorbell rings.

Zoe's voice fills the house. "Morning, everyone! The cavalry has arrived!"

She's as bright and bubbly as ever, a whirlwind of energy in her chic blazer and heels. Her nails are painted hot pink with diamantes, her subtle rebellion against the power suits of our industry. She religiously gets them done every few weeks, and the designs are purposefully as far from corporate as possible.

Jade is right behind her—young, casually stylish, her wavy brown hair and warm smile instantly putting me at ease.

"Charlotte, this is my cousin, Jade," Zoe says, gesturing to the young woman beside her.

"Hi, Jade." I reach out to shake her hand. "Thanks so much for helping out."

Jade waves off the thanks with her own smile, and I'm struck by how similar she and Zoe look. "No worries at all. I love kids, and Zoe's been telling me all about your two. I'm excited to hang out with them."

Meadow comes bounding into the hallway, her unicorn dress billowing behind her like a cape. She stops short in front of us. "Who are you?" she asks, her eyes wide with curiosity.

Jade crouches down, beaming at her. "I'm Jade. And you must be Meadow. I hear you're a unicorn expert."

Meadow nods enthusiastically. "Yes! I have a unicorn dress!"

Jade's eyes widen in mock amazement. "No way! That's the coolest thing ever. I bet we're going to have so much fun today."

Noah appears next, hanging back with a slightly more reserved expression, but Jade handles it like a pro, asking him about his favorite dinosaurs which immediately ignites his interest.

Jade's natural ease with the kids puts me at ease too, and I can feel some of the tension in my shoulders start to melt away.

Zoe claps her hands together, bringing my attention back to her. "See? Jade's got this covered. You, on the other hand, need to focus on kicking ass at the office today."

"Wow, thanks. No pressure, right?"

Zoe rolls her eyes, thrusting a massive coffee cup out towards me. "I figured you might feel that way. So, I brought you this—extra strong, no syrup or cream, just how your weirdo ass likes it. Dark and bitter, like your soul."

I take the coffee, laughing despite myself. Zoe's energy is infectious, a force of nature that sweeps you up and carries you along with it. It's one of the things I've always loved about her. When my own confidence wavers, it's like she has enough for both of us. I've leaned on that energy more times than I can count, and today is no different. Just being around her makes me feel like I can handle whatever the day throws at me.

"Yes, because caffeine is *great* for anxiety," I tease, but when she moves to snatch it back, I hold it out of reach. "No no, this is too strong for you. I should drink it just to spare you."

"Thank God," Zoe sighs dramatically. "I took one sip on the way here and it burnt my taste buds directly off my tongue. I'm pretty sure I can smell colors now."

I snort, taking a sip of the coffee that's somehow exactly how I like it, the caffeine hitting like a promise. "Thanks. I needed that."

"Good," she replies, nudging me playfully. "And stop fussing with your hair or whatever you've been doing up there. You look fantastic. Remember, you've got this job because you're a total badass. Now come on, we've got an office to wow."

I say goodbye to the kids, pausing at the door to watch them for a moment longer. Meadow's laughter rings out as she shows Jade her favorite doll, while Noah is already deep into his toys, lost in his own world. My heart tugs a little, knowing how much I'm asking of them with this move, how much they've already had to adjust.

Swallowing the lump in my throat, I remind myself this is all for them. Every sacrifice, every moment of doubt—it's all to give them a better life. But as I finally step out the door, I can't shake the feeling of how hard it is to balance being a mom with everything else.

We head out to Zoe's car, and as we drive towards the office, my nerves start to settle into a more manageable buzz. The drive to Pulse is short but feels longer as Zoe chatters away, filling the silence with stories about the office, the clients, the team. I try to focus on her words, but my mind keeps drifting back to the daunting task ahead. When we pull into the parking lot, my heart is pounding.

The building itself is impressive, sleek with glass walls and high ceilings that amplify the sense of urgency in the air. Everything here is precise, on-the-minute. It's a stark contrast to the laid-back energy of New Zealand, but that's exactly what I need right now.

Zoe leads me through the maze of desks and offices, greeting people as we pass. Everyone seems to know her, and it's clear she's well-liked. She introduces me to a few colleagues along the way, but I can barely keep track of the names and faces. It's a blur.

Finally, we reach a corner office with a view of the city skyline. "This is you." Zoe pushes open the door and ushers me inside.

It's modern, airy, and a lot more than I expected. My eyes settle on a framed photo of the kids that she must have set up on my desk, and I feel my throat tighten.

Zoe drops into a chair across from me, arms crossed. "So, what do you think?"

"It's amazing," I say, though my voice wavers. "It's a lot to take in."

She gives me a look, leaning forward. "It's okay to be nervous, Charlie. This is a big step. Just remember, you're here because you're damn good at what you do. And trust me, you're gonna knock their socks off."

Before I can respond, there's a tap on the door, and a man steps inside. He's tall and lean, with sharp features and a confident air. "Morning, ladies."

"Morning, Marcus," Zoe says with a grin. "Charlotte, this is Marcus Li. He heads up our tech accounts."

"Nice to finally meet you," Marcus says, extending a hand. "I've heard great things."

"Great to meet you, too," I say, smiling politely. He squeezes my hand a little firmer before letting go.

"I'm looking forward to working with you on some big accounts."

"Likewise," I reply, feeling his eyes lingering on me a little too intensely.

Zoe seems to pick up on it, because she gives Marcus a playful nudge with her elbow as she stands from her chair. "Careful, Marcus. Charlotte's a heartbreaker."

He chuckles, holding up his hands in mock surrender. "I'll behave, I promise."

He takes his leave, and Zoe turns back to me. "He's harmless, I swear. But watch out—he's got a reputation."

"Noted," I reply. "I'm not here for that anyway."

Zoe smirks, clearly unable to resist. "Look, you're gonna have to date again someday, but let's just say Marcus isn't exactly the Cinderella story I envision for you." She smooths her blazer down then looks at me. "So we have some meetings lined up for you this morning, but I'll be there every step."

I nod, choosing to ignore her comment on dating entirely. At this point, I'm determined to be a spinster. "Thanks, Zoe. I really appreciate it."

She shrugs a shoulder. "Don't mention it—I'm beyond thrilled to have my best friend here. Naturally, I volunteered to be your buddy."

I raise a brow. "Hope the Board approved that decision."

"Pfft, those guys don't need to know everything." She waves a hand like she's dusting the thought away.

As we leave my office and head down the hallway, I feel like I'm on the edge of a make or break moment. This is it. The start of something new. And while I'm still terrified, I'm also determined. I'm going to make this work.

Before we reach a board room for our first meeting, Zoe nudges me with her elbow. "Oh, and by the way, I've got something fun planned for this weekend."

"Oh yeah?"

"An ice hockey game! The Colorado Storm have their home opener, and I've got great seats. You can't live in Denver and not go to a game. I won't allow it."

I chuckle, appreciating Zoe's enthusiasm. "Alright, sounds fun. I've never been to an ice hockey game before."

"Trust me, you're going to love it," she says, her excitement building. "And who knows, you might even get to meet some of the players afterwards. They're pretty cool guys."

CHAPTER THREE

IS THAT A FOAM FINGER, OR ARE YOU JUST HAPPY TO SEE ME?

✦

Charlotte – 12 Years Ago

I flinch as the first crack of thunder reverberates through the woods, my heart leaping into my throat. The sky, bright and clear only an hour ago, is now dark and churning with the promise of rain.

"Uh, Jake?" I glance over at him, struggling to keep my voice steady. "Is this normal?"

He looks up at the sky, a small grin tugging at his lips. "Yeah, summer storms roll in pretty quick around here. No biggie, but we should head back."

Another bolt of lightning splits the sky, so close I swear I feel it, and I clench my fists as my nerves jangle. Back in New Zealand, storms are nothing like this. Here, the air feels charged, like it could spark at any second.

Jake chuckles, clearly amused by my reaction. "Don't tell me you're scared of a little thunder and lightning?"

"Not usually," I say, my voice wavering as the wind gusts and rustles the trees around us. "But this is different."

As if to prove my point, a bolt of lightning flashes followed by a thunderclap so loud it feels like it's shaking the ground beneath us. I yelp, grabbing onto Jake's arm.

The rain starts, hard and sudden, drenching us within seconds. The path back to camp quickly blurs in the downpour, and I can barely see past the sheets of rain cascading down in front of us. Jake's expression changes, noticing the worry I'm trying to hide.

"Hey, it's okay," he says, his tone softer. "I was just messing with you. We're safe, I promise."

But the thunder's relentless rumble makes my heart race, and I feel a panic rising in my chest that I can't quite stifle. I keep clinging to him, needing his solid presence.

Jake reaches an arm out, pulling me in. "I've got you, Charlie girl."

With his arm around me, we start moving again, picking our way carefully through the woods. Despite the chaos around us, Jake's calmness feels like an anchor, steadying me with every step.

When we finally reach the edge of camp, soaked but safe, I let out a shaky breath. We duck under the porch of a nearby cabin, the rain still pounding down around us, but it doesn't seem as frightening now.

"You okay?" Jake asks, brushing a wet strand of hair away from my face. A line of concern deepens between his brows, and it warms me from the inside out.

"Yeah," I say, my voice still a little shaky. "Thanks to you."

He responds with a soft smile. "You're tougher than you think, Charlie. You weathered the storm."

The way he says it, like it's a fact that's plain as day, makes me believe it. Even if it's just for a moment.

***

Charlie – Present Day

I pull my newly acquired burgundy-and-blue scarf tighter around my neck as Zoe practically drags me through the crowded concourse of the arena. She insisted I wear Colorado Storm colors tonight, and now I see why. Without this scarf, I'd stick out like a sore thumb in a sea of jerseys, face paint, and foam fingers. Even with it, I feel conspicuously out of place.

I'm barely two weeks into my new life in Denver, and Zoe's already taken it upon herself to make me a hockey fan. Tonight is the Storm's season home opener—a huge deal, apparently. Honestly, I wouldn't know. Ice hockey barely exists in New Zealand. I've never seen a game live, but Zoe's been hyping this up for days and I'm keen to see what the fuss is about.

As we enter the arena, the hum of excited voices, the smell of buttery popcorn, and the distant scrape of skates against ice hit me all at once. I feel like I've stepped into a completely different world. Everyone here seems so at home, and here I am, just hoping to blend in.

"You're going to love this!" Zoe says, practically bouncing towards our seats as the Colorado Storm players skate around for warm-ups. "Plus, number 27 is out there tonight—total legend. Incredible player. Women go nuts for him."

I nod absently, half-listening as we settle into our seats. Zoe's enthusiasm is infectious, but my mind's wandering. I'm still trying to figure out the rules of this sport. We're sitting close enough that I can see the sweat on the players as they whiz past, but they all look like armored giants out there. The only way to really tell them apart is by their numbers.

"There," Zoe says, pointing toward the ice. "Number 27. He's like... an ice god."

I laugh. "*Ice God?*"

"Well, he moves like one." She raises her eyebrows suggestively. "Trust me, once you see him up close, you'll get it."

I snort, sipping my beer as she rattles off the team roster like she's naming items on a menu. I may not know much about hockey yet, but I can appreciate the buzz. The warm-up drills fade into anticipation as the players leave the ice and then come back a while later for the anthem and face-off. The arena hums with energy, a charged excitement that's hard not to get caught up in.

Beer in hand, I nibble on a pretzel and try not to look too out of place as the game begins. The puck drops, and the players explode into action, their movements fluid and powerful like it's second nature. And that's when I hear the announcer.

"Jake Brooks with the puck!"

I freeze mid-sip. What the fuck did they just say? *Jake Brooks*? I glance at the ice, scanning the players as they whizz around, but my eyes can't seem to focus. Zoe's still talking through plays, oblivious to the mini heart attack happening right next to her.

I squint at number 27 as he skates past. Broad shoulders, strong jawline, a face that's... holy shit. My beer almost slips from my hand as my heart gives a weird little lurch.

It's Jake. *My* Jake. From camp.

I slowly blink as my brain scrambles to process. My pulse races, and I grip my cup a little tighter as I do a quick mental calculation. Twelve years. It's been *twelve years* since I've seen him. I could kick myself for not connecting the dots sooner. Zoe's been yapping about him nonstop, and he's *right there*, gliding on the ice like he owns the place, all stubbled and chiseled like some rugged superhero. Like an *ice god*.

The memories rush back, and suddenly I'm not at an ice hockey game. I'm at camp, sitting by a fire under the stars, talking all night about dreams, fears, and life. Laughing for hours until our eyes were shiny with tears. We never got together back then, but I wanted to. I think he did, too. But we were so young, and life happened *to you* back then. So we said goodbye, thinking the world was too big for us to hold onto each other.

"Everything okay?" Zoe asks. I break out of my trance to see her frowning. "You look like you've seen a ghost."

"Uh..." I try to play it cool, but I'm rattled. "Yeah. I'm fine."

But I'm not. Not even close. My stomach's flipping around like a pancake on speed.

"You're acting weird."

"I'm not!" I blurt, forcing a smile and taking a slug of my beer. "I'm just—"

Before I can finish, the Jumbotron flickers, and I appear on the screen. I'm met with a giant version of my startled face, in fucking *high definition*.

I choke on my drink, sputtering beer down my chin as I try to hide behind my napkin. Zoe cackles beside me. "Oh my God, *wave*, you weirdo!" She nudges me, but it jolts the beer in my hand, sending it splashing all over my top.

Perfect.

The arena erupts in laughter as I sit there mortified, dabbing at my shirt with the most useless paper napkin to ever grace the earth. I'm covered in soggy pretzel, and my face is stuck on the jumbotron like a bad Tinder profile.

I hesitate, cheeks burning, but finally lift my hand in an awkward wave to the cheers of the crowd.

"I'm going to die. Right here, right now," I mutter, trying to shrink into my seat.

After what feels like 143 years of Zoe cackling and trying to help dab at my shirt, the camera pans away. I let out a shaky breath and glance back at the ice, only for my pulse to cartwheel again. Jake's staring.

Right at me.

Our eyes lock for what feels like an eternity. I gulp. He stares. I dart my eyes away, then back again. He's still staring. He looks... surprised? Confused? Maybe both. I don't dwell on it because now I'm panicking, wondering if there's any way I can crawl under this seat and live there for the rest of my life.

And what does he do? He *smiles* at me. A slow, familiar grin that makes my heart ache with memories. One that makes me think he hasn't even registered the absolute clown show I've just performed to a full arena. My breath catches in my throat, and I force myself to look away as all the feelings I buried years ago come rushing back.

This is insane.

I stare down at my half-spilled beer, trying to regain some semblance of normalcy, but my heart's still racing like I've downed three espressos. Jake's here, on the ice, looking like some Greek God who traded Mount Olympus for a hockey rink.

And I've just done my best impression of a soggy human pretzel in front of him. Brilliant.

The periods pass in a blur, with Zoe narrating each play in my ear. As the game goes on, I steal glances at him, my heart leaping every time he comes near our side of the rink. At one point, there's a scuffle on the ice. I look over to see Jake locked in a heated exchange with an opposing player.

The crowd goes still, holding its breath as the other guy shoves him. Jake doesn't flinch, his jaw set, eyes blazing as he knocks the player to the ground. He's utterly unbothered, and the confidence radiating off him is attractive as hell.

The ref intervenes to separate them, and as Jake skates past us, he glances in my direction and locks eyes with me again. Then, as if he's done it a thousand times, *he fucking winks at me.*

My stomach flips. Zoe, oblivious to my internal meltdown, sighs dramatically. "He's so great with the crowd, such a media darling."

"Uh-huh," I manage, cheeks heating up all over again.

After the final buzzer sounds, the crowd starts to pour out of the arena. But instead of heading for the exits like a sane person, Zoe grabs my arm, steering me toward the tunnel.

"What are you doing?" I hiss.

"Just wanna congratulate the boys and see if I can get a quick Insta update," she says breezily as we weave through the crowd.

Before I can object, we're at the tunnel, the noise of the crowd fading into the background. My heart's pounding and I can't decide if I want to run, hide, or spontaneously combust. I'm about to see Jake. After twelve freakin' years. What am I supposed to say?

Hey, remember me? The girl you stayed up all night talking with at camp, but never kissed?

I run through my options. Act casual? Pretend like seeing him doesn't feel like being hit by a semi-truck? Laugh it off? Get very drunk in the next five minutes? The only thing I know for sure is that my heart is pounding so loudly, I'm sure he'll hear it.

One by one, the players start emerging and I lose all brain function. They're all towering giants in suits and ties. Zoe's camera is already out, snapping photos like she's on a red carpet. Chase Walton, the team's notorious playboy and perpetual thorn in Zoe's side, is the first to appear. He's exactly how Zoe described him: pure swagger. He lights up as soon as he spots Zoe.

"Well, if it isn't my favorite PR Queen."

"Go away, Walton." She rolls her eyes but lifts her camera for a quick snap. "Don't you have fangirls to tend to?"

"I'm free for drinks if you are," he fires back with a wink.

"I'd rather eat glass," she retorts, but her lips twitch like she's fighting a smile. "Now, stand still so I can get a photo and be done with you."

Watching them banter is almost enough to distract me. Almost. Because then, like a figure pulled straight from my most vivid memories, someone steps into my peripheral vision. My heart stutters when I look over, and there he is. Jake Brooks. Our eyes meet, and he freezes, like he's just been caught staring.

"*Charlie?*" He says my name like he's not sure if he's dreaming, slowly closing the distance.

His voice is deeper now, but I'd know it anywhere. And God, he's grown into himself. Taller than I remember. Broader, more self-assured, with those same hazel eyes that once felt like the safe harbor in my storm. Warm, piercing, and entirely too familiar.

"Uh, yeah." I give a small wave, then instantly regret it because who waves at someone standing right in front of them? "Hey, Jake." My voice comes out embarrassingly breathy, and I immediately want to crawl under a rock.

For a heartbeat he just stares at me, eyes sweeping over my face like he's trying to fill in twelve years of missing memories. "I can't believe it's you."

"Yeah, I—uh—same," I laugh, nerves bubbling up. "You look different. Good! I mean, really good. Not that you didn't before, but now... yeah." *Stop talking, you fool. Just stop.*

To my relief, he chuckles, and it's that same soft laugh I remember. "You too. Better than good, actually." His gaze moves over me again like he's cataloging every change.

Heat rises to my cheeks. I barely know what to do with my hands, or my heartbeat, or any part of me at all. His presence feels familiar but magnified, like everything about him has somehow sharpened since we were younger. It's unnerving.

"Hang on," Zoe interrupts, her eyes bouncing between us with barely restrained glee. "You two know each other?"

I let out another nervous laugh, unable to peel my eyes from Jake even as I answer her. "We, uh, met at summer camp. A long time ago."

"Camp?" Zoe's eyebrows shoot up. "Wait, wait, wait. You and Jake Brooks were *camp buddies*?"

"Something like that," Jake says, his eyes still on me like he's remembering every detail. Every time I'd tease him about his ego, every night we'd stay up too late talking, every moment we almost-but-never crossed the line.

"Oh, this is too good," Zoe says, practically vibrating. "I need details."

Before I can reply, Chase butts in, sliding an arm around Zoe. "Details? This sounds like a fun conversation."

"Get off me, Walton!" Zoe shrugs him off, which only seems to widen Chase's grin. "This is important."

I steal another glance at Jake, who's still watching me. Everything feels surreal in this moment. The memories of our past have collided with this very real moment, somehow threading us back together. Like time is folding in on itself, bringing us right back to the beginning.

"So..." Jake steps a little closer, hands in his pockets, voice casual. "Are you here now? In Denver?"

I nod, tucking a stray piece of hair behind my ear. "Yeah, we just moved. New job, new city, new everything."

His eyebrows lift, barely a fraction. "We?"

"Me and my kids. Noah and Meadow."

Jake's expression shifts slightly, something like surprise flashing across his face. I can practically see him trying to piece things together. He nods slowly. "That's amazing, Charlie. I bet they keep you busy."

"Oh, you have no idea," I laugh, shaking my head.

Jake chuckles, but I can tell there's another question lingering behind his eyes. "So, is it just you and the kids here, or...?"

There it is. I feel the tiniest jolt at his question, even though I know he's trying his best to ask politely.

"Smooth," I say playfully, covering my nerves. "But it's just me and the kids. No husband if that's what you're asking."

His shoulders relax and his mouth curls at the edges. "Still sharp as ever, huh?"

Our eyes lock as we grin at each other, and in that instant it's like we're back under the stars at camp, two kids with dreams bigger than we could even understand. There's so much I want to say, but every word feels tangled up in my chest.

Just as Jake's about to speak, Chase swoops in again. "If you ever need a babysitter so you can catch up with this guy, I'm available."

Zoe makes a sound of utter disbelief. "You? *Babysit*? Please. They'd be zip-lining off the roof within an hour."

"I'm a fun uncle," Chase retorts, his eyes twinkling mischievously as they lock on Zoe. "I could keep 'em entertained, you could tag along. It'd be a blast."

Zoe's expression turns deadpan. "Over my dead body, Walton."

Jake smirks but his eyes drift back to me, a trace of hope in them as he steps just a little closer. "So... drinks?" His voice is quietly hopeful. "To catch up?"

There's an eagerness in his gaze, and for a moment I want to say yes. But the kids are at home, and Jade's on the clock. I gesture awkwardly over my shoulder, like the answer is there waiting. "I can't. Babysitter, jet lag, the whole bit."

Zoe, ever the gatekeeper of my energy, jumps in. "Yeah, sorry boys. My favorite Kiwi can't be tuckered out before she even gets started. But I'll see you both on Monday for the team catch-up."

"Are you back on Monday, too?" Jake asks, a hopeful smile still on his face.

I let out a soft chuckle. "'Fraid not, I'm not the sports gal at the agency—I'm FMCG."

Jake's smile falters just a bit, but he nods. "Maybe another time?"

I give a small noncommittal shrug, feeling my stomach twist. "Maybe. It's just... a lot right now."

He studies me for a second, like he's trying to gauge how real that answer is. "Well, whenever you're ready, it'd be so good to catch up."

Sensing the tension, Zoe swoops in. "Alright, time for us to head out before Walton involves us in some depraved fangirl pick'n mix."

Chase gives a dramatic sigh. "Ladies, you're missing out. It could've been epic."

"Hard pass," she fires back, already grabbing my arm and steering me away.

I glance back over my shoulder one last time to find Jake still watching me, his expression thoughtful, almost like he's holding onto the weight of every word we just exchanged.

He raises a hand in a small wave, and I return it, my heart still racing.

Back in Zoe's car, she takes a deep breath and turns to me with the biggest shit-eating grin I've ever seen. I do my best to look clueless.

"What?"

"Don't *what* me—you know *exactly* what!"

Sighing, I lean my head back against the seat. "Fine. We met one summer at Camp America when we were like, eighteen. Both counselors for a group of sports kids. Nothing happened."

Zoe arches an eyebrow, unconvinced. "Just friends?"

"Just friends. And I haven't seen him for *twelve years*!"

She bites her lip, clearly plotting something, her cinnamon eyes sparkling with mischief. "For the love of God, just say whatever you're thinking," I mutter, bracing myself.

She laughs as she clicks her seatbelt. "Fine, I'm thinking thaaaat... this is the perfect way to give a giant fuck you to Alex."

I scoff. "*What?*"

She puts the car in drive, backing out of the lot slowly. "Oh, come on! It's perfect. Jake is so hot, you could fry an egg on his abs."

I laugh, shaking my head. "No. No Zoe. I can't mix work and men."

"Technically, you're not. He's one of *my* clients—not yours."

I shake my head again, firmer now. "I'm not here to get laid. I'm here to start a new life."

Zoe scrunches her nose. "As a *nun*?"

"Yes..." I pause, thinking it over. "No. But I need to sort my shit out before I jump into anything. My mind is a mess right now."

Her face softens and she's quiet for a beat, like she's mulling something over. "Well, Sister Charlie, he looked at you like he was ready to eat you alive. And hockey players have huuuuge... appetites."

I close my eyes. "Unbelievable. You know you're unbelievable, right?"

Zoe beams, unbothered. "I'm regularly told I'm hard to believe, yes," she says, turning up the music as we pull onto the street.

She glances one more time at me as we stop at a red, but doesn't say anything else. I'm grateful she's not pushing me too much on this. I close my eyes, trying to ground myself, but it's no use.

His smile, his laugh, his warmth—it's all there, exactly where I left it.

CHAPTER FOUR

I'D FORGOTTEN THE FRECKLES SCATTERED ACROSS HER NOSE

———————·✦·———————

Jake

I can't believe it's her. Charlie. *My* Charlie. From camp.

She still has that light, that warmth and quiet strength that always pulled me in. And fuck, it's pulling me in now, harder than ever.

Her dark auburn hair falls in loose waves, catching the light and making her ethereal. I'd forgotten the freckles scattered across her nose and cheeks, but seeing them now brings back a flood of memories. I regret not counting every single one of them back then and committing the number to memory. I wonder how many more there are now, and how many stories they carry.

She's standing right in front of me, her green eyes a little guarded. There's a heaviness there, something I don't know yet. But God, I want to know. More than anything, I want to know everything about her from the last twelve years.

Have you been happy?

The question slams into me, and I hate that I don't know the answer. What's her life been like? Has she found joy? Did she chase the dreams we whispered about under the stars? Or has she been carrying something heavy, something I should've been there to help lift?

Have you been loved? Did you love someone else?

I swallow down the bitterness rising in my throat at the thought. I never had the chance to love her, not the way I wanted to. I wonder if someone else did. If they treated her right. *Loved* her right, the way I would've. If they made her laugh and feel like the center of their world. Or did they let her slip away, the way I did?

Did they see you the way I do?

Because that's what I've always done. Seen her. Not just the way she looks—though she's a goddamn showstopper—but the way she *is*. Charlie's always been light itself, the kind that makes you feel better just by being near it.

I'd give anything to bask in that light again. To feel the warmth of it, even for a few minutes.

That connection we had was rare. The kind you don't come across twice, and I was too young and too damn stupid to realize it at the time.

Now I'm standing here staring at her, and all I can think about is her laugh, and the way it warmed me from the inside out. The way we stayed up, talking for hours under the stars. It always felt like something more was going to happen between us, but it never did.

I ask about her kids and her life now, desperate for a glimpse into the world she's built without me. When she teases me for asking if there's a husband in the picture, it's like she's seen straight through me.

She knows exactly what I'm getting at, and I love that she's bold enough to call me out on it. Caught. I smile, trying to play it cool, even as I hold my breath waiting for her to answer.

No husband.

The relief is instant but tangled with so much else. She's single, but that doesn't mean she's open. She's here, but that doesn't mean she's staying. And God knows I have no claim to her. Not after all this time.

But fuck, I want to. I want to know how her days go, what makes her smile now, what makes her laugh. What hurts. What's healed. I want to know about Noah and Meadow—tiny pieces of her walking around in this world, carrying her spirit.

And I want to know about him. The guy who hurt her. Because I can see it now, the weight behind her smile, the battle wounds she's learned to hide.

What happened, Charlie?

I don't have the right to ask, not yet. So instead I practically beg her to come for drinks, hoping she'll say yes. Hoping she'll let me into her world for just a bit longer. But when she says no, I see it. The walls she's built, the fear she's carrying. The responsibility that weighs on her.

And I hate that I wasn't there to help carry it.

I should've been there.

"Maybe another time?" I try to keep my voice casual, though it's harder than I expected.

Her smile is soft but there's distance in it. "Maybe. It's just... a lot right now."

It's not a promise. It's a real maybe. The kind that feels fragile, like it could shatter if I push too hard.

But I don't want *maybe*. I want yes. I want more.

I want to hear about the last twelve years in all their messy, beautiful detail. I want her to tell me everything. The highs, the lows, the dreams, the fears.

Did you ever think about me?

Zoe pulls her away, but my eyes stay glued to Charlie as she moves toward the exit. I force myself not to follow, even though every part of me screams to. She glances back, and there's something in that unguarded look that's unmistakable.

Her lips part slightly, and her eyes catch mine like she's trying to make sense of it all. Like she hasn't just remembered me, but everything we left behind.

It tugs at something deep, a familiar ache I haven't felt since the morning I watched her leave all those years ago. A thread still hanging, waiting to be pulled.

And God, I want to pull it.

***

I lean back in the booth, letting the cold beer soothe the adrenaline still running through me. Partly from the game, partly from seeing *her*.

The bar hums with the familiar post-win energy, but I can't shake the image of Charlie. She's been on my mind since that second our eyes met on the ice.

"Dude, you're miles away." Chase nudges me, scanning the VIP section. "You should be celebrating. That was a killer game."

I force a grin, taking a sip of my drink. "Yeah, just... thinking"

"Thinking about something or *someone*?"

I don't answer right away, my mind drifting back to that moment on the ice when I first saw her on the Jumbotron. She looked out of place in the best way, like she didn't quite belong but was still the most captivating thing in the entire arena.

"*Charlotte.*" Chase teases. "Pretty, huh?"

Pretty doesn't even begin to cover it. I nod and take another sip of my beer, letting the image of her settle deeper. Fuck, she's stunning.

The memories hit me with surprising clarity, pulling me back to that summer. I was on the edge of the draft, looking for something that felt real. Working with kids in sports felt meaningful, especially after years of feeling like my own goals didn't matter to those around me.

On the last night, we hiked up to the highest point in camp, where the Milky Way felt close enough to touch. I can still hear her laughter, feel the warmth in her words that made me feel like I belonged, like I mattered for just being me.

I wanted to kiss her that night but held back, knowing we'd soon be worlds apart. I told myself it was better that way, yet in that one night, she made me feel more important than I ever had. *She was glad I existed.* Not for my skills or potential, but just because. No one had ever said that to me before.

Life moved fast after that. She went back to New Zealand, I got drafted, and everything turned into a blur of training and games. But the promise we made to follow our dreams stayed. Maybe that's why I've pushed myself so hard all these years.

Ryan gives me a look. "How'd you know her again?"

I take a sip. "We met at a sports camp in Boulder, both eighteen, just before the draft. She was only here for the summer. Was one of the best summers of my life."

"Were you guys...?"

"Nah, we were just friends." I pause, shrugging as I finish my beer. "But fuck, if I could do it all over again..."

Chase whistles from farther down the booth. "That's wild, man. And you just run into her here, out of nowhere?"

"Yeah," I say, still reeling. "The second I saw her, I knew it was her."

I glance around at my teammates unwinding after the game. The bar keeps this VIP space reserved after our home games—a private spot, our usual.

Ryan wanders over to the pool table with his wife, Claire, who's expecting soon. Watching him juggle hockey with a family on the way is something I've never even considered, but he makes it look easy. I follow over, and stand next to Elijah and his girlfriend, Tamara. I helped him select a ring recently, and now he's just waiting for the right moment to propose. The way he looks at her, like she's his whole world, that's something I've never let myself want.

And then there's Chase, chatting up a girl at the end of the bar, her hand resting on his arm as she laughs. He'll probably take her home, and tomorrow there'll be another one. It's the same story every night, and I can't say I don't get it. Hell, I lived that life in the past, too.

Part of that is because of the demands of my lifestyle. Hockey is my life, and I've dedicated everything to it. But it's not just the game that kept me from settling down, it's what I grew up with. My dad was a workaholic, completely checked out. He barely noticed me, didn't give a damn about hockey, even when I got good. Not once did he come to a game, not once did he try to understand the joy it brought me.

I spent years trying to impress him, trying to get an ounce of his attention. Anything. But he just didn't see the merit in hockey, or in me as a whole. Sometimes I wonder if, given the choice, he'd have chosen not to have me at all.

My mom was different. She tried, but the sadness was always there, like a heavy fog she couldn't shake. I could see it, even as a kid before her diagnosis. I remember her crying when she thought I wasn't looking, remember the way she couldn't get out of bed, like the world was too much for her. Like it was draining her very soul.

For years, I thought maybe I was the problem. That I was too much, needing too much. I learned to take care of myself pretty young. And while I later understood it wasn't about me, the feeling of being both too much and not enough hasn't faded.

Therapy's helped. It's been one of the privileges of being a pro: access to good doctors. I've been able to help Mom too, but I don't know if she'll ever fully shake that sadness.

But I swore I'd never end up like my dad, ignoring a family for the sake of work, or letting someone else's misery seep into my life. So I kept my focus on hockey, stayed out of anything serious, and let the rest fall away.

"Are you gonna see her again?" Ryan asks, pulling me back.

"I want to," I admit, feeling an pang at the thought of not seeing her again. "But I'm not sure she's open to anything."

"Doesn't mean you can't catch up," Eli chimes in. "You guys were friends, right? No harm in reconnecting."

I nod, but the thoughts linger. I've never done relationships, barely ever tried. It's not just the schedule, it's that I've seen what happens to guys who try—they're torn between hockey and home, and sometimes lose focus. I convinced myself that wasn't for me.

But seeing Charlie again tips every one of those thoughts off balance. I don't even know what that means, but there's something about her that shifts things, stirs questions I haven't let myself ask. She doesn't fit neatly into my life, but somehow seeing her again makes me wonder if I suddenly want to try fitting a circle through a square.

"I've never been that guy," I say, leaning back and gazing over the crowded room. "The game's always come first."

"You're overthinking, man." Chase claps me on the shoulder. "Just see where it goes."

He's right, though I hate to admit it. I've always been about the game and the next win, but watching my friends find the real thing has changed something. Maybe there's more out there for me, too.

"Yeah," I say finally, a small smile tugging at my mouth.

A woman sidles up to the pool table, her eyes bright with interest as they scan me up and down. It's a look I've seen a hundred times but haven't acted on in months. I smile politely, but I'm already looking past her, my mind still caught on the way Charlotte's eyes held mine.

"Wanna buy me a drink?" she asks, leaning in a little too close, her perfume heavy.

"Uh, not tonight" I say, nodding toward Chase. "He's your guy."

The woman pouts, but I'm already turning back to my thoughts.

I need to see Charlotte again.

CHAPTER FIVE

IT'S BRIBERY BY BROWNIES ALL ROUND TODAY

———— ✦ ————

Charlotte - 12 Years Ago

The campfire crackles merrily as the kids toast marshmallows, sending sparks up into the darkening sky. I sit beside Jake, watching as he skewers a marshmallow and holds it over the flames, the golden glow highlighting his smile. This camp tradition feels so American, something I'd only seen in movies back home.

"You ever had a s'more before, Charlie?" Jake asks as he adds a piece of chocolate and a graham cracker to his marshmallow.

I shake my head, still marveling at the idea. "Nope, first time."

"Well, I'm about to blow your mind." He reaches into his backpack, pulling out a small container.

"Brownies?"

He winks, breaking off a piece and adding it to the s'more before handing it to me. "Trust me, this takes it to the next level. I call it a Mega S'more."

I take a bite, and the combination of gooey marshmallow, chocolate, and brownie melts together in my mouth. "Oh my God, this is incredible," I mumble.

He chuckles. "Told ya. My gran used to make the best brownies. She always said a brownie could fix anything."

"Smart lady." I glance at him, touched by the small glimpse into his life.

"Yeah, she was," he agrees, a bit wistful. "Made these every summer when I was kid. I've been trying to perfect her recipe ever since," he pauses for a moment, then flashes me a smile. "So, what do you think? Are you a fan of the Mega S'more?"

"Officially a fan," I say, wiping a crumb from my lip. "You gonna share the recipe with me?"

Jake shakes his head, a playful glint in his eyes. "Nope, that's a family secret. Only special people get the recipe."

I nudge him playfully. "Special, huh? I'm not special enough?"

"Maybe one day," he teases, popping the rest of his s'more into his mouth. "For now, you'll just have to enjoy the perks of my secret stash."

I roll my eyes, laughing. "Fine. But don't be surprised if I figure it out myself."

"I wouldn't expect anything less," he says with an easy grin.

***

Charlie - Present Day

It's Monday, and instead of diving into client work, I'm elbow-deep in brownie batter.

I'm still sorting life admin since our move, especially for the kids. Today, I'm interviewing a nanny, hoping she's the answer to the stability we need. If she has any reservations about working with my little angels, hopefully these brownies might make her reconsider.

I love my kids fiercely, but they can be spirited. Right now, they're in the living room watching *Frozen*, singing "Let It Go" at the top of their lungs while tossing popcorn around like it's snow. The kitchen smells of rich chocolate and melted butter, mingling with the faint hint of popcorn from the other room.

Sighing, I feel a pang of guilt as I wonder if they're acting out just a bit because of all the changes. Moving across the world, starting over—it's a lot for anyone, let alone a six and three-year-old. I wanted this fresh start for us, but it means they've lost familiar faces, familiar routines. It's hard not to second-guess myself sometimes.

"Mama, are brownies ready?" Meadow's voice pipes up as she scampers into the kitchen, hair tousled and cheeks flushed.

"Almost, honey bee," I say, smiling as I gently pick a few pieces of popcorn from her hair. "What's the rule about throwing food in the house?"

She looks at me with those innocent blue eyes. "Only when Olaf sings."

I try to keep a straight face. "No, the rule is no throwing food, even popcorn. So go tell your brother to help clean up before our guest arrives, okay?"

"Okay, Mama!" She scurries back to the TV room, and I hear her ordering Noah to help clean up, her tiny voice so full of authority that I have to stifle a laugh.

I turn back to the kitchen, the smell of brownies filling the space, a small comfort amidst the chaos. Baking has always been my solace. A way to gather my thoughts, to feel grounded. It's my space, something Alex never understood. I can still hear him scoffing, telling me I should be spending my time doing *real jobs*. Probably things like cleaning his laundry.

But standing here now, batter in the bowl and memories of Jake's campfire brownies in my mind, I feel more myself than I have in years. It's funny how something as simple as baking brownies can remind me of the girl I used to be and the dreams I had before the kids; before Alex and his indifference.

My phone buzzes on the counter, the screen lighting up with Zoe's name. I quickly grab the phone and answer, setting it on speaker.

"Hey, Charlie!" Zoe's voice is as bubbly as ever. "Quick question—how's the brownie situation?"

I glance at the counter where a batch is cooling. "Almost done..." My eyes narrow suspiciously as I try to figure out her motives. "Why?"

"Because I need *bribes,* girl! I've got a marketing meeting with the Storm guys soon, and I need to convince them to get involved in a video idea. Think you could spare some for the cause?"

I smile, knowing full well that Zoe has been parading my baking around since I arrived. Within the first few days of my arrival, I'd baked her a thank-you-for-helping-me-find-a-house cake, some thanks-for-staying-up-late-to-Facetime-me-from-the-other-side-of-the-world cookies and a please-convince-me-I've-made-the-right-decision apple pie.

"Alright, fine. How many do you need?"

"Enough to make them fall in love with me—and by extension, you."

I laugh, slicing the first batch into neat squares. "Consider it done. Just swing by and grab them."

"Have I told you lately that I love you?"

"Only every time I bake you something," I retort. "But I don't mind. Baking's my happy place."

"Yeah, you're practically a sugar fairy," she says with a mock sigh. "You should seriously consider doing something with that talent of yours, Charlie. I'm talking bakery, cookbook, the whole shebang."

I chuckle, shaking my head as I lean against the counter. "Maybe in another life. Right now, I've got my hands full with the kids and this new job."

There's a part of me that's secretly pleased at the idea. The truth is, if I wasn't a marketer, I'd probably be a pastry chef, spending my days creating sugary masterpieces that make people smile. There's a certain magic in it, transforming simple ingredients into something beautiful, something that brings people together.

"Hey, have you heard from Jake since the game?" Zoe's voice is casual, but I sense the curiosity.

I hesitate, images of Jake at the game flashing in my mind. His intense gaze, the warmth in his smile. It felt like an echo from years ago, stirring up feelings I haven't been able to shake since.

"No, haven't heard from him," I say lightly, hoping it sounds casual. "Why?"

"Oh, no reason," Zoe replies, too innocently. "You two just seemed to click."

I laugh, but it's forced. "It was one summer, Zoe. We were just kids."

"Kids with some serious chemistry," she says.

I brush her off, but my thoughts linger on Jake. That entire summer had been such a whirlwind, but I'd loved every single minute of it. I'd befriended some of the other team leaders too, but Jake and I just seemed to get each other. We shared something, a kind of easy connection I haven't found since. But life moved on, and we grew apart.

When the news hit about his draft a couple months later, I felt so proud of him for living his dream. We emailed briefly to start with, but the demands of his career coupled by time differences and him forgoing social media back then meant our connection just fizzled out.

Before I can reply, Meadow bounds into the kitchen with a crayon drawing clutched in her hands. "Mama, look! I drew us in snow!"

"It's beautiful, honey bee," I say, crouching down to admire her art, feeling a surge of gratitude that I get to be here with her. I may have left a lot behind, but what matters most came with me.

Zoe chuckles through the speaker. "Alright, Supermom, I'll let you get back to it. See you soon!"

After hanging up, I finish packing the brownies, trying to resist the urge to snag a corner piece. I know they're delicious—years of perfecting this recipe has made sure of that. Baking has always been my go-to, a stress reliever, a ritual that reminds me who I am outside of all the noise. And these brownies in particular have always been a comfort. A little bit of sweetness amidst the bitterness.

Memories of Alex surface, unbidden. I try to push them away, but it's hard. Hard to forget how he dismissed moments like these as trivial, how he never truly saw the joy these little rituals brought me or the kids.

I take a breath, nudging away the thought of everything that led us here. I want Noah and Meadow to grow up feeling valued, in a home where love is easy to give and receive.

Alex never understood that. The cracks were always there, and in the end they shattered. I thought Alex was the love of my life, but over time it became painfully clear that I wasn't his, and neither were the kids.

My heart cracked too many times watching Noah's sweet face mask his own disappointment when Alex didn't show, like he needed to remain unaffected by his father's disinterest and soldier on. It was those small hurts, stacking up year after year, that finally gave me the strength to walk away.

Meadow would rain adoration down on him like he was a damn king. I would have thought being on the receiving end of that kind of pure, unconditional love would bring a man to his knees. But not Alex. He never indulged her, never sat for five minutes to play. Never batted an eyelid at the way she'd cling to his leg when he left in the morning. It broke something inside me to see her try so hard for so little in return.

I spent years trying to make it work, trying to be enough for him despite the constant berating and blame. Spent years hoping he'd notice us, only to realize he'd been doling out all that love to flings on his business trips.

Leaving him was the hardest decision I've ever made, but I did it for us. We deserve better—deserve to be seen, loved, chosen. My kids deserve to grow up in a home where they're valued, where love isn't just an afterthought. And I deserve to be with someone who sees me, who wants to be here, who isn't going to put everything else before me.

I pack the brownies into a container, giving myself a small, quiet nod. Today is just another step forward, another piece in the life I'm building. And thanks to Zoe, I've got a friend who keeps pushing me to see the possibilities, reminding me that there's more ahead than what's behind.

Zoe arrives a moment later, her energy filling my home as she breezes in. "Speak of the devil," I murmur, approaching the foyer.

"Charlie, my love, my light, my *angel*. These look amazing!" she exclaims, peeking into the box. "You're a brownie genius."

I shrug a shoulder, waving off the compliment. "They're just brownies. It's not rocket science."

"Yeah, well, these *just brownies* are about to make me a hero, so thank you."

"Zo Zo!" Meadow appears from the living room doorway, looking chaotic and excited to see her new favorite person. She slides in her socks across the polished wooden floor as fast as she can, barreling into Zoe's legs.

Zoe passes me back the brownies so she can pick Meadow up in her arms. I watch as she presses her nose against my daughter's in the cutest form of greeting I've ever seen.

"How's my favorite three year old today? Being good for Mama?"

Meadow beams with a nod, her hair swishing around her shoulders as she does so. "We gonna have brownies!"

Zoe grins back. "Me too! We are pretty lucky to have your Mama's brownies, aren't we kid?"

"It's bribery by brownies all round today," I mutter as I watch Meadow wriggle out of Zoe's arms and scuttle off again. I hand her back the box of brownies.

"Bye guys!" Zoe yells down the hallway. "Don't make the nanny run for the hills!"

I follow her to the door, suddenly feeling a bit nervous about where she's going and who might be eating the brownies. "Hey... don't tell them I made them, okay?" I struggle for an excuse. "I don't want to be *that girl* trying to impress the hockey team."

Zoe snorts. "Your secret's safe with me. But seriously, be proud of these."

With that she's gone, leaving me to clean up the kitchen and trying to shake off the lingering thoughts of Jake.

CHAPTER SIX

IS THIS ABOUT THE BROWNIES OR THE GIRL?

————————— ✦ —————————

Jake

Zoe's marketing updates are barely cutting through my thoughts as I replay the game on Saturday and the unexpected shock of seeing Charlotte again. The girl who kept my head in the clouds that summer. The girl who's been haunting my thoughts ever since we locked eyes across the rink.

God, she looked good. I'd tried to be respectful and not look, but my eyes had scanned her body on their own accord, and this woman was fire to all my senses. Curves for days, those little golden rings in the middle of her green eyes, that quiet air of strength she's always had.

Zoe's been droning on about fan engagement and some new social media ideas, and I'm trying to keep up, but all I keep seeing is Charlie's smile. Just as I'm thinking this meeting can't get any less interesting, Zoe tosses a white bakery box onto the conference table, snapping me out of my trance.

"Alright, boys," she says, sliding the lid off to reveal squares of thick, chocolate brownies. "A little treat to keep you going. Don't say I never give you anything."

Chase is already halfway into the box before Zoe can finish, his hand darting for the biggest piece. "Damn, Carlson, you've been holding out on us," he says, taking a bite. "Oh God, *they're still warm.*"

I reach for one, letting the rich chocolate scent fill my nose. They smell good. I've tried brownies from just about every bakery in Denver, always on the lookout for the best, trying to find a decent replica for the ones my Gran used to make. I'm a brownie snob and proud of it.

As soon as I take a bite, I freeze. The chocolate melts on my tongue, the perfect balance of sweet and bitter, with a hint of espresso. I can feel the familiarity and nostalgia in every bite as I chew. It's like a little piece of heaven in my mouth, and I need to know where Zoe got them.

"Holy shit," I mutter, earning a chuckle from the guys around me. "Where did you get these?"

Zoe just grins and shrugs. "A secret bakery." She eyes me with a look that's more than a little smug.

I narrow my eyes at her. Zoe knows damn well how much I love brownies. "Secret, huh? C'mon Carlson, you can tell your favorite client."

"Not a chance," she says, tapping her pen against her notes. "Consider it a trade secret."

I blow out a low laugh and lean across the table, trying my damndest to not reach out for another slice. "Don't hold out on me. You know I'm good for it."

Ryan nudges me, laughing. "You look like you're in love with a baked good."

"You'd think he'd found the Holy Grail the way he's eyeing that brownie," chuckles Eli from across the table.

"Guess we've just found Brooks' weak spot," Chase adds with a smirk. "Who knew it'd be brownies?"

I roll my eyes, but they're not wrong. The taste of this damn thing is unlocking memories I thought I'd buried years ago. The crackle of a campfire flashes across my mind—smoke, marshmallows, a soft laugh.

Zoe just shakes her head, tapping the whiteboard with her marker. "Sorry, Brooks. My lips are sealed. And we have some work to do."

The meeting drags on, and Zoe's doing her best to keep our attention, but analytics and marketing stats just don't do it for me. I'm here to play hockey, not be a poster boy. Leave that to Chase. He's good at it, and he adores the attention.

My mind—and my eyes—keep drifting back to those damn brownies. Every time I take another bite, I'm more convinced I need to know where they came from. It's driving me nuts.

Eli leans toward me and whispers, "Can you make it through this meeting without eye-fucking the brownie?"

I ignore him and try again a bit later when there's a pause in the presentation. "So, Zoe, this *secret bakery...* is it downtown? Maybe somewhere close by?"

She clamps her lips together, eyes sparkling with amusement. "Nice try, but no dice."

Chase chuckles from a few seats over. "Dude, let it go. It's just a brownie."

But I can't. It's not just a brownie, it's *the* brownie. As I chew, something clicks. Another distant memory hits me—and there's only one person I know who could make them *this* good, who'd care enough to rework a recipe to perfection.

Charlie.

By the time the meeting wraps up, I'm two brownies deep, with a third one in hand. I can't leave without knowing. As everyone starts gathering their things, I lean in close to Zoe, lowering my voice so only she can hear.

"Zoe, level with me. Did *she* make these?"

She shuffles her notes, giving me a calculated look, like she's debating whether I'm worth her time. I hold her gaze, pouring every ounce of charm into what I hope looks like my best puppy dog expression.

Finally, she sighs and leans in conspiratorially. "Fine, Sherlock freakin' Holmes. Yes, Charlie made them. She just didn't want anyone to know."

A slow smile spreads across my face. Of course they're hers. It's just like Charlie to make something this good and then duck out of the spotlight. That's the girl I remember, the one who could outshine anyone but never cared about the attention.

"She's incredible. How is she?"

Zoe folds her arms. "Brooks, is this about the brownies or the girl?"

"Can't it be both?" I take another bite, letting the rich chocolate melt in my mouth, wondering what else of Charlie's would taste incredible on my tongue. But I rein it in—she deserves more than my perverted thoughts. For now.

"Has she mentioned me?" I ask before I can stop myself. *Because I've sure as shit been thinking about her.*

I want to know everything. Where she's been, if she's thought about me, if she's still the same girl who used to laugh by the campfire, who made me feel like I mattered.

Zoe tilts her head, studying me. "You're such a goner. Yeah, she's mentioned you. She didn't expect to see you either, you know."

Something warm floods through me. Knowing my name has been on her lips matters more than it probably should.

"Is she... happy?" The question comes out quieter and more serious than I intend, but I need to know.

Zoe's expression softens. "She's making it work, Jake. She's got two amazing kids, a good job, but yeah, she's handling a lot. Moving across the world, raising kids on her own. She's tough. But you already know that."

Two kids. Charlie, a mom. It's still sinking in that this is her life now. And hell, I like kids. I've always loved working with them through my foundation, but it's different when you're someone's whole world like that.

"Right, the kids." I clear my throat. "How old are they?"

"Noah's six," Zoe says proudly. "Sweetest kid you'll ever meet. And Meadow's three—she's a firecracker. Definitely takes after her Auntie Zoe."

I nod, trying to picture it. Charlie with two little ones, each carrying a piece of her spirit. It feels right somehow, like she's exactly where she's meant to be, even if it's a long way from that summer. I bet she's the best mom in the world.

"And their dad?" I ask cautiously, unsure if I want to hear the answer.

Zoe's face hardens. "He's in New Zealand, barely in the picture. She doesn't talk about him much, but what I *do* know is that he's a giant cock waffle."

Something protective stirs in me. Zoe's a sharp judge of character, and if she hates him, he's earned it. There's a history there, a past that's left its mark on Charlie. I already feel the urge to throttle him if he's the reason she's not happy.

"Sounds like a lot to handle," I say carefully.

"It is." Zoe nods, her tone growing serious. "But she's not one to complain. Charlie's been through a lot, but she's here to build something new for her and her kids. So, if you're thinking of anything more than just getting your hands on her *brownies*, you'd better be ready to step up."

I nod, feeling the weight behind Zoe's words. Charlie's always had that quiet strength, the kind that draws people in without them realizing it. But the way Zoe talks, it sounds like she's carrying too much. And even though we've only just reconnected, the pull between us hasn't faded. I still feel tied to her, like if she asked me to jump, I wouldn't hesitate to ask how high. That look she gave me Saturday night keeps replaying in my mind—like she remembered how much we meant to each other, too.

"I'm just... interested, that's all," I say, trying to downplay the burn in my chest. "She's good people."

Zoe smirks, clearly seeing right through me. "She is. And I've got her back, just so you know."

"Noted," I say with a grin, but inside my thoughts are already spinning with possibilities. She's single. She's here in Denver, with a new life ahead. For the first time in a long time, I'm not just thinking about the next game or the next win. I'm thinking about her.

A thought flickers through my mind, and I seize it before I can second-guess myself. My upcoming charity event is the highlight of the year, a day filled with games and activities for the community's kids. It's personal to me—giving kids the support I wish I'd had growing up.

"Got a proposition for her," I say casually. "That charity event I mentioned, the one for the kids? We could use some baking for the spread. Might be a good way for her to meet some folk around here, you know. Get the kids involved, too."

"Oh, you sly bastard." Zoe's eyes sparkle. "I like it."

I can already see it. Charlie's baking front and center, her kids laughing and running around, and a chance for me to see her again. Sure it's an excuse, but it's one I'd bet would mean something to her, too.

Zoe dips her head to catch my eye. "I'll let her know you're interested. In, you know, *the brownies.*"

I laugh, shaking my head as I stand up. "Thanks, but could I just grab her number instead?"

She lets out a dramatic sigh as she holds out her hand for my phone. "Fine," she says as I eagerly pass it to her, watching her type the number in. "But don't fuck with her, Brooks. I mean it."

I nod as she hands my phone back to me. As I head out of the board room with Charlie's number burning a hole in my pocket, Zoe's words echo in my mind.

I'm not going to mess this up. This is just the beginning, and for the first time in years, I feel certain that whatever this is, I'm all in.

CHAPTER SEVEN

JUST A QUICK CONVERSATION ABOUT BAKED GOODS

───────── ✦ ─────────

Charlotte - 12 Years Ago

Jake and I collapse under the shade of a massive oak tree, sheltering from the relentless, blazing sun. We've just finished playing a round of tag with a group of kids, and their laughter still rings out in the distance. But all I can focus on is the boy next to me. Jake, with his easy grin and playful energy that's made the start of this summer unforgettable.

"You know what this camp really needs?" Jake asks, still catching his breath. There's that mischievous glint in his eyes, the one that always seems to promise fun.

"What's that?"

"Superheroes," he declares, his grin widening. "Every camp needs them, right?"

I chuckle. "And you'd be who? Superman?"

"Nah, I'm thinking more like Captain Thunder. You know, because of my voice. You're always saying it's loud enough to get all the kids in line."

I laugh, nodding in agreement. He's not wrong—his voice can carry across the entire camp with ease, booming out commands or jokes with the same effortless charm. "Captain Thunder suits you."

"But as we know, you can't have thunder without lightning. And you... you lighten the mood wherever you go. Plus, you did great during that storm the other night. You should be Lady Lightning."

I feel my cheeks heat up, but I play along, pretending to consider it seriously. "What, like your sidekick?"

He shakes his head. "More like a partner. I bring the thunder, you bring the flash."

"Lady Lightning, huh? I like it."

Jake smiles, clearly pleased with himself as he extends his hand to me. "Captain Thunder and Lady Lightning, partners in crime. Saving the camp one kid at a time."

I take his hand, feeling the warmth of his grip as I grin. "Deal."

***

Charlie – Present Day

Today's been busier than I expected. The interview with the new nanny, Nina, went well. She jumped right in, hosting Meadow's dolly tea party and swapping space facts with Noah. It's a relief to finally find someone who clicks with the kids. And best of all, she's local, so she knows all the best spots to introduce them to their new city.

After Nina left, I braved the grocery store with the kids. Everything feels different here, even basic things like groceries. The kids did well, despite the store's size—though Meadow treated me to an epic meltdown in the cereal aisle. I did my best to stay calm, but the stares from other adults were piercing. It's hard enough managing a meltdown without feeling like the entire store is silently judging you.

With my hands braced on the kitchen island, I take a long breath, savoring the calm as the busy afternoon fades into evening. Noah's absorbed in his latest LEGO creation in the living room, while Meadow is happily coloring at the dining table, tongue poking out in concentration as she carefully fills in the lines. She's completely forgotten about her earlier meltdown—and that's how it should be. But after moments like that, I do miss having someone there to tell me I'm doing okay. A partner in crime who'd get it, pour me a glass of wine, and tell me I'm not alone in this.

I'm still pottering in the kitchen, debating what to do for dinner, when my phone buzzes on the counter. I wipe my hands on a dish towel and glance at the screen. It's an unknown number. I hesitate for a moment before picking up.

"Hello?"

"Hey, Charlotte? It's Jake. Jake Brooks."

The deep timbre of his voice slides through the phone, familiar yet startling. It's been years, but somehow it still feels like coming home. I stand a little straighter, gripping the phone tighter. "Oh, hey, Jake. How are you?"

"I'm good, thanks. I, uh, got your number from Zoe—hope that's okay? I wanted to ask you about something."

My heart does a little flip. "Sure, what's up?"

"Well..." He pauses, and I can almost hear him gathering his thoughts. "I've got this charity event coming up, and I thought... well, your brownies were a hit at the meeting today. Tasted very *familiar*," he pauses, waiting for me to react.

My stomach dips. *Shit.* I clear my throat, thankful he can't see my cheeks heating. But before I can conjure a reply, he continues.

"So I was wondering if you'd be interested in baking some for my event."

I blink, caught off guard by the request. "You want me to bake for a charity event?"

"Yeah, exactly." His tone is lighter now, like he's relieved to have asked. "It's a big event I'm passionate about, and I think your baking would be a perfect addition. We could use something like that to make the day extra special for the kids."

His words wrap around me, unexpected but welcome. I love the idea of helping out, especially if it's for a good cause. "Um, wow... okay. That sounds great, Jake. I'd love to help out. When do you want to discuss the details?"

"How about now?"

"Now?" The surprise is obvious in my voice, earning a soft chuckle on the other end of the line.

"Yeah, if you're free. It'll be easier to talk in person."

I glance around, hyper-aware of the toys and the mess that comes with two young kids. But this is us, our everyday life. If he wants my brownies, he'll have to handle a little bit of chaos. "Uh, sure, I guess that works. The kids are here though, so it's a bit... lively."

"That's fine with me," he replies, his tone light. "I'll see you in a few?"

I agree, ending the call before I can overthink things, especially how he knows where I live. Zoe's doing, no doubt. I stare at my phone for a second, processing what just happened. Jake Brooks is coming over. To my house. Right now.

I do a quick, frantic clean-up, picking up scattered toys and stashing the last few groceries in the pantry. I'm still tidying when the doorbell rings, and Meadow, as eager as ever, beats me to it.

"Mama, someone's here!" she calls out as she flings open the door.

I hurry over, wiping my hands on my jeans, my breath catching when I see Jake standing there. He's dressed casually in a t-shirt, jacket and jeans, but he fills the doorway in a way that's impossible to ignore. Meadow, wide-eyed, stares up at him like he's the most fascinating thing she's ever seen. And honestly, I don't blame her.

"Hi there," Jake says, his smile warm as he crouches down to her level. "You must be Meadow."

Meadow's usual shyness vanishes. She sticks her hand out toward him just like I taught her, all business. "I'm Meadow. I'm three."

Jake chuckles, gently taking her tiny hand. "Nice to meet you, Princess. I'm Jake."

The nickname makes me melt. Let's hope I'm not a complete puddle by the time he leaves. He just stepped into her world so naturally, and watching him with her, it's hard to reconcile the boy I knew with the man he's grown into. He's hot. All man now. And the easy gentleness he shows Meadow just magnifies it.

When his eyes meet mine, my throat goes dry. He rises slowly, towering over me, and I can't help but notice every inch of him. He's tall, lean, and if I'm being honest, probably the best-looking man I've seen.

"Hey, thanks for coming over," I say, trying to sound composed.

"Thanks for letting me barge in." His eyes crinkle at the corners, and I don't miss the way they sweep over me, taking in every detail. My pulse quickens, but I shake off the distraction, determined to stay focused.

Taking a breath, I open the door wider. Letting him step into our space feels like a whole wave of memories and possibilities all at once.

Brownies. He's here for brownies. For his brownies.

"Come on in."

***

Jake

I'm not one to overthink, but as I pull up to Charlotte's place, I realize I've done exactly that the whole drive here. What the hell am I doing? I've seen her once, and here I am pulling up outside her house like a lunatic because I can't stop thinking about her.

Because of the brownies. Gran's brownies.

But I know there's more to it. She's stuck with me since I saw her at the arena. Maybe it was her surprised look that day, like she couldn't believe I was real. Or the memory of that summer, when she was my whole world for ten unforgettable weeks.

I look up at her house as I approach. It's cozy, with a big porch that looks made for family dinners and lazy Sunday mornings. A swing hangs on one side, and I can picture her there, reading to her kids or watching them play in the yard. A thought suddenly stirs in me: I want that. Want to be part of something like that.

Before I can overthink, I ring the bell. There's a scurry of activity before the door flies open, and a tiny strawberry-blonde tornado in a unicorn dress appears. Her eyes are bright blue, her expression one of fascination, like I've just arrived straight out of a fairy tale. She looks just like a mini version Charlotte. With lighter hair and different eyes, but with that same spark of light.

"Hi there," I say, crouching down to her level. "You must be Meadow."

She hesitates for only a second before she pops her little hand out, surprising me. "I'm Meadow. I'm three."

I shake her tiny hand and chuckle. "Nice to meet you, Princess. I'm Jake."

Her face lights up, and for a second, I'm completely disarmed. I've always had a soft spot for kids, but she's a whole new level of adorable. Her innocence, her trust. It's a lot to take in.

Behind her, Charlotte appears, looking a little flustered but still pulling off that natural grace she's always had. "Hey, Jake. Thanks for coming over."

"Thanks for letting me barge in." I stand and take her in. She gives me a warm smile, and for a second, the tension eases.

Damn, she looks good. I immediately notice how her clothes hug her curves, how her hair falls in soft waves around her face. It's hard to focus on anything else. I can't believe how nervous I am about this, like I'm desperate not to fumble this opportunity to spend time with her.

"Come on in," she says, gesturing me through the door.

I step inside, absorbing the house's warmth and color. Toys are scattered around, a half-finished LEGO spaceship sits on the coffee table, and there's the faintest hint of vanilla and coffee in the air. It's a real home, cozy and alive. Unlike my condo downtown, which feels more like a pit stop than a place to settle. Here I feel grounded, like I could stay a while.

Noah, focused on his LEGO creation, glances up when he sees me, his eyes going wide. "Are... are you that hockey player from the TV?"

I can't help but chuckle as I approach him, noticing Charlotte's cheeks pinken slightly as she replies, "Yeah, buddy, this is Jake."

He looks at me with awe, as if I've just promised he can eat cereal out of the Stanley Cup itself, but then, just as quickly, it fades.

"I'm building a spaceship. It's gonna be really fast, maybe even faster than you!"

"Good call," I say, squatting down to get a closer look at his creation. "We could use some spaceship speed on the ice."

He smiles, and I can't help but feel the pull of these kids' open acceptance. It's genuine, uncomplicated. They don't care about your status, your money, or your contracts. They just see you for who you are in the moment, and there's something pure about that.

It's something I've been missing. These real connections, not overhyped interactions with people who only care about my points or how many sponsors I have.

Charlie catches my eye and nods toward the kitchen. "Wanna chat while they play?"

"Sure," I say, though I'm reluctant to leave this room that feels full of life.

As I follow her towards the kitchen, I'm unable to shake this feeling of wanting to know every detail of her world. I walk close enough behind her to catch a faint scent of vanilla—or maybe it's something floral. I'm not entirely sure, but it's distracting as hell, and I have an immediate urge to bury my face in the crook of her neck and inhale deeply.

Instead, I force myself to take a seat at the breakfast bar, stealing glances at her while she gets me a water. As she hands me the glass, our fingers brush just for a moment, but it sends a charge through me. She glances at me briefly, and I wonder if she feels it, too. *God, I hope so.*

She quickly goes to help Meadow find stickers for her coloring page, and my eyes trail after her. Watching her with Meadow, I feel a pang deep in my chest and try to name it. Longing, maybe. For something I've never had but suddenly want.

I shake my head, mentally chastising myself as she walks back over to sit next to me. I need to keep it light. But somehow, with Charlie pulling up a barstool next to me, so close I could reach over and tuck that stray strand of hair behind her ear if I wanted to, it feels impossible. *Inevitable.*

Damn, she's beautiful. The kind of beautiful that makes you forget why you're here in the first place. She smiles at me, crossing her legs and raising an eyebrow. I remind myself that I'm here to talk about the charity, not to get lost in those mossy green eyes tinged with gold.

"So, tell me about the event," she prompts, looking at me with genuine interest as she takes a sip of her water, waiting for my reply.

I inhale deeply, watching the way her throat moves as she swallows. *Get it together, you creep.*

"It's for my foundation called *Play It Forward,*" I begin, feeling the pride swell in my chest. "We give underprivileged kids the chance to play sports—equipment, training, even mentorship."

Her expression softens as I speak, her smile growing. "That sounds like a wonderful cause, Jake. I'd love to help. How many brownies are we talking?"

"Ahh... maybe more than just brownies." I pause, giving her a pointed look. "Though I'd be lying if I said those weren't my favorite."

Her eyes twinkle with knowing, but she doesn't comment, waiting for me to continue.

"So definitely more brownies than I could ever eat, and maybe a spread of cookies, cupcakes, whatever you think would be a hit."

She nods thoughtfully. "I can do that. And it's a family-friendly event?"

"Absolutely," I say. "It's all about the kids. No stuffy banquet, just fun, games, and dessert. Bring Noah and Meadow, too. They'd love it."

Her smile widens, and for a second it feels like the years haven't stretched between us. Like it's just me and Charlie again, building something together. She reaches for her glass, taking another sip, and for a moment I'm caught watching her tongue flick out to catch a stray droplet. She's so close, the warmth of her body a reminder of what I want. More time, more moments, just more of her.

I force myself to look away, scanning the kitchen to keep my hands from doing something stupid, like brushing my thumb over her moistened lower lip. The place mirrors her—warm and full of life. My eyes shift back to Charlie, lingering on the soft curve of her neck, the delicate sweep of her collarbone peeking out from beneath her sweater.

"This place, it suits you," I say, desperate to extend this time together.

Her smile shows a flash of pride, and I can tell how much effort she's put into making it home.

"Thanks. Zoe really hit the jackpot finding it," she says. "It's been an adjustment, but it's starting to feel like ours."

I nod, trying to imagine what it took to uproot her life halfway across the world. "Must be a lot to handle—new city, new country. You seem to be managing pretty well."

She pauses, her expression thoughtful. "I won't lie, there are moments when I wonder if I've made the right choice. The kids are my priority, so as long as they're happy, that's what matters."

Admiration floods through me. She's strong in a way a lot of people aren't, carrying so much with such grace. "You're doing a good job, Charlie. They're lucky to have you."

Giving me a shy smile, she glances down at her hands. "And what about you?" she asks, shifting the focus back to me. "How's the season treating you so far?"

I lean back in my chair again, smiling at the question. There's something disarming about the way she's asking, like she genuinely cares about my answer. "It's been good. A lot of pressure, but that's the norm. I guess I've been at it long enough to know how to manage."

She tilts her head slightly. "You've always been like that. So focused, so determined to go all the way. And now, here you are." Her voice is thoughtful, and for a second it feels like we're both slipping into the past, remembering who we were back then.

I hold her gaze, my voice dipping deliberately lower. "Guess I'm pretty good at focussing on what I want."

Her lips part just slightly, and a charged beat passes. I track her eyes as they flick to my mouth before she quickly clears her throat and looks away, shifting in her seat slightly.

"And good ol' Camp America, eh?" She changes the subject with a playful smirk, leaning her arm out on the counter to gesture her finger back and forth between us. The movement draws my attention to the subtle curve of her wrist. It's such a simple thing, but I have to fight the urge to reach out and trace the line of her fingers with my own. "I have to say, it's a bit surreal seeing you after all these years."

"Actually, I'm surprised you didn't recognize me sooner, *Lady Lightning*."

A genuine, warm laugh fills the room. "Oh my God, I can't believe you remember that nickname."

I grin, a little sheepish but mostly pleased she remembers. "Hard to forget the girl who kept saving the day all summer."

Charlotte shakes her head, still laughing. "I'm pretty sure you were the one doing most of the saving. I just kept the kids from tying you up with the jump ropes."

I chuckle as the memories come back in a rush. The way she looked back then, her eyes full of mischief, not all that different from now. The way she'd lighten up even the toughest days with just a smile. But there's something more to her now, a maturity that makes her even more captivating.

"Who would've thought we'd end up here, of all places?"

"Life has a funny way of working out," she agrees, her eyes scanning over my face, lingering like she's seeing right through me. "I always wondered what happened to you after that summer."

The sincerity in her words strikes me, and I realize how much I wanted to hear her say that. To know I wasn't the only one who held onto those memories.

"I wondered about you, too," I murmur.

There's another beat of silence. I scramble for words, to say anything to stop myself from doing something stupid like telling her how much I regret not kissing her. Or telling her how much I want to kiss her right now.

"Mama, look what I drew!" Meadow's voice calls out from the living room.

The spell breaks, and Charlotte's focus shifts entirely to her daughter, her expression softening in a way that has nothing to do with me.

"I should go check on her," she says, offering me a quick smile as she stands.

A part of me wants to reach out, to pull her back and keep her in this moment with me just a little longer. But Charlotte's a mom first, and that's one of the things I respect most about her.

"Yeah, of course," I say, pushing my own chair back to stand. "I should get going anyway. But thanks for agreeing to help. It means a lot."

"Thanks for thinking of me," she replies, her words tugging at something deep inside me.

"Always." The word slips out before I can stop it. But fuck it, it's true. And it feels good to say out loud.

I know I should leave, but I can't quite make myself walk out the door. "Maybe... I could come by and help with the baking?"

Her laugh is playful, the sound curling low in my gut. She raises a brow at me, clearly skeptical. "You bake, Jake?"

It's flirtatious, and it's a challenge I'm more than willing to rise to.

"Oh, I can handle a spoon and batter. Worst case, I burn something and you put me on dish duty." I wink, confident it'll land how I want.

"Well, maybe I'll take you up on that."

"Good," I say, savoring the hint of pink on her cheeks. "Just text me the ingredients you need."

As I turn back to the door, Meadow rushes over, holding a unicorn picture. "Look, Jake! I made this for you!"

I crouch, taking the artwork. It's a colorful swirl of rainbows and sparkles with a very enthusiastic unicorn front and center. "This is awesome, Princess. Gonna put it in my locker for good luck."

Her wide eyes light up. "Really?"

And just like that, this kid has me wrapped around her tiny finger. I'm tempted to drive straight back to the arena and immediately frame this in my locker.

"Really," I promise, giving her pretty hair a soft ruffle before looking back up at her equally pretty mother. "Even Captain Thunder needs a little magic, right?"

Charlotte's eyes flicker with recognition, the corner of her mouth lifting in a knowing smile. "Right," she echoes softly.

"See you soon, Lady Lightning," I say, unable to help the warmth in my voice.

"See you soon," she says, her voice a little breathless. I'm definitely having an effect on her, and damn it feels good.

I hesitate at the door, wanting to keep this conversation going so I can find other ways to get under her skin. But the words are caught somewhere between my heart and my throat.

What the hell am I doing? This visit was supposed to be about the charity event, but now I'm leaving with a thousand unspoken questions, the biggest one flashing like a neon sign: *Wanna go on a date?*

Instead, I give her one last smile and tap the doorframe lightly. "Text me," I say softly before stepping outside.

As I walk to my SUV, something's shifted. Not just in her, but me too. The pull's still there, a spark that feels like it's been waiting years to ignite.

And this time, Captain Thunder is ready to strike.

CHAPTER EIGHT
SWEETENERS ARE FOR THE WEAK

———————— ✦ ————————

Charlie

Two days have passed since Jake came over, and I still haven't texted him. It's not that I don't want to, I do. But every time I pick up my phone, I freeze. I've spent most of my free time researching dessert table ideas, trying to figure out what would work best for the event, but the thought of actually texting him makes my heart race.

It's Wednesday morning, and I'm sitting at my desk staring at my screen. My focus is supposed to be on a report due by the end of the day, but my mind keeps drifting back to Jake's visit and the way he looked at me.

With a heavy sigh, I lean back in my seat and glance at my phone, lying innocently on my desk. What do I even say?

Hey, Jake. Thanks for coming over. About those ingredients...

No, too lame. Too stiff. I'm not stiff, I'm *fun*. I huff out a breath, feeling ridiculous. It's just a text, for God's sake.

Before I can overthink it anymore, there's a soft knock on my office door, and Zoe peeks her head in. "Morning! Got a minute?"

"Of course," I say, grateful for the distraction. "What's up?"

She steps inside, holding out a coffee cup, and I take it with a smile. "Just wanted to check in. And," she adds with a teasing grin, "I haven't had the chance to properly talk to you about Monday."

I sigh, already knowing where this is headed. "Oh, that."

"Yes, *that*." She settles into the chair opposite my desk. "Mr. Hockey Star casually turns up on your doorstep, and I've been dying to know more ever since. So, spill."

Stalling for time, I take a sip of my coffee, but I can feel my cheeks betraying me as they heat with the memory of Jake's smile. I take a breath, relishing in the taste of the dark brew as it hits my tongue.

"There's nothing to spill," I say, trying to sound casual even though my heart's still doing that annoying stutter whenever I think about him and that little dimple on his left cheek when he smiles. "He asked me to bake for his charity event, that's all."

Zoe raises an eyebrow. "And?"

I frown, a blend of excitement and anxiety bubbling up. "And... we talked about the event. He was just really nice. Supportive, actually. Even offered to help me with the baking."

"Nice? Supportive? You know, I've known the guy for a while now and I've never heard him described as *just* nice and supportive. Try again."

I shake my head, smiling despite myself. "Okay, fine. He was more than nice. He was sweet. And maybe a little flirty."

Zoe laughs. "Sweet and flirty, huh? So, what's the problem?"

Setting my coffee down, I shrug. "I don't know. It's just... I haven't seen him in years, and suddenly he's back in my life, and I'm supposed to... what? Text him about baking like it's no big deal?"

"Charlie, it's a *text*, not a marriage proposal. You're overthinking this."

"I know," I say, running a hand through my hair. "But it's not just the text. It's everything. I'm not the same person I was back then, and neither is he. He's *Jake Brooks*. And I'm just me."

Zoe waves her hand dismissively. "Oh, please. You're amazing, and if he doesn't see that, then he's a fool. But from what you're telling me, he's definitely not a fool."

I smile, feeling a little better but still unsure. "He's... I don't know. We haven't seen each other in years. This is probably just nostalgia."

"Nostalgia doesn't make a guy like Jake offer to help you bake," Zoe says, folding her arms again like she's ready to debate me into the ground. "This is real, Charlie. And you deserve something real."

I want to believe her, but I still feel that nagging doubt. "I just don't want to assume something that's not there."

She leans forward, her tone softening but still laced with that Zoe-branded determination. "Listen. You're not imagining this. You guys are like magnets. Freaky, once-in-a-lifetime, defy-the-laws-of-physics magnets. It's honestly uncomfortable to witness, but that's why it works."

I scoff, but she keeps going before I can interrupt.

"Just take it slow, see what happens. No one's saying marry him tomorrow. But don't be that person who misses out because you're scared of falling."

"Was that a pep talk or a secret audition for motivational speaking? Because I feel like you could trademark the magnet thing."

She narrows her eyes, feigning offense. "Wow. I try to inspire you, and this is the thanks I get? I could've gone with something boring, like *connection*, but magnets felt more iconic. You're welcome."

I laugh in disbelief. "You're way too invested in this."

"Damn right I am." She stands, stretching her arms like she's just won a championship. "Because I'm rooting for you, Charlie. And trust me, whatever this is—it's real. So can you just hurry up and text him?"

"Ugh, fine. I'll text him... eventually."

"Good. And when you two get married, I'll expect my name in the thank you speeches."

She heads to the door, but before she leaves, she turns back with a smirk. "Oh, and by the way, I've got a meeting in a few minutes with some of the Storm players. Just thought you should know. In case you want to, ya know, *accidentally* bump into someone."

"Zoe!" I launch a pen at her, but she dodges it with a cackle, and disappears down the corridor.

Shaking my head, I try to refocus on my work, but now all I can think about is the possibility of running into Jake in the office.

I glance at my coffee cup, now empty on my desk—drank that too fast. I stare at it for a moment, like it holds the answers to all my questions, but all it does is silently shout at me for a refill. And who am I to argue with the needs of questionable amounts of caffeine in my bloodstream? I swipe it up, deciding to refill it in the office kitchen.

Stepping out of my office, my stomach flips when I see Jake heading down the hall. He's all tailored suit and effortless confidence, and when his slow grin lands on me, my pulse stumbles.

"Charlotte," he says, his voice holding a mock professionalism as he closes the distance. "Fancy seeing you here."

I arch a brow, channeling every ounce of cool I don't feel. "Yeah, I work here, remember?" *He smells ridiculous—like cedar and trouble.*

He chuckles, the sound curling around me in a way that makes it hard to focus. "Hard to forget."

We fall into step together, his arm brushing mine as we walk. I'm hyper-aware of how close he is, how his cologne sinks into me, and I can feel my brain short-circuiting. Somehow, I manage to keep walking without tripping, which feels like a small victory.

When we reach the kitchen, I busy myself with the coffee machine, gripping the handle like it's the only thing tethering me to reality.

"What can I get you?" I ask, keeping my voice light. *It's just coffee, Charlie. Not a life-or-death situation.*

He leans casually against the counter, the corner of his mouth curving upward, dimple on full display. "How about you tell me what's good? Just don't make me drink that dark, bitter stuff you're into."

I glance at him, fighting a smile. "Sweeteners are for the weak." *And I'm about as weak as they come.*

His laugh is deep and entirely too distracting. "Zoe warned me you'd say something like that."

I roll my eyes, grabbing a cup. "I just like my coffee strong." *And you in a suit, apparently.*

Our fingers brush as I hand him the cup, and the brief contact sends a ripple through me. "I'll take your word for it," he says, studying me with those intense hazel eyes. His voice drops just slightly, like it's meant only for me. "I've been waiting for your text."

My heart kicks into overdrive. "I was meaning to, I just... I've just been busy." *Keep it together, Charlotte Renee Andrews.*

He tilts his head, smirking like he can see right through me. "Busy, huh? Too busy to text me about brownies?"

I force myself to meet his eyes, even as my pulse hammers. "I've been researching ideas. Wanted to make sure I got it right."

"Is that so?" He sips his coffee, watching me over the rim of the cup. "Well, don't overthink it. Just tell me what you need." *Why does this feel like we're no longer talking about brownies?*

I nod slowly. "Okay. I will."

We stand there, the air charged with tension. Then, with a wink that's equal parts infuriating and charming, he sets his cup down and steps away.

"See you later, Charlie girl," he says, and walks out.

The way his voice wraps around my name feels like he's looking right into me, like there's something inside worth revering. I stand there, heart still racing as his words linger.

As I head back to my office, my mind spins. Jake Brooks just *called me out* for not texting him, while wearing a suit and looking like some kind of ice god. And as much as I plan on killing Zoe for placing that term in my head, I think I enjoyed every minute of it.

***

An hour or so later, I'm up to my eyeballs in report data, still processing everything that happened with Jake earlier, when Marcus strolls into my office. "Hey, Charlotte. Got a minute?"

I glance up, shifting gears. "Sure. What's up?"

Marcus leans casually against the doorframe, smiling. "Just wanted to chat about the project you're helping me with. You've been doing great work, as always."

"Thanks," I say, brushing off the compliment. "What do you need?"

He steps in further, leaning a little too close over my desk. Normally, I'd laugh it off or redirect, but today I'm hyper-aware of how hollow his actions feel. Especially after this morning with Jake.

"Well," Marcus begins, his tone tipping from professional to something a lot more informal. "I was thinking maybe we could grab lunch sometime? You know, to discuss the project... And get to know each other a bit more."

Before I can respond, there's a sharp rap on the open door, and I jump slightly. Jake stands in the doorway, his expression unreadable, but his presence fills the space like a thundercloud rolling in. His gaze flicks to Marcus, then to me. "Am I interrupting?"

Marcus straightens, caught off guard. "Oh, hey, Jake. No, not at all. We were just chatting about grabbing lunch."

Jake nods once, his face neutral but his posture anything but relaxed. "Charlotte, could I borrow you for a second?"

"Of course," I say, my pulse picking up speed. Marcus gives me a quick, almost nervous smile before excusing himself. I watch as Jake's gaze tracks him, holding steady until Marcus is halfway down the corridor. Then he steps into my office and closes the door firmly behind him.

The air shifts instantly. Jake turns, his eyes locking on mine, direct and unrelenting. It sends a shiver down my spine, every single nerve suddenly awake.

He steps closer, and for one idiotic second I think he's going to pull me into his arms. But my eyes refocus on his hand as it moves towards me, and I realize he's holding out a notepad and pen. "I was thinking, you should write down what you need for baking tomorrow. I'll pick it up."

I blink, caught off guard. "You don't have to do that. I can handle it—"

"I want to. Then we can bake together tomorrow afternoon at your place, if that still works for you."

I nod and reach for the notepad. His fingers brush mine deliberately, and I falter for a moment. "Yeah, that works."

I jot down the list quickly, focusing on my pen moving across the paper and not the way he's watching me, or the fact that I'm imagining us baking together in my kitchen. It feels intimate, maybe too soon. But when I glance up at him, the sincerity in his eyes holds me there. Keeps me from pulling back.

I hand him the notepad, and his lips curve into a grin as he scans the list. "Simple enough. Just promise not to be too impressed when I turn out to be a natural in the kitchen."

I scoff, tilting my head. "Big talk for someone who might just end up covered in flour before we even preheat the oven. But I'll try to keep my awe in check... if you can keep up."

"Oh, I can keep up, Charlie girl." He steps a little closer, his voice dropping to a low rumble that makes me feel like I'm quietly crumbling. "But now you've got me curious—what happens if I don't? Do I get extra lessons? Maybe some one-on-one tutoring?"

His voice dips just enough to make my breath hitch, but I recover quickly, raising an eyebrow at his blatant innuendo. "We'll see how you do, Captain Thunder. Just don't be surprised if I have to take over when you burn the first batch."

Jake laughs, and it's impossible not to smile back. "Challenge accepted, Lady Lightning. But don't say I didn't warn you when I turn out to be your star pupil."

I bite my lip and his eyes flick down briefly, catching the movement. The flash in his eyes tells me he's having just as much fun with this as I am.

He clears his throat, holding my eyes for a moment as he slaps the notepad into the palm of his other hand. "Thanks for this. I'll see you tomorrow."

"Tomorrow," I echo, barely above a whisper.

Giving me one last lingering smile, he turns and walks out, leaving me standing there.

Tomorrow.

CHAPTER NINE

DON'T INNOVATE TOO HARD AND BREAK SOMETHING

———————— ✦ ————————

Jake - 12 Years Ago

I'm sitting by the lake, the fire crackling softly as the night settles in. The kids are long asleep, and the other leaders are still laughing and talking around me, but it's just noise. I stare at the edge of the water, letting it all fade.

Charlie sits down beside me, close enough that our shoulders touch. The soft breeze ruffles her hair as she stares out over the shoreline, and I know she can tell something's off. She always does.

"You okay?"

I force a smile and avoid her eyes. "Yeah..."

She doesn't press, just pulls her knees to her chest and mirrors my gaze toward the water. The way she slips into the quiet with me makes it easier to relax, like she knows what I need before I do.

I sigh, rubbing a hand over my face. I'm not used to talking about my dad and how he's never really there. But tonight, it slips out anyway.

"Just... stuff with my dad," I offer.

Charlie leans into my shoulder a bit more, her quiet presence like a lifeline. I'm used to holding it in, but with her beside me, I feel like I don't have to. She's the one person who doesn't look at me like I have to have it all together. And tonight, I'm too tired to pretend everything's fine.

"He's never around," I finally say. "Always working. And when he is home, it's like he's not even there. Like he doesn't care."

Her hand curls under my arm and wraps around it, linking us together. The gesture's simple, but it feels grounding, holding me in place while I find my way through the words.

"My mom," I pause, swallowing hard. "She's not okay. Hasn't been for a while. She's tired all the time, kind of... out of it. She's on meds now, but I don't think they're helping. And he doesn't notice. Or maybe he does and doesn't care. I don't know which is worse."

The bitterness in my words is clear, and I hate how it sounds. But it's the truth. He's checked out, and I'm the one left picking up the pieces.

"Have you talked to him about it?" She asks gently.

A short, cold laugh escapes me. "Yeah. It's like talking to a wall. He thinks everything can be fixed with a few pills. Get her on medication and problem solved, right?" I pause, my chest tightening. I don't want to break in front of Charlie, but it's hard to keep it all inside.

"But it's not solved," I mutter, hands clenching into fists. "Not for her, not for me."

I hear my words, and they cut deeper than I expected. Charlie stays quiet, her touch still steady on my arm. She's not trying to fix anything or give me advice, and somehow that's exactly what I need.

"Guess that's why I threw myself into hockey," I murmur. "I love it, and I can control it. Work hard, get results. You don't rely on anyone but yourself."

Her fingers tighten slightly on my arm, and I glance over. Her eyes are soft and steady when she speaks. "But you don't have to do everything alone."

"I just—" My voice cracks, and I pause. "I don't want to be like him, you know? I don't want to be the guy who checks out when things get hard. I'm terrified of that. I don't wanna fail the people I care about."

"You won't, Jake," she says. "You're not him."

I shake my head, the fear bubbling up so raw and exposed now. "What if I do, though? What if I get so wrapped up in hockey that I lose sight of everything else? It's already happening. I'm obsessed. And if I make the NHL, it'll only get worse. Half in, half out. I can't do that."

There it is—my biggest fear laid out in the open. The thing I've never let spoken words claim. That I'll never be enough. Not for hockey, not for my family. Not for anyone.

Without a word, Charlie's hand slips from my arm and finds my jaw, her grip firm as she turns my face toward hers. "You're not going to fail." She holds my eyes, her conviction sinking into me. "You care, Jake. And one day you're gonna make someone so happy, just by being who you are."

I stare back at her, the words settling into the spaces where my doubt lives. And for a moment, with her eyes on mine, I let myself believe her.

***

Jake - Present Day

The echo of blades on the ice should be grounding, pulling my focus back to morning skate—but not today. Not with Charlotte taking up space in it.

I haven't stopped thinking about her since I left her office yesterday: the way she grinned and rolled her eyes at my teasing, the way her teeth sunk into her bottom lip. Being around her feels both nostalgic and new. Like a past I've missed and a future I've been waiting for, buried so deep inside I didn't realize its significance until now, has finally breached the surface.

Seeing Marcus leaning a little too close over her desk made my hands clench. It took everything in me not to drag him aside. But in a way, he did me a favor. Just cemented what I already knew. With Charlie, it's like a fog lifts, and everything feels sharper and more alive. It terrifies me how quickly I've realized how much I want her, how much I always have. I think I've been waiting for her all along.

"Hey, Brooks, you awake?" Ryan's voice snaps me back. I've been standing still, the puck just sitting on the ice in front of me. He skates up beside me, eyebrows raised. "What's up?"

"Nothing," I lie, taking a quick shot at the net. The puck glides in smoothly, but doesn't bring the usual satisfaction. "Just a lot on my mind."

Ryan doesn't press, but I know he's not buying it. He's been my captain for years and knows me too well. But I'm not ready to talk about it. Not yet.

We return to the drills, and I push myself to focus, forcing Charlotte from my mind. But before long, the routine blurs, and she slips back into focus with that flash in her eyes when she flirted right back.

I skate over to the bench, grab a drink, and reach for my leather notebook—glancing over notes on plays, trying to find something to ground me. It's something I keep on me for everything I can't keep in my head. My therapist recommended it a few years back, as a way to manage stress and keep things in perspective. I don't need the sessions as much anymore, but the notebook stayed. Mostly it's filled with game strategies and scattered notes.

Lately though, I've started adding tiny stars in the margins each time Charlotte crosses my mind. Just a quick mark, small enough to miss, but it's becoming a habit I can't seem to break.

"Brooks! You in or what?" Chase skates over as I slip it back into my bag.

"Just warming up, man. Don't get too ahead of yourself."

Chase laughs, speeding toward the net where some of the other guys are shooting. I pick up my pace, letting adrenaline and muscle memory take over.

"Late night?" Eli asks as I line up beside him.

"Nah, just have a lot on my mind."

"Uh-huh." He gives me a sideways glance before refocusing.

We go through the drills, and while I'm concentrating, I'm also running through the rest of my plans of the day. I'm picking up ingredients and heading to Charlie's place this afternoon. The thought has my stomach flipping, excitement tangling with nerves.

I'm nervous, because I don't want to mess this up. And I'm excited, because I know I won't.

After the drills, we break into smaller groups, working on specific plays. Chase skates over to me, his expression turning mischievous. "So, what's got you so distracted, Brooks? It's not like you to be this quiet."

I shrug, trying to play it cool. "Just thinking about some stuff. Got plans later."

"Plans, huh?" Chase smirks, glancing around. "Would those plans involve a certain redhead from the Pulse office?"

I can't hide the smile tugging at my mouth. "Maybe."

Chase claps a hand on my shoulder, testing his luck. "You know what they say about redheads... lady in the streets, fiery in the sheets." He waggles his eyebrows. "Bet she'd keep *you* on your toes, or maybe I should say your knees."

"Careful," I warn, but he doesn't take the hint.

"Just saying man, she's hot! And I wouldn't mind—"

"Fuck off, Walton. She's not some hookup for your list."

Chase raises his hands in mock surrender, smirk in place. "Alright, alright. Didn't peg you as the jealous type, Brooks. Gotta say, it's kinda cute."

"Chase," I say, the edge unmistakable now.

He grins, clearly thrilled with himself. "Okay, Romeo. Just keep that fire on the ice too, huh? Wouldn't want you slipping because you're too busy playing *lover boy*."

"This coming from the guy who loses his mind every time Zoe scowls at him from the stands?"

"Touché," he laughs. "But don't go getting soft on us, Brooks."

"Not a chance." I give him a playful shove. "I'm fully focused."

"Yeah, on something that's definitely not hockey," he teases, skating off.

Coach blows the whistle, signaling the end of our practice. We gather at center ice, listening as he runs through the week's schedule, but my mind's already on what's next — getting those ingredients and heading to Charlotte's.

As we start to head off the ice, I spot Zoe standing near the boards, her camera in hand. "Jake! Smile for the camera!"

I laugh, giving her a mock salute as I skate over. "What're you doing here so early?"

Zoe shrugs, lowering her camera to scroll through shots. "Just getting some content. Plus, Chase said you guys were doing new drills, so I thought I'd capture some of them."

I glance over at Chase, who's giving Zoe his classic lopsided grin. I smell bullshit. That guy will say anything to get her attention. "*New drills*, huh?"

"Yeah, we're all about innovation," Chase calls back, laughing.

Zoe narrows her eyes. "Uh-huh. Try not to innovate too hard and break something, Walton. I'm not in the mood for a PR disaster today."

Chase chuckles, slinging his stick over his shoulder. "Don't worry, Zoe. I'll be a good boy for you. Wouldn't want to get you all worked up."

Zoe shakes her head, but she lingers on him for a moment before turning back to me. "Anyway, how's your morning going, Jake?

I shrug, feeling a little exposed under her knowing watch. "Good. Got some plans this afternoon I'm looking forward to."

"Oh? Care to share?" Her tone is light, but I know better. The way girls talk, she probably already knows exactly what I'm up to.

I smirk, leaning in slightly. "Let's just say I'm working on a special project close to my heart."

Zoe raises an eyebrow, biting her tongue to hold back a smile. "Well, good luck. I'm a *big fan* of special projects when the heart's involved."

I give her a nod. She knows exactly what I mean. And as Charlie's closest friend, it feels good to have her as an ally.

As I head toward the locker room, I catch Chase circling back to Zoe. Her eyes roll at whatever he says, but a smile tugs at her lips. Those two are like a storm waiting to happen, but I've got my own shit to handle.

By the time I'm showered and changed, most of the guys are gone. I grab my keys, my mind already set on the afternoon with Charlie. I swing by the store, checking off her list and feeling that surge of determination again.

This isn't just about baking. It's about showing her I'm here for more than just a good time. This feels significant—like maybe one of the most important things I'll ever do. I want her to let me in, to trust me enough to see where this could go.

And if she's not ready, then I'll wait. Because I'm not going anywhere, not this time.

When I finally pull up to her place, I take a deep breath, looking down at my notebook on the passenger seat. I jot a couple of stars onto a page, then tuck it back in my bag and grab the groceries, my nerves humming.

I ring the doorbell, hearing the sound echo inside. A few moments later the door swings open, and there she is. Red hair catching the light, her bright smile already disarming me.

"Hey, Charlie." My grin sharpens as I let my eyes roam over her just a little. "Or should I call you Chef?"

CHAPTER TEN

WHAT DO YOU MEAN YOU DON'T KNOW HOW TO FOLD?

---·✦·---

Charlie

The sound of the doorbell jolts me, and I nearly spill my wine. I set the glass down quickly, hands shaky with a mix of nerves and excitement.

Zoe's voice echoes in my mind: *Pour yourself a glass of wine and stop being a pussy.* Well, I took her advice, but now that Jake's actually here, one glass may not cut it.

I smooth down my apron, take a deep breath, and walk to the door. I can do this. It's just baking, just an afternoon with an old friend. But nothing about this feels like *just* anything.

When I open the door, Jake's standing there with bags of ingredients, looking as effortlessly handsome as ever. That nervous flutter in my stomach turns into a full-blown storm.

"Hey, Charlie," he says. "Or should I call you Chef?" *That smile should come with a warning label.*

I raise an eyebrow, leaning on the doorframe. "That depends. Think you can follow orders?"

His eyes glint as he steps inside. "Guess we're about to find out."

He follows me to the kitchen, moving like he's been here a hundred times before, filling the house with an energy that feels both familiar and unnervingly new. There's something both thrilling and terrifying about it.

"So, what's the plan?" Jake asks, setting the bags down on the counter. "I'm at your mercy, Chef." *Oh, there are several things I would have you do at my mercy.*

I laugh a little too loudly, and grab my wine glass for a quick gulp. "Alright, first thing's first—do you know what folding is?"

His eyebrow quirks up, smirk edging into a grin. "Folding? Like... laundry?"

"Like *baking*," I correct, trying to keep a straight face. "It's a technique, not just stirring. You have to be gentle, so you don't knock the air out of the batter."

The grin widens. "So, it's like stirring but fancy. Got it."

I narrow my eyes at him with mock seriousness. "This is very important. I don't think I trust you with it."

He puts a hand over his heart. "You wound me, Charlie. But alright—what am I allowed to do?"

"Measuring," I say, pointing to a bowl. "Everything needs to be exact. You can handle that, right?"

"I think I can manage."

I hand him the measuring cups and recipe, watching as he carefully scoops flour into the bowl, his focus almost comically intense for such a simple task. The scene is so absurdly domestic, it makes my heart twist. *Measuring flour isn't hot, measuring flour isn't hot.*

"So," he says, glancing at me. "How long have you been perfecting your control-freak baking methods?"

Biting back a grin, I try to sound authoritative. "It's not control-freakishness. It's precision."

He leans in, close enough that I catch a hint of his cologne. "It's cute." *Oh my God.*

I roll my eyes, ignoring the flush creeping up my neck. "Less talking, more measuring." *Get it together, Charlie.*

He chuckles, but not before brushing past me, his arm grazing mine, sending a tingle through me. As we work, the conversation flows easily with the kind of light banter that feels effortless. It's just like camp. Easy, familiar.

But underneath it all, there's tension. It hums between us, unspoken but obvious. *Is he as terrified as I am?*

At one point, Jake glances over and his eyes turn more serious. "So, what made you decide to move here? With the kids and everything?"

I pause, caught off guard. I've thought about it a thousand times, but hearing him ask in that non-judgemental way makes it feel more real. I focus on folding the batter like it's the most important thing in the world. "It was time for a change. Things with my ex weren't good because he was more focused on his career than on us."

Jake nods, his expression thoughtful. "That must've been hard."

"It was," I say softly. "But staying would've been harder, you know? I tried for a long time to... I don't know, make it work. Make him love us. But it was always one-sided. I couldn't keep letting him break my babies' hearts. I had to do what was right for them—and for me."

He's quiet, his eyes focused on measuring, but there's a tension in his jaw. "You did the right thing. My dad... well, you might remember he wasn't around much. My mom stayed, but it wasn't easy for her, or for me. I always thought she should've left. So, I think it's pretty damn brave that you did."

His words hit me, stirring memories of a late-night conversation by the lake. I look up, surprised by the raw honesty. There's a depth in his gaze that makes my heart ache. "I remember."

"And you shouldn't have to make someone love you," he says softly. "It should be effortless." His eyes catch mine, holding them. "Loving you would be the easiest thing in the world."

For a moment, the air feels heavy with everything unsaid and the weight of all the time between us. My chest thunders, like it knows he's reached across the years and touched a part of me I thought I'd hidden away. His eyes linger on mine as though he wants to say more, and I stare back, not sure what to say myself.

And then the oven dings, shattering the moment into pieces.

I clear my throat, turning toward the oven. "Looks like the first batch is done."

Jake steps back, giving me space to open the door, but there's a look in his eyes that says he felt it, too—whatever *it* was.

As I pull the tray out, he leans against the counter, watching me with that easy smile. "So, how'd I do on the measuring? Star pupil or what?"

I laugh, grateful for the mood lightener. "Pretty good. But don't get cocky. There's still plenty of work to do."

He winks at me. "I'm not scared of a little work." *I'm not going to survive this day if he keeps winking at me like that.*

We keep baking, tension ebbing and flowing as we move around the kitchen. I feel his eyes on me, watching every move. The way he finds any excuse to get close, brushing his fingers against mine or reaching an arm around my back for something, only stokes this thing building between us. When we both reach for the same spoon, his fingers linger on mine, and it takes everything in me not to react.

Eventually, I pour myself another glass of wine and offer him one. He accepts, and for a moment we stand there, sipping in comfortable silence.

"You know," he says finally, breaking the quiet, "I'm glad we're doing this. Feels like we picked up right where we left off twelve years ago."

His words catch me off guard, and I glance at him trying to gauge them. *Pretty sure where we left off involved us both trying not to jump each other's bones.*

"You're right," I say with a smile. "It's like no time has passed."

"Yeah." He looks at me, eyes softening. "We should've kept in touch."

I nod, turning to the oven and pulling out another tray of cookies, the caramelized sugar filling the air. "Yeah, we should have," I admit, setting the tray on the counter. "But life just got in the way, I guess."

Turning back, I expect him to still be by the counter, but he's right there—closer than before. Our eyes lock, the distance between us feeling paper-thin.

"I looked for you online for a while, but then I got rid of my socials. Too much pressure from the media, too many people wanting to know every detail."

I blink, surprised. "I didn't know that. I just assumed you got busy with your career taking off and everything. And I was at uni, then met Alex..." I trail off, not wanting to bring up my ex again.

Jake nods, his expression darkening for a moment. "Yeah. Guess we both got busy. But I thought about that summer a lot, Charlie. I didn't forget you."

There's something in his words that sounds like a confession, like he needs me to know it. The space between us feels like it's caving in, and I swallow, suddenly very aware of how close he is. His eyes drop to my lips before flicking back to my eyes.

"Those cookies smell amazing," he says, like he's not talking about cookies at all.

"Yeah..." My voice barely comes out, my pulse thundering in my ears.

Neither of us move. We just stand there, inches apart, the heat from the oven mingling with something far more authentic. My heart pounds so loud I'm sure he can hear it. *I'm gonna die. I'm gonna pass away surrounded by cookie dough and Jake Brooks.*

His hand twitches like he's about to reach for me, and I stop breathing, waiting.

But then the front door clatters open, and seconds later, Noah and Meadow's voices fill the air, reality crashing back around us.

We both step back, the heat dissipating as quickly as it came.

Jake clears his throat, giving me a sheepish smile. "Looks like we've got some extra helpers."

"Yeah," I reply, voice shaky. "Perfect timing."

"Perfect," he echoes. But he doesn't seem annoyed by the interruption. In fact, there's warmth in his eyes as he turns toward the kids.

"Mama!" Meadow's voice rings out as she runs into the kitchen, wrapping her arms around my legs. "We're back!"

I bend down to scoop her up, her little arms squeezing tight around my neck. "Hey, honey bee. Did you have fun?"

She nods eagerly, catching sight of Jake over my shoulder. "Hi, Jake!" She wriggles out of my grasp, rushing over to him.

Jake crouches down, giving her a huge smile. "Hey, Princess. You've got perfect timing—cookies are almost ready."

Noah steps forward, eyeing Jake with a mix of curiosity and familiarity. "Did you make donuts, too?"

Jake chuckles, reaching out to ruffle Noah's hair. "Not this time, buddy. But we did make some awesome cookies."

After Nina leaves, the next half hour becomes a whirl of flour, sugar, and laughter. Jake is amazing with them—patient, playful, completely present. At one point, Meadow ends up with flour all over her, and Jake laughs along with her, gently wiping it off with a kitchen towel. It's a simple gesture, but the tenderness in it makes my heart swell.

Watching him with my kids feels almost too natural, as if he's always been here. *Stop it, Charlie. This is just baking.*

Eventually, we gather around the table to sample our creations.

"This is the best cookie ever!" Noah announces, mouth full of chocolate chips.

Jake takes a bite of his own. "I agree, bud. Your mom's a pretty great baker."

I feel heat rush up my neck and quickly take a sip of my wine to hide it. "Thanks. But you did most of the work."

Jake raises an eyebrow, the dimple in his cheek appearing. "Pretty sure you didn't let me do anything more complicated than measuring."

"Someone had to keep you and your lack of folding skills in check," I joke, and he laughs, the sound warm and full of genuine happiness.

After the cookies are devoured and the kids start to get sleepy, I take them upstairs, tucking them in with promises of more baking adventures. When I return, Jake's wiping down the counters, looking so at home it hits me like a punch. *This is dangerous territory, Charlie.*

"Thanks for helping out," I say, leaning against the doorframe, trying to steady the strange mix of contentment and longing building in me.

"Anytime," he replies, meeting my eyes. "This was fun. We should do it again."

I nod, feeling the tension spark again now that we're alone. "Yeah, we should... if you can handle the chaos."

He laughs, tossing the cloth in the sink. "Meadow and Noah are adorable. I'd be happy to hang out with them anytime."

His words wash over me, but I control the urge to climb this man like a tree. We stand there, eyes locked like we're both weighing the risks, deciding if we're ready to cross whatever line we're toeing.

But then he blinks, breaking the moment with a soft, bittersweet smile. "I should go. Gotta be ready for the event tomorrow."

I nod, feeling a pang of disappointment. "Yeah, of course. We'll see you there."

"You better," he says, the corner of his mouth curling up.

He grabs his jacket and walks to the door, but he pauses while opening it. "For the record, you're an amazing mom, Charlie. I mean it."

There's something about Jake saying that to me without any hesitation that has me swallowing hard. He knew who I was and sees exactly who I am now. Somehow, he bridges both versions of me, filling the gap with a warmth I haven't felt in years. Maybe not since him.

"Thanks," I say softly, unsure if I can say more without getting weird and emotional.

He gives me one last, lingering look before heading out, leaving me standing there with my spinning thoughts.

While tidying up, I find his cap on the floor by the dining table. I pick it up, feeling the worn fabric between my fingers. It looks identical to the one he used to wear at camp. *Don't smell it. Don't be a fucking psychopath, Charlie.*

I take it upstairs with me and place it on my dresser. Once I'm in bed, I settle under the covers, but my thoughts keep drifting back to Jake. I grab my phone from the nightstand, intending to check the time, but my fingers hesitate.

Without overthinking it, I shoot him a quick text.

Me: You forgot something

Jake: Did I? Was it important?

I snap a picture of the cap and send it.

> **Jake:** Oh, that. For a second there, I thought you meant something else.

> **Me:** Like what?

> **Jake:** A kiss? My dignity? I lose track around you.

My heart skips as I read his message. I bite my lip, warmth spreading as I type back. Maybe it's the wine making me bold, or maybe it's just him.

> **Me:** Maybe you did

> **Jake:** In that case, I'm definitely coming back

> **Me:** Haha. You should feel lucky I didn't fire you as my sous chef.

There's a pause while I watch the little dots move, and then—

> **Jake:** Lucky, huh? How about I make it up to you tomorrow?

> **Me:** What, by not burning down the kitchen?

> **Jake:** No guarantees. But I might aim for a promotion.

> **Me:** To what? Head dishwasher?

> **Jake:** Nah. Head taste tester.

My pulse picks up as I think of a reply, but then my phone pings again.

Jake: I had a great time tonight, Charlie.

Me: Me too. Night, Jake

Jake: Sweet dreams, Chef.

I laugh softly, placing my phone down and closing my eyes.

There's something about the way Jake pays attention to me. It's always felt different. Under his gaze, I feel steady and weightless all at once, like I'm standing on solid ground but still capable of reaching for more.

With him, I feel seen. Heard. Respected. He notices the little things, listens like every word matters. His eyes never waver, like I'm the only person in the room. Like he genuinely cares, not because it's convenient, but because it's who he is.

It might be the familiarity of old memories clouding my judgment, but it's been so long since someone looked at me like that. Back then, his attention felt almost accidental, like he didn't realize how much of it he gave me. But tonight was different. That flirting wasn't innocent. It was deliberate, focused, intentional. And I felt it, every charged word and lingering glance.

Alex was always too busy, too wrapped up in his own world to really see me. I was an afterthought, a convenience, something to check off a list.

But Jake makes me feel like I matter. Like I'm worth the time, worth the effort. Even with something as small as teaching him how to fold batter.

Still, I can't ignore the past, and I need to remind myself to be cautious. Because letting myself fall without a safety net feels risky as hell.

CHAPTER ELEVEN

YOU'RE THE DESSERT THAT SHOULD BE ON THIS TABLE

———— ✦ ————

Charlotte - 12 Years Ago

T he kids are buzzing, their excitement spilling over as they gather around us for the nature hike they've been talking about all day. Jake stands beside me, hands shoved in his pockets, wearing a grin that almost hides the nerves radiating off him. Almost. He's been a little on edge ever since we were asked to take this group out, but I know he'll be great. He just doesn't realize it yet.

"Alright, kids!" I clap my hands to focus their attention. "Who's ready for an adventure?"

A chorus of cheers erupts, and I catch Jake's eye as I continue. "We're going to explore the woods, find some cool rocks, and maybe even spot a few animals. But first, we need to make sure we stick together. No running off, okay?"

The kids nod, their eyes wide with anticipation, and I bump Jake's shoulder lightly. "You ready, Captain Thunder?"

"Ready as I'll ever be, Lady Lightning," he says, voice steady but shoulders tense.

We set off, and as expected, the kids are a tornado of energy—darting after bugs, tripping over rocks, and shouting about everything they see. Jake keeps pace, his voice calm but firm as he wrangles the chaos. He doesn't realize it, but he's got this quiet authority that makes people listen.

When a little girl named Lily trips and scrapes her knee, Jake's by her side in an instant. He crouches down, his voice low and soothing. "Hey, tough cookie. You're okay. Know what I used to do when I got a scrape like this? Pretend it was a battle scar from fighting dragons. Wanna try?"

Her sniffles turn to giggles, and she nods. He helps her to her feet, dusting off her shorts. "There you go. Now, let's get back to our adventure."

When he looks back at me, I smile warmly. His expression is a mix of surprise and something softer, like he's still processing that he's capable of this. That he's good at this.

By the time we return to camp, the kids are worn out but happy. The tension has eased from Jake's shoulders, and I give him a playful nudge. "You were great out there, you know."

He glances at me, a little sheepish. "I don't know about that. You did most of the work."

"No, Jake. They listened to you. They look up to you." I meet his eyes, holding his gaze. "You make people feel safe. That's not something you can fake."

For a moment, he just looks at me, like he's trying to figure out why I believe in him so much. Like I've given him something he didn't know he needed. Then he nods, his voice soft. "Thanks, Charlie."

That night, as I lie in my bunk, I replay the events of the day and the way he looked at me. Vulnerable, uncertain, and quietly grateful.

It's small, but it sticks with me. Because in that moment, I saw something in him—a need to be seen and valued—and it made me want to be that person for him.

The one who always believes in him, no matter what.

***

Charlie - Present Day

The Play It Forward fundraiser is a busy, bright mix of laughter, voices, and kids darting around tables. Everywhere I look, clusters of people are deep in conversation, all here to support Jake's foundation. I didn't expect to feel so proud of him, but I am.

Jake's completely in his element, moving from group to group, his smile wide, his laugh carrying across the room. He's magnetic. And I'm just as captivated as everyone else, watching him interact with the kids and seeing firsthand just how much this means to him. Kids crowd around him, clinging to his every word as he crouches down, engaging each of them with such genuine warmth.

My kids are no exception. Noah's wearing Jake's cap from last night, excitedly describing his latest LEGO build. Jake listens with a focus most adults skip over, nodding as if Noah's explaining something groundbreaking. Meanwhile, Meadow's taken to Jake like she's known him forever. When she's not perched on his knee, she's riding on his shoulders, her giggles loud enough to turn heads. Watching him with them feels *unsettlingly* attractive. Like I'm seeing a glimpse of something I shouldn't be letting myself want.

Every so often, I catch him glancing my way. There's something steady in his look, like he's tuning the whole room out for just a second, focused entirely on me. Each time our eyes meet, my chest thunders with a mix of excitement and terror knotting together. *I need air.*

"Someone's got it bad." Zoe sidles up to me, pretending to peruse the desserts before snagging a cupcake.

I pluck it from her hand and set it back on the display. "I don't know what you're talking about."

"Oh come on, Charlie." She sighs dramatically, like she's dealing with a clueless child. "He's been giving you heart eyes since you walked in."

"We're just friends," I argue, but even to my ears the denial sounds weak.

"*Friends?*" She raises a brow. "Friends, my ass. Right now, he's staring at you like *you're* the dessert that should be on this table."

I roll my eyes, but I can't ignore the way my heart skips at the thought.

"Humor me," she says, tilting her head. "Look across the room and tell me who he's staring at right now."

I laugh, nudging her. "Zoe, please. You're making this sound like some middle-school crush."

Despite myself, I sneak a glance at Jake across the room. He's talking with some of his teammates, but even as they laugh and clap him on the back, his gaze drifts my way. And the second our eyes meet, the crowded room seems to narrow, like it's just the two of us tethered by some unspoken connection. A smile tugs at his lips, his dimple on full display like he's been saving its presence just for me.

"See? Heart eyessss," Zoe singsongs, using the distraction to grab the cupcake again and biting into it before I can take it off her.

"You're being ridiculous." I try to brush her off, but she's right. That look of his is impossible to ignore. "He's probably just making sure the event's running smoothly."

"Riiight," Zoe says, dragging the word out between her mouthful of cake. "As smoothly as the way he just tracked you across a room full of people."

I shake my head, trying to focus on rearranging the gap in the cupcakes. "He's busy. This whole thing is for his foundation. Which, by the way, is amazing. I had no idea he was this involved."

"He is," Zoe says, softening. "He puts his whole heart into this foundation. Every off-season he's visiting schools, organizing events, talking to kids... He never wants them to feel like they're on their own."

I nod, understanding the depth behind Jake's dedication probably more than Zoe realizes. Each smile, word, and laugh with these kids is genuine. This isn't just showmanship for him; it's his heart on display. A chance to give kids the support he didn't have growing up.

But before I can respond, Zoe's smirk reappears. "Anyway, don't let me distract you. I'm sure you've got to make sure that *cock-um-booch* is ready. I have a feeling he'll be *very* impressed."

I groan at her mispronunciation. "It's *croquembouche*. And he probably doesn't even know what it is."

"Bet he will when you tell him. Now, if you'll excuse me…" She grabs another cupcake and saunters off to schmooze more guests, grinning at my disdain for her outright cake theft.

I try to lose myself in organizing the desserts, but it doesn't last long. That feeling prickles at my skin again—the weight of a gaze. When I glance up, I catch Jake looking my way again. His eyes hold mine for just a beat, his lips tugging into a quiet smile before he nods at something his teammate says.

My pulse roars in my ears. I don't know how much longer I can keep pretending I don't notice his eyes on me. With a quiet sigh, I slip into the kitchen to catch my breath and double-check the remaining desserts. I've been in and out all day, but the space is empty now, giving me a chance to breathe.

But even in here, away from the crowd, I can't shake the warmth of his eyes on me.

CHAPTER TWELVE

YOU AND ME, WE'RE HAPPENING

———————✦———————

Jake

"**D**ude, are you even listening?" Eli's voice snaps me back to the present, and I realize I've been staring at Charlie again.

I look back to my teammates, watching me with varying degrees of amusement. The event's in full swing, and I should be right in the thick of it, running on the energy in the room. But I'm only half present. The other half? Laser-focused on Charlie.

"Yeah, sorry," I mumble, trying to follow the conversation. But it's impossible. Not when Charlie's just a few feet away, looking so damn beautiful it hurts.

Eli chuckles, following Ryan's gaze to where Charlie's in a cupcake stand-off with Zoe. "You've been watching her like she's gonna vanish if you blink."

Ryan claps me on the shoulder. "You've got it bad, Brooks."

I don't even care that they're giving me shit. My brain's on one track.

"Not denying it," I mutter, eyes back on her. She's laughing at something Zoe said, and it's like I'm magnetized, drawn to every expression, every movement. The guys are right, and I couldn't care less.

Chase smirks. "Whole room's here for you, and she's the only one you're looking at."

"That's rich coming from you, Walton. How *is* Zoe?"

93

"She's onto her third cupcake and has threatened me with physical violence eight times so far."

The guys all laugh, but I'm restless. I've been antsy all day, and no matter how hard I try, I can't stop thinking about Charlie. My eyes track her again, watching her walk back towards the kitchen.

Ryan gives me a nudge in that direction. "Go. Put us all out of our misery."

I don't argue. Sliding away from the crowd, I head toward the kitchen. Each step picks up my pulse, sharpening my focus. I've been in a fog of speeches and handshakes, but now I know exactly what I want.

Charlie's been incredible all day, moving between the kitchen and the dessert table, making sure everything's perfect. I've watched her from a distance, and she's seamless. So natural, so at ease.

But what gets me is how she is with my teammates. She's met most of them today, along with their families, and somehow she fits right in. Like she's always belonged here, in my world. And in my arms and bed, if I get my way.

Every now and then, she's caught me watching her, and those green eyes meet mine like they're tuned just to me. Crashing right through the surface, through all the bullshit, and seeing right into the core of what's real.

When I step into the kitchen, she's at the counter carefully arranging a tower of desserts. Her hair's fallen slightly from her clip to frame her face, and she's humming softly to herself. It's a simple thing, but watching her is a reminder of every reason I fell for her all those years ago.

I'm not even trying to be subtle as I lean against the doorframe. With her back to me, I unashamedly watch the way her body moves as she works. It's intoxicating.

"Need a hand?"

She startles slightly, glancing over her shoulder, and when our eyes meet the oxygen leaves my lungs. Her smile's warm, a little surprised.

"I'm good, thanks," she says, turning back to her work. But I see her hands falter just for a second, her focus shifting as she decorates her tiny tower of cakes.

I push off the doorframe and step closer, hands in my pockets. I want to be near her. Need to be closer.

"You're good with that thing," I say, nodding toward the tower, trying to keep it casual.

"It's called a croquembouche," she says, her mouth tugging in a slight smile.

"I'm not even going try to pronounce that," I chuckle, taking another step. "But it looks amazing."

She shrugs, but there's a quiet pride in her expression. "Years of practice."

"It's impressive, Charlie girl."

She doesn't look at me, just keeps focusing on the dessert. But I see the way her shoulders tense with her breath. I'm getting to her, and it feels damn good to know I have this effect.

"You're supposed to be out there, schmoozing everyone," she says, trying to sound nonchalant.

"Well, you looked like you might need a hand."

"Ever the gentleman," she retorts. "Didn't think you'd be the type to hide back here."

"Wouldn't call this hiding. Just wanted to be wherever you are." I take another step.

Her lips twitch, even as she tries to hold her composure. "Think you can just charm your way into my kitchen, Brooks?"

"Maybe." I move closer still, gaze dropping to her lips before meeting her eyes again. "Though if I wanted to charm you, I'd start by telling you I've spent twelve years trying to hold onto the way you made me feel the last time I had you this close."

She lets out a small scoff. "You're still a smooth talker, that part hasn't changed."

"Only with you."

Her eyes dart to me briefly, and I see it. Hesitation, curiosity, a flicker of want. It's subtle, but it's there, and all I want to do is fan it. She sucks her plush lower lip between her teeth, glancing away, and that's it. I'm gone.

Every good intention I've clung to—giving her space, not rushing things—shatters in an instant. Because fuck it. Fuck waiting. Fuck caution. I've spent twelve years wondering if this moment would ever come and now she's right here, standing in front of me like a goddamn miracle. I'm not wasting another second.

"Charlie." I reach out, brushing a loose strand of hair from her face, letting my thumb drift along her cheekbone. Her skin is warm beneath mine, and her breath hitches just enough to wreck any resistance left in me.

She leans into my touch, eyes locked on mine, and it's like this thing between us, this fire that's been smoldering since we last saw each other, finally lights up.

Her eyes drop to my lips, and I feel my heartbeat trip. I move my thumb to trace her lower lip, feeling her breath tremble against my skin.

"Jake..." Her voice is barely a whisper, like she's not sure if she should pull away.

"I'm right here," I murmur. "If you want me to stop, tell me."

Her eyes widen, flicking between mine, but I wait, giving her the choice. I want this kiss, I've wanted it for so many years, but I need her to want it, too.

"God, you're beautiful." The words escape before I can catch them, but I don't regret a single syllable. Instead, I let my eyes trace the lines of her face, waiting, hoping she'll lean in.

For a second, I think she might step back. Her eyes hold mine, uncertainty flickering like she's still deciding if this is allowed—if *we're* allowed. But just when I think I've read this wrong, she leans up to close the distance, her lips brushing against mine in a tentative, soft touch.

It's barely there, a whisper of a kiss, like she's testing the waters. But it's enough to set every nerve in me alight. The second her mouth parts slightly, every ounce of restraint I've been clinging to crumbles.

The heat between us ignites, flaring like a spark catching dry tinder. My hand slips into her hair to tilt her closer, my other finding the curve of her waist to steady us both. Her fingers twist into the front of my shirt, holding on like she's afraid to let go. But as she melts into me, her arms wind up around my neck, pulling me in as if we're both starving for this.

Time collapses around us, every missed moment and unspoken word filling the spaces between each drag of our lips. Every night she's felt alone and I've felt lost, every memory that's lingered with an ache—it's all right here, in this kiss. She tastes like red wine and something uniquely her, and I realize this is it. I want to fill every corner of her heart that's been left waiting, every dark space that's ever been hurt or broken. I don't ever want to stop.

Her fingers flex in my hair, a soft sound escaping her as the kiss deepens. A groan slips from me, rumbling into her as I press her closer, needing her to feel how real this is. It's every unsaid promise, every piece of me I want to give her.

When we finally pull back, we're both breathless, and the air between us feels charged and fragile. Her eyes are wide and searching mine, her lips flushed and slightly parted. It takes everything I have not to pull her back in, to show her how far gone I am for her.

Fuck.

She stares at me with her fingers pressed to her lips, and I can see the doubt creeping in, the rush of thoughts crashing over her.

"Oh God, Jake, I... I'm sorry. I shouldn't have—"

"Hey, hey." I catch her hand, keeping her close. "Don't apologize." My thumb brushes over her knuckles, hoping to ground her. Ground *me*.

Her eyes search mine hesitantly, like she's waiting for the other shoe to drop. But all I feel is relief. Relief that I've finally kissed her, finally shown her how I feel.

"I just... I wasn't sure if... this is what you wanted."

"What I *wanted*? Charlie, I've wanted to kiss you since that last night at camp," I confess, the words spilling out before I can stop them. "And now that I have, I'm not letting it go."

I can see her wrestling with herself, the mix of emotions flashing in her eyes. Relief, fear, hope. Gently, I tug her back into me, not ready to let her go just yet. This is it for me.

"But you know what *else* I want?" My eyes roam her face, trying to read her. "A date. With you."

She blinks, processing. "A date?"

"Yeah. Because after that kiss, I'm not stopping at just one."

Her brows knit together, a hint of doubt crossing her face. I can see her struggling, sorting through all the reasons to say no.

"Jake, this... it's moving fast. I'm not sure—"

"Maybe it feels fast to you," I say, cutting in softly. "But I've been waiting for this moment for twelve years." I cup her jaw, thumb brushing slowly over her cheek. "I know what I want. And I think you do, too."

She hesitates and looks down, but I'm not having it.

"Don't second-guess this." I lift her hand to my lips, pressing a kiss to her knuckles. "This is real, Charlie. You and me, we're happening."

She looks at our joined hands, and I can see it—the spark she's trying to push down and ignore, but she can't.

"Please, Charlie girl?" My thumb traces slow circles over her skin. "All you need to do is say yes."

She looks up slowly, and when her eyes meet mine, I see her decision in them. The edge of her lips curl, and she whispers, "Okay."

A smile spreads across my face, a quiet victory. "Tomorrow," I say, giving her hand a final squeeze as I step back. "I'll pick you up at seven."

She nods, cheeks still flushed, and I see the thrill mixed with nerves in her eyes. I want to kiss all that doubt right out of her, to hold her close and remind her how real this is. Tell her I'm all in, and I'm not going fuck this up. But I hold back, knowing I need to give her time.

At least, I try to.

"Wait," I murmur, stepping back into her space. Her lips part, breath catching as I cup her jaw again. "One more, just one."

I kiss her again, softer this time, less urgency and more promise. Her fingers curl into my shirt, and I feel her smile against my mouth when I pull back. But it's not enough.

"Okay," she whispers, cheeks pink. "We should—"

"Hang on." I cut her off, hands still framing her face as I steal another kiss. Her laugh is muffled against my lips, and when I pull away, her brows lift in amusement.

"Jake—"

"Last one, I swear." I dip my head to kiss her again, savoring the way she softens against me. Her hands slide to my shoulders, and I can tell she's trying not to laugh. I peck her softly once, twice, and then reluctantly pull back.

"We really should get back out there," she says, swiping at her hair and nodding toward the hallway.

She's right, but it takes all my self-control to let her go.

"Okay, okay. I'm done... for now," I say, feeling the ache of separation already. I push down the need to keep her close, even though every cell is screaming at me to do the opposite.

Stepping back into the event is like a cold splash of reality. The noise and lights are a sharp contrast to the quiet intensity of what just happened. All I want is to bundle her and the kids into my car to take them home, and hold her in my arms until the sun comes up.

Instead I force a smile, shake hands and make small talk, but none of it feels real.

The only real thing is her. Charlie, the promise of tomorrow, and the certainty I've waited twelve years to feel.

CHAPTER THIRTEEN

JAKE'S #1 FAN CLUB

———————◆———————

Charlie

The kiss.

That perfect, toe-curling, mind-stilling kiss. It's all I can think about as I drive home. The way Jake's hands gripped my waist like he couldn't bear to let go replays on a loop in my mind. It felt like opening a door I'd shut years ago, stepping into a moment that was always meant to happen. A rewrite of something unfinished, yet intense and new.

I've been kissed before, but nothing like this. Nothing that felt so consuming, like every part of him was aligned to me in a pull we couldn't resist. The kiss was a cataclysm, rearranging the ground beneath us, making me feel more seen and alive than I have in years.

It felt like a kiss that had been made just for us, one he'd been saving to give me. And he was ready to break through every wall I'd carefully built to make sure I knew it.

Now that it's happened, I can't imagine going back. I can't imagine a world where I don't know the feeling of his lips on mine ever again. And I don't think I want to. *Fuck.*

As soon as I get home, I tuck the kids into bed, their sleepy faces blissfully unaware of the turmoil raging inside me. Once they're settled, I pour a glass of wine, hoping it'll calm my nerves. But it doesn't. It just makes the butterflies flutter harder. I'm stressing out, and I know I am because now I'm overthinking whether butterflies *fly or flutter*, for fuck sake.

My fingers itch to text Zoe, the only person who can talk me down from this ledge.

Me: Fuck fuck fuck

My phone rings immediately with her name flashing on my screen. I answer, and before I can even say hello, she's talking.

"Did you kiss him?!" Zoe's voice is full of anticipation, and a pang of exhilaration hits me.

"Oh my God, I kissed him," I blurt out, my words a jumbled confession. "Actually, no—he kissed me! But I might have leaned in first. And it was *amazing*, but now I'm freaking out."

Zoe laughs. "Well don't do *that*! How was it?"

I start pacing, spilling every detail. "Incredible. Terrifying... What if it's too much, too soon? What if I just complicated everything? And now he wants to take me on a date tomorrow. What if I'm not ready?"

"Charlie," she says gently through her amused chuckle. "You kissed an amazing guy who's clearly into you. Don't overthink it—just enjoy it. You deserve this!"

I let out a breath, feeling the tension ease a little. "He said he's wanted to kiss me since the last night we had at camp."

She gasps dramatically down the phone. "Oh my God, he's been *pining for you for years*! Charlie, that's disgustingly romantic!" She pauses. "Why are you freaking out again?"

"I don't know! What if this complicates things with the kids? Or what if I'm not what he's been imagining all this time?"

Zoe scoffs. "Please. You're even better. And you deserve to be happy, babe. Does Jake make you happy?"

"Yes." My whispered answer comes without hesitation. *He always has.*

"Then go the fuck to sleep, and enjoy tomorrow."

I close my eyes with a sigh, holding the phone tightly to my ear. "Okay..."

"Trust me, this is a good thing. Take it one step at a time and see where it goes."

I smile, feeling a bit lighter. "Thanks for another stellar motivational speech."

"And if he rocks your world, I expect a full report. Charts, graphs, and a dramatic reenactment."

Chuckling, I end the call. I set my phone down, but before I walk away, it buzzes with a new notification from Zoe.

Zoe changed the chat name to: Jake's #1 Fan Club

> **Me:** Cute. Real cute.

> **Zoe:** Welcome to Jake's #1 Fan Club, Madame President!

I snort, shaking my head as I snuggle into the sofa. I'm about to text her back again when another message comes through.

> **Jake:** You get home okay?

My heart thunders.

> **Me:** Yeah, just got the kids settled. You?

> **Jake:** Just got in. Any idea why Zoe just texted 'finally'?

Fucking Zoe. I'm mortified.

> **Me:** Ignore her, she's meddling

> **Jake:** I'm not ignoring it. 'Finally' feels like the right word

I blink, his words sending a thrill through me. Before I can respond, another text pings.

> **Jake:** Can't stop thinking about that kiss.

> **Me:** Same. It was intense

> **Jake:** In a good way, I hope

> **Me:** Yeah. Definitely in a good way

> **Jake:** Good. Because I don't think I can wait until tomorrow night to see you again

I bite my lip, smiling as another message pings.

> **Jake:** Maybe I should come over and help you freak out about this kiss in person

> **Me:** How exactly would that help?

> **Jake:** We could talk it out. Or kiss it out. Your call

> **Me:** You're a bad influence, you know that?

> **Jake:** Only when it comes to you

My stomach flips wildly as another text rolls in, and I take a sip from my glass.

> **Jake:** So… what are you wearing?

I choke on my wine. Is he serious? Oh God, he's serious. I'm giggling like a teenager, thanking God Zoe can't see me right now.

Me: You're impossible

Jake: But you're not answering the question...

Nibbling on my lip, I play along.

Me: I'm still in my dress from the event. Happy?

Jake: Very. That dress looks incredible on you. Bet you look even better out of it, though

I laugh again, pulling the sofa blanket up to my chin like I'm hiding. *I am going to pass away, and all we've done is kiss.* I channel Zoe's confidence and type back.

Me: You'll have to wait and see.

A pause. I wonder if I've gone too far, but then the three little dots appear again.

Jake: I'm counting down the hours already

Me: See you tomorrow, Captain Thunder

Jake: Sweet dreams, Lady Lightning.

I set my phone down, the giddiness of our exchange mixing with lingering anxiety. Zoe's right—I should enjoy this. I've spent so long worrying about everything that could go wrong, I've forgotten how to enjoy something that feels right. And Jake and I feel right. We always have.

As I settle against the cushions, the memory of our kiss floods back. His lips on mine, the way my walls felt like they were crumbling around me. How he held me like he knew it. Like he was anchoring me, promising he wasn't going anywhere. A warmth spreads through me, soft and terrifying all at once.

Because *shit*. Tomorrow, I'm going on a date with Jake Brooks.

And he wants to see me out of my dress.

CHAPTER FOURTEEN

LIONS AND TIGERS AND ONE GIANT HOT HOCKEY PLAYER, OH MY!

Charlie

> **Nina:** Hey Charlotte, I'm so sorry, but I've come down with a nasty bug. I won't be able to watch the kids tonight.

My stomach sinks as I frantically think through options. Zoe and Jade might be able to help, but I remember Zoe mentioning they're both tied up at a family event tonight.

Still, I quickly text her, hoping by some miracle I misunderstood.

> **Me:** Zo, just checking—are you free tonight?

> **Zoe:** Sorry, babe. I'm at that family thing with Jade xx

Of course. Just my luck. I sigh, running a hand through my hair as I try to come up with another solution. But without the nanny, a babysitter, or Zoe, I'm out of options. Nerves tangle in me as I type out the dreaded message to Jake.

> **Me:** Hey, my sitter is sick. I don't think I'll be able to make our date tonight. So sorry

Closing my eyes, I hit send. My phone buzzes almost immediately—he's calling. I pick it up, bracing for his disappointment.

"Charlie girl," his voice is warm, but there's a hint of concern. "You're not flaking on me, are you?"

"No! I swear, I'm not," I blurt, my words rushing out in my anxiety. "I really don't have anyone to watch the kids. I've tried everyone, and I'm fresh out of options."

He's quiet for a beat, and I chew my lip, waiting for him to say it's okay and we'll try another time. But instead, his voice softens, full of understanding.

"It's okay Charlie, I get it. How about this... I'll come over to yours. We can still hang out, just the four of us. I'll bring lunch, and we'll make a day of it. Maybe take the kids somewhere fun."

Surprised relief floods through me, and I feel a smile tug at the corners of my lips. "Really?"

"Of course. I'd love to spend the day with you and the kids. We can hit the zoo or the park, whatever they're into."

I smile, unable to help the warmth spreading through me at his willingness to adapt. "They'd love the zoo. That sounds perfect."

"Great. I'll be over in a bit. Don't stress—this is all good. Okay?"

"Okay," I breathe, the weight lifting off my shoulders. "Thanks, Jake."

"Anything for you, Charlie girl," he says softly before hanging up.

I stare at the phone for a moment, grinning like an idiot at the way he's so understanding, so willing to be part of my life, kids and all. He's not just tolerating them, but embracing them. And of course I should expect that, but it's still overwhelming how naturally he does it.

With Jake due any moment, the kids are bouncing with excitement. Noah's at the window, eagerly awaiting Jake's arrival, while Meadow twirls around the living room, her giggles filling the air. I've calmed down, but when I hear Jake's SUV pull up, my heart starts racing again.

"Mum, he's here!" Noah shouts, darting toward the front door.

I open the door just as Jake steps out, looking way too good in a jacket, t-shirt and jeans, sunglasses on and his cap turned backward. Some of his dark brown hair flicks out underneath, and I wonder how he hasn't been arrested yet for disturbing the peace.

He's holding a brown bag of deli food in one hand and two stuffed animals peeking out from the crook of his arm. My heart does a flip at the sight—he's brought lunch and something for the kids.

"Hey, guys!" he calls, kneeling down as Noah barrels into him.

"Jake!" Noah's face lights up as Jake ruffles his hair. "What did you bring?"

"Something for lunch," Jake says, glancing up at me with a wink that makes me weak on the spot. "And maybe a little something for you and your sister."

He pulls out a lion with a soft mane and hands it to Meadow, who gasps with delight. "For me?" she whispers, her big eyes wide.

"For you," Jake says, eyes crinkling with a smile. "Every zoo visit needs a lion."

Meadow clutches the toy to her chest, glowing with happiness. "Thank you, Jake!"

Watching them, my heart swells. He's so natural with them, so caring. It hits me just how different this is from what I've known.

"Hope you're hungry," he says huskily as he brushes past me, following the kids into the living room. *I definitely am, but it's not for lunch.*

We settle down for a 'picnic' in the lounge, the kids chattering as they dig into the sandwiches Jake brought. Noah tells him all about his favorite animals, and Jake listens, asking questions and engaging with both of them like it's the most fascinating thing in the world. Noah and Meadow are completely at ease, clearly adoring him.

At one point, Meadow spills her juice, and before I can react, Jake's there calmly mopping it up with a napkin and reassuring her it's no big deal. It's a small thing, but he handles it with such care and understanding that my chest tightens.

When we finish eating, I glance at the clock. "We should probably head out if we want to make it to the zoo before it gets too crowded."

Jake nods, already standing to help clean up. "I can transfer their carseats to my car, if you like. We can leave whenever you're ready."

I watch him move to get the kids' seats, rooted to the spot. It's such a simple gesture, but it means the world. He's not just here for me, he's showing me he's here and thinking of them, too.

Once the kids are strapped in, I slide into the passenger seat, sneaking glances as Jake navigates the city streets. His hand rests on the gear shift, but when we stop at a red light, he reaches over, gently placing it on my leg. The warmth of his touch seeps through the fabric of my jeans, grounding me.

"You okay?" he asks quietly, his thumb brushing my thigh.

I nod, turning to meet him. "Mhmm."

His smile is reassuring, and I feel the tension ease in me. "Relax, Charlie," he says, giving my knee a squeeze. "Today's gonna be fun."

***

At the zoo, it's like watching Jake come to life in a new way. He's in his element, guiding the kids from one exhibit to the next, his enthusiasm matching theirs. He lifts Meadow onto his shoulders so she can see the giraffes, and when Noah insists on reading every sign, Jake listens patiently, encouraging him. Noah's only just started at his new school, and I'm so proud watching him sound out words, Jake cheering him on.

When we reach the penguins, Noah practically fizzes. "Jake, look! They're swimming!"

Jake laughs as he watches Noah's delight. "They're pretty fast, huh?"

"Yeah! Do you think I could swim that fast?"

"I bet you could, buddy," Jake says, ruffling his hair again. "Maybe even faster."

I smile at the exchange, feeling a lump rise in my throat. This is what I've been missing. And seeing it now, it makes me realize how much I want this for them. Someone who's present, who genuinely loves being around them.

As we move through the zoo, Jake effortlessly shifts between being playful with the kids and attentive to me, making sure I'm included in every moment. At one point, he catches my eye and winks, and I feel my cheeks heat, turning away with a sheepish grin. He knows he's getting to me, and he's enjoying it.

Later, we stop for ice cream, and Meadow takes an eternity to decide on a flavor. I'm helping her, crouched down by the display and explaining each one, when Jake leans down beside me, his hand finding my lower back.

"How are my girls doing? Too hard to decide?"

I turn my head slowly to him, raising an eyebrow. *My girls.* The twinkle in his eye says he knows exactly what he's said.

"I can't deciiiide, it's too haaaard!" Meadow whines, and I brace myself for a meltdown.

I glance back at Jake with a mock grimace, signaling we're treading into tantrum territory. As I turn back to try and cajole Meadow, Jake steps in first.

"C'mere, Princess. I'll hold you up so you can see better." His hands bracket my hips lightly as he brushes behind me, reaching for her to lift her up. She giggles, clearly a fan of his attention, and honestly, I don't blame her.

It doesn't take long for me to realize that Jake Brooks and Meadow Grace are a charm offensive. No one is safe—not even the server at the ice cream stand, who happily hands over sample after sample.

I clamp my teeth down on my lips. This man just saved me from a three-year-old's public meltdown, and it might be the hottest thing anyone's ever done for me.

Actually, second hottest. Because now he's turning toward me, extending a sample of chocolate fudge ice cream on a tiny spoon.

"Open wide, Mama." He smirks, using the name only Meadow calls me, feeding me the sample.

I can't help what I do next. I hold his gaze as he places the spoon in my mouth, and I slowly close around it. His smile falters as I make a small moan in the back of my throat as I swallow, eyes dropping to my lips as I lick them clean.

I smile, teasing. "Mm, I'd definitely choose this one."

He doesn't look away. "Me too."

Internally, I die. I know neither of us is talking about ice cream anymore. Externally, I keep my cool, reminding myself we're in public, surrounded by families. It's a miracle Jake hasn't been recognized, and I realize that's what the sunglasses and cap must be for.

Either way, I'm glad we've so far had his undivided attention, so I'm not about to draw attention to him now by jumping the man in public. And I'm hyper aware of Noah and Meadow seeing us interact, so I'm trying to keep it friendly. Apart from that one ice cream spoon moment, but I'm maintaining that he goaded me.

The rest of the day passes in a blur of laughter, and by the time we reach home, the kids are asleep in their seats. I glance at Jake, silhouetted by the evening light, and feel a surge of emotion so strong it almost takes my breath away.

When we pull up to the house, he cuts the engine, and we both sit in the quiet for a moment, the only sound the soft breathing of the kids in the backseat.

"Thank you," I say softly, breaking the silence. "For today."

Jake turns to me, warm and a little serious. "You don't have to thank me, Charlie. I wanted to do this. I loved every minute of it."

His sincerity makes my pulse race, and I lean over to press a gentle kiss to his cheek. "Still, I appreciate it."

He smiles at that, his eyes meeting mine in the dim light. There's something unspoken between us—a promise, or maybe just an understanding that today was important. That this, whatever it is between us, is becoming something important.

***

111

Jake

"Should we get these two inside?" I nod toward the kids, still fast asleep in the backseat.

Charlotte nods, and we both quietly exit the car. I carefully unbuckle Noah and lift him out, cradling him against my chest. His head lolls against my shoulder, completely out cold.

As I carry him inside, his little arms wrap instinctively around my neck, and my heart swells with a fierce protectiveness I didn't know I was capable of. This little guy, who's already been through a lot, trusts me enough to hold him close. It's a responsibility I don't take lightly.

Noah stirs slightly as I walk up the stairs, his eyes blinking open for just a moment. "Jake?" he mumbles, his voice thick with sleep.

"Yeah, buddy. I've got you," I whisper, making my voice as soothing as possible.

"Kay," he breathes, his head dropping back onto my shoulder. Then, barely audible, he mumbles, "I like that you're my Mum's friend."

I pause, overwhelmed by his sleepy words. It's so simple, so innocent, but it settles deep in my chest. Because this isn't just about Charlie. It's about all of them.

Once he's tucked in bed, I linger for a moment, a quiet protectiveness settling in me. There's something about this kid that hits me hard—maybe because I know what it's like not to have someone there when they should be.

He deserves better. Someone who sticks around. Someone who gives a damn.

I ruffle his hair softly. "Sleep tight, buddy."

When I step out, Charlie's just coming out of Meadow's room, gently closing the door. She gives me a tired smile, equal parts exhaustion and contentment.

"Thank you for helping me get them to bed," she whispers, as if talking any louder might disturb the quiet.

"Thank you for letting me be a part of it," I reply, just as softly.

I follow her back down the stairs and into the living room, and a comfortable silence settles between us. For a moment, neither of us says anything. The weight of the day, the significance of it all, lingers in the air. It's not just about a fun day at the zoo or moments shared with the kids—it's about what all of this means.

"Jake..." She stands there, wringing her hands with hesitation, and I feel compelled to put her mind at ease.

I take a step closer, my hand instinctively moving up to cup her face, thumb brushing gently along her cheek. "Charlie, I'm all in. Whatever this is between us, I want it. I'm not going anywhere."

The words spill out before I can second-guess them, but I know they're true. I've never felt this sure about anything. Seeing the way she looks at me now, with this mix of hope and vulnerability, only strengthens that certainty.

It might seem fast, but I don't care. I just hope she feels the same way.

"I want this, too," she admits, her voice barely above a whisper. But it's enough. It's everything.

I chuckle with relief, leaning in to press my lips to her forehead. "God, I'm glad you said that."

She closes her eyes, and I feel her relax into me, the tension of the day finally ebbing away. It feels right, like this is exactly where we were always meant to end up—together.

"Stay..." she whispers, her voice soft but sure, looking up at me. "Just a bit longer?"

For a second, it knocks the air out of me, because I'm already so far gone for her. And if I stay, I know I'll get to a point where I never want to leave. I search her eyes for any sign of doubt, but all I see is the same desire that's been building between us all day.

"You sure?"

She nods. "I'm sure."

That's all I need. With a low groan I can no longer hold back, I close the distance, capturing her lips in a kiss that's anything but soft. It's hungry, intense, and full of everything I've held back all day.

Her hands tangle in my hair as I deepen the kiss, pulling her close, needing to feel every inch of her against me and making damn sure she can feel every inch of me, too.

We stumble back toward the sofa, neither of us willing to break the kiss. By the time she falls back onto the cushions, pulling me down with her, my skin is buzzing with anticipation. My hands skate up her sides, gently pushing her top up to brush against the warm skin at her waist.

The quiet moans she lets out as she tilts her head back, giving me access to drop warm kisses along her throat, nearly undoes me. Her fingers tighten in my hair, and she pushes her hips up, grinding against me.

But as much as I want her, as much as I want to let this happen, I know I need to slow down. I don't want to lose control tonight, I want to do this right.

"Charlie," I whisper into her neck, my breath coming in ragged gasps. "I want you. God, I want you so much," I say, pulling back so she can see my face. "But I need you to know this isn't just a hook-up for me."

She looks up at me, breathing deeply, dragging her fingertips from my hairline down to my jaw. "I know..."

I search her eyes, finding only sincerity. Still, I want to be sure. "Okay... Then let's take it slow. As much as I want to get you naked right now, I wanna do this right."

For a second, I think she might argue, might pull me back down. But instead she nods with a smile, leaning in to kiss me softly. "Slow is fine."

I kiss her again, savoring the taste of her, before pulling back and helping her sit up with me. We both take a moment to catch our breath, the intensity gradually ebbing into a quiet sense of calm.

Pulling her close against my side, we settle into the sofa. My fingers trace patterns up and down her arm as the weight of the day settles over us. It's not overwhelming—it's comforting. Holding her here, feeling her steady breathing, I know that this is exactly what I want. All of it. The hurried frantic moments, the chaos, and all these slow, easy moments, too.

I feel her shift slightly, like there's something on her mind.

"Jake..."

I tilt my head down to look at her. "Mm?"

She hesitates, staring at her hands. I can see the battle playing out in her head, like she's deciding whether to let me in on something important. She's searching for the right words, and I wait, giving her the space she needs. "There's something you should know. About my time here in the States."

I sit up a little, giving her my full attention, my arm still around her. "Okay..."

She bites her lip, and I can see the struggle in her eyes. "When I left New Zealand, Alex gave me an ultimatum. He said I had a year to prove that the kids were settled here, that this life was better for them. Otherwise, he wants me to bring them back."

A protective instinct flares inside me. The thought of her ex trying to control her and the kids from halfway around the world pisses me off more than I can say.

But I keep my voice calm for her sake. Charlie and her kids have already become important to me, and the thought of losing them—of them being forced back into a situation that's less than they deserve—lights a fire in my chest. "That's not fair, Charlie. He's using the kids to control you."

She nods, her expression a mix of frustration and sadness. "I know. It's been weighing on me since we got here. I don't want to go back. I want to stay, but I need to be sure that this is the right choice for Noah and Meadow."

I'm quiet, processing her words. I can tell she knows this move was a good choice for her, but her ex is clearly still in her head, manipulating her with doubt. The weight of it all hangs heavy, but I know one thing for sure, I'm not letting her go again.

After a beat, I reach up and gently brush a strand of hair behind her ear. "That's a lot to carry, Charlie girl," I say softly. "I'm glad you told me."

She exhales, like sharing this has lifted some of the burden. "I didn't want to keep it from you. I want to make sure the kids are happy and settled, but there's always that worry... like it's not enough."

I tighten my grip, brushing my thumb over her shoulder. "It is. You're a great mom. I've seen how much Noah and Meadow love it here already. You're doing everything right."

Her expression softens. "Thanks. I just needed to say it out loud, I guess."

Tilting her chin, I make sure she's looking right at me. The kiss that follows is slow, tender, full of what I feel for her. Her lips are soft against mine, and her response is full of that same deep pull.

I want her so badly, but it's more than that, it's a fierce need to be here for her and the kids, to fight for this chance to keep them here. I pull back, pressing a kiss to her forehead. "We'll figure it out, Charlie. One step at a time."

She settles into me, and I feel her relax further. "Yeah... one step at a time."

The house is quiet, save for the soft sound of her breathing. I didn't think I'd feel this attached so quickly, but it's there, clear as day. Something about this family feels right, like they're where I'm supposed to be.

Noah's sleepy words replay in my mind, the way the little guy instinctively snuggled closer as I tucked him into bed. He'd mumbled that he liked I was his mom's friend, and the innocence of it sinks into me like an anchor. I want to be someone they can rely on, someone *she* can rely on.

And a damn bit more than just her friend.

CHAPTER FIFTEEN

YOU'VE GONE FULL DAD MODE

———————◆———————

Jake

T he ice feels different tonight. It's an away game and the crowd's loud, hostile even, but that's nothing new. I'm used to it. Away games always bring a different kind of intensity. But tonight, as I skate out, there's this nagging thought in the back of my mind, one I've been trying to push away since we left town.

I haven't seen Charlie or the kids since our zoo date last weekend. It's only been about a week, but damn, I miss them more than I thought I would. It's like there's this empty space in my chest that only they can fill, and being away is harder than I expected.

As we line up for a face-off, one of the other team's wingers skates by, smirking. "Hey, Brooks, heard your contract's up this season. Think you'll get another one, or are you headed for the retirement home?"

I shoot him a look. "Keep talking, kid. Maybe you'll figure out how I keep scoring on you."

He laughs. "Easy, Grandpa. Don't pull a groin on us."

I tune him out, focusing on the puck and the play. I've heard it all before, the chirps about my contract, but tonight it digs a little deeper. Not playing with the team I love is a possibility I've been pushing aside, but it's creeping in tonight.

The game moves fast. We're back and forth, trading hits and shots, and I'm determined to make my presence known. The cold air bites at my face as I streak

117

down the ice, skates slicing through the noise of the crowd. I take the hit against the boards hard, shoulder-first, the impact rattling through my chest. But I push through, adrenaline dulling the pain as I focus on the puck, the play, the goal.

Midway through the second period, I finally get the chance I've been waiting for. We're on the power play, moving the puck around, looking for a gap. Logan threads a perfect pass my way, and I don't even settle the puck. I wind up and let it fly—a clean one-timer that beats the goalie glove-side. The puck snaps into the twine with a satisfying thud.

I raise my stick as the red light flashes, a grin splitting my face as the boys swarm me, clapping my helmet, celebrating the goal. I point at Logan as I skate past, letting him know that was all him—the perfect assist. He grins like he's just won the lottery.

As I pass the other team's bench, one of their defensemen mutters loud enough for me to hear, "Enjoy it while you can, old man. That contract's ticking down."

I smirk as I skate backward, locking eyes with him. "Keep counting the days, kid. I'll still be scoring on you when I'm collecting my pension." His scowl deepens, but I turn away, knowing I've made my point.

The game is a battle, but we hold our ground, and when the final buzzer sounds, we're on top. In the locker room, the atmosphere is light, full of laughter and banter as we strip out of our gear.

Chase sidles up as I'm tossing my pads into my bag. "So, big man," he says, voice dripping with mischief, "we all saw that little unicorn drawing in your locker back home. You got a mini fan club now?"

A few of the guys chuckle, and I roll my eyes, smirking despite myself. "It's from Meadow. Charlotte's little girl."

Chase nods sagely. "Because a crayon drawing keeps you focused on hockey, right?"

I grab a towel, slinging it over my shoulder, and turn to face him with a mock-serious expression. "You'd know, Walton, if you ever managed to get past a first date and actually spend time with someone who has kids."

There's more laughter, but it's all in good fun. The guys can joke all they want about that drawing, but it means more to me than any trophy.

Ryan chimes in from his locker. "Leave him alone, Walton. At least Brooks has got something real going on."

"You've gone full dad mode already, huh?" Eli chuckles from the bench. "Next thing we know, you'll be driving a minivan and coaching little league."

I snort, shrugging it off as I unlace my skates. "I'll stick to hockey, thanks. But yeah... get used to the idea of me being around her more."

Ryan gives me a serious look, something between approval and warning in his eyes. "You know it's a big step, right? Being with someone who has kids."

"Yeah, I know." I grab my notebook from my bag. "This isn't a game to me, though."

Flipping it open, I jot down some thoughts from the game: the goal, the plays, even some of the chirps. I add three stars to the page, too.

Logan, still riding the high from his assist, glances over as I finish up. "What's that for?"

"Just a tool for getting my head right, game-wise. Helps me go over plays or whatever's on my mind."

Chase can't help himself. "Yeah, or maybe it's just your poetry journal, Brooks. 'Ode to a Rookie' and all that."

I roll my eyes. "Fuck off, Chase. At least I have more to write about than beer and bad dates."

As the locker room starts to empty, Ryan sticks around, glancing at me more seriously.

"You good, man?" he asks, lowering his voice so the others don't overhear.

I nod, knowing I can't hide much from him. "Yeah, just been thinking about a lot lately. Balancing everything, you know?"

Ryan leans back against his locker, arms crossed. "Yeah... But you've always been good at handling pressure."

"It feels different now," I admit, running a hand through my hair. "Didn't expect to get this attached this fast. And then there's the contract stuff, the chirps tonight... it's getting to me. Makes me wonder if I can really do this—be there for them and still give everything to the game."

Ryan studies me before speaking. "You're not alone, Brooks. We've got your back, especially me. And as for Charlotte and the kids, sounds like they're worth the effort. You can balance it, man. Don't let the noise get to you."

I nod, appreciating his words more than he realizes. Ryan's always been the voice of reason, keeping me grounded when things start to spin out of control. "Thanks, man. I'll figure it out."

His expression softens. "Trust me, I get it. With Claire pregnant, I'm already trying to figure out how to balance this. It's a whole new game when there's more than just you to think about."

The mention of Claire and their baby on the way makes me smile. Ryan's been a rock on this team, and seeing him so settled, with a family on the way, gives me hope.

"By the way, Claire and I are hosting Thanksgiving this year. First time in the new house. Eli and Chase are coming, and we want you there, too. And Charlotte and the kids are welcome, if things are... you know."

I nod, appreciating the gesture. "Thanks, man. I'll see how things are going by then."

The idea of bringing Charlie and the kids to Thanksgiving at Ryan and Claire's is both exciting and nerve-wracking. It's only a few weeks away, and it feels like a big step. But the truth is, I want them there. I want to share this part of my life with them.

***

Back in my hotel room, the adrenaline from the game still pulses through my veins. The post-game high usually sticks with me, especially on the road. Normally, a win is enough. But tonight, I can't shake this restless energy. The thrill of the game, the chirps from the other team, the roar of the crowd—all distractions. Now that it's silent, all I can think about is Charlie.

I head into the bathroom to shower, hoping the scalding hot water will clear my head. I know the team's physio hates it when I do this, but there's something about the heat of the water that I can't resist. Under the spray, my mind keeps drifting to Charlotte—her laugh, her smile, the way she looks at me when she thinks I'm not paying attention. The way she trusts me.

Closing my eyes, I imagine her here with me. And that's probably the worst thing I could've done, because now I'm rock hard. I lean a hand against the wall, letting the water cascade over me, and reach down with the other to grip myself.

I let out a low groan as I work my hand up and down, picturing Charlie right here with me, her warm freckled skin pressed against mine, so damn soft. And God, her lips. Those soft, inviting lips I could kiss for hours.

My hand motions grow jerky at the thought of pinning her against these tiles, wondering what shade of pink her nipples are and how I'd take them into my mouth, making her moan as they turn to hard peaks between my teeth. Tasting her, feeling her go weak under my touch—it's all it takes. I shudder, coming hard against the tiles, her name slipping out softly.

I stand there for a moment, letting the water spray over me, washing away the evidence. For fuck's sake. I want her bad.

Turning off the water, I grab a towel and step out, staring at my reflection in the fogged-up mirror. I see the tension in my own eyes. I need to figure out how to balance this—my career, my feelings for Charlotte, the life I'm starting to imagine with her and the kids.

As I towel off and get dressed, I think about texting her. I just want to see her name light up my screen, maybe hear her voice. Before I even pick up the phone, it buzzes. My pulse kicks up when I see her name.

Charlie: Congrats on the win! That goal you scored in the second period was unreal. And the way you took that hit - ouch. Your shoulder okay?

A grin spreads across my face. She watched the game. No one I have ever truly cared about has watched my games. Knowing she was watching, thinking about me, sends a thrill through me I can't shake. I type back quickly.

Me: Thanks, Charlie girl. Shoulder's fine, just a little sore. You turning into a hockey fan now?

Charlie: When the star player is someone special, it's hard not to pay attention

I laugh softly, flopping down on the bed, feeling lighter already. I can almost hear her playful tone in that message, but the fact that she watched, was cheering me on and thinking about me, makes me feel like I'm playing for more than just the win.

Me: Someone special, huh? I'm flattered. Maybe next time you'll have to come in person

Charlie: Hmm, I dunno. Sounds like a lot of ego stroking is involved.

I resist the urge to tell her there's plenty of other stroking I'd prefer for her to do right now.

Me: Trust me, I can think of a few other things I'd rather have you stroke than my ego.

I did not resist the urge. I grin at my own audacity, waiting to see if she'll let me get away with that.

Charlie: Wow. You have a very vivid imagination, Brooks. Must be lonely in that hotel room.

Me: You don't know the half of it. I miss you.

Charlie: We miss you, too. The kids asked about you tonight, especially Noah. You've got a number one fan here.

The idea that they're thinking of me, missing me, makes everything else fade. It's not just Charlie—it's all of them. And damn, I want to be there.

Me: Tell Noah I'll be back soon. And that I'm bringing him a surprise. I've got something for Meadow, too.

Charlie: Now you're just spoiling them! But they'll be stoked. Thanks, Jake x

The way she says my name, even in text, feels like I can hear her voice, soft and warm. And that little kiss she added? I want to be with her right now, pressing my lips to hers for real. Not in some hotel room hundreds of miles away receiving typed ones.

I hover over the screen, fingers itching to type something flirty again, something to make her smile. But beneath the easy banter, there's a seriousness I can't shake. This isn't just some fling. Not even close. When I finally type my response, it's with the hope she feels it too.

Me: It's gonna be hard to sleep tonight

Charlie: Who says you'll be sleeping?

Her reply sends a jolt of desire straight through me, already conjuring all the ways I wouldn't 'not sleep' with her in my bed. This woman—she has me completely.

> **Me:** You sure you don't want to fly out here? I could make it worth your while.

> **Charlie:** Tempting. But I don't think your team would appreciate me distracting you

> **Me:** I'd risk it.

> **Charlie:** Of course you would.

> **Me:** Can't help myself when it comes to you.

There's a beat—just long enough for the words to settle.

> **Charlie:** Night, Jake. See you soon xx

> **Me:** Sweet dreams, Lady Lightning x

I stare at her last message for a moment, heart pounding in a way that has nothing to do with the game. Setting the phone down, I lean back and close my eyes.

But all I see is her.

CHAPTER SIXTEEN

SHE SEES THE CRACKS IN MY ARMOR AND FILLS THEM WITH HER WARMTH

———————•✦•———————

Jake - 12 Years Ago

I slip away from the group, my heart pounding harder than it should after a simple game of capture the flag. It's not the physical exhaustion—I can handle that—but the pressure in my chest, like something's about to cave in.

I lean against a tree, the bark rough under my palms as I try to focus on my breathing. In, out. In, out. But the air doesn't reach my lungs, no matter how hard I try. My vision blurs at the edges, a weight settling like lead in my stomach.

Not now. Not here.

I ball my shaking hands into fists against the bark, willing the anxiety to go away. I've felt it creeping in before—usually when I think too much about the draft, about what comes next. But I can usually push it down. Not today.

My pulse quickens, chest tightens. It's like everything is closing in, and I can't breathe.

"Jake?"

Her voice is soft, but it cuts through the noise in my head. I don't want her to see me like this. Not Charlotte. Not when I'm supposed to have everything together.

I try to straighten, but my legs feel unsteady, my breathing shallow and ragged. She steps closer, her face full of concern as she stops in front of me.

"You okay?" she asks.

"I'm fine," I manage to choke out, but even to my own ears it sounds weak.

She doesn't buy it. *Of course she doesn't.* She's always seen right through me. Without a word, she reaches for my hand, her touch gentle and grounding. "Jake, it's okay. Just breathe."

I squeeze my eyes shut, my breath still coming in shallow bursts. I hate her seeing me like this—exposed, falling apart—but I can't stop it.

She stays quiet, her thumb tracing small, soothing circles on the back of my hand. "I'm right here," she whispers. "You're safe. Just breathe with me, okay? In... and out."

I focus on her voice, letting it anchor me as I try to match her slow, steady breaths. In, out. In, out. The world stops spinning so fast, the tightness in my chest loosening bit by bit.

Finally, I open my eyes. Charlie's still there, her hand wrapped around mine, her expression calm.

I feel exposed, like she's seen a part of me I've tried so hard to hide. But she doesn't say anything. Doesn't ask questions or make me feel small. She just stays there, solid and real, willing to carry whatever weight I can't.

"Thanks," I mutter, embarrassed. "I don't... I don't know what happened."

She gives a small, understanding smile. "It's okay. You don't have to explain. Sometimes things just get overwhelming."

My throat bobs. I've always handled things on my own. Told myself I could tough it out.

"I just..." I hesitate, the words catching in my throat. "The draft... and everything. It's a lot."

She nods, her hand still holding mine. "I get it. You're allowed to be overwhelmed. You're allowed to take a break."

Her words settle into the tight spaces in my chest, easing some of the tension. For the first time in what feels like forever, I feel like I can actually breathe.

I glance down at our intertwined hands and give her a small squeeze. "Thanks, Charlie. I mean it."

She smiles, that light, familiar smile that always makes things feel warm. "Anytime, Captain Thunder."

I laugh softly, the nickname a welcome distraction. "I guess Lady Lightning saves the day again, huh?"

A mischievous glint flashes in her eyes. "What can I say? We make a good team."

We stand there for a while longer, not saying much, just breathing together under the trees. And for the first time, I think that maybe I don't have to carry everything on my own.

***

Jake - Present Day

I stare at the muted highlights of the game playing on my TV, each mistake replaying in my mind like a bad dream. The thrill of winning our previous away game has evaporated, replaced by the sting of the recent loss we shouldn't have had. But it's more than just this game. Doubt creeps in, that insidious fear that maybe I'm not as good as I used to be.

When the plane touched down last night, I wasn't ready to face the silence of my condo. Ryan went home to Claire, Eli to Tamara, and Chase hit a bar, probably hunting down a bunny. I should've done the same—gone home, tried to shake this mood—but instead, I drove aimlessly through the city, not ready to be alone with my thoughts.

The memory of the loss, the media speculating about my contract, the doubts swirling in my own head—they all collide, making it impossible to think straight.

My phone's been buzzing, but I haven't had the energy to check. I know Charlie's been texting, her messages getting progressively more outrageous, trying to pull me out of this funk. They've gone from sweet to blatantly flirtatious, but I can't bring myself to reply. Not in this headspace.

The phone buzzes again on the coffee table, pulling me out of my thoughts. I pick it up, half-expecting another one of her attempts to cheer me up. But it's just a notification from a sports app, another article speculating about my future. I toss the phone back down, not even bothering to read it.

A soft knock at the door pulls me from my spiral. For a moment, I think it's one of the neighbors, but no one ever comes by unannounced. When I open the door, my heart stumbles in my chest.

"Charlie?" I blink, trying to process that she's standing here in my hallway, casual in a sweater and jeans, but looking like a godsend.

"Hey," she says, stepping inside without waiting for an invitation. "I took the afternoon off."

I'm caught off guard, surprise morphing into relief as I take in the sight of her. "What are you doing here?" *I'm so glad you came.*

"You've been kinda MIA, and I was starting to worry," she replies casually. "Plus, I sent you some seriously ridiculous texts, and you didn't even reply. So, here I am."

I can't help but smile at that, despite the dark cloud hanging over me.

She smiles back, her eyes scanning mine. "I thought you might need to talk it out. Or, you know, not talk at all. Whatever you need."

This girl. Her words, her thoughtfulness. The fact that she's here, that she took the time to check on me. It's something I'm not used to, someone caring like this.

A part of me wants to tell her I'm fine, to shrug it off like I always do. But another part of me, one I'm not used to acknowledging, is relieved she's here.

"You didn't have to do that," I say, but my voice lacks conviction.

She shrugs, glancing around the condo. "I wanted to," she says simply. "And I'm kinda pissed you didn't reply to my amazing texts."

I grin despite myself. "Sorry about that."

"You should be. I put a lot of effort into those, you know."

Her light tone, the way she's trying to bring humor into the situation, makes something inside me unclench. I step back to fully let her in, feeling the tension ease from my shoulders. "Well, I appreciate the effort."

She nods, venturing into the living room, her eyes roaming the space. "So, this is the famous condo," she says lightly.

"It's nothing special. Just a place to crash between games." I follow her as she moves around the room.

"You don't really let yourself settle, do you?"

Her words catch me off guard, and I'm not sure how to respond. So instead, I just watch as she walks over to the windows, looking out at the city.

"This place is incredible," she says, her voice softer now.

I sigh, rubbing the back of my neck. "Yeah... I don't know. Doesn't really feel like home."

She turns back to me, eyes searching mine. "What *does* feel like home?"

I stare back at her, the question hanging in the air. I've never thought about it before, but suddenly it's clear as day. *You. You feel like home.*

"I don't know," I lie.

She holds my gaze for a beat, then glances toward the kitchen. "Why don't you sit down?" she suggests, heading toward the counter. "I'll make us some tea."

Tea. The simplicity of it almost makes me laugh, but there's comfort in it too. I sit on the couch, watching her move around my kitchen. Her presence is like a balm to the rawness I've been feeling since the game.

She doesn't push me to talk, doesn't press for answers I'm not ready to give. She's just here without fuss or fanfare, and somehow that's exactly what I need.

As she potters around, she comments on little things she notices—the artwork on the walls, the view from the window. She makes a joke about my perfectly organized kitchen, and I can't help but laugh, the tension in my chest easing a little more.

"I didn't mean to worry you," I say, my voice rougher than intended. I watch as she pours hot water into mugs, the steam curling up in lazy spirals.

The gray light filters through the windows, casting soft shadows across the room, matching the overcast mood inside me. But watching her move around, so calm and sure, it's like she's bringing a bit of warmth into the space—and into me.

She glances over her shoulder. "Don't apologize. Just wanted to make sure you're okay."

Her simple words hit me in a way I'm not used to. I'm not used to someone caring, taking the time to come to me when I'm shutting down. I've learnt to deal with this on my own. But with Charlie, I welcome it.

She walks over, handing me a mug of tea. I take it, the warmth seeping into my hands. For a moment, we sit in silence, the quiet between us comfortable. The chaos in my mind settles into a dull roar.

"This condo is nice," she says after a while, her voice light. "But I'm starting to think you could use a little more disorder in your life. Maybe some mismatched cushions, a few dying plants."

I chuckle. "Mismatched cushions, huh? Sounds like something Zoe would suggest."

Her eyes sparkle. "She's already mentioned she'd love to style this place. Consider yourself warned."

I shake my head, a smile tugging at my lips. Her light-heartedness is infectious.

The silence creeps back in, though. It's comfortable, but I can feel her waiting, giving me space to talk. I sip my tea, searching for the right words, but they feel heavy in my throat. I stare into my mug, the steam swirling and dissipating into the air, just like my confidence did on the ice yesterday.

"It was a rough game," I finally say. "We shouldn't have lost. And the chirps... that stuff usually rolls off, but it got to me. Then the media's all over me. Maybe they're right..."

She doesn't interrupt, her presence a steadying force.

"My contract's up at the end of the season," I continue, the words spilling out. "And I'm starting to feel like maybe I'm losing my edge."

The confession hangs between us. I'm not used to being this vulnerable, letting someone see the cracks in my armor.

But Charlie doesn't flinch. Doesn't say anything at first, just listens, her eyes full of understanding. She sees those cracks and fills them with her warmth.

"You're not losing your edge, Jake," she says, steady and sure. "You had a bad game, everyone does. But that doesn't change who you are or what you've accomplished."

I shake my head, the doubt still gnawing at me. "It feels like it's all slipping. The pressure, the media, the expectations... it's getting to me. I'm supposed to be the guy who has it all together, but right now I feel like I'm falling apart."

She shifts closer, her hand resting gently on my knee. "You're allowed to struggle, to doubt yourself. No one expects you to be perfect. But that doesn't mean you're not enough."

I take her in, letting my eyes slowly roam over her face, and I see how deeply she understands. She gets me more than anyone ever has. And she's here, sitting with me in a dark moment, just being here. Not trying to fix me.

"It's hard to talk about this," I confess. "I've always dealt with this stuff on my own. But I'm glad you're here, Charlie."

She squeezes my knee. "I'm not going anywhere."

The words wrap around me, warm and comforting, and I realize how much I've needed to hear them. I reach out and lace my fingers with hers, holding on like she's my lifeline. "Thank you." *You're my favorite person in the world.*

"You don't have to thank me," she says. "This is what we do for each other, right?"

I lean into her, the scent of vanilla in her hair grounding me. "But what if I can't do it?" I sigh. "What if I can't balance it all. Hockey, this thing with you... What if I fail?"

She turns to face me, eyes locking onto mine. "You're already doing it. Small steps, remember?"

Her words echo my own from a week ago, resonating deeply. I pull her closer, wrapping my arms around her, needing to feel her close.

I nod, letting my eyes trail over her face, taking her in—every freckle, the curve of her smile, every piece of her that feels like it was made just for me. She's the calm in my chaos, the quiet when everything else is too damn loud. I don't know how I lived so long without this, without *her*. "Yeah, I remember." *I remember everything about you.*

She smiles, leaning in to press a soft kiss to my lips. "Good. Because you're enough, Jake. And I think you need to hear that more often."

The conviction in her voice makes me believe it, even just for a moment. I bury my face in her hair, letting her calm the last of the storm inside me.

We sit there in silence, holding onto each other, and I realize this quiet understanding, this shared vulnerability is what I've been missing. Charlie doesn't see the star player who has to have it all together.

She sees me, just me.

CHAPTER SEVENTEEN

HELLO, BRAIN? KINDLY FUCK OFF.

---◆---

Charlie

I stare at my computer screen, scrolling through page after page of analytics for a major client meeting tomorrow. Facts and figures blur in front of me. I know there's data I should be paying attention to, but it's all a haze.

I wonder what he's doing right now?

It's been a few days since I showed up at Jake's condo after he got back from his string of away games. I needed to make sure he was still alive and hadn't sunk too deep into post-loss gloom. But since then, our schedules haven't aligned. I've missed him more than I want to admit, and it's messing with my concentration.

Ridiculous. Missing someone I've only ever kissed. The audacity of me.

Except it's not just me. Noah's been asking if he'll see Jake again soon, too. He's been quieter than usual this week, and I've been desperately trying to cajole him. Even Meadow, as I tucked her into bed the other night, mumbled sleepily that she missed Jake and his shoulder rides.

It's sweet, but it also fills me with so much anxiety. Jake's only been in our lives for a short time, and yet he's already become a part of our little world. It feels risky. Like I should be pulling back, moving slower.

I feel protective and guilty, like I should be doing more to rein myself in. The last thing I need is for my kids to get attached to someone who might not be around for the long haul. I've already done that to them once. This move to

Denver was supposed to give them a fresh start—the opposite of what they had with the last man in their lives, their own father.

But I can't get Jake's words out of my head, the ones he said to me after the zoo. *I'm all in.*

How can he be so sure? It actually pisses me off a little, thinking he's saying these things so casually. He can't just say that to a single mother with two kids. It's not fair. Unless, of course, he means it. Which he might. And the way he looks at me... it feels like he really does.

I huff, clicking my mouse a bit too aggressively as I scroll through the data on my screen. I'm a bloody mess. I need my overactive brain to kindly fuck off for a bit.

The way my thoughts and emotions are swinging from side to side is driving me nuts. This isn't what I came here to do. I should be able to focus. There's too much at stake if I don't.

A light tapping on my office door pulls me from my spiraling thoughts. Zoe saunters in, her mischievous smirk faltering a bit when she sees my stormy expression. "What's with the face?"

I smile, composing myself and shaking my head. "Just... stuff."

"Oh, *stuff,* huh? Would that stuff happen to be six-foot-three, ridiculously handsome, and play professional hockey, by any chance?" Zoe's eyes twinkle.

I sigh, leaning back in my chair, but I can't help the small smile tugging at my lips. "Maybe."

Zoe plops down in the chair across from me, propping her feet on the edge of my desk. "Wanna talk about it?"

I hesitate, searching her face. I *do* want to tell her, but I already know what she's going to say—that I need to give this a chance. And while I love her for her support, I don't think she fully understands just how fiercely I need to protect my kids.

"I'm feeling... conflicted," I finally admit.

Zoe raises an eyebrow. "Conflicted because...?"

The words spill out before I can stop them. "Isn't it obvious? I'm a single mother who uprooted her kids to the other side of the world. I swore I'd keep them safe, keep them from getting hurt again. And now they're missing Jake more than I expected. I'm scared I'm setting them up for another fall. I feel like a hypocrite."

Zoe's expression softens, her usual teasing replaced with concern. "You're not a hypocrite, Charlie. You're *human*. You're doing the best you can for those kids. And I don't think you're giving Jake enough credit. From what I've seen, he's missing you guys just as much, probably even more. He's got this whole tortured soul thing going on." She waves her hand for emphasis. "That man's not going anywhere unless you push him away."

I bite my lip, her words hitting closer to home than I want to admit. "But what if I'm wrong? What if this all ends up hurting them? I can't let that happen again."

Zoe leans forward. "You're a great mom, Charlie. You'd never let anything hurt those kids if you could help it. But maybe it's time to believe Jake is all in, like he said."

I open my mouth to respond, but before I can, my phone buzzes loudly on the desk, the screen lighting up with *Noah's School.* My heart drops.

"Hold on," I say, picking up the phone. "Hello?"

"Hi, Ms. Andrews? This is Mrs. Lopez from Noah's school. I wanted to inform you that there was a small incident today. Noah was involved in a scuffle with another student."

My stomach tightens. "A scuffle? What happened?"

"It seems another student was picking on Noah, and he... well, he defended himself. He's not in any trouble, but I thought you should know. He was pretty upset afterward."

"What were they picking on him about?"

Mrs. Lopez hesitates. "It was about his accent, Ms. Andrews. Some of the kids were teasing him for the way he pronounces certain words. I've spoken to the other students involved, and we're addressing it, but I thought you should be aware."

My heart sinks. "Thank you for letting me know. I'll come pick him up shortly." I hang up, a heavy weight settling in my chest.

Zoe's frown deepens. "What's wrong?"

"Noah's had a rough day. Some kid was bullying him, and he lashed out."

Zoe's expression darkens as she swings her feet off the desk. "What the hell? Is he okay?"

"They said he's not in trouble." I take a deep breath, staring down at my phone, trying to process it all.

"Are *you* okay?"

I nod, but I'm not. I'm stressed, worried, and angry all at once. Noah's been so excited about school, and now he's being teased for something he can't control. And I'm the one who did this. I moved him here, to this new country, and he's paying the price. And on top of that, this will be perfect ammunition for Alex. The kids need to be happy and settled here, or he'll insist they come back to New Zealand.

Zoe watches me closely, her usual playfulness gone. "What were they bullying him about?"

I swallow, the words thick in my throat. "His accent. They're teasing him for the way he talks. He's been trying so hard to fit in, and now..."

Zoe reaches across the desk, resting a hand on mine. "Charlie, you're doing your best. Noah's lucky to have you. And you're not alone, okay? You've got people who care about you and the kids."

I squeeze her hand, grateful for the support but feeling the weight of my worries pressing down. "Thanks, Zo. I'm gonna head home and pick him up myself today. I need to be there."

As I gather my things, Zoe stands, still looking at me thoughtfully. "I'm heading to the arena soon, but if you need me to come kick some elementary kid's punk ass, I will."

I manage a grin, but the idea of leaning on anyone else right now feels wrong. The fact I even have to text Alex to update him on this is doing my head in. I've always handled these things on my own. It's not just pride; it's about protecting my kids from any more upheaval.

"Nah, I'll deal with it."

***

Jake

The pucks echo off the boards as morning skate wraps up. It's been a pretty good session. But even as I go through the motions, my mind keeps drifting back to Charlotte. It's been days now since she came to my condo, and we haven't seen each other since. I'm not sure how much longer I can go without seeing her, and the thought of it gnaws at me.

As I unlace my skates in the locker room, footsteps echo in the corridor, followed by Zoe's familiar voice. She's chatting with a few staff members, but when she spots me, she waves them off and heads straight over.

"Hey, superstar," she says with a small smile, but there's something serious in her eyes that puts me on alert.

"Hey, what are you doing here?" I stand, tossing my skates into my bag.

"I have a meeting upstairs. But, uh... I wanted to talk to you first," she says, her tone shifting from playful to concerned.

"What's up?"

She hesitates, glancing around to make sure we're out of earshot of the other guys, then lowers her voice. "It's Charlie. Noah had a rough day at school. He got into a scuffle with some kids who were picking on him because of his accent."

A surge of protectiveness rises in my chest. "*What?* Is he okay?"

She nods quickly, probably noting the fire in my eyes. "Yeah, he's okay. Charlie's heading home now so she can go pick him up herself," Zoe explains. "But she's spiralling a bit. She feels like it's her fault for bringing the kids here, for uprooting their lives. And you know how she is—she's trying to handle everything on her own."

I frown, shaking my head. "She doesn't have to handle it alone."

Zoe sighs. "You know what she's like, she doesn't ask for help even when she's stressing out. And I bet Alex won't help matters when he finds out."

I let out a slow breath through my nose, jaw clenched tight at the mention of his name. I've seen the stress he puts on her, how it weighs on her every decision.

And now, knowing that Noah's being bullied over something as simple as his accent—something tied to where he comes from, where they *all* come from—it's no wonder she's feeling overwhelmed. It doesn't sit right that she's doing this alone, bearing all that weight when I could be there.

"Thanks for telling me, Zoe." I grab my jacket and sling my bag over my shoulder. "I'm gonna head over there, see if she needs anything."

"Jake—" Zoe hesitates, her concern flickering as I turn back. "Maybe just call her first. Give her a heads up before you charge in."

I nod, already pulling my phone out as I head towards the exit. Zoe gives me a small, encouraging smile as she waves me off, and I dial Charlotte's number.

After a few moments, she picks up. "Hey, Jake." Her voice is tense, guarded, and a bit muffled—she's clearly on her car speaker. There's an edge of tiredness in her tone that tugs at me.

"Hey," I say, keeping my tone soft. "Zoe told me what happened with Noah. You okay?"

There's a pause. I hear her breathing, the sound of traffic faint in the background. I can almost visualize her walls going up. "I'm fine. I'm just on my way home before I go pick him up."

I know her too well, even after all these years. She's holding back, trying to sound unbothered, but I hear the strain. A pang of frustration hits me—she's shutting me out, carrying all this weight on her own, and I'm damn tired of watching her carry it alone.

It's like she's desperately rebuilding a wall I'm trying to break through. *Let me in, Charlie.*

"Do you want me to come with you? I can be there in a few." I keep my tone steady, but inside, I'm pleading.

Another pause. "It's okay, I've got it handled." There's a coldness to her words, a barrier she's put up. I know it's because she's stressed, trying to protect herself and the kids, but it still stings.

Handled, she says. Like I'm not even an option to lean on.

I force a nod she can't see. "Alright." The word tastes bitter. I don't want to push her away by coming on too strong, but I can't just sit by and do nothing. "You know I'm here if you need anything, right?"

"Thank you," she replies politely, like she's talking to one of her clients. "I'll talk to you later."

The call ends before I can respond. I stare at my screen, frustration and help-lessness churning hot in my chest.

Fuck this.

She thinks she's protecting herself and the kids, but she's wrong. She doesn't know how to lean on someone, to *trust* someone, but I'm going to show up for her. Prove I'm not going anywhere. That she doesn't have to carry this alone.

I grab my keys, tossing my bag into the back of my car, and slam the door shut. Her place isn't too far—if I move fast enough, I'll get there before she does. She might not have asked for help, but I'm going to be there with it anyway.

***

Charlie

I pull into the driveway, my mind still a chaotic swirl of worry and guilt. This day has turned into a nightmare, and all I want is to get inside, change, and pick up Noah. I feel like I'm teetering on the edge of a cliff, trying to hold it all together. So, the last thing I expect to see when I turn the corner of my street is Jake.

But there he is, leaning casually against his SUV, arms crossed, waiting. It feels like a double-edged sword seeing him here. A wave of emotions collide in me—nerves, frustration, and something that feels suspiciously like relief. The sight of him both calms and unsettles me, and I realize I've missed him. God, I've missed him. But I can't focus on that. Not now.

As I pull into my driveway and step out of my car, he straightens up with concern etched in his eyes, which only makes me feel more on edge.

"Hey," he says softly, eyes searching mine.

"What are you doing here?" I ask, frustration sneaking in, betraying my attempt at calm.

Jake's brows knit together for half a second before smoothing out. "I told you, I'm here if you need anything." His voice holds a steady resolve, a quiet promise that he's not going to let me push him away. "I thought you might want some help."

"I already said, I've got it handled." I let out a sharp breath, torn between clinging to my independence and the overwhelming relief of having him here. I want to lean on him, but I can't shake the feeling that it means I'm losing control. He gives me a look like he wants to tell me how wrong I am, but I continue before he does.

"You don't have to keep doing this, you know." I bite out, but the words feel brittle. "You don't have to keep showing up like this. What if—"

"I know I don't have to," he interrupts, frustration clear as he steps closer. "I choose to. I'm here because I *want* to be. I'm not making promises I can't keep, Charlie."

I look away, not sure how to respond. The wall I've been holding up to keep him at a safe distance feels fragile. Part of me knows he means it—whenever I look into his eyes, I can see that he does. But another part of me, the part that's been burned before, can't help but wonder if it's all too good to be true. That he'll get tired of this. Of *us*. The very thought of it makes my throat burn, so I go for half the truth.

"I just... I'm worried about Noah. I brought him here, to this new place, and now he's being bullied because of it. It's my fault."

Jake exhales slowly, his expression softening as he steps even closer, reaching out to gently touch my arm. "It's not your fault. And you're doing an amazing job. But right now, you don't have to do it alone."

"I'm scared, Jake," I blurt before I can stop myself. "I'm scared of letting you in, of letting the kids get attached to..." I wave my hand between us. "Whatever *this* is. I can't handle them getting hurt again."

He doesn't flinch, just stands there, his presence like gravity pulling me in. Too close. It's been days since I let myself feel this pull, and now it's like a dam threatening to break. I can see the determination in his eyes, the way he's fighting his own frustration to be patient with me. It's enough to make me *want* to believe him, even if it terrifies me.

His hand slides from my arm up to cup my jaw, tilting my face so I'm looking directly at him. The warmth of his touch sinks through me, unraveling the defenses I've spent time rebuilding. "I get it, I do. But I'm not going anywhere, Charlie. And *whatever this is*," he repeats my words back to me, "I'm all in."

Looking into his eyes, I see that steady sincerity I always see when he says these things. There's something so unwavering in his gaze that it makes me want to trust what he's telling me. That I don't have to do this alone.

"Okay," I finally whisper. "Okay. Let's go get Noah."

Jake nods, visibly relieved that I'm letting him in, even just a little. "I'll follow you there."

I make a sound of agreement and turn towards the house, but then I feel his hand on my arm again. "Unless... Do you wanna ride together?"

The idea feels like a big step, but when I meet his eyes, I know it's a step I want to take. "Yeah, okay. Let's ride together."

I rush inside to change, and then head back out to Jake's car. As he opens the passenger door for me, I catch his eye and offer a small, grateful smile. He returns it with one of his customary winks that sends my heart racing.

With Jake beside me, his hand tentatively sliding into mine as he drives, something inside me feels like it's slowly unraveling. His calm presence is exactly what I needed today, I just didn't know it. I glance at him out of the corner of my eye, watching the way his focus stays steady on the road, but his hand lingers against mine like he's afraid I'll pull away.

I don't.

***

When we pull up outside Noah's school, the usual buzz of parents and kids milling around hits me, but today it feels different. There's a noticeable shift in the air as Jake jumps out of the car and walks around to open my door. I hadn't considered that I'd be stepping out of a giant SUV with an equally giant NHL player beside me.

A few parents glance our way, recognition flashing in their eyes before they whisper to their kids. Even some of the teachers by the entrance look over, their expressions a mix of confusion and curiosity.

As we approach the front office, a group of kids by the playground notice us, wide-eyed as they point in our direction. One nudges his friend, and I hear their excited whispers: "That's Jake Brooks! He's here!"

Mrs. Lopez in reception stumbles momentarily over her words when she sees Jake beside me. "Ms. Andrews, and... Mr. Brooks," she greets us, keeping her professionalism despite her surprise. "Thank you for coming in."

"Of course," I say, brushing off the attention and focusing on what matters. "Can we see Noah?

She nods, regaining her composure. "Noah's in the counseling room. He's calm, but I think he'll feel a lot better seeing you, Ms Andrews."

As we walk down the hallway, Jake's quiet presence beside me feels like an anchor. He's not trying to take control, or steamroll in. He's just here, ready to act if I need him to. When we reach the door, Mrs. Lopez glances at Jake. "I'm sure Noah will be thrilled to see you too, Mr. Brooks."

Jake gives her a warm smile, but his focus is on me, silently offering support.

I nod at Mrs. Lopez, and she opens the door, letting us enter. Inside, Noah sits on a small couch, his shoulders hunched, staring blankly at a book in his hands. He looks so small, so dejected. His face lights up when he sees me, then his eyes widen when he spots Jake behind me.

"Mum! Jake!" He jumps up, running over.

I kneel down, pulling him into a tight hug, feeling the tension in his small frame ease as he buries his face in my shoulder.

"Hey, buddy. You okay?"

Noah pulls back and nods, his eyes filled with unshed tears. "I didn't mean to, Mum. I just... He wouldn't stop."

Brushing his hair back, I smile gently. "It's okay, Noah. You're not in trouble."

"Hey, Noah," Jake says softly, crouching to our level. "Tough day, huh?"

Noah nods, glancing back and forth between us.

I catch Jake's eye in a silent exchange, his soft eyes meeting my glassy ones. His presence is grounding, even as I try to hold my fraying edges together.

"Come on," I say, standing and reaching for Noah's hand. "Let's go home."

Noah nods, his hand slipping into mine. Jake slowly stands, his quiet support unspoken but tangible. I feel his hand slide over my shoulder and squeeze gently, but I don't dare look at him because I know I'll break. My wounds are on full display, and he's seeing right into my biggest fears.

As we step outside, the stares from parents and kids hit us like a spotlight. A group of boys from Noah's class hangs nearby, their eyes widening at the sight of Jake. "Whoa, Noah, you know *Jake Brooks*?"

Jake grins, clearly enjoying the attention his presence is affording Noah. He ruffles Noah's hair and says, "Yeah, Noah's cool. We're buds."

The boys gape in awe, and I see Noah's posture straighten a little, his shy smile breaking through.

As we reach Jake's car, he leans close to Noah, his voice dropping so only he can hear. "Remember buddy, those things that make you different? They're your superpowers. Don't let anyone tell you otherwise."

Noah nods, gripping my hand tighter as he climbs into the backseat. I catch Jake's eye, mouthing a silent "thank you." He just smiles, his gaze lingering on mine for a beat too long. He wants me to see this. wants me to see how much he cares.

As Jake drives us away from the school, his quiet presence fills the car again. I glance over at him—this man who keeps showing up, and something in me softens. The weight that's been pressing down on me all day begins to lift.

And it's all because of Jake.

CHAPTER EIGHTEEN

YOU'RE PRACTICALLY PART OF THE FURNITURE

---·✦·---

Jake

We pull into Charlie's driveway, and I kill the engine but linger in the driver's seat as Charlie gets Noah out. I can feel the weight of something unspoken—like we're both waiting for the other to make the first move.

Once we're all out, I hover near the front door as she finds her keys, hesitating as she unlocks it, unsure if I should follow her in or give her space. It's been days since I've properly seen her, and it's driving me crazy. Every part of me wants to be close, but I don't want to push—especially not today, when everything feels so fragile. Still, leaving without making sure she's alright isn't an option.

Noah tugs on my sleeve, blissfully unaware of the tension between his mom and I. "Are you coming inside, Jake?"

I glance at Charlie, searching her face. Her hesitation is brief, and she quickly nods.

"Yeah, come in. You're practically part of the furniture now." Her voice is teasing, but her eyes have questions—uncertainty about us. *Fuck that. I'm not letting you doubt this.*

Inside, Noah practically launches himself onto the sofa, grabbing the remote. "Can we watch hockey? I wanna learn the rules!"

"Absolutely, buddy." Settling next to him, I start flipping through channels until we find a game.

As the game unfolds, I explain the rules, pointing out plays and strategies. He's never played hockey before—hell, he's probably never even seen a game up close. The idea that I might be introducing him to something he could come to love fills me with a surprising sense of pride.

"You know," I say, glancing at Charlie as she watches us from the kitchen, "we should get you some skates and take you out on the ice sometime. I can show you a few tricks. What do you think?"

Noah beams. "Yes! That'd be awesome!"

"And maybe," I add, turning back to him, "if it's okay with your mom, you could come to one of my home games soon. I'll get you the best seats in the house."

Noah's face practically splits with excitement. "Really? Can I, Mum? Please?"

Charlie pauses from pulling things out of the fridge, a soft smile playing on her lips. "Sounds like a lot of fun. I'm sure we can make it happen."

I linger on her, imagining them front and center at a game, wearing my jersey and cheering me on. The idea of them being there, making the game mean so much more... It's something I want more than anything. "I'd love that." *I think I love more than just that.*

As I sit with Noah, explaining the game, I glance over at the kitchen and notice Charlie distracted, her eyes glued to her phone. She steps around the corner as it rings, her posture tightening, and I catch the strain on her face. I try to focus on Noah's questions, but something's tugging at me, making it impossible to ignore.

After a beat, I make an excuse to Noah. "Just grabbing some water, buddy. Be right back."

I step into the kitchen and grab a glass, catching the tail end of her conversation.

"Look, it was an isolated incident, Alex," she says. "I don't think you need to—"

"Right. Isolated. Sounds like everything's already falling apart over there, Lottie. Maybe if you weren't so intent on playing account manager in Denver, our son wouldn't be getting into fights at school. But no, you had to prove you could do it all." Alex lets out a mocking laugh. "And now Noah's paying the price."

My fingers tighten around the glass as a surge of fury courses through me. Who the hell does this guy think he is? I keep my composure for her sake, but it takes every ounce of self-control not to storm over and grab the phone off her.

Charlotte's shoulders slump, her voice barely steady. "Noah's adjusting fine, Alex."

Another low laugh. "Yeah? We'll see how long that lasts."

The line clicks, and she stands there, her expression shattered. She exhales slowly, pressing her phone to her forehead like it might hold her together for just one more second. Her head lifts slightly as she notices me, a flicker of embarrassment in her eyes. The anger inside me solidifies, quiet but unyielding.

I'm about to say something, but before I can say a word, Meadow charges through the front door like a burst of sunshine, Nina following close behind.

"Jake!" Meadow races over, throwing herself into me. "I missed you!"

I scoop her up with a laugh. "I missed you too, Princess. What have you been up to?" I meet Charlotte's gaze over Meadow's shoulder with a silent promise. He's not getting in her head like that while I'm around.

Meadow babbles about her playdate and her new friend she's made. I listen, hanging on every word, feeling something churn deep inside me. She's grown attached to me in such a short time, but so have I.

Before long, Meadow's up on the sofa with Noah, both of them hanging on my every word as we watch the rest of the game. I steal glances at Charlotte as she moves around the kitchen, her hands busy and shoulders slowly relaxing. She's using the time to decompress from that phone call, no doubt—but I can't stop watching her.

I want nothing more than to march over there, pin her against the counter, and kiss the stress right out of her. Feel her soft curves press into me as I remind her, with my hands and mouth, that she's not in this alone.

***

Charlie

Once Nina leaves, I retreat to the kitchen to collect myself. Noah and Meadow's excitement is contagious, and despite the tension coiled inside me from the call with Alex, I can't help but smile as I watch them, happy and carefree. The worry etched into Noah's shoulders from earlier is all but gone.

He seems so light, so thrilled to be discussing sports and planning activities. Meadow is just happy to be involved and in Jake's presence. She's always been a tactile kid, seeking cuddles and affection from those she trusts. The thought breaks my heart, because it's not something she's always received so freely.

I watch Jake wrap an arm around Meadow as she snuggles up beside him on the sofa, like he's been doing it for years. Jake isn't just filling a gap—he's creating experiences my kids have never had. And he's doing it effortlessly, like he was always meant to be here. *I want you to be here.*

I start making spaghetti bolognese, the kids' favorite. The scent of garlic and tomatoes fills the air, mingling with their laughter from the living room. I glance over at them every few minutes, my heart thundering with each laugh and story he shares with them. But a small voice that sounds annoyingly like Alex, keeps whispering. *This won't last.*

"Dinner's ready," I finally call out, setting plates on the table.

The kids come running, but Noah stops halfway, turning back to Jake. "You'll stay for dinner too, right?"

Jake hesitates, glancing at me as if he's unsure. "I don't want to intrude..."

I quickly shake my head, the words spilling out before I can stop them. "You're not intruding. Stay. The kids would love it."

He smiles, a warm, genuine thing that makes my heart skip. "Alright, if you're sure."

But as he says it, the doubt creeps in. I don't want him to feel obligated. "I am, but if you have other places to—"

"I don't. I'm *starved.*" His eyes lock on mine with a flash of frustration, like he's daring me to second-guess him again.

The last word is pointed, and it's true. It's been days since we've seen each other, and my body aches for him in ways I don't want to admit. I've been overthinking everything, over-analyzing every small moment, while Jake's been waiting for an opening; waiting for me.

Dinner is filled with the kids' chatter, but Jake and I are more reserved, both of us stealing glances at each other when we think the other isn't looking.

As dinner winds down and the kids get sleepy, Jake surprises me again. "How about I read them a bedtime story?"

Noah and Meadow immediately light up, and I can't help but smile. "That would be great," I say softly, grateful for the suggestion.

After I get them ready for bed, Jake follows the kids upstairs to read. The house feels different tonight—warmer, more alive. I've been so focused on keeping everything under control that I didn't realize how much we were missing.

When the dishes are done, I head upstairs to check on them. I stop just outside Meadow's door, holding my breath as I peek inside. Jake is sitting on her bed, with Noah and Meadow snuggled up on either side of him, listening intently as he reads. He's using different voices for each character, making them giggle and gasp at all the right moments.

My chest aches at the sight. I've never seen the kids so happy. They've needed this. And seeing Jake like this, so completely at ease, makes me realize just how much I've needed it too.

He glances up mid-sentence, catching me spying, and I feel heat creep up my cheeks. Instead of looking embarrassed, he just smiles at me, a look of understanding passing between us. He's making himself part of this, whether I'm ready to admit it or not.

When the story's over, I tuck Meadow in, brushing the hair out of her face. "Mama, I love Jake's stories," she mumbles sleepily as I pull the covers around her.

I smile, stroking her face. "Yeah, he's good at stories, isn't he?"

"Can he read me stories every night?"

I hesitate, unsure how to answer. "Well, that might be a bit tricky for him. But you know I can read them, too."

"You're not funny like Jake, Mama," she says matter-of-factly, her innocent honesty putting me in my place.

A chuckle comes from behind me. I look back to see Jake leaning in the doorway with a grin. I glare at him, but his smile only widens as he walks over.

Crouching down, he whispers to Meadow. "I'm honored, Princess. I'll read you stories anytime you want."

My heart stumbles in my chest for two reasons. One, because of how naturally he cares for my kids. And two, because you can't make promises like that to a three-year-old and not keep them. I find myself hoping he means every word because if I have to pick up the pieces, there'll be hell to pay.

"Jake's not here all the time though, honey bee. Sometimes he'll be away, and sometimes he'll be busy," I add, needing them both to understand this might not be a permanent thing.

Jake turns to me, his eyes resolute, before turning back to Meadow. "We'll figure it out, Princess. Promise."

I wait until he's wished Meadow sweet dreams and has gone back downstairs before quietly checking on Noah. He's already half-asleep, curled up under the blankets, but there's a peace about him now. Like he's had a tough day but come out the other side, thanks to the love he's received.

I close his door softly and head downstairs, my heart still racing from the sight of Jake with them. As I reach the bottom step, he's there, waiting in the foyer, eyes on me and hands clenching slightly by his sides.

"Thanks for today," I say softly, almost hesitantly. "I'm sorry that—"

Before I can finish, he's closing the distance between us. I don't have a chance to think as he crowds me up against the wall, tilting my face up to lock his eyes with mine. He takes a breath, like he's about to say something, but stops himself. Instead, his lips crash against mine in an urgent, hungry kiss.

He kisses me like he's desperately trying to make me understand something. Like there's something with words he can't quite say right now. His hands tangle in my hair as he presses into me, and I can't fight it anymore. I don't want to. A low groan escapes him as he pulls me closer, his grip in my hair tightening, and I melt into him.

"Jake," I whisper against his lips, my voice trembling with a mix of need and hesitation.

He pulls back just enough to meet my gaze, his eyes dark and intense as he cups my jaw again. "Please don't doubt this, Charlie," he murmurs.

So, I do what any respectable woman would do in this moment.

I surrender.

CHAPTER NINETEEN

I WANT YOU. DO YOU WANT ME?

—————— ·✦· ——————

Jake

A soft moan escapes her, hands gliding up my chest and over my shoulders, pulling me closer. I step into her, my fingers traveling down her back, gripping her hips and tugging her flush against me.

I lift her effortlessly as her thighs tighten around me, like she's been waiting for this as much as I have. The need between us is electric as I carry her to the nearest flat surface—the kitchen counter— and set her down gently. My hands slide up her thighs, fingers tracing the curve of her hips as I lean in, capturing her mouth in another frantic kiss.

"Been waiting all week to do this," I murmur against her lips, pushing her back on the countertop. She breathes hard as my hands slide up her top, planting soft, heated kisses over her stomach. Her skin is warm beneath my lips, and the way she arches up into my touch drives me crazy.

"Oh my God," she breathes, fingers raking into my hair.

I grin against her skin as I inch her top up higher, exposing her black lace bra. Her skin is so soft, and I can't resist dotting kisses and gentle bites across the pillowy flesh of her breasts, savoring the way her breath catches each time.

Looking up, I catch the need and hesitation warring in her eyes. *I can't have that.*

"You're fucking perfect," I rasp, one hand sliding up to cup her breast through the sheer lace, the other stroking her jaw as I claim her mouth again. My thumb finds her nipple, and I roll it in slow, deliberate circles above the fabric, pulling a deep moan from her throat.

Trailing down to her jeans, my fingers unbutton them with a roughness that mirrors my own need. My mouth drags along the delicate skin of her throat, inhaling her scent and nipping at her, drinking down every sound she gives me. Soft, breathy whimpers.

Fuck, I want more.

I slip a hand under her waistband, then look up, seeking permission. Her eyes are hazy with desire as they meet mine.

"Tell me to stop, Charlie."

She bites her lip, the softest plea escaping her. "Don't stop. Please."

Something in me snaps at her words. I'm done for. This isn't just want anymore, it's *need*—bone-deep, primal, and only for her.

"God, you're soaked," I groan, my finger sliding through her wetness and dragging a slow, teasing circle over her clit. "That all for me, baby?"

"Yes," she breathes, her hips lifting and begging for more.

I won't deny her. Not tonight.

Tonight, I want her writhing and wrecked, her voice breaking as she sobs my name. I want to show her how good I can make her feel, and I want her craving more. To think about this for days to come, and remember that it was me, *only me*, that made her feel this way.

I slowly run a finger through her again, swirling over her clit and eliciting the sweetest sounds from her mouth. Then I pull her jeans and thong down in one motion, peeling them off her body. She's laid out before me like the most tempting feast I've ever seen, and I'm fucking starving.

My hands slide up her legs, gripping her thighs and spreading them wider. And when I look down at her, I nearly lose my goddamn mind.

Pink. Glistening. Absolutely drenched.

Lifting my eyes back to hers, a low sound leaves my throat as I slide a finger inside her, watching her body swallow it down. Then another.

"Oh my God, Jake..."

The breathy way she says my name is everything.

With my eyes locked on hers, I lower myself, lips tracing slow kisses up her thighs, inching closer to her center until I finally reach her clit. I suck slowly, and her head falls back, exposing her throat. Her hands tangle in my hair, and I let out a vibrating hum of pleasure that makes her hips jolt.

Fuck, yes.

Satisfaction spreads across my face as I lap at her. She tastes like heaven, and I know I'll never get enough. Crooking my fingers, I hit a spot that has her throwing an arm over her face to keep her voice down.

No fucking way.

"Eyes on me, baby." My voice is a rough command as I look up at her from between her legs. Her eyes meet mine, flickering with desire as I suck her clit, and I swear to God I could come just from the way she's looking at me right now.

She's so outrageously gorgeous and doesn't even realize it, her head lifting between her peaked nipples to watch me, like the best sunrise I've ever seen.

"Fuck, you taste so good," I grunt, pumping my fingers and feeling her tighten. I curl them, coaxing every ounce of pleasure from her, our gazes locked.

"Please Jake, don't stop. God, that feels so—" She gasps, her head falling back, mouth open in a silent cry.

I press a hand against her thigh, keeping her spread and increasing the pressure, my tongue swirling as she bucks against me. Her breathing turns ragged, fingers tightening in my hair, thighs trembling as she teeters on the edge.

"*Eyes*, Charlie." Her eyes find mine again, glazed over with pleasure, and the look in them is enough to undo me. "That's it, baby. Such a good girl, riding my mouth. You want more?"

A shudder rolls through her, and a soft whimper slips out as her nails dig into my scalp. I can barely breathe from how fucking perfect she looks like this. Needy. Desperate. *Mine.*

"Yes," she breathes, her hips lifting to meet my mouth, chasing every flick of my tongue. It's the sexiest damn thing I've ever seen.

"You gonna come for me?" My voice drops low in between strokes. "I want you to come on my tongue, let me taste you."

"Jake—oh my God—" her voice breaks as I curl my fingers and press one last open-mouthed kiss against her clit, before sucking it in deep.

"That's it, baby. Soak my tongue. Make a fucking mess of me."

She shatters with a cry, her body arching and thighs trembling around my head, and I take every bit as her climax pulses through her. I don't stop, won't even consider it until I've wrung out every last drop, until every desperate little moan has been mine to devour.

A half-crazed prayer fists in my chest, begging the universe to let me be the only man who ever gets to do this to her over and over again. Only me.

Charlie's body relaxes and she lets out low, uneven pants, her fingers still tangled in my hair like she doesn't want to let go. Good. *She won't have to.*

I press one final kiss to her inner thigh, before dragging my tongue over my lips, making sure she sees how wrecked I am for her. My eyes roam over her gorgeous body sprawled out on the counter, a masterpiece of my own making.

"Sweetest thing I've ever fucking tasted."

Leaning in, I brush my mouth over hers, letting her taste herself on me. She hums softly, deepening the kiss as her fingers slide down to my waistband, ready to return the favor.

But I catch her hand, holding it firm.

"Jake," she whispers, still breathless, her eyebrows drawing together in confusion as I shake my head.

"Not tonight, Charlie girl." My voice is low and laced with a restraint my cock is definitely not listening to. "Tonight was for you. I needed you to feel how much I want you—beyond reason, beyond anything else."

Her eyes search mine, wide and questioning. "But I—"

I press a finger gently to her lips. "Shh, let this be enough. Let me be enough."

Her breath hitches like she wants to argue, but instead she slowly nods. I can see the flicker of doubt in her eyes, the way she's clinging to control, trying to keep her vulnerability at bay. But I'm not letting her hide again. Not with me.

I run my fingers through her hair, tangling them in the strands as I cradle her face. "You've been carrying so much, and you've been doing it so damn well. But you don't have to do this alone... let me in."

Her lips part, a breath slipping out, but no words follow.

She stares at me for a moment, her face unreadable except for a flicker of something vulnerable.

A shiver runs through her as she speaks, like it's taking all her effort to form the words. "I'm scared, Jake. I don't want to mess this up. I don't want to get hurt, or hurt the kids, or *you*. What if..."

Her voice trails off, swallowed up in the space between us.

I lean in, tilting my forehead to hers, breathing in her hesitation, looking that abyss of doubt in the eye. Then I softly kiss her, reminding her how real this is. How real I am.

"You're not going to mess anything up. We'll figure this out together, one step at a time. I want you... do you want me?"

She nods again and sways into me, gripping my arms. "I want to trust this... us."

"That's all I need," I murmur, letting my lips skim down her collarbone, sealing my promises into her skin. "I promise you I won't break it."

The weight of everything we've just shared hangs between us. The fear, the hope, and the quiet, slow shift of her walls starting to give.

Exhaling shakily, her eyes flick between mine, and I can see it.

She's letting me in.

I don't know what I did to deserve this, but I'm ready to fight tooth and nail to keep it.

Helping her off the counter, her fingers linger against my chest as she moves, shimmying back into her jeans with a soft blush painting her cheeks.

I smile, watching as she tucks her hair behind her ear—like she's trying to pull herself together, but there's still a part of her floating in the moment with me.

She steps back into my arms, like it's instinct, like she's done it a thousand times, like it's second nature.

And just like that, my heart fucking stutters again.

"Thanksgiving's soon," I say, pressing a kiss to her forehead. "Ryan's hosting, and I want you and the kids there. You'd love it."

She blinks up at me with surprised eyes. "Thanksgiving? I mean, I know it's soon, but we've never celebrated it. It's not a thing back home."

I grin, already imagining the day. "Then you and the kids are definitely coming with me. We'll eat too much food, watch football, and you'll get the full American experience. I want you guys to be part of it."

There's a quiet softness behind her gaze as she studies me. "Okay. I'll think about it."

"Good." I hook an arm around her, pulling her close. "Let's go get comfortable. I'm not staying, but I wanna hang out a bit longer. Is that okay?"

"More than okay," she whispers, tucking herself against me as we make our way to the living room.

"Stay as long as you want, I'm not ready to say goodbye yet."

Neither am I.

Not now. Not ever.

CHAPTER TWENTY

THE PIZZA WAS DEFINITELY... GOURMET

———————◆———————

Charlie

The morning sun filters through the windows, casting a warm glow across the kitchen counter. The very counter where everything changed last night, where Jake literally devoured me. I close my eyes, still feeling the ghost of his touch, the way he looked at me like I was the only thing in the world that mattered.

When we said goodbye last night, he'd cradled my face as if he was afraid to let go while reminding me how much he wants this, wants *me*. I'd tried to respond, tried to tell him I felt the same way and he didn't need to convince me. But the words were tangled in my fear and uncertainty. So instead of speaking, I'd kissed him one more time. It was desperate, a little clumsy, but it was all I could offer in that moment—my way of conveying what I can't say out loud yet. *I'm all in too. I want this too.*

His parting words play on a loop in my mind.

I'm not going anywhere.

I swallow hard, struggling to hold back the emotions. He means every word, and I know it. But that only makes this more complicated, because if he's serious, then I have to be too. And that scares the hell out of me.

I've been up for hours, replaying everything in my head. The house is quiet except for the soft hum of the fridge and the kids' occasional laughter in the living room. All I can think about is how much I want to believe him, how much I want to throw caution to the wind and just let myself fall.

But the other part is screaming to slow down, to protect myself and the kids from potential heartbreak. I don't know how to navigate this. How to balance my life, my kids, my job, and this overwhelming feeling growing between Jake and me. I'd planned everything: relocating, setting up life here, even quizzing Zoe endlessly to nail the new job.

Nowhere in my notes had I planned for Jake.

To bump into him after twelve years, to have him dig deep beneath my skin, burrow right through my ribcage, and cup my heart in his hands like it's something precious. He's done it so quickly, so effortlessly.

Like it was always meant to be his.

It's making me fucking crazy that I can't control this, but I can't stop the little voice in my head telling me this is exactly what I need—to relinquish the control I've so tightly clutched and just *live.*

The doorbell rings, snapping me back to the present. When I open it, Zoe's standing there practically vibrating with excitement. I sent her a crisis text after Jake left, so I know she's here for one reason: a debrief.

"Morning, lover girl," she singsongs as she steps inside, blowing kisses to the kids in the living room before sauntering into the kitchen, grinning at me like an idiot.

"Sooo...?" She plops down onto a barstool, not even trying to hide her curiosity.

I roll my eyes but can't help the smile tugging at my lips as I sit down next to her. "We need to be careful with what we say," I whisper, nodding toward the living room.

"Got it. Code names and metaphors." She winks.

I hand her a cup of coffee, but she barely acknowledges it as she leans forward with a smirk on her face. "So, Charlie. How was the... pizza?"

"Pizza?"

"Yeah, you know, the *pizza.*" She waggles her eyebrows suggestively. "Was it everything you wanted it to be? Cheesy, hot, maybe a little... *spicy?*"

I nearly choke on my coffee.

"What?" she says innocently. "I'm just asking if the *pizza* was worth it."

I shake my head, a smile slipping through despite myself. "It was... Let's just say it was *gourmet*. Way more than I expected."

"That good, huh? Sounds like it *hit the spot*."

"Oh, it did," I reply, lowering my voice. "It was amazing. But it's not just the... toppings. It's everything else. The way the pizza... looks at me, the way it... makes the kids so happy. It's an intense pizza."

Zoe's eyes, glittering with barely contained amusement, soften as she clinks her coffee mug with mine. "Sounds like you've got yourself a *five-star meal*, Charlie."

I sigh, leaning back in my chair. "But what if it's too good to be true?"

She tilts her head. "He's not a *fast-food* kinda guy, Charlie. Can't you tell?"

I take a deep breath, trying to steady myself. "Yeah, it's just... it's a lot. But in a good way."

"That's because the pizza is head-over-heels, can't-think-straight into you, babe."

"Yeah, but what if it doesn't last?" I blurt out, the fear that's been gnawing at me finally surfacing. "Alex seemed all in too, and look how that turned out."

Zoe's playfulness fades at the mention of Alex's name. "The gourmet pizza is *nothing* like that stale loaf of bread. And you're not the same person you were back then, either. You're stronger now, smarter. You're allowed to want this, Charlie. You're allowed to be happy."

I snort at the comparison, but try to absorb her words. "I just don't want the kids to get hurt. They're already getting attached to him, especially Meadow."

Zoe gives me a knowing look. "Which means *you're* getting attached, too."

I look down at my coffee, her words hitting me hard. "Maybe."

"Look," she says firmly, "you don't have to have all the answers. Just take it one day at a time. And trust that he's in this for the right reasons. I've known him for a few years now, and honestly? I've never seen him like this with anyone."

"You think he's ready for all this?"

Before she can answer, Meadow runs in, her eyes bright with excitement. "Mama! Can Jake read me a story again at bedtime?"

I chuckle, scooping her up into my arms. "We'll see, honey bee. Jake might be busy tonight."

"He promised." Meadow pouts, resting her head on my shoulder.

Zoe shoots me a gleeful look. "And there's your answer."

I ignore her and turn back to Meadow, kissing the top of her head. "We'll figure it out, honey bee."

Zoe stands and stretches with a satisfied grin. "Well, I think that's my cue to leave you with your gourmet meal—I mean, your *thoughts*."

She gives me a quick hug and waves to the kids before heading for the door. With a last wink, Zoe leaves me alone with my thoughts, and a little girl who's already halfway in love with Jake.

As I watch Meadow wander back to the living room, I feel the weight of Zoe's words. *One day at a time.*

Maybe that's all I can do right now.

***

Jake

Ryan and I step into my condo, still laughing about something one of the guys said at practice. The door clicks shut, and it's quiet, almost too quiet after the buzz of the arena.

I drop my bag by the door and stretch, the adrenaline from practice still humming in my veins. Ryan heads straight for the fridge like he owns the place, grabs two bottles of water, and tosses one my way.

"Man, I think we might actually have a shot at the playoffs this year," he says, cracking his bottle open.

I lean back against the counter, nodding. "Yeah, we've got a good rhythm going. Just gotta keep it up."

Ryan takes a long swig, glancing my way. "Definitely. About time we got our act together. And if Eli keeps playing like that, we're golden."

We trade a few more jabs and inside jokes about the team, but I can feel Ryan's tone shift. He's got something on his mind, and I know him well enough to recognize it.

He sets his bottle down, crossing his arms. "So... Thanksgiving. You bringing Charlotte and the kids?"

I pause mid-sip, glancing at him. "Yeah, that's the plan. Mentioned it to her last night. She's hesitant, but I think she's on board."

Ryan quirks an eyebrow. "Last night?"

"Yeah. Noah got into some trouble at school, so I offered to help out. Then I hung around for a bit."

He smirks, leaning against the counter. "You thinking about making it exclusive?"

I frown. I hadn't considered I needed to ask outright, I just assumed we were. "She's mine." I sound like a caveman, but I don't care.

He chuckles, lifting his water. "Does *she* know that?"

My thoughts race at the question, the weight of it settling over me. *She better fucking know it.*

"I don't want to push her too fast. She's been through a lot, so I don't wanna screw this up by rushing things."

Ryan's expression turns serious. "You're all in with her, aren't you? The way you talk about her, man..."

"All in, one hundred percent. She appeared right in front of me after twelve years, there's no way I'm not letting her go again."

"Dude, you're in deep."

I run a hand through my hair, sorting out everything in my head. "I just don't want to scare her off, you know? She's got the kids to think about, but I don't want her thinking I'm not serious either."

His head shakes, amused. "I've never seen you like this over anyone. Surely she knows."

I glance at him, trying to gauge how much is friendly reassurance and how much is truth. "I don't wanna screw this up. I…" I trail off, unable to voice my deepest feelings out loud—not yet. Not until I've said them to her first.

Ryan claps a hand on my shoulder, giving it a squeeze. "You're doing everything right, man. Just keep being yourself. She's already halfway there."

Nodding, I take in his words. He's right. I've put it all out there, and I've got to trust that she feels the same. Still, the idea of making our relationship official is a lot to process.

I'd do it in a heartbeat, but I have to be careful. Losing her now, before we've even really started, scares the shit out of me.

We finish our waters, the conversation lightening up as we talk about the upcoming game, Chase's escapades, and the usual locker room banter. But after Ryan leaves, the condo feels even more sterile, the silence pressing in around me.

I take in the sleek lines and pristine surfaces. It's the kind of place that looks good in a magazine. Impressive on the outside, but hollow at its core. The same way I've felt without her these past twelve years.

I think back to Charlie's house and how warm it felt; how alive. There's a coziness there, a sense of home my place is missing. The thought crosses my mind to make my condo more inviting for her and the kids. It's not something I've thought about before, but now it feels important. I want them with me. *I want to be with them.*

With a sigh, I pull out my phone, scrolling until I find Charlie's name. My thumb hovers over the screen for a moment before I hit the call button. It rings a couple of times, and I hear chaos in the background when she picks up.

"Hey, Jake," she says, voice frazzled. A high-pitched wail sounds in the background.

"Hey, Lady Lightning," I reply, a smile tugging at my lips. "Everything okay over there?"

"Sorry, it's a bit crazy right now." Her words are nearly lost in the noise—sounds like Meadow is in full meltdown mode.

"You okay?"

She lets out a tired laugh. "Just another standard night at Casa Charlotte. Meadow's decided that bath time is the end of the world, and Noah's arguing with me about whether broccoli is necessary. You know, the usual fun and rainbows."

I chuckle, picturing the scene. "Sounds like a full house."

"Yeah, it's... something," she says, then quickly changes the subject. "How was practice?"

I ignore it, instead focusing on the strain in her voice. She's tired in a way that goes beyond physical—a kind of tired that comes from doing everything alone, day after day.

"I should come over," I say, the decision made before I even realize it. "I promised my favorite three-year-old a bedtime story anyway."

"Jake, you don't have to—"

"I'm on my way," I insist, already grabbing my keys. "Be there soon."

There's a pause, then a sigh. "Alright. But don't say I didn't warn you."

"Bring it on, baby."

CHAPTER TWENTY-ONE

PAJAMAS ARE THE ABSOLUTE WORST

―――――――――✦―――――――――

Jake - 12 Years Ago

I'm heading toward the mess hall when I spot Charlotte sitting on the steps of her cabin, her head in her hands. She's usually right in the thick of things, helping the kids and organizing other leaders with a smile in place. Something's off.

"Hey, Charlie," I call, keeping my tone light. "Everything okay?"

She looks up, and the exhaustion in her eyes hits me like a punch. "Just a long day," she says, her voice missing its usual spark. "I'm fine, really."

I don't buy it. "You don't look fine." I sit down beside her on the steps, stretching my legs out. "Wanna talk?"

She sighs, running a hand through her hair. "You know how it is. Some days are just harder than others. Today was one of those days."

I nod, not pushing. Camp can be exhausting, and it's more than the physical stuff—it's the emotional weight of being 'on' all day. I've had my rough days too, but I've never seen her like this.

"Anything I can do to help?"

She shakes her head. "Not unless you've got a magic wand that makes kids listen the first time."

"Hmm, fresh out of those. But I'm a pro at sitting..."

A small, tired smile appears. "Yeah, that helps."

If that's all it takes, I'll gladly sit beside her for as long as she needs. We sit in comfortable silence, the distant chatter of campers and the rustling of leaves around us. It's still. Peaceful.

After a while, she straightens, rubbing her hands over her knees. "I just wanna feel like I'm doing a good job. Like I'm not letting anyone down."

I frown, because I've had that same thought a hundred times myself, but I never would've guessed she felt the same. Seeing her like this stirs something deep in me. It's hard to reconcile this version of her with the strong, confident person I know. But maybe that's the point—maybe even light needs a place to rest.

"You're not letting anyone down," I say firmly. "The kids adore you. Hell, this whole camp would fall apart without you."

She doesn't respond right away, but I see the faintest smile tugging her lips. For the first time since I sat down, she looks lighter. Less weighed down by whatever's been gnawing at her all day. It's small, but I feel the victory. Like maybe just being here with her is enough. "Thanks, Jake."

"Anytime, Lady Lightning."

I glance at her, and for a moment, I see her in a new way. Not just as a friend or camp leader, but as someone who also needs to hear that they're doing okay. That they're valued.

And if she needs that reminder, I'll do it. Every damn day.

***

Jake – Present Day

When I pull up to Charlie's house, the sounds of mayhem are almost audible from the driveway. I knock, and when she opens the door, she looks frazzled—hair slightly out of place, tracksuit still somehow managing to look sexy on her.

"Hey," she says, breathless. "You really didn't have to come."

"I wanted to," I reply, stepping inside.

165

The scene is just as chaotic as I expected. Meadow clutches her towel, red-faced and wailing at a pitch that could shatter glass. At the table, Noah glares at his broccoli like it's personally offended him, while Charlotte juggles a handful of pajamas and a sippy cup.

I drop to one knee in front of Meadow, softening my voice. "Hey, Princess. What's got you so upset?"

She pauses mid-wail, blinking at me, but then she remembers her grievances and starts up again, even louder. "Don't wanna wear pajamas!" Her lower lip trembles, tears streaking her cheeks.

"Pajamas are the worst," I agree solemnly, glancing up at Charlie with a wink. "But bedtime stories are the best."

Meadow's eyes briefly light up before suspicion returns. "No! No pajamas!" She pulls the towel tighter like it's a shield against the idea.

"How about a deal?" I say, keeping my voice gentle. "You get into your PJs, and I promise you the best story ever. I'll even do all the voices."

She hesitates, her little brow furrowed in contemplation. Before she can decide, Noah pipes up, frustrated. "Do I *have* to eat the broccoli? It's gross!"

I glance over at him, seeing the broccoli standoff. "Tell you what, buddy," I say, balancing between Meadow's tantrum and Noah's broccoli battle, "if you finish it, you get to pick the story tonight. Deal?"

Noah grumbles, but finally stabs the broccoli and takes a tiny, dramatic bite, grimacing the whole time.

"Good job, Noah," I say, before turning back to Meadow. "So, what do you say, Princess? Pajamas, then stories?"

She's still sizing me up, her grip on the towel firm. I can see the wheels turning in her little mind, deciding whether she trusts me enough to keep my promise.

Charlotte steps in, her voice soft but tired. "Honey bee, let's get into your PJs, okay? Then story time."

Meadow's lip quivers, but instead of bursting into tears, she lets out a small defeated sigh. "Only if Jake reads the story," she concedes, looking at me with big, watery eyes.

I shoot Charlie a grin as she quickly helps Meadow into her pajamas. "Deal."

Once she's dressed, I lift Meadow onto my shoulders, drawing a few giggles. As we head upstairs, I hear Charlotte let out a quiet sigh of relief. Noah, still grumbling, shuffles up to his room to get ready.

Getting Meadow into bed isn't as easy as I hoped. She squirms and protests, complaining about the covers, and at one point, throws herself onto the floor in frustration. With a lot of patience and coaxing, she finally settles, clutching her favorite stuffed unicorn.

Noah arrives with a stack of books, each one thicker than the last. "You said I could pick the story," he reminds me, holding up a book that will take hours to read.

I chuckle, ruffling his hair. "How about we save that one for the long weekend and pick something a little shorter?"

He pouts but eventually hands me a different book. I settle in with them on Meadow's bed, putting on all the silly voices. But even as I read, Meadow fidgets, scrunching her face up. "No, not like that! You're doing it wrong!"

I laugh and adjust my voice, deeper and more dramatic, and that seems to satisfy her for now. She's testing, the way little kids do when they're figuring out how far they can go. Maybe it's her way of checking if I'll still be here when the story's over—if I'm someone she can count on.

After the story, I close the book and look at the two sleepy faces beside me. Noah's already half-asleep, but Meadow's still fighting it, her eyes fluttering as she tries to stay awake. It's damn near the cutest thing I've ever seen.

"More stories tomorrow?" Meadow yawns, her tiny fist rubbing at her eyes.

"You got it, Princess," I reply, brushing her hair back. She finally settles, her breathing evening out.

I stand, feeling a mix of contentment and something deeper—something that feels a lot like belonging. This house, hectic and vibrant, is everything my condo isn't. It's not quiet or neat, and it sure as hell isn't simple. But it feels alive. It feels like a place where love happens, even in the middle of broccoli standoffs and bedtime battles. And that's something I didn't even know I was missing. Not until them.

As I turn to take Noah to his room, I spot Charlotte at the door, leaning against the frame with a soft smile.

"I'll tuck her in," she whispers, stepping in. I nod and head with Noah to his room, pulling his covers back.

"You did good, Jake," he mumbles, barely coherent as he snuggles under his covers.

"Thanks, buddy." I smile. "Sleep tight."

I head back downstairs and stop by the bathroom to wash my hands, taking a moment to breathe while Charlotte finishes up with the kids.

Everything tonight has been a whirlwind, exactly as she promised. But it feels right. Even in the chaos, there's a warmth here that I love.

Back in the kitchen, I find Charlie pulling out a bottle of wine from the fridge. There's a tension in her shoulders, like she's still processing the evening. She doesn't hear me approach, so I place my hands on her shoulders, kneading slowly. She jumps slightly, but then stands there, letting me work out the tension in her muscles.

"You okay?" I ask softly, pressing a kiss to her neck.

She chuckles, though there's weariness there. "I'm fine. This is just... life."

I smile, releasing her as she turns to me. "Wouldn't change it for anything."

She sighs, offering me a glass, but I shake my head.

Taking a small sip, she studies my face. I smile serenely back at her, and brace for the hit. I know her. I know exactly what she's going to say. This is where she'll tell me that this is too much for me to take on.

"You don't have to pretend, you know. It's okay if this is a lot."

Bingo.

"It is," I admit, my fingers trailing up her arm. "But I like it."

She swirls her wine, processing my words. "You say that now, but what about when it gets harder?"

"Charlie girl, the easy parts are great, but I'm here for all of it."

She looks down into her glass, doubt flickering in her eyes. "I don't want you to feel obligated because of the kids."

I place my hand over hers, stilling the motion of the glass. "Charlotte. I'm here because I want to be. Not out of obligation, but because I care about you—and them."

She meets my gaze, her eyes softening. "I'm trying to believe you," she whispers. "But it's still scary."

I nod, understanding her fear. Cupping her cheek, I brush my thumb up her jaw to her earlobe. "I know. Life's messy, and this isn't easy for you. But I don't wanna be anywhere else, or with anyone else."

A small genuine smile appears, her defenses lowering. We stand there for a moment, just enjoying the quiet after the storm. Then I lean down, pressing a tender kiss to her lips. When I pull back, I let my eyes coast over her face, savoring her. *God, you're beautiful.*

"So, about Thanksgiving..."

Her smile fades slightly, but I give her hand a reassuring squeeze.

"It's just a holiday," I say. "A chance for us to spend time together with everyone there, Zoe too."

She sighs, still torn. "It's not just the holiday Jake, it's everything. I'm a package deal. My life isn't simple, and there are a lot of highs and lows. I need to know that you've thought this through."

"Trust me, I've thought about this a lot. I know it won't always be easy, but I want you and the kids to be a part of my life, and I want to be a part of yours."

She lets out a shaky breath. "Okay," she finally says. "We'll go to Thanksgiving."

Relief and warmth wash over me. "You know, you could make this a little easier by just admitting I'm irresistible."

Charlie laughs, her eyes twinkling. "Oh, is that what I'm supposed to do?"

I nod. "It'll be fun. I promise."

She takes another sip, still smiling. I watch her for a beat then reach for the glass, taking it from her hands and setting it down.

"Come here."

Her breath catches slightly as I reach for her, my fingers brushing back her hair, lingering at the nape of her neck.

This time when I kiss her, I let everything pour out—the intensity, the longing, the quiet certainty that's been building since the moment she walked back into my life.

Her lips part beneath mine, and fuck, I swear I could get drunk off her. She tastes warm and sweet, but there's something else too. Something distinctly Charlie that I've been chasing for twelve years without even realizing it.

A low hum escapes her as her fingers tug into my shirt, pulling me closer. My hands drift down, tracing the curve of her spine until they settle firmly on her hips. She presses into me, and a sharp breath leaves me as the heat of her body sinks into mine.

Griping her ass, I squeeze just enough to feel the way her breath stutters against my lips. She moans, and I swallow the sound down as I deepen the kiss, teasing her lower lip between my teeth before soothing it with my tongue. Fuck, I want her.

When I pull back, her eyes stay closed for a moment, her lips parted and breathy. I press a lingering kiss to the corner of her mouth, memorizing the way she feels against me. She exhales, eyes still closed, gripping my shirt like she's not ready to let go, and I fucking love it.

I love you.

"See?" I murmur, studying her. "Told you this would be fun."

She opens her eyes, and the look she gives me is all I need to know I'm right where I'm meant to be. Whatever comes next, whatever challenges we'll face, I know one thing for certain.

With Charlie, I'm home.

CHAPTER TWENTY-TWO

DON'T YOU KNOW A VPL CAN RUIN AN OTHERWISE FANTASTIC OUTFIT?

---◆---

Charlie

I'm staring at the mirror, debating whether this dress is too much.

It's not what I'd usually wear, especially not to a Thanksgiving dinner with Jake's friends, but Zoe insisted it was *the one*. With my makeup done and hair cascading over my shoulders, I have to admit it does look good. Tight, yes, but not over-the-top.

My phone buzzes with a message from **Jake's #1 Fan Club**

> **Zoe**: Send me a pic. I wanna see if my hard work's paid off x

I snap a full length mirror selfie, flipping her off with my free hand. Her response is almost immediate.

> **Zoe:** HOT. But girl, are you seriously wearing those panties?

> **Me:** What's wrong with my panties?

171

Zoe: VPL! Can see it from here. Lose them.

Rolling my eyes, I glance in the mirror, tilting my hips. Shit. She's right. It's a faint but undeniably visible panty line.

Me: Fine, commando it is. But if I flash Jake's friends, I'm blaming you.

Zoe: You'll be thanking me when Jake can't keep his hands off you. Trust me.

Laughing, I toss my phone aside. Zoe makes everything sound so simple, but today feels like a big step. Bigger than the fundraiser, where I was just 'the friend who made cakes.'

Today, I'm... what? His date? His something-more? Everything's been moving fast, and we haven't defined it yet, which ties my stomach in knots.

My phone buzzes again.

Jake: Just leaving mine. Be there in 15

Me: K. Warning—Meadow's bouncing off the walls!

Jake: Good. I'll bring the tranquilizers

Me: If only...

Jake: You look beautiful, by the way. I'm already picturing that dress on the floor later.

I grin at his words, which make absolutely no sense as he hasn't seen me. I'm not used to this kind of effortless flirtation. This easy confidence. Especially from someone who sets my skin on fire. It's been so long since I felt like this with anyone, and I can't deny how much I enjoy it.

Me: You haven't even seen what I'm wearing

Jake: Don't need to. I already know you'll look perfect

Me: Flattery will get you everywhere, Brooks

Jake: That's the plan, Lady Lightning

Smiling, I tuck my phone away and head downstairs to check on the kids who are watching cartoons. Meadow twirls in her princess dress, her little face lit with joy, while Noah sulks on the couch, casting a baleful eye down at his outfit.

"You look like a prince," I say to him, adjusting his collar as he squirms.

"I don't wanna be a prince," he mutters. "Can I just wear my hoodie?"

"Not today," I say, ruffling his hair. "Besides, Jake's friends are going to think you look really cool."

He grumbles, but his shoulders relax a bit. Progress. He's been becoming more independent, but his moodiness usually fades whenever Jake or Zoe is around.

The doorbell rings, and Meadow bolts for it. "Jake's here!"

Taking a deep breath, I give myself a final glance in the foyer mirror—tight dress, no VPL—and open the door. Jake stands there holding a bouquet of flowers, looking far too good in a casual shirt with rolled-up sleeves.

"Wow," he stammers. "You look..." My heart does a little flip when his eyes roam down my body.

"Happy Thanksgiving," I say, taking the flowers as he steps in, his hand slipping to the small of my back. His touch is grounding, and I can feel the warmth of his palm through the fabric of my dress.

"Happy Thanksgiving," he replies, pressing a soft kiss to my cheek. His hand lingers at my waist, thumb grazing my hip. "I brought something for the kids, too."

Meadow's eyes light up as Jake pulls out two boxes wrapped in shiny paper. "What is it?"

"Open and see," Jake says, crouching to their level.

The kids tear into the paper, revealing a new animal family set for Meadow and a LEGO box for Noah. Seeing their delight, I feel a swell of gratitude for this man who just gets it.

"Thank you, Jake!" Meadow squeals, hugging his leg. Noah gives a shy smile, mumbling his thanks before retreating slightly, still holding the gift.

"You're welcome," Jake chuckles, picking Meadow up with one arm, tendons rippling his forearm as he does so. I try to restrain myself at the sight of it.

"You ready?" Jake asks, eyes on mine.

I nod, composing myself. "Yeah, let's go."

The drive to Ryan and Claire's is filled with Meadow's excited questions and Noah's attempt to play it cool, though he keeps sneaking glances at the LEGO box on his lap. Jake reaches over and gives my knee a gentle squeeze.

"You doing okay?" His voice is low and intimate, just for me.

I smile as his thumb sweeps up and down. "Yeah, think so. A little nervous."

"You look incredible, by the way."

"Thanks," I say, feeling my cheeks flush a little as we stop at a red light. "Zoe insisted I wear it. Said it was a winner."

"She was right." He gives me a once-over, slow and deliberate. I turn to the window, biting my mouth closed to keep it from spreading across my face.

At Ryan and Claire's, the warm, savory scent of butter and sage mingles with the faint tang of citrus, carrying a richness that feels unmistakably like Thanksgiving. Ryan greets us with a broad grin, while Claire stands beside him, her hands resting on her growing belly.

"Welcome!" Claire says, pulling me into a quick hug. We've met once before, but she's so warm and welcoming it's hard not to feel like I've known her forever. "We hoped Jake would bring you all."

"Thanks so much for having us," I say, nerves dissolving. "Your home is beautiful."

Inside, the place is buzzing with conversation and laughter. It's exactly what I would imagine Thanksgiving should feel like—cozy, welcoming, and full of life. This isn't some formal event. It feels relaxed, like I'm already part of the family.

Zoe swoops in, hugging me tight. "I'm so glad you're here!" She turns to Meadow and Noah, leading them excitedly toward the rec room. "Games and snacks this way, guys!"

Elijah ambles over from the sofa and claps Jake on the shoulder. "Well, if it isn't the man of the hour, finally bringing Charlotte around." He turns to me. "We hoped you'd come and put us out of our misery."

"Oh really?" I shoot Jake a teasing glance. "Been talking about me, huh?"

Jake chuckles, completely unrepentant as he tightens his arm around me. "Only the good stuff. Maybe a few of the bad, just to keep them interested."

"You're too kind," I say, giving him a playful nudge. He squeezes my waist in return, his hand lingering a little longer than necessary.

"Chase is here somewhere too... probably trying to convince the kids to play indoor football. You might want to rescue them," Claire says, gesturing toward the hallway.

I laugh, feeling some of the tension ease. "Thanks for the heads up."

Jake squeezes my waist once more before I drag myself out of his grip and head toward the large rec room, leaving him to speak to his friends for a moment.

I walk into a scene of organized chaos: Zoe is leading Meadow and Noah in a game of tag, while Chase is trying to convince them to play indoor football instead. The room is large enough that the kids are zipping around, both Zoe and Chase trying to convince them to be on the other's team. Meadow is giggling, her cheeks flushed with excitement, and even Noah looks like he's having fun.

"Hey, boss lady!" Zoe calls out, waving me over. "Come join the fun!"

I laugh, shaking my head. "I think I'll leave the running around to you. Besides, someone has to keep an eye on Chase. I don't trust him not to throw a football at one of my kids' heads."

Chase scoffs. "I would never!"

Zoe rolls her eyes, clearly not buying it. "Don't listen to him, Charlie—he's been trying to convince me to play tackle football all afternoon."

"I'd pay to see that," I say.

Chase waggles his eyebrows. "I'm sure we can arrange something."

Zoe swats him with a playful glare.

The banter is light and easy, and I feel a sense of belonging creep a little further in. This is Jake's world, and he's invited me into it, giving me a place beside him that feels comfortable.

Jake appears at my back, his hand instinctively finding the curve of my waist, head dipping close to my ear.

"Hey, Coach," he calls out to Chase, keeping his grip anchored on me. "You thinking about switching careers?"

Chase grins, shaking his head. "Nah, just trying to keep the kids from tackling Zoe. She's already threatened to break my kneecaps if I don't keep it *non-contact*."

"I said no *tackle football*, Walton. They're children, not linebackers." She turns her attention back to the kids. "Who's ready for some snacks?"

We watch the kids cheer and careen off with Zoe, having the best time of their lives. "See?" Jake says, breath tickling my neck. "They're having a blast."

I hum, leaning back into him. "They're gonna be hyped on sugar thanks to her."

Before he can respond, Claire steps in, inviting me into the kitchen with her and Tamara. Jake squeezes my hand once, as if to let me know he's here if I need him, and then I follow Claire.

The kitchen is a warm, inviting space, filled with the sounds of bubbling pots and the occasional clatter of utensils. Tamara is already pulling out wine, pouring a glass and handing it to me when we enter. I take it gratefully.

Claire hands me a bowl of fresh cranberries and a recipe card, her easy smile calming something restless in me. They're not just welcoming me—they're folding me in, like I belong here. "Are you any good at cranberry sauce? It's a family recipe, but I'm terrible at it."

Tamara looks over from the stove, her eyebrows shooting up. "Wait, you're making cranberry sauce? Like, from actual *cranberries*?"

Claire nods, wincing slightly. "Yeah. I know it's a crime, but my mom insisted on homemade every year, so it's a habit."

Tamara groans dramatically, leaning her hip against the counter. "Homemade cranberry sauce is an abomination. Nobody likes it. You know what's better? The stuff in the can that comes out solid with the little ridges still on it. *That's* cranberry sauce."

"What?" I blink at her, completely lost. "Cranberry sauce comes in a can?"

"Oh, Charlie," Tamara says, her expression serious, like she's about to deliver earth-shattering news. "Yes. And it's glorious. You open the can, it slides out in one perfect jiggling tube, and you slice it like a loaf. None of this homemade nonsense."

Claire shakes her head, laughing as she turns back to her chopping board. "You're terrible."

"No, I'm right," Tamara fires back, waggling her spoon in Claire's direction. "Be honest, when's the last time anyone actually ate the homemade stuff?"

Ryan walks in, grabbing a roll from the counter. "What are we arguing about?"

"Homemade cranberry sauce," Claire answers, shooting him a look. "And how *someone*—" she glances at Tamara, "—thinks the canned stuff is superior."

"Because it is!" Tamara says, throwing her hands up.

Ryan pauses mid-chew, considering. "I hate to say it, but Tam's got a point. That canned stuff is weirdly addictive."

"Thank you!" Tamara says triumphantly. "See? Ryan knows what's up."

Claire rolls her eyes, turning to me. "What about you, Charlie? What's your take?"

I hold up my hands in mock surrender. "I have no idea. We don't do Thanksgiving in New Zealand, let alone this whole cranberry sauce debate. This is uncharted territory for me."

Tamara grins, leaning closer. "Okay, here's the deal. If your cranberry sauce actually turns out, I'll eat it. But if not, I brought a can with me and I'm not afraid to use it."

I laugh as I set to work on the recipe. "No pressure, then."

As the afternoon goes on, the conversation flows easily, and I find myself enjoying their company more than I expected. Claire is sweet and nurturing, while Tamara has a dry sense of humor that catches me off guard in the best way.

"So, how's it *actually* going with Jake?" Tamara asks after a while, her tone casual but curious.

I shrug. "It's going well. We're still figuring things out."

"He's crazy about you, you know. He talks about you nonstop," Claire replies knowingly. "He seems happier."

I glance at her, unsure what to say. "Really?"

Tamara nods. "Agreed. He's always been great, but there's something different about him now. It's a good thing."

Her words warm me, but they also make me think about how much has changed for me, too. Jake has been a constant in a time of uncertainty, and being here today surrounded by his friends, makes me realize just how much I really do want him in my life.

My cheeks heat, but I manage to keep my tone even. "Yeah, well, he's pretty great."

"And today's going to be great, too," Tamara says confidently, noting my blush and topping up my glass of wine.

As the day turns into evening, I realize I haven't seen the kids for a while and wander down the hallway towards the rec room to check on them.

To my left, a bathroom door opens and Jake steps. He gives me a slow, devilish smile and grabs my hand, pulling me back inside with him.

The door clicks shut behind us, and suddenly I'm caged up against the bathroom wall.

"Hi," he murmurs, face inches from mine.

"Hi," I reply, my voice barely a whisper as my hands settle on his chest, feeling the strong beat of his heart beneath my fingertips.

"You doing okay?" His breath is warm against my skin as he dips his head, pressing his lips to the curve of my jaw.

Laughing, I tilt my head to give him better access. "Are *you* doing okay?"

His mouth brushes just beneath my ear, and I can feel his subtle smirk that's now my undoing.

"No... it's agony keeping my hands off you." A hand slides down to my hip.

I stifle a laugh, leaning into his chest. "Really? In here?"

"Just one kiss," he says, lips grazing my earlobe. "Maybe two."

I swallow. This is far too dangerous for me to remain composed for just one kiss. The man is a walking pheromone, all I want to do is shred his shirt right off him.

"Jake Brooks." I nudge his chest to create some distance, but he doesn't budge. "This is a family-friendly event"

"Not in this bathroom, it isn't."

"Get off me, you creep," I chuckle, pressing against his chest again.

"Make me."

He's too close, too magnetic, and my brain scrambles. I clear my throat, trying to regain some control. "Seriously, Captain Thunder? That's the best you've got?"

"Stick around and you'll find out, Lady Lightning," he husks, the edge in his voice deliciously dangerous. Before I can retort, he speaks again. "And it should be illegal that you're allowed to walk around like this."

"Like what?"

His voice drops to a low rumble. "Why aren't you wearing any underwear?"

"VPL," I say matter-of-factly. "Don't you know a visible panty line can ruin an otherwise perfect outfit, Jake?"

He chuckles, gripping my sides. "You're killin' me."

"Only if you're lucky."

"I'm feeling very lucky," he says, head dipping closer. His eyes roam my face as he lets out a tortured groan, then his lips are on mine. Hands skim down over my hips, finally settling at my ass as he pulls me tighter against him. I melt into him as he deepens the kiss, his mouth stealing every coherent thought.

His lips are warm, and I can taste the faint hint of the beer he had earlier. The bathroom suddenly feels too small as he presses me back further against the door, his touch everywhere.

Finally, he pulls back, breath hot against my lips as he rests his forehead on mine. "You have no idea how hard it is to stop."

I exhale shakily, my hands still gripping his shoulders. "Maybe I don't want you to stop…"

"Then we better get out of here before I bend you over the sink."

Letting out a shaky laugh, I step back as he reluctantly releases me, eyes still filled with heat as he adjusts himself. He opens the door, brushing a final kiss to the corner of my mouth, thumb grazing my cheek as if he's memorizing every second of this.

I smile as he takes my hand and leads me out, his lips still lingering on my skin as we rejoin the gathering.

CHAPTER TWENTY-THREE

FASHION CRIME OR NOT, I'M NOT COMPLAININ'

———————— ✦ ————————

Jake - 12 years ago

The camp buzzes with energy, a mix of excitement and chaos as kids race around, getting ready for the evening's big event.

We've spent the past week planning this; our very own mini celebration for the kids. It wasn't on the official schedule, but we thought they could use a night to look forward to before summer ends.

"Think they're going to like it?" Charlotte loops another balloon around the makeshift party area by the campfire, stepping back to assess her work.

"They're going to love it." I grin. "You did great, Charlie."

She returns the smile, a little shy but proud. "*We* did great. Couldn't have pulled this off without you."

I shrug, playing it cool, but inside I'm buzzing. The planning, the decorating, the skits we put together—it's been a highlight of my summer. And the best part is I got to do it with Charlotte.

As the sun sets and the kids gather around, faces bright with anticipation, a surge of pride hits me. We did this. We created something special, something they'll remember long after camp.

The night unfolds perfectly. Laughter, music, and surprises fill the air. Charlotte convinced a couple of the other leaders to perform a silly dance that had the kids in stitches. I can't take my eyes off her, watching as she moves through the crowd, making sure everyone's having a good time.

At one point, she catches me staring and walks over, nudging me with her elbow. "You look like a proud dad watching his kids," she teases, her eyes twinkling.

I chuckle, shaking my head. "Nah, if I'm camp dad, that makes you camp mom. And I think we're a little cooler than that."

She nods. "You're right. We've got nicknames for a reason, Captain Thunder."

I smirk, crossing my arms. "Exactly, Lady Lightning. Best duo this camp has ever seen.

Her laugh is warm, her eyes softening as she looks out over party. "Yeah, I like that."

We stand there, watching the kids dance, and toast marshmallows over the fire, their faces glowing in the flickering light. The air is filled with smoke and laughter, one of those moments I know I'll carry with me for a long time.

"This is what it's all about," she says quietly. "Creating moments, making people feel special... like they belong."

I nod, my chest whirring. "Yeah."

When the kids head back to their cabins, Charlotte and I stay to clean up. It's quiet now, the energy fading into a comfortable silence between us.

"Thanks for doing this with me," she says after a while, her voice soft as she picks up a stray marshmallow stick. "It wouldn't have been the same without you."

"Anytime," I reply, meaning it more than she probably realizes. "I'm always up for making something special."

She looks at me, her expression thoughtful. "You're really good at it, you know. Making people feel like they're part of something."

***

Jake – Present Day

The warmth of Charlie's hand in mine is something I don't think I'll ever get used to. As we walk back through to the kitchen, I steal a glance at her. She's fit into my life so easily, like she's always meant to be here.

And damn, it's hard to keep my hands off her when she's all flushed from our little bathroom encounter. Any longer in there, and I would've kept my promise to bend her over the sink.

Laughter and the clatter of plates greet us in the kitchen. Claire's checking on the turkey, and Tamara's stirring something on the stove, her expression set with that familiar glint, the one that means she's about to say something I'll regret hearing.

"Well, look who's back," Tamara says, her voice dripping with playful sarcasm as she glances over her shoulder at us. "What were you two up to? Or should I not ask?"

I squeeze Charlotte's hand before letting go to grab a dish towel. "Just soaking in the chaos of the day, Tam. You know how it is."

"Uh-huh," Tamara replies, her tone skeptical but amused. She turns back to her pot, but I don't miss the glance she throws our way. "Soaking in *something*, alright."

Charlotte turns about three shades of pink before mumbling something about finding Zoe, leaving me to fend for myself. She's always so composed, but I love knowing I'm the reason for that blush creeping up her chest.

"Tam, leave the poor girl alone," Ryan says, walking in with a tray of drinks. "She's already gotta deal with Walton trying to woo Zoe."

Tamara snorts, turning off the stove. "Please. Chase wouldn't know what to do with Zoe even if she gave him a manual."

Ryan chuckles, handing out the drinks. "True. But it's fun watching him try."

I laugh, thinking about Chase's hopeless attempts with Zoe. It's a miracle she hasn't punched him yet. She gives as good as she gets though, which makes it even more entertaining.

As if on cue, Chase walks in. "Did I hear my name being mentioned? Talking about my undeniable charm again?"

"More like your undeniable failure rate," Tamara shoots back. "How's Zoe today? Managed to avoid the death glare?"

Chase smirks, leaning against the doorframe and glancing out to where Zoe and Charlie are deep in conversation. "She loves me. She just needs time."

"Time, and maybe a restraining order," I mutter, grabbing a drink from Ryan.

"She's playing hard to get," Chase says with a shrug. "I respect the long game."

"Yeah, and we respect your delusion," Tamara fires back, tucking a stray piece of hair behind her ear.

Before Chase can respond, Claire gasps. "Is that—Tam, is that a ring?!"

Tamara smiles, letting Claire grab her hand for a closer look. "Yep. Eli proposed last night in our backyard."

I turn to Eli, who's hovering by the doorway, and slap him on the back. "Congrats, man! Took you long enough."

Eli shrugs, looking unbothered. "Had to make sure she'd say yes."

"Enough about us," Tamara says, waving off the attention and lowering her voice. "What's going on with you and Charlie, Jake? You've been glued to her all day."

"Can you blame him?" asks Ryan. "The guy's clearly smitten."

I glance toward the living room, where Charlie is laughing with Zoe and the kids, completely oblivious to our conversation. My chest tightens at the sight. She fits. Here, with my friends, with me. And the thing is, it doesn't feel forced. It feels right.

"Yeah," I say, almost to myself. "I am."

"Good," Eli says, slapping my back. "Now stop being a pussy and lock it down."

"You guys are relentless," I mutter, shaking my head.

"Only because we care," Claire says. "And because we want you to be happy, Jake."

I am happy. She makes me happy.

Before I can dwell on it, Meadow and Noah come barreling into the kitchen, Meadow's curls bouncing as she skids to a stop in front of me.

"Jake! Jake! Can we play tag outside? Please?" she pleads, tugging on my hand.

I glance out the window, where the sun is dipping lower, casting the yard in golden light. "It's getting a bit late, Princess. Maybe we should stick to indoor games."

"Noooo." She pouts, her eyes pleading. "Please, Jake?"

I sigh, unable to resist those eyes. "Alright, but just for a little while."

Meadow cheers, dragging Noah toward the back door. I glance at Charlotte, now lounging on the sofa with Zoe. She raises an eyebrow and makes a whipping gesture in my direction, her smirk pure mischief. Brat.

I shake my head, laughing as I follow the kids outside. The cool evening air greets us, and soon enough, everyone joins in for a chaotic game of tag. Meadow's giggles fill the yard as she chases Ryan, and Noah laughs as Eli pretends to trip over his own feet.

"Tag, Jake! You're it!" Meadow shouts, whacking me before darting off.

I pretend to stumble as I charge after her. She giggles uncontrollably as I scoop her up in my arms, and I feel a surge of pride in making her so happy.

When Charlotte steps outside, her soft gaze finds me. I can see the affection in her gaze, and it makes me want to be the reason she continues to feel that way.

"Alright, you two," I say, gesturing to Noah and Meadow. "Dinner time!"

As we head inside, Charlie lingers for a moment, her eyes catching mine, and that smile of hers nearly undoes me.

She doesn't realize it yet, but she's already mine. And tonight I'll make sure she knows it.

***

As we all gather around the table, the energy in the room shifts from playful banter to something more meaningful. The table is packed, brimming with plates of turkey, mashed potatoes, cranberry sauce, all the trimmings.

Claire's gone all out, and the warm scent of roasted turkey and spices fills the room. I look around at everyone—my friends, Charlie, the kids—and I can't help but feel a swell of gratitude.

This is what it's all about. Family, found or otherwise.

Ryan's sitting at the head of the table, looking every bit the proud dad-to-be as he glances over at Claire, who's glowing in that way pregnant women do. He's older and has been my rock since I joined the Storm. We've shared a lot of highs and lows, and seeing him so settled with Claire makes me think maybe there's hope for me yet.

"Alright, everyone," Ryan says, raising his glass. "Before we dig in, I just want to say how thankful I am to have all of you here. This year's been a lot, but having you guys has made all the difference."

There's a murmur of agreement around the table, and I catch Charlie's eye, giving her a small smile. She's beside me, close enough that our knees brush. I reach for her hand under the table, loving how her fingers curl into mine. Natural. Right. Like her hand belongs in mine.

Claire nods, hand resting on her bump. "And I'm thankful for this little one on the way," she says softly, looking at Ryan with so much love it's almost too much to witness. "And for all of you, for being our family, especially when mine is so far away."

Her family's on the East Coast, and she doesn't get to see them often, especially not during the season. She's strong, like Charlie.

"Let's not forget Eli and Tam," Chase cuts in, always ready to steer the moment somewhere lighter. "Or should I say the soon-to-be Mr. and Mrs. Parnell?"

All eyes turn to Eli and Tamara, who exchange a look before Tamara lifts her hand dramatically, the giant rock on her finger catching the light.

"Finally someone made an honest woman out of you, huh?" Zoe jokes.

"Long overdue," I add, raising my glass.

Eli and I have been through a lot together. We came up in the league around the same time, and he's always been the romantic of the group, always talking about finding 'the one.' Tamara keeps him grounded, challenges him in the best way. They're good for each other.

"And let's not forget the real hero of the day," Tamara says, straight-faced. "The canned cranberry sauce. Without it, Thanksgiving would've been a total disaster."

Laughter erupts around the table, Claire groaning as she buries her face in her hands. "It wasn't that bad!"

"Oh, come on, Claire," Tamara teases. "Your homemade sauce looked like it was plotting revenge on all of us."

Charlie leans into me, laughing. "I had no idea cranberry sauce was such a hot topic in this country."

Ryan grins. "It's not Thanksgiving until someone defends the can. Tam's just carrying on the tradition."

Tamara lifts her wine glass with a smug smile. "And I do it with pride."

The laughter dies down, leaving a warm, lingering glow. Claire turns to me next, her expression soft. "Jake, what are you most grateful for this year?"

I clear my throat, caught a bit off guard, but then I look at Charlie and the kids, and the answer feels easy. "Honestly? I'm grateful for family—the one I was born into, but especially the one I've chosen."

There's a moment of silence, and then Ryan raises his glass. "Well said, man. To family."

"To family," everyone echoes, glasses clinking.

I catch Charlotte's gaze as we sip, her smile shy but touched. Her warm hand is still in mine, and I stroke my thumb lightly over her knuckles. She glances down at our joined hands for a second, the faintest hint of color dusting her cheeks before her eyes meet mine again.

I love you.

As the conversation flows, I catch Chase laughing at something Zoe said. He's the wildcard, but I've noticed the way he looks at Zoe when he thinks no one's watching. It's obvious he's got a thing for her, but whether he'll ever make a move is another story. Chase has a reputation, and I know he won't want to screw things up with Zoe, who's become a big part of our crew.

"So, Chase," I say, leaning back in my chair, "you gonna tell us what you're grateful for?"

Zoe raises an eyebrow. "Yeah, Chase, what makes *you* thankful?"

Chase's smirk falters for a moment as he looks at her, but he recovers quickly. "What can I say? I'm a man of mystery."

"More like a man of bullshit," Ryan quips, earning a round of laughs.

The banter is light, and I can see Charlie sinking right into it, laughing along. She's fitting in like she's always been here, and watching her be part of this is one of the most satisfying things I've ever felt.

As we pass plates around, I lean close to her. "How you holding up?"

Her eyes shine bright. "Really good. Everyone's amazing. Thanks for inviting us."

"Thanks for being here." I squeeze her hand under the table. "Wouldn't have been the same without you."

Dinner's a flurry of conversation, laughter, and the occasional argument over who got the last bit of stuffing. Charlotte fits in seamlessly, laughing at all our old stories—like when Ryan and I got lost on a road trip and ended up at a bar in the middle of nowhere, or the time Chase nearly burned down his kitchen trying to impress a girl with homemade pasta.

Across from me, Noah's eyes are bright as he watches Chase make goofy faces at him, trying to make him laugh. Meadow, on Charlotte's other side, is happily chatting away to Tamara, who listens with genuine amusement.

It's perfect.

After dessert, the kids are fighting to stay awake, eyelids drooping. I catch Ryan's eye, and he gives me a knowing look. He doesn't say it, but I can hear it: *You've got something good here. Don't screw it up.*

And he's right. I do have something good—something incredible. And I'm not letting it slip through my fingers again.

I start gathering their things while Charlotte says her goodbyes. Crouching down, I scoop Meadow up in one arm, carrying some of their things in the other. "Come on, Princess. Let's get you and your brother home."

Meadow yawns, resting her head on my shoulder. "Okay. Can you read a story?"

"Of course," I reply, pressing a kiss to the top of her head. "Anything for you, Little Lightning."

By the time we step out into the cool night air, Meadow's half-asleep on my shoulder, and Noah's holding onto Charlotte's hand, his eyes heavy.

The drive back to Charlie's place is quiet, the kids knocked out in the backseat. I glance over at her, and she gives me a tired but happy smile, resting her hand on my thigh. I reach down and give it a gentle squeeze, grateful for the connection between us.

"Thank you for today," she says softly. "It was perfect."

I take her hand and bring it to my lips. "You are."

Back at her place, I help settle the kids into bed. Meadow mumbles something as I tuck her in, her tiny hand clutching my shirt for a moment before letting go. "Sweet dreams, Princess."

When the kids are finally asleep, we head downstairs, the house quiet except for the soft creak of the floorboards. Charlie pauses at the bottom of the stairs, turning to face me with a look that tells me everything I need to know.

"Wanna stay for a bit?"

My heart hammers as I step closer, my hands finding her waist. "Is that a trick question?"

"Depends. What's your answer?"

I lean in, brushing my lips against her ear, my voice low and teasing. "Whatever gets me upstairs with you."

Her laugh is soft and entirely too tempting as she tilts her head, eyes glinting with mischief. God, I'm so gone for her.

"You talk a big game, Brooks."

I chuckle, the sound vibrating between us as I close the final inch. "That's because I always back it up."

She relaxes into me, fingers curling into the fabric of my shirt, and her eyes flick to mine, holding them for a beat longer than feels safe. Something passes between us—a question, a dare, an inevitability.

Her breath hitches, and my gaze drops to her lips. That's all it takes.

Our mouths collide, and the world falls away. It's not just a kiss, it's a collision that's been building all day, maybe even longer. Her lips slide against mine, and when her tongue brushes tentatively before tangling with mine, my head spins.

Gripping her hips, I pull her firmly against me, deepening the kiss until I can feel her heartbeat racing alongside mine. She lets out a soft moan, and it's everything I can do to keep from losing control right here at the bottom of the stairs.

I pull back just enough to catch my breath, resting my forehead against hers as I try to steady myself. "You've been driving me crazy all day, Charlie girl."

She smiles, a wicked little grin that makes my blood run hot. "Good," she whispers, sliding her hands into my hair. "Because I've been waiting for this all day."

This time when I kiss her, there's no holding back. The world narrows to her—her touch, her laughter, the way she looks at me like I'm someone worth waiting for. I lift her effortlessly, her legs wrapping around me as I carry her upstairs. I'm so ready to lose myself in her that I can barely think straight.

We stumble into her room, kicking the door shut behind us. Setting her down gently on the bed, I take a moment to drink her in. Her hair is mussed, her lips red from our kisses, eyes heavy and full of desire.

"You're so fucking beautiful," I say, my hands skimming over her waist as I lean down to kiss her again. She arches into me, her hands slipping under my shirt, nails dragging across my skin, and I'm gone.

My hands find the hem of her dress, slowly lifting it as she lets out a soft moan against my mouth. The fabric slides up her thighs, baring her to me, and I remember our earlier conversation.

"You weren't kidding about the VPL."

She laughs softly, her breath deliciously hitching under my touch. "Told you. Fashion crime, Jake."

"Fashion crime or not, I'm definitely not complaining."

Her laughter turns into a gasp as I push her dress higher, my hands gliding up her bare skin, warm and soft under my touch. It's intoxicating the way she responds to me, the way she bites her lip like she's trying to hold back. She's as wound up as I am.

I lean in to kiss her, pressing myself against her so she can feel exactly what she's doing to me. Her hands slide up into my hair, tugging me closer, and the electricity between us feels like every second of waiting has been worth it for this.

"Charlie, you're killing me," I murmur, barely able to contain myself.

She smiles, that wicked, playful grin that makes my heart race, and begins unbuttoning my shirt, fingers slow and deliberate. "I'd say I'm sorry, but I'm not."

A low rumble escapes me as I trail kisses along her neck, savoring the way she shivers. "You're a brat, you know that?"

"Only when I'm winning," she says, arching into me, her breath warm against my neck.

"Well consider this game on."

The need to feel her, to claim her, to show her exactly how much she means to me, it's overwhelming.

Charlotte Andrews has changed everything for me.

Tonight, I'm gonna make sure she knows it.

She's mine.

CHAPTER TWENTY-FOUR

I'LL TAKE THE CHAOS, THE LAUGHTER AND ALL YOUR MIDNIGHT FREAK-OUTS

————————✦————————

Charlie

"Oh my God." Jake swiftly pulls my dress over my head, leaving me in just my bra.

I press my lips together, holding back a grin as his hungry gaze sweeps over me. I'd hoped tonight would lead us here, and judging by the look in his eyes, he'd been hoping the same.

"God, you're beautiful," he murmurs against my skin. His lips drag down my neck, hands sliding up my thighs. "So fucking beautiful."

"Jake..."

Reaching behind me, he pulls me flush against him as he unhooks my bra one handed. "This is coming off," he says, voice rumbling against my ear.

"Then you're losing these." I fumble with his jeans, yanking them down his hips.

He chuckles low as he kicks them off, and I trace my hands over him, feeling tension coiling in his muscles. He groans, tipping his head back, and I let my hand drift down to stroke him slowly.

"Fuck, Charlie..." His voice is taut, like he's barely holding himself in check.

There's nothing restrained about him—he's all hard lines, raw strength, barely contained power. Like a god above me as he peels off his boxers.

He catches me admiring him, mouth curving in a dark smile as he leans in, cupping my breast. "Like what you see, sweetheart?"

"Hmm, the view is *okay*," I tease, but my facade crumbles as he rolls my nipple between his fingers, the bite of sensation sending a thrill through me.

"Don't tease me, baby." His words are a rough demand, his mouth recapturing mine in a searing kiss that brands me.

After a beat, he pulls back, hands tracing up to frame my face, his expression turning serious. "I've got condoms," he says hesitantly, but frowns when I laugh.

It's not a mean laugh, it just feels like an awkward moment straight out of high school. Two responsible adults about to sleep together, and we're both hesitating like it's our first time.

"Would you prefer to?" I ask, and he raises an eyebrow. "I've had the injection," I clarify, trying to sound casual.

His frown shifts into a slow, relieved nod. "Oh. Right. That's, uh, good." There's a pause before he clears his throat. "I get checked regularly, you know. With the team and all." He pauses, scratching the back of his neck. "But I mean, it's been a while since, uh, anyone else."

I can't help it; a small snort escapes me. "Same. A very long while."

"Right," he says again, his lips twitching. "Cool. So we're, uh, good?"

"Super good."

His smirk finally breaks through as I reach up to brush my thumb over his bottom lip, but he ruins the moment by catching it between his teeth and biting.

"Ow!" I yelp, jerking my hand back. "What the hell was that?"

"Payback for laughing at me, Lady Lightning. It's a serious topic."

"Oh, very serious," I deadpan. "So serious I can't believe you didn't write out a formal agreement first."

"Don't tempt me. I've got a pen around here somewhere," he says, pretending to look around before tackling me back onto the bed.

We laugh and both move at the same time, colliding again, hands exploring, lips claiming, a tangle of breathless touches and heat. Every nerve in my body is attuned to him, and the tension that's been building all day explodes. Nothing else matters now. Only him.

"Open up for me, Charlie girl," he says, positioning himself over me and nudging my legs apart.

My breath hitches as his cock slides against me, slow and deliberate, teasing every nerve.

"Look at you, spread out and dripping for me like this. You're fucking stunning."

"Jake... please..." The words come out shaky, my hips tilting up in desperation.

His tip slides up and down, grazing over my clit, making me gasp. I squirm beneath him, desperate for more, but he just grins.

"Patience, baby," he murmurs, like it's a lesson I'm about to fail. "Tell me how much you want this."

"I want you... I want this," I manage, my voice breathless.

The dimple in his cheek deepens as he smirks, his thumb brushing over my cheek like he's savoring every second of my unraveling. "Say it again," he commands, daring me to hold back. "Tell me exactly what you need. Use those sweet lips."

Heat floods my cheeks, but his gaze pins me there, and the desire roaring through me drowns out any hesitation. "Fuck me, Jake. Please. I need you."

The second the words leave my mouth, his lips are on mine, stealing my breath. "That's my girl."

He draws back and positions himself at my entrance, eyes flicking up to lock on mine as he slides in.

"Holy shit," I squeak, feeling him everywhere.

"Fuuuuck," he moans into my ear, dotting wild, wet kisses along the column of my throat.

"Jake..."

"You feel that?" His voice is thick with restraint. "That's us, baby. Perfect."

I can't even respond, my head tipping back with each wave of heat spiraling through me. My breath leaves me in a shudder as he moves, and he cups my face to hold me steady. "Look at me," he murmurs.

I meet his gaze and everything stops for a beat, every inch of him pressing into me. He's looking at me like I'm the only thing in the universe, something precious to behold.

"God, you feel amazing." He finds a rhythm, each movement driving me higher. "Like you were made for me, Charlie. Only me."

I've never been looked at like this—like I'm everything. His gaze burns into mine, anchoring me as if he's afraid I'll slip away. The intensity of it drags a sigh from my throat that feels like surrender.

"Yeah, that's it, I wanna hear you."

"Jake," I moan, arching up to meet him. Every touch of his skin against mine feels electric, like he's rewiring something deep inside me. "You feel so good. Don't stop."

"Fuck," he rasps, his voice fraying at the edges as his gaze flickers down to where we're joined. "Tell me where you need me, baby. Right here?" He circles his hips, drawing a desperate cry from my throat. "Yeah, thought so."

"Harder." I grip his shoulders, nails biting into his skin as I meet each thrust. He watches me like he's committing every reaction to memory, like he's hungry to give me exactly what I need.

"You want harder?" His lips curl into a wicked grin. "I'll give you everything, Charlie girl. Every. Fucking. Inch."

We move together, my body responding to every word, every touch, as if we've done this a thousand times. His lips graze my neck, teeth catching my skin, and I clench around him.

"Such a good girl, taking me so well."

"I'm... I'm close..."

"Then give it to me," he commands, his grip tightening on my thigh as he pulls me flush against him, his own movements becoming erratic. "Come for me, Charlie. I wanna feel you come all over me."

My release tears through me, his name a broken cry on my lips as I shatter. I cling to him, my body trembling as waves of pleasure ripple through me.

"That's it," he groans. His hips falter as his own climax overtakes him, body shuddering as he buries his face in my neck, hot breaths dragging over my skin. "Fuck, that's my girl."

Everything around me falls away and rebuilds in a heartbeat, and in this moment I know there's no going back.

"You're so gorgeous when you come, you know that?"

All I can do is let out a breathy chuckle in reply. He brushes my damp hair from my forehead, pressing a lingering kiss there as his hand skims down my neck.

After a moment, he pulls out, his gaze softer now but still filled with that same possessive intensity. He stays close, hand tracing light patterns along my back as his breathing slows. "I don't think I'll ever get enough of you."

"You might need to pace yourself," I tease, though my voice comes out breathy.

"You okay?"

I manage a nod, pressing a kiss to his collarbone.

We fall into a comfortable silence, his hand dragging slowly up and down my spine, grounding us in the moment. But then I sense a shift in him, like he's about to say something deep. Something important.

So of course, I ruin it by sitting up.

Jake's hand shoots out, catching mine. "Where are you going?"

"Just... need the bathroom." I give him a weak smile, slipping out of bed and grabbing my robe.

Closing the door behind me, I sit on the toilet and take a deep breath, my head falling into my hands. Why am I being a weirdo? That was fucking perfect. The best. *Gourmet.* It was so good I almost feel as if it wasn't real.

But it was real. It was Jake.

Jake, who looks at me like I'm the only thing he's ever wanted.

I shake my head, trying to slow my racing heart. I need a minute to get my head straight, because that was not just sex. It was everything.

And here I am, on the verge of a freak out, while the hottest man I've ever seen is in my bed.

I wash up and catch sight of myself in the mirror. My hair's a mess, makeup smudged, but it's my face that catches my eye. I have that glow. The glow people have when they're in... I can't say those words. Nope. I'll settle for a safer phrase.

It's a freshly fucked glow.

Yeah. Definitely not a glow that comes from a man slowly handling every broken piece of me with reverence, clicking each one back into place like he owns the very blueprint of who I am. No, definitely not *that* glow...

Shit.

I just left him out there, while I freak out in here like a complete psychopath. I close my eyes, willing myself to quit being the biggest flake of all time. Then I take a deep breath and open my eyes, glaring at my reflection.

"Get it together, bitch," I whisper. I know I want him. Every nerve in my body is screaming it.

I step back through the ensuite door, the soft click echoing in the stillness. The silence wraps around the room until Jake rises from the bed, eyes immediately locked on mine.

He steps closer, that irresistible grin deepening the dimple in his left cheek. "Charlie," he says. "I'm just gonna say this before you freak out again... Be mine."

I arch an eyebrow, crossing my arms in mock defiance. "Is that a question or a demand?"

He chuckles, undeterred as he takes another step. "A heartfelt request," he amends.

I tilt my head, pretending to ponder, stalling to steady myself. "Hmm, I don't know. Sounds like a lot of work."

"Oh, it definitely will be," he agrees, reaching to tuck a strand of hair behind my ear. "But I'm good at heavy lifting."

"Is that so?" I quip, trying to suppress a smile. "Because I've got two kids, a full-time job, and a leaky kitchen faucet that says otherwise."

He laughs, hands settling on my hips. "I've got two strong arms, a flexible schedule, and a toolbox ready for anything you need."

"You make a tempting offer, but I'm not sure you know what you're getting into."

His thumbs trace slow circles on my sides. "I know exactly what I'm getting into," he murmurs, leaning in close so his breath brushes my cheek. "And I want it all. The chaos, the laughter, these midnight freak-outs. Everything."

I feel my resolve slipping, but I muster a playful retort. "What makes you think I'd want to share my freak-outs with you?"

"Because sharing is caring," he says, lips ghosting over my ear. "And I promise to bring wine."

A laugh escapes before I can stop it, and I shake my head, lightly pushing his chest. "You really have an answer for everything, don't you?"

"When it comes to you, absolutely." His tone is light, but his eyes hold something deeper that makes me nervous.

I take a step back, trying to regain control. "Jake, this isn't just about you and me. There's more at stake here. The kids, our jobs..."

"I know. I care about them too Charlie, you know that. I'm not looking to rush or disrupt their lives. We can take it slow, be careful... But I want you to be mine. I want to know that when I look at you, I'm looking at the woman who's mine. Who was *always* mine."

"And what happens when things get tough? When life throws curveballs?"

He steps forward, his hands warm and steady as they frame my face. "Then we swing together," he says softly. "I'm not afraid of the hard stuff. I don't wanna miss out on this just because we're scared of what might happen."

The honesty in his voice wraps around me, and when I look into his eyes, I see a depth of emotion that's so intense it's almost terrifying. The thought crosses my mind that he actually might be insane, but if he is then I definitely am, too.

"You really don't give up, do you?"

He just smiles, thumb brushing tenderly across my cheekbone. His hazel eyes flicker with gold, unrelenting but not demanding. "Please, Charlie girl... Be mine. Let me be yours."

I bite my lip, searching for a good comeback, but the way he's looking at me like I'm everything makes my heart race. I'm done for.

"Jake," I finally whisper. "I'm scared..."

"I know you are." He leans his forehead to rest against mine. "But I'm not going anywhere. I'm in this, all the way. And I promise I'll be careful with your heart, and with the kids. I'll be careful with all of it."

I search his face, looking for any sign of doubt, but all I see is unwavering certainty.

"You're impossible, you know that?" I say, shaking my head with a small smile.

"And you love it." He leans in, pressing his lips to my ear, his voice a soft plea.

How is it possible to feel this wanted? This seen? It terrifies me, because if I let myself believe him, there's no going back.

I release a long breath, feeling the last bit of my resistance melt. "You're not going to stop until I say yes, are you?"

"Not a chance," he whispers, lips dragging to my jaw. "Say it. Say you'll be mine."

I tilt my head like I'm considering it. "What do I get in return?"

His eyes glint with mischief. "Everything. All of me. But you already knew that."

"You're awfully sure of yourself, Brooks," I tease, letting my fingers trail up his chest.

"I've never been more sure of anything in my life."

I close my eyes, letting the warmth of his touch and the weight of his words wrap around me. "Fine," I finally whisper, heart pounding.

His grin breaks wide and unrestrained. Before I can respond, he's kissing me, hard and desperate, like he's been holding back far too long. And maybe he has, because the intensity nearly takes my breath away.

"You're mine," he murmurs, kissing me like he's staking his claim in every breath.

I melt into him, kissing him back fiercely, my hands threading through his hair as I pull him closer and allow myself to feel it all.

"You have no idea how happy that makes me."

My fingers brush the back of his neck as I softly smile. "I might have an inkling."

"Want me to show you?"

"Hmm, I don't know," I grin, like I'm actually considering it. "It's late, and I have a busy day tomorrow..."

He growls low, scooping me up before I can protest. "Too late, no take-backs."

Our laughter dissolves into something more intense as he throws me onto the bed. Hovering above me, his gaze roams my face, memorizing every detail. "Mine."

He kisses me again, hands slowly removing the robe I'd hastily wrapped around myself. The rasp of his stubble against my skin sends shivers cascading through me, and I arch into him, silently begging for more.

"I've wanted you to be mine forever," he murmurs, like it's a truth he's been holding onto for too long.

"Me too," I whisper, my hand moving down to grip him and loving the way he hisses at the contact. A smirk pulls at my lips as I slowly pump him. "You gonna claim me now, Brooks?"

His control snaps, and he's suddenly kissing me with a hunger that's both feral and tender, like he's laying claim to every part of me. I lose myself in the sensation—the taste of him, the warmth of his body, his hands exploring every inch.

"You're perfect." His voice is rough with emotion as he presses lingering kisses along my collarbone. "And you're all fucking mine."

"Flattery will get you everywhere," I say breathlessly, earning a low chuckle.

"Good, because I plan on going everywhere."

Our playful banter dissolves as he pushes inside me again. My name slips from his lips in a breathless moan as he fills me completely, the sensation almost overwhelming. He grabs my leg, bending it up toward his shoulder, setting a new pace that has me seeing stars.

"Shit, God, don't stop," I groan, my nails biting into his thighs.

"Not planning on it, baby," he grits out. "Gonna make you come so hard you never forget you're mine."

One hand coasts up my stomach, the heat of his palm branding me as it glides between my breasts and gently collars my throat. He pauses, searching my face for any hesitation, but he won't find any. Instead, I press my hand over his, squeezing his fingers tighter in permission.

His chest rumbles in approval, and he thrusts deeper.

"That's it."

Thrust.

"Take all of me."

Thrust.

"All. Fucking. Mine."

A loud, raspy noise escapes me as the rough skin of his palm tightens slightly against my throat, grazing the sensitive skin there. Every touch, every kiss, every word pulls us closer, deepening the connection I can no longer deny.

"Look down." His voice is steady despite the strain as he slows his pace. "I want you to see how good you look wrapped around me."

"Jake, please. I need you, I need all of you." My words make him curse softly, but he continues to go slow, teasing me at the edge.

"Say you're mine," he commands. "Need to hear it again, Charlie."

My eyes lock with his, breath coming in shallow pants.

"Say it, Charlie." His eyes blaze, grip tightening.

"I'm yours, Jake."

"Mmm, good girl." He leans down, kissing me again, his movements more erratic. I grind up against him, meeting him thrust for thrust, breathless as I reach my breaking point.

"Come with me," I plead, my voice husky as I cling to him.

"Christ," he croaks, burying his face in my neck. That's all it takes for me to lose control, his name falling from my lips as I come hard, nails digging into him. He follows, his grip on me fierce, holding himself deep as his own release tears through him

When he collapses beside me, a sense of belonging settles over me. I've never felt so connected, so utterly consumed as I do lying in his arms.

He presses a tender kiss to my forehead. "That was fucking incredible."

I smile, nuzzling closer to him. "Agreed. You definitely earned a repeat performance."

"You won't have to wait long for that, trust me."

His fingers trace slow, soothing patterns along my arm as we lie there catching our breath in the quiet darkness.

"You alright?" he asks, breaking the silence.

It's the same question he asked earlier, before I had my little freak-out. But this time, I feel no fear.

"More than alright," I reply, tilting my head up. "I don't think I've ever been this happy."

His eyes soften, and he leans down, capturing my lips in a tender kiss. "You deserve all the happiness in the world, Charlie."

I smile, a warmth spreading through me that has nothing to do with what we just shared and everything to do with the man holding me

We lie there and talk in hushed tones about everything and nothing, sharing secrets and dreams under the cover of darkness. I'm reminded of that night years ago—when we lay under the stars on that hill at camp, talking about everything we wanted in life.

It feels almost fated, like an invisible string has been quietly tying us together, pulling us through time and space, even when we didn't realize it. Every thread has led to this connection, this trust, this sense of home I feel only with him.

As the conversation slows and his body remains wrapped around mine, sleep begins to claim us, the only sound his gentle breathing against my hair.

It feels so easy and natural, like we've been doing this forever. As my eyelids grow heavy, I drift off to the sound of Jake's steady heartbeat—a rhythm that feels like home.

***

A soft rustling stirs me from sleep, and I blink groggily as I adjust to the faint pre-dawn light. Jake sits on the edge of the bed, pulling his shirt back on with careful movements.

"Leaving so soon?" I mumble, my voice thick with sleep as I push up onto my elbows.

He turns at the sound of my voice, a guilty smile tugging his lips. "Didn't mean to wake you," he whispers, leaning over to press a soft kiss to my lips. "But I should get going—don't want the kids finding me here in the morning."

I sigh, reaching up to run my fingers through his tousled hair. "I know. Doesn't mean I like it, though."

He chuckles softly, capturing my hand and pressing a kiss to my palm. "I don't wanna go either. But we agreed to take things slow for them, right?"

"Yeah, yeah, Mr. Responsible," I tease, tugging him down for a proper kiss. "Who knew you could be so mature?"

He grins against my lips. "Don't spread it around. I've got a reputation to maintain."

I laugh quietly, but it fades as I trace my fingers along the collar of his shirt. "You sure you can't stay just a little longer?"

"You have no idea how much I want to." His voice drops. "But Noah's sharp as hell, and Meadow's always watching. They'd figure it out in a second."

"Right." My heart twists a little, even though I know this is the right decision for now. "Will I see you later?"

"Try and stop me." He stands and smooths his clothes. "I'll bring coffee and donuts for breakfast. How's that sound?"

"Like you're trying to win me over with baked goods."

"I think I won you over enough last night," he says with a wink, then pauses at the doorway. "Get some more sleep, Lady Lightning. I'll see you soon."

"Drive safe," I reply softly, watching as he slips out the room, the door clicking shut behind him.

I flop back onto the pillows with a contented sigh, a smile firmly planted on my face as I pull the covers up around me. The bed still smells like him, a comforting mix of his woody cologne that lulls me back towards sleep.

CHAPTER TWENTY-FIVE

THAT WAS FOR YOU, CHARLIE GIRL

————————✦————————

Jake

The arena is already humming with energy. The sound of skates slicing the ice, sticks clacking, and the steady thrum of the crowd gathering outside is like a familiar rhythm that always gets my blood pumping.

After finishing our drills and pushing through warmups, I head back to the locker room. It's alive with the usual pre-game rituals. Eli is taping his stick, his brows furrowed in concentration. Chase is bouncing on his feet, hyping himself up. It's the calm before the storm, and we all feel it.

Normally I'd be focused, but today my mind keeps drifting back to Charlie. To what we are now. Official.

I can't stop thinking about the nights I've spent with her since Thanksgiving—the way she looks up at me, sprawled on the bed like an angel, the feel of her body against mine, the sound of her laughter.

She's intoxicating.

"Thinking about Charlotte again, huh?" Eli's voice cuts through my thoughts.

I chuckle, pulling out my pads. "My girl's never far from my mind."

"I'm happy for you, man. She's a catch."

His words warm me, but they also stir up that lingering worry in the back of my mind. I keep thinking about the kids, too. They're a package deal, and I'm not just falling for Charlotte, I'm falling for them just as much.

"So, what's next?" Eli asks, catching my expression.

I shrug, but there's a smile playing on my lips. "I don't know. We're taking it slow, especially with the kids. But I'm in this, all the way."

Eli nods, his expression serious. "Good. If anyone deserves happiness, it's you, Brooks."

I laugh, knowing he's right but still feeling the weight of it all. "How did you know Tamara was the one? I mean, when did you know you wanted to marry her?"

Eli's face softens, his gaze distant for a moment. "There wasn't one big moment, you know? But I remember this time after a rough game. I was beat up, felt like I'd let the team down. Tam didn't say much, just showed up with my favorite takeout and a movie she knew I loved. Didn't try to fix it, just sat with me. That's when I realized I didn't just want her around when things were good—I wanted her there when things were tough, too."

The words hit home. Charlie did something similar recently, showing up after a rough game when I'd felt like shit. She just slipped into the condo, made me tea, and let me know she was there. That's how she's always been—quietly present, like she sees the parts of me I'm not always sure are worth seeing. And she makes me feel like they are.

I nod and turn back to my locker, the familiar mix of sweat and adrenaline thick in the air. My eyes land on the small, crayon-drawn unicorn taped to the door—Meadow's masterpiece.

Reaching out, I tap the picture lightly, almost unconsciously. It's silly, but it centers me.

"Touching the unicorn for luck, huh?" Ryan calls from the bench.

"Can't mess with the routine," I shoot back as I grab my helmet.

The banter continues, but I'm already slipping into game mode. I close my locker, my mind focused and ready. Tonight's game is going to be a battle, but I've got more than just the win on my mind.

"You ready for this?" Ryan asks as I take a seat beside him.

"Always," I reply, tightening the straps on my pads. "But it's gonna be a tough one."

"We'll handle it. Just stick to the plan."

When we finally hit the ice, the roar of the crowd is deafening, and it's like flipping a switch. The nerves disappear, replaced by the fierce focus that comes with game day.

The arena is buzzing as the national anthem plays, the crowd on their feet. I'm standing in line with the team, dialed in. But as I scan the stands out of habit, something catches my eye in the WAGs box.

Charlie. She's sitting with Tamara, Claire and Zoe, looking like a damn miracle. Dressed casually but still mesmerizing, her face is lit with excitement. Meadow is on her lap, bouncing with the same energy thrumming through me, and Noah sits beside her, wide-eyed at it all.

She brought the kids. I'm so caught off guard, I almost miss the start of the anthem, barely catching myself in time as I grin like an idiot.

Charlotte meets my gaze, her eyes lighting up as she realizes I've spotted them. I can't help but smile wide, a silent acknowledgment that I'm glad they're here.

I make a mental note to get them all jerseys with my name and number on the back. They're part of this now, part of me. As the anthem finishes and we take our positions on the ice, I keep that image in my mind: Charlie and the kids cheering me on.

The puck drops, and the game begins.

Right from the start, it's clear this is going to be a battle. The other team's aggressive, throwing everything they've got at us, and we're not backing down. There's a lot of chirping on the ice, guys trying to get under each other's skin, but I'm locked in and keeping my cool.

Both teams are playing hard, but I'm on fire tonight. When I finally get the puck and see an opening, I don't hesitate. I charge forward, weaving through the defense, and with a powerful shot, I send the puck flying into the net. The red light flashes, the horn blares, and the crowd erupts in cheers.

As my teammates swarm me in celebration, I glance up at the WAGs box, locking eyes with Charlie. She's cheering, her face lit with pride, and I give her a wink and a grin. *That was for you, Charlie girl.*

Midway through the second period, things start to heat up. We're tied, and the tension is thick. I'm digging hard in the corner for the puck when I feel the hit. Hard and fast. The glass rattles with the force, and my helmet smacks hard against the plexiglass. The sharp sting in my shoulder makes me suck in a breath as the world tilts for a second. The roar of the crowd becomes distant, muffled by the blood rushing in my ears.

"Brooks, you good?" Chase's voice cuts through the fog, and I nod, even though my vision blurs slightly as I push myself up.

"Yeah, I'm fine," I grunt, shaking off the stars in my vision as I push to my feet.

The ref's arm is up—boarding, two minutes for the other guy—but all I can think about is the ache spreading through my shoulder and the fact that Charlie and the kids just saw that.

It's hell sitting on the bench, especially when I see a few scuffles breaking out on the ice. But I know better than to push it. The last thing I need is to make whatever this is worse.

By the time I'm cleared to get back on the ice, we're in the final period, and the score is still tied. But then Eli wins the faceoff, and the puck lands on my stick.

I push forward, weaving through the defense like my life depends on it. As I approach the net, I glance up instinctively. Charlie's watching, her face a mixture of nerves and hope, and the kids are on their feet, eyes wide with excitement.

It's all the motivation I need.

I wind up and let the shot fly, the sound of the puck hitting the back of the twine like music to my ears. The arena erupts in cheers, and my teammates crowd me, everyone shouting and slapping my back.

We hold onto the lead for the remaining minute, and when the final buzzer sounds, the relief and joy that washes over me is indescribable. We did it.

All I can think about is getting upstairs to see Charlie and the kids. But as soon as the game ends, reality hits. The media is already gathering, waiting for post-game interviews, and I know what's coming.

When I get back to the locker room, I pull off my gear and hit the showers quickly, knowing what's waiting outside.

As I step back out, the media is already there, gathered around Ryan first. He's answering questions with his usual calm, and then it's my turn. I grab the nearest towel to swipe the lingering sweat from my face, plastering on a game-ready smile as the reporters close in.

"Jake, incredible goal tonight! How's the shoulder feeling after that hit in the second?"

"It's fine," I say, keeping my tone steady. "Nothing serious. Just part of the game."

"What was going through your mind during that last play?"

I shrug, leaning on the bench behind me. "Just focusing on getting the puck in the net. The team's been working hard on creating opportunities like that, and it paid off."

The questions keep coming, veering from the game to playoff prospects, and then inevitably, to my personal life.

"Jake, there have been rumors about someone special in your life. Any truth to that?"

I grit my teeth behind my smile, deflecting with practiced ease. "I'm just focused on talking hockey right now. That's where my head's at."

I glance toward the locker room entrance, itching to get out of here. The thought of Charlie and the kids waiting for me upstairs is enough to keep me grounded, but it doesn't stop the reporters from pushing for more.

"Jake, do you think having family in the stands tonight gave you an extra boost?"

The question catches me off guard, but I recover quickly, the grin on my face more genuine this time. "Having people who believe in you always helps," I say simply, dodging the specifics. "Now, if you'll excuse me, I've gotta catch up with them."

I step away before they can ask anything else, making my way toward the private exit that leads to the suites.

My heart's pounding, but it's not from the game or the media—it's from the thought of seeing them.

CHAPTER TWENTY-SIX

JUST FRIENDS, REALLY REALLY GOOD FRIENDS

———————✦———————

Jake

W hen I finally reach the box, the sight that greets me is enough to make everything else fade away. Meadow is perched on Charlie's lap, both of them chatting away, while Noah is excitedly chatting with Tamara and Zoe.

Charlotte stands when she spots me, gently setting Meadow down. Her eyes scan me, concern flashing. I smile, closing the distance between us.

"You okay?" Her voice is worried as her hand rests on my chest.

"Now I am," I reply, pulling her into a hug and pressing a kiss to her temple. "Just a little knock, nothing serious."

Her hand lingers, fingers moving to my face as she looks me over, searching for any signs of injury. The casual intimacy makes my heart surge. *I love you.*

"You didn't tell me you were coming," I murmur, keeping a hand on her hip.

"I wanted to surprise you. Noah's been begging to watch you play."

"I'm glad you're here." My hand squeezes her slightly.

For a moment, her eyes lock on mine and she leans in like she's going to kiss me, but then they flicker with awareness. She pulls back, cheeks flushing as she glances toward the kids.

Meadow's wide, curious eyes are fixed on us, and Noah watches too, his expression thoughtful. It hits me that this might be the first time they've seen us being so openly affectionate. We've been careful, keeping things light and easy, but I wonder if they're piecing it together.

"Jake okay, Mama?" Meadow asks, clutching Charlotte's leg.

Charlotte forces a smile, bending down to pick her up. "Yes, honey bee, Jake's just fine. See? He's right here."

Meadow surveys me, her bright eyes taking in every detail. Damn, if it doesn't nearly break my heart. I lean in to plant a gentle kiss on her cheek. "I'm fine, Princess. Your unicorn picture kept me safe."

She beams, while Noah, who's been quiet until now, looks up at me with a serious expression. "You were really good out there, Jake," he says, his tone almost adult-like in its sincerity. "But you got hit. Did it hurt?"

I crouch to his level, giving him a reassuring smile. "Thanks, buddy. And yeah, it hurt a little, but it's part of the game. I'm okay, though."

Noah nods, accepting that. Then he glances between Charlie and me, brow furrowing. "Are you and my Mum... together?"

Before I can answer, Charlotte jumps in, her voice slightly strained. "We're... friends, Noah."

What. The fuck.

But Meadow's not satisfied with that. She tugs on Charlotte's sleeve, her brow furrowed. "Is Jake a boyfriend?"

Her innocent question makes my heart ache with a fierce need to tell her yes, I'm here and I'm not going anywhere. That I want to be the man they can rely on.

But before I can respond, Charlie cuts in again, her voice a little higher than usual. "We're, um, friends. Really good friends."

She stumbles over the words, and I can see the conflict in her eyes. She's trying to protect them, to keep things simple for them, but it stings that she didn't just say yes.

Noah, still observing, suddenly pipes up. "Are you guys in love?"

I hear a laugh that turns into a cough and glance over to see Zoe and Tamara suddenly very engrossed in their phones, both trying not to smirk. My eyes narrow at them.

Charlotte's eyes widen, and she glances at me, searching for words. But before she can respond, I kneel in front of him, wanting to be on his level for this. This moment could shape everything, and I need to get it right.

"Your mom and I care about each other a lot." My eyes flick to Charlotte's, hoping she hears what I can't say, then I look back at Noah. "We're still figuring out what that means, but we're very close. And I want you to know that you guys are really important to me."

Charlie exhales slowly, clearly relieved that I didn't dive in too deeply. But Noah watches us both, his expression still serious.

"So, you're *not* in love?" His tone is skeptical, like he's not buying it.

I hesitate, glancing at Charlotte, who's chewing her lip like she's about to draw blood. "We're... really good friends," she says yet again, her voice wavering slightly.

The fuck we are. I'm not in love with my friends, Charlotte.

Noah considers this, his eyes narrowing, but he eventually seems satisfied. Meadow, who's been trying to follow along, looks up at Charlotte with a frown. "*Best* friends?"

Charlie nods quickly, trying to keep her tone light. "Yeah! Best friends."

Frustration twists in my gut. This conversation is slipping away from what I wanted. She's holding us at arm's length when all I want is to pull her and the kids closer. I know she's trying to keep things simple for them, but every time she says *friends*, it intensifies my need to show her just how much I'm *not* her fucking friend.

I especially don't want Noah to be confused. It's important to me that he understands that I'm committed to this, that he can rely on me. Something I never had.

"I'm going to be around, and I'm going to be here for all of you." I look Noah in the eye, hoping he understands.

He seems to accept this for now, though I can tell he's still processing. Finally, he nods. "Okay. But you better be good to my mum."

His words are so earnest, so full of unspoken worry, that it tugs at my heart. I reach out and ruffle his hair gently. "I promise buddy, you have my word. I'll be the best to her, *and* to you and Meadow."

The tension in the room eases, and Charlie gives me a small, grateful smile. But I can see the uncertainty lingering in her eyes.

As we gather our things to leave, I feel a mix of emotions. The game was tough, but these questions from the kids were tougher. The whole evening stirs something deep. But despite it all, I'm over the moon knowing they were here cheering me on.

Outside, the crisp night air bites at my skin, mingling with the lingering adrenaline from the game. I glance at Charlotte holding Meadow, Noah by her side.

I force myself to keep some distance, to act like we're *just friends*, though all I want to do is wrap Charlotte and the kids in my arms and take them all home.

When we reach the parking lot, Charlie gives me a small, apologetic smile. "Thanks for tonight, Jake. The kids had a great time."

"Yeah, it was really good," I reply, voice tight with the effort of holding back as the kids clamber into the car. "It meant a lot to have you all here."

She nods, her smile growing. "We'll have to do it again sometime."

"Definitely."

I crouch down to wave to the kids as I close the car door, then turn back to her with one more smile. Leaning in, I press a light kiss to her cheek, my lips lingering by her ear as I murmur, "See you soon." *I love you.*

On my way back to my car, I hear footsteps. Charlotte's rushing over, her car only a few spots down. She crashes into me, pulling me down the side of my car, out of view of her own.

"You forgot something."

My hands slide to her waist. "What's that?"

She stretches up on her tiptoes, pressing her lips to mine with a soft urgency, her smile curling against my mouth as her tongue flicks along my bottom lip. The taste of her, the warmth, pulls a groan from my chest. I pull her closer, the kiss turning needier.

But just as fast as it starts, it's over. She pulls back, her cheeks flushed from the chilly air. "Talk later?"

"Among other things, yes." I swat her ass playfully as she walks back to her car, and she grins over her shoulder.

God, the chokehold this woman has on me.

As I watch them drive away, a familiar determination settles in my chest. We might be taking it slow, but there's no slowing the way I feel about them.

Later that night, after a long hot shower that barely eases my restlessness, my phone buzzes with a text.

> **Charlie:** I'm surprised you didn't melt the ice out there tonight

> **Me:** Oh yeah? Liked what you saw?

> **Charlie:** Liked? I was worried that they'd need to bring out the Zamboni early

I chuckle, her playful teasing bringing a smile to my face.

> **Me:** I love it when you hit on me, Lady Lightning.

> **Charlie:** Just stating facts You sure you're okay, though?

> **Me:** I'm fine. Just wish my "best friend" was here to see for herself.

> **Charlie:** Ouch, I deserve that. But seriously, you're okay?

> **Me:** Want me to come over and show you?

There's a pause before her next message arrives.

> **Charlie:** Tempting, but you need rest, not another workout

Me: Resting? I was thinking more along the lines of recovery... with you as my masseuse

Charlie: Smooth, Brooks. You've got an away game to win in 2 days, though. Someone has to keep you focused.

I let out a frustrated sigh, knowing she's right but not liking it.

Me: Fine, I'll stay put. But tomorrow, you're mine

Charlie: I better be

Me: Night, beautiful

I set my phone down, still feeling the ache of wanting her close, tempered by the promise of tomorrow.

CHAPTER TWENTY-SEVEN

YOU'VE REACHED YOUR QUOTA ON THE WORD 'FRIEND'

Charlie

Mondays always feel chaotic. The office hums with the usual morning buzz of clacking keyboards, ringing phones, and the occasional burst of laughter from down the corridor. I stare at an email, but my mind drifts back to last night.

The game. The kids. The way Jake looked at me when I called him a friend.

I press my hands to my face. I could have handled that so much better. The kids caught us off guard, but the sting in Jake's eyes when I stumbled over my words still lingers in my chest.

Seeing him get hit was terrifying. Instinct pulled me to him, forgetting the kids in my rush to make sure he was okay. I didn't think twice. Being so openly affectionate with him in front of his teammates and our friends doesn't bother me at all, but in that moment, I forgot the kids were there too.

I'm trying to ease the kids into this, but last night I went and did the opposite. And then I doubled down, confusing them even more by insisting Jake and I were just friends.

"Morning, lover girl," Zoe's voice breaks through my thoughts, and I glance up to see her grinning from the doorway.

"Hey," I reply, trying to sound casual. "Aren't you supposed to be in the boardroom?"

"I've got a few minutes." She waves her freshly manicured hand dismissively and steps in, closing the door behind her. "So, how was the rest of your night with your *good friend* Jake?"

I groan, dropping my head to the keyboard. "Don't start."

"Oh, I'm starting," she says, sliding onto the edge of my desk. "It was pretty entertaining. Every time you said the word *friend*, he looked ready to haul you over his shoulder like a caveman to stake his claim."

"It wasn't like that," I argue, though my cheeks heat at the memory. "The kids were confused, and I didn't want to make it more complicated."

"Complicated? Charlie, those kids are *smart*. Anyone with eyes can see there's more going on than friendship."

I run a hand through my hair, trying to sound firm. "We agreed to ease the kids into this. It's not as simple as jumping into his arms forever."

"It's exactly that simple," she counters. "You've got a guy who's crazy about you and the kids. So why are you still holding back?"

Before I can respond, there's a knock at the door. Marcus peeks his head in, a bright smile on his face. "Morning, Charlotte. Zoe."

Zoe gives me a pointed look before hopping off my desk. "Catch you later, Charlie." she says, muttering something about popcorn as she brushes past.

Marcus steps inside, his gaze lingering a moment too long before he speaks. "I was wondering if you'd like to grab lunch today? My treat."

"Oh," I stammer, caught off guard. "Thanks Marcus, but I've got a lot to get through."

"Everyone's gotta eat," he says with an easy laugh, leaning casually against my desk. "Besides, it's a new place. Great reviews. Thought it'd be nice to, you know, get to know each other better."

Before I can find a polite way to brush him off, there's another loud knock, and the air in the room shifts. Jake steps inside, his presence commanding without effort. His eyes sweep over Marcus, then land on me, and I feel my stomach do a flip. There's a tension in him that immediately sets me on edge.

"Morning, Charlotte," Jake says, but there's an edge to his tone. "Zoe said you were in here."

Of course she did.

"Hey," I reply. "What can I do for you?" His eyes flash at the question, because I know *exactly* what he wants me to do, and I stifle a grin.

Marcus pipes up, still oblivious to the vibe. "Hey, Jake. Good to see you again. How's the team doing?"

Jake's gaze cuts to Marcus, polite but sharp. "We're good. Just gearing up for an away game."

"That's great," Marcus replies, continuing like he's not about to be the target of a seething pro hockey player. "Charlotte and I were just talking about grabbing lunch later."

I feel the blood drain from my face. I shoot a glance at Jake, a fierce flash of something primal crossing his eyes. I know that look—it's the one he gets right before he slams an opponent into the boards.

"Actually," Jake says smoothly but pointed, "I'd already made plans with my *good friend* here."

I shoot Jake a look, trying to ease some tension. "Your good friend, huh? Thought I was your *best friend?*"

Jake smirks, but his eyes burn into mine. "You're pushin' it, Charlie."

Marcus blinks, clearly taken aback. "Oh, I didn't realize—"

"You wouldn't." Jake cuts him off with a shrug. "We've been keeping things low-key."

The air feels hot, the weight of Jake's words settling over the room. Marcus glances between us, his smile faltering as he heads for the door. "Right, well... Maybe another time, Charlotte."

As soon as he's gone, I whirl on Jake. "What was that?"

He doesn't answer immediately, his gaze still on the door Marcus just walked out of before clicking it shut and turning to me. "That was me making it clear you're off-limits."

"Off-limits?" I echo. "You can't just—"

"What was I supposed to do? Stand there while he kept hitting on you?"

I cross my arms. "I can handle myself, Jake."

"Oh, I know you can." He steps closer, eyes blazing into mine. "But I'm not going to stand there and watch some guy act like you're fair game. I know we agreed to keep things low-key for the kids, but I'm not okay with you pretending we're just friends, especially after last night."

"Jake—"

"No. You've now hit your quota on calling me your friend, Charlie. I'm the guy who's spent the last few weeks in your bed with my face between your legs. I'm not your friend. I'm never going to be okay with that word when it comes to us. You get that, right?"

I bite back a smile, hoping to lighten his mood. "Okay, but what about *best* friend? Does that still count?"

His lips twitch but the fire in his eyes doesn't waver. "Not even close. You're not just a best friend, you're not *just* anything. You're mine, and I won't let you pretend otherwise."

"I was just trying to keep things simple," I explain, guilt starting to gnaw at me.

Jake runs a hand through his hair, clearly struggling to find the right words. "I get that, but I won't sit back and watch some guy act like you're available. You're not, Charlie. You're with *me*."

I take a deep breath, trying to steady myself. "I know, but we still need to be careful. I need to protect the kids, and the media... they complicate things. We can't just tell everyone without thinking about the consequences."

His expression softens, though frustration still simmers beneath the surface. "I'm not saying we need to broadcast it, but I'm not hiding. I'm proud you're mine."

Those words hit their mark, and I feel the weight of everything we've been navigating. "You know I'm proud to be with you too, right?"

He steps closer, his eyes crinkling. "Yeah, I do. But when Noah asked if we were together, that was our opening. I could've told him the truth—hell, I wanted to—but then you jumped in with the *just friends* line again and again. You don't know how much that sucked."

I look away, his words sinking in, heavy and undeniable. "I hate that I made you feel like that. I'm scared that if the kids don't adjust or if things get too intense, Alex will find a way to take them back. I'm scared of the media, of how they might spin things. What if all of this blows up in our faces?"

Jake lifts my chin. "It won't. Because I'm not going to let it. But I need to know that you're with me on this."

I search his eyes, finding nothing but steadfast certainty and something deeper, something I'm not ready for him to admit yet.

"I'm with you, Jake," I say, leaning into his touch. "I just... I need to protect the kids."

He nods, brushing his thumb gently across my cheek. "I know, Charlie girl. I want to protect them, too. But I'm not going to hide what we are, and I'm sure as hell not going to stand by while some guy acts like he has a shot with you."

His words hang between us, heavy with meaning, and I take a shuddering breath. "I don't wanna mess this up."

"We won't. We'll figure it out together. But don't push me away, especially not in front of the kids. They need to see that we're solid, even if we're still figuring it out."

I nod slowly. "Okay."

"Good." He smiles, the tension easing as he leans down to kiss me, but I stop him with my fingers on his lips, nodding toward the clock.

"You should get to your meeting with Zoe."

"Yeah, I should." But he doesn't move. Instead, he leans in again with more determination. This time I let him kiss me, his mouth slowly dragging over mine deliberately. When he pulls back, his eyes are blazing. "Don't ever call me just your friend again, Charlie."

Before I can respond with anything more than a snort, he's out the door, leaving me standing there, mind racing from the intensity of his words. I take a deep breath, steadying myself as I prepare to face the rest of the day.

Sinking back into my chair, his voice echoes. Jake protects the people he loves without hesitation, like it's instinct.

And now, he's asking to do the same for me.

CHAPTER TWENTY-EIGHT

I DON'T WANT TO KEEP YOU
IN THE SHADOWS

———————✦———————

Charlotte - 12 years ago

The camp is quiet, the kind of stillness that only comes in the dead of night when everyone's fast asleep. I lie in bed, staring at the dark ceiling of my cabin, trying to shake off the uneasy feeling that has settled over me. It's probably just the usual camp noises, but something doesn't feel right.

Then I hear it—a soft sniffle outside the cabin. I slip out of bed, careful not to wake the other girls, and crack the door open. Tyler stands there, clutching his stuffed dinosaur, tears streaking his cheeks.

"Tyler?" I whisper, crouching down to his level. "What's wrong?"

"I had a bad dream," he mumbles, voice shaky.

My heart squeezes. "It's okay," I say softly, brushing a tear from his cheek. "Do you want to sit on the porch for a bit?"

He nods, his grip on the dinosaur easing slightly.

The wooden porch creaks as we sit down on the steps, Tyler's small feet dangling off the edge. I wrap an arm around him, and he leans into me, his shivers easing.

"It's okay to be scared sometimes," I tell him, keeping my voice low. "But you're safe here. I'm not going to let anything happen to you."

We sit in comfortable silence, the night wrapping around us like a blanket. Tyler's eyes start to droop, and I know it's only a matter of time before he nods off. I stand, ready to carry him back to his cabin, when a shadow moves out of the corner of my eye.

It's Jake, coming back from the bathrooms. His expression shifts from curiosity to something softer when he notices us.

"Hey," he says quietly, walking over. "Everything okay?"

I nod, adjusting Tyler. "Bad dream. I was about to take him back."

His smile is soft as he nods. "He's lucky to have you."

"He just needed someone to be there." I shrug, trying to play it off.

Jake tilts his head, studying me. "You're good at that."

"At what?"

"Being there for people." He rubs the back of his neck like he's unsure about admitting it.

I feel my cheeks heat up. "Well, someone's gotta do it."

There's a pause—not exactly awkward, but uncertain. Like neither of us knows if we're supposed to say more or just let the moment settle.

"Want me to carry him?" Jake finally asks, nodding toward Tyler.

"Sure," I say, gently handing hin over. "Thanks, Jake."

"No problem." He settles Tyler in his arms with ease, like he's done it a hundred times.

We walk back to Tyler's cabin in silence, the night air cool against my skin. As we tuck him back into bed, I catch Jake looking at me thoughtfully.

"What?" I ask, feeling self-conscious.

"Nothing," he says quickly. "Just... you're pretty great, you know?"

My cheeks flush again, and I look away, pretending to adjust Tyler's blanket. "You're not so bad yourself, Captain Thunder."

He chuckles softly. "Get some sleep, Lady Lightning."

***

Charlie - Present Day

The house is quiet, the kids are finally asleep, and I'm stuck doom-scrolling on the couch, my mind replaying the tension from earlier today.

I hear the front door open and close softly. A bag drops, and then Jake walks into the living room, his eyes immediately finding mine.

"Hey," he says, dropping down beside me. "Everything okay?"

I nod. "Yeah, just thinking."

"About earlier?" His tone is gentle, but there's an edge to it, a reminder of the tension.

I take a deep breath, setting my phone down. "Yeah. I've been thinking about everything. About the kids and us. About how complicated this all is."

Jake reaches out, taking my hand in his. "It's not that complicated, Charlie. We can figure it out."

I look down at our joined hands, feeling the warmth of his calloused skin. "I just... Alex will be looking for any reason to drag the kids back to New Zealand."

His thumb brushes over the back of my hand, soothing but firm. "That's not happening. Those kids aren't going anywhere. Alex can try all he wants, but he's not taking them away from you. I won't let it happen."

I search his eyes for any hint of doubt, but there's none. Just the steady, determined gaze of a man ready to fight for me.

"I don't want to keep you in the shadows, but I'm scared of what could happen if we don't."

Jake shifts closer with a frown, his grip on my hand tightening. "In case you've forgotten, I want this, Charlie. So you tell me—what are we doing here?"

I open my mouth to respond, but the words get stuck in my throat. The fear, the doubt, it's all there, but so is the desire—the overwhelming need to be with him, to let go of everything else.

"No, I need to know," Jake presses, his voice intense but not harsh. "Because I'm not going to play a game where I pretend you're just a friend when you're not."

Inhaling deeply, I look away, but Jake's hand on my chin gently turns my face back to his. "I'm not asking you to rush into anything, but I need to know where we stand. I need to know that I'm not the only one who wants this."

His words slice through my hesitation, leaving nowhere to hide. I can't keep pretending either, not when every part of me is screaming for him.

"You're not," I whisper. "You're not the only one."

Relief flickers across his face, but he doesn't let up. "Then let's stop with the mixed signals. We're in this together, okay? No more denying ourselves for the sake of anyone else."

"Okay." I nod, finally letting go of my fears. "Okay, let's do this."

A slow, relieved smile spreads across his face, and he leans in to kiss me, his lips soft but firm against mine.

When he pulls back, he rests his forehead resting against mine. "You're my Lady Lightning. Don't you forget it."

A thrill rushes through me at the possessiveness in his tone. "And you're mine, Captain Thunder."

"Damn right I am."

"But we need to be careful," I say, as he brushes a strand of hair behind my ear. "The kids... they come first."

"Of course. They always come first."

The tension between us is a living thing, pulling us closer, drawing us into the inevitable. I nod again, feeling relief wash over me as I submit to the feeling.

"Okay."

He pauses, searching my face. "Why don't we spend Christmas at my cabin? Just us, the kids, and some time together."

I blink. "Your cabin?"

"Yeah, it's where I go to get away from everything, clear my head. And I want to share that with you and the kids."

Excitement and fear twist in my chest. But the way he's looking at me, it's impossible to say no. "I'd like that."

"Yeah?" His smile is slow, lighting up his face.

"Yeah."

"C'mere , then." Jake's hands slide down my back, pulling me onto his lap.

Lips capture mine in a kiss that's anything but gentle, filled with all the need that's been building between us. I lose myself in him, letting go of everything else.

His fingers thread through my hair, tugging me closer. When he deepens the kiss, I softly moan into his mouth, running my tongue against his.

The kiss turns hungry, and I can feel the tension in his body, the way he's holding himself back, trying to stay in control.

But I don't want control, I want him. All of him.

"Jake," I breathe, pulling back just enough to look into his eyes. "I want you."

He stands, my legs wrapping around his waist, and he carries me toward the stairs, hands firm and possessive on my thighs. There's a desperate urgency between us, a need to erase every inch of distance and hesitation that's lingered.

We barely make it to the bedroom before our clothes are gone, discarded in a trail behind us. Jake's hands are everywhere, his mouth crushing mine with a hunger that borders on desperate.

He leaves a hot, open-mouthed trail down my neck, sucking at my collarbone before moving lower, and I arch up, desperate for more. His touch is almost feral, like he's staking a claim and marking me with every press of his lips.

"You're mine, Charlie," he murmurs low against my skin. "No more hiding, no more pretending. Say it."

"Yours," I breathe, shuddering as his fingers trail down my sides.

"Good girl. Now come here." His grip tightens as he flips us over, settling me on top of him. His hands lock around my hips, holding me steady. "Ride me, baby. Show me who you belong to."

My lips part, feeling the heat between us build as I sink down onto him, his cock stretching and filling me completely. A breathy groan escapes him, his hands gripping tighter as he watches.

"Fuck, that's it," he growls, eyes glued to where our bodies meet. "You feel like heaven, Charlie. Move for me."

His words send a jolt through me, and I start to roll my hips, grinding down on him, his hands guiding me with every movement.

"You're so damn beautiful," he rasps, one hand moving up to roll my nipple. "Look at you, riding me like a queen."

I throw my head back and move faster. "Oh God..."

The pleasure builds sharp and fast, and his hand slides up, fingers curling gently around my throat. His eyes search mine, a question unspoken but clear.

"More," I gasp, my hands bracing against his chest. "Don't hold back."

His chest rumbles with approval, fingers flexing as he leans up. "My good girl," he murmurs, pulling me to him, his hand tight as he presses his mouth to mine. "Not just my friend. Fucking *mine*."

A sharp breath escapes me as his hand moves and smacks my ass, the sensation sending a jolt of pleasure through me. I press harder against him, finding a rhythm that matches the movement of my hips with his.

"Christ, you're wet," he breathes, voice strained. "So fucking perfect, Charlie. You don't know what you do to me."

"Show me," I whisper, challenging him, nails scraping his chest as I move to meet his every thrust.

He lets out a dark chuckle, his eyes glinting with a fierce need. With effortless strength, he flips me onto my back, hands capturing my wrists and pinning them to the mattress. His thrusts are deep, each one claiming me relentlessly.

"Is this what you wanted?" His voice is rough as he moves. "Taking me so fucking deep you can't think straight?"

"Oh my God, just like that, don't stop..."

"You're so tight around me," he grits out. "You feel that, baby? That's me ruining our friendship."

A breathy laugh escapes me, but it's swallowed by a moan as he bottoms out. "Fuck friendship."

"You gonna come for me, then?" His hand slips down, circling my clit. "Fall apart for me, right here on my cock."

I cry out, my entire body igniting as the orgasm crashes over me. But just as I'm riding it out, he flips me onto my stomach, pulling my hips up until I'm on all fours.

"On your knees," he rasps, his palm landing on my ass with a sharp smack that sends a fresh jolt of pleasure through me. "Give me one more. I wanna hear my name on your lips when you come."

A hand slides up my back, threading into my hair, pulling me upright until I feel his breath against my ear. "Tell me again, Charlie."

"I'm yours," I pant, the words spilling from me as he moves.

"Damn right you are. Mine. Every single part of you." His hand moves around to my throat, holding me steady as his pace quickens. The world fades, every sensation focused on the way he's claiming me completely.

"Come for me," he demands, voice husky as he thrusts. His hand drifts lower, brushing my clit before delivering a sharp slap. "Come, Charlie. Show me you're mine."

"Holy shit, Jake!" I choke out, my body shattering as I come hard for a second time.

"Fuck yeah, baby. That's what I want—everything you've got."

His voice breaks as he buries himself deep one final time, my name falling from his lips as his release tears through him. The grip on me softens, his hands sliding over my hips to hold me close as he dots a trail of kisses up my spine, murmuring reverent words against my skin.

I collapse underneath him in a melting heap, and he crashes down beside me, his chest rising and falling with rapid breaths. The air between us is thick with the aftermath, but there's a quiet intimacy in the way his arm drapes over my waist, anchoring me close.

Jake presses a kiss to my shoulder, trailing up my neck until his lips hover just below my ear. When he finally lifts his head, his eyes find mine, and the heat in them gives way to something softer.

"You okay?"

"Yeah," I murmur, still breathless as I move into him.

His arm wraps tighter around me, stubble grazing the soft skin beneath my ear. "You're *my* fucking girl, Charlie. And I'll remind you like this anytime you forget."

A hum of contentment escapes me as I move closer, resting my head against his chest. The steady rhythm of his heartbeat matches the way his hands stroke down my back, but the thought of him leaving tomorrow hangs over us.

"You're staying tonight, right?" My voice has an edge of vulnerability I can't quite hide, and I know he'll catch it.

He nuzzles into my hair, inhaling deeply. "Yeah, I'm staying. Got my bag right by the door."

"I'm gonna miss you," I whisper, fingers tracing the curve of his bicep.

"Mm, get ready for a week of calls and texts," he says, his grip tightening like he's never letting go.

And I don't want him to.

CHAPTER TWENTY-NINE

GO KICK SOME ASS, CAPTAIN THUNDER

---------------✦---------------

Jake

Morning light filters through the curtains as I stir, still caught between sleep and waking. It's too early to be conscious, but it's time for me to get going. I feel Charlotte's hand reach out, pulling me back as I try to move.

"Charlie," I whisper, my voice rough with sleep, "I've gotta get going or I'll miss my flight."

She mumbles something incoherent as she nuzzles into me, her warmth tethering me to the moment. I'm supposed to leave before the kids wake up, to slip out quietly and catch my flight, but the way she holds onto me makes it impossible to pull away.

"Just five more minutes," she murmurs.

I groan softly. "You know I can't say no to you."

Just as I'm settling back, the soft click of the bedroom door handle catches my attention. I freeze, glancing up to see a small figure standing in the doorway.

"Mama?"

It's Meadow, clutching her stuffed unicorn, her eyes wide and teary. She looks so small, so fragile, and every protective instinct in me flares.

"Meadow, honey, what's wrong?" Charlie asks, her voice calm even though I can feel her pulse quicken under my hand on her arm.

"I had a bad dream," Meadow whispers, her voice trembling.

Without a second thought, I sit up and hold out my arms. "Come here, Princess."

For a second I think she'll hesitate, but she doesn't. Meadow climbs onto the bed and snuggles up between us like it's the most natural thing in the world. I pull her close, feeling her small body relax against mine, and my heart swells in a way I didn't know it could. I glance at Charlotte, who looks as surprised as I feel.

This wasn't part of the plan. We were supposed to ease the kids into the idea of us being together, to protect them from any confusion. But as Meadow settles in, her eyes drifting shut, I realize this might be how it was meant to happen all along.

Charlie watches us, her eyes soft as she takes in the scene. She reaches out, brushing a strand of hair from Meadow's face. "Jake was just about to leave for his trip."

"Stay," Meadow mumbles, her voice already heavy with sleep as she clings to me.

I drop a kiss to the top of her head, the weight of this unexpected moment hitting me hard. "I'm not going anywhere just yet."

As Meadow drifts off, I glance at Charlie, our eyes meeting in the quiet morning light. This wasn't how I imagined it, but holding Meadow here, trusting me to keep her safe, makes everything else seem unimportant.

"Charlie," I whisper, careful not to wake Meadow, "when I get back, we'll figure out how to tell them. Properly."

She nods, her eyes soft with something that looks a lot like love. I feel it too—this need to protect, to cherish, to be the man both she and the kids can count on. I've never wanted anything more.

I listen to Meadow's small, sleepy breaths as she falls back into a deep sleep. Charlie has drifted off too, her face peaceful, the gentle curve of her lips slightly parted. I let myself watch her for a few moments, taking in her beautiful face, her eyelashes soft against her cheeks.

I love you.

Finally, I slip out of bed as quietly as I can, careful not to wake them. The room is still dark, just the faintest hint of dawn sweeping through the room. I press a kiss to Charlotte's temple and let my lips linger on her skin for a moment, before heading downstairs.

The house is silent, the kind of stillness that only comes before the world wakes up. It's way too early, but I've got a flight to catch, and leaving before the kids wake up was the plan. After Meadow's appearance though, it feels like a step forward—unexpected, but somehow perfect.

After freshening up in the downstairs bathroom, I head to the kitchen, scrolling through my phone while I wait for the Uber. The only sound is the soft ticking of the clock on the wall.

It's almost too peaceful, like the calm before the storm. I can feel the weight of the next week pressing down on me, the distance that's about to stretch between us.

A creak of a floorboard pulls my attention up, and I see a small figure in the doorway. Noah's wide eyes lock on mine, and I can tell he's still half-asleep, piecing together what he's seeing.

"Hey, Noah," I say softly, careful not to startle him. "It's just me."

He blinks, rubbing his eyes. "Jake?" His voice is sleepy, a little confused, but there's no fear.

"Yeah, buddy. Just waiting for my ride."

Noah steps into the kitchen, holding a small cup. "I was getting some water."

I nod, watching as he moves to the sink, filling his glass. He's quiet, more observant than I would've expected. As he takes a sip, he glances at me, and I can see the wheels turning in his head. He's sharp for his age, but instead of questioning, he just nods to himself, like this is all perfectly normal.

"You're going?" he asks.

"Yeah, got a flight to catch. But I'll be back soon."

He nods again, taking another sip. "Okay."

His matter-of-fact tone catches me off guard. He's not surprised; not questioning why I'm here so early. It's like he's already accepted it, and that makes me feel a little more at ease.

Soft footsteps on the stairs make us both look up, and there's Charlie in mismatched pajamas, her hair tousled. She freezes when she sees us, her eyes flicking between me and Noah, a mix of surprise and something like relief crossing her face.

"Noah," she says gently, moving toward him, "what are you doing up so early?"

"Just getting some water." He holds up his glass as proof.

Charlotte glances at me, her eyes softening as she places a hand on Noah's shoulder. "It's still really early, bud. Why don't you go back to bed for a little while longer?"

Noah nods, his eyes flicking to me again. "Bye, Jake," he adds before heading back upstairs.

"Bye, buddy," I reply.

Charlotte waits until Noah's door clicks shut, then turns to me, a soft smile tugging at her lips. "He didn't seem too surprised to see you."

I chuckle, shaking my head. "No, he didn't. He's a sharp kid."

She steps closer, wrapping her arms around my middle as she rests her head into my chest. "Guess we might have underestimated how much they're aware of."

"Yeah," I murmur, resting my lips to her hairline. "But I think that's a good thing."

Charlie tilts her head to look up at me, then leans in to press a soft kiss to my jaw. "I'm gonna miss you like crazy."

"Same, but I'll be back before you know it..." I brush my lips slowly against the tender skin where her neck meets her jaw. "And I'm not leaving you alone, remember? You've got the world's *best friends* upstairs to keep you company."

She groans softly, playfully smacking my shoulder. "Seriously, Jake, let it go."

I chuckle, the sound rumbling in my chest. "We'll talk to them properly when I get back, okay? Make sure they know what's going on."

She nods, her fingers tightening slightly on my shirt. "Okay."

We stand there a moment, holding each other, neither wanting to let go. But then the app for my ride pings, shattering the quiet. I want to throw my phone across the room and crawl back into bed with her, but I have to go.

I pull back and tilt her chin up to kiss her thoroughly, like I'm trying to make it last the whole week.

When we finally pull apart, I rest my forehead against hers. "I'll call you when I land."

"Safe travels," she whispers.

I grab my bag and head for the door, but stop and turn back to look at her one last time. She's standing there, watching me with a soft smile, and I know on the spot this week apart is going to be harder than I thought.

"I'll see you soon," I say, forcing a smile, hoping it hides the unease gnawing at me.

"See you soon," she echoes.

Opening the door, I pause and glance back one more time. "Remember, I'm just a call away. If you need anything, you know I've got you."

Her smile widens as she leans against the doorframe. "I know. Now go kick some ass, Captain Thunder."

"You got it, Lady Lightning." I flash her a grin before heading out into the early morning.

As I walk down the driveway, the chill in the air biting at my skin, I can't shake the feeling that I'm leaving a part of myself behind, right there in that house with Charlie and the kids.

***

Charlie

After Jake leaves, I linger in bed a while longer, watching Meadow sleep. Her little face is so peaceful, her breaths soft and even. I brush a hand over her hair, marveling at how angelic she looks like this. The room feels quiet—almost too quiet without Jake beside me.

But the quiet doesn't last long. I hear the familiar creak of Noah's door, and soon enough, his sleepy figure appears in the doorway, rubbing his eyes. "Mum? Is Jake gone?"

I nod, giving him a soft smile. "Yeah, sweetie. He had to catch his flight."

Noah shuffles over and climbs into bed, settling himself on the other side of me. He's quieter than usual, and I can tell something's on his mind. I wrap my arm around his shoulders, pulling him close. "You okay, buddy?"

He shrugs, looking down at his hands. "I just... I like having him around. It feels nice."

I swallow the immediate lump rising in my throat, pulling him even closer. "It *is* nice, isn't it? Jake loves being here with us, too."

He nods, leaning into me. "I hope he's not gone for too long."

"He won't be," I assure him. "He'll be back before you know it."

The three of us stay like that for a while, huddled together under the covers, soaking up the warmth of the morning. Meadow eventually shifts, waking up and blinking her sleepy eyes at us.

"Morning, honey bee," I whisper, brushing a hand over her hair.

"Hi Mama," she murmurs, snuggling closer. "Where's Jake?"

"He's gone to work, but he'll be back soon." I tell her, and she nods slowly, not fully awake yet.

As we lie there, I think about how seamlessly Jake has woven himself into our lives, how natural it feels to have him here, to talk about where he is and when he'll be back. Noah's calm acceptance, even after seeing Jake here early this morning, surprises me in the best way. Maybe this isn't as complicated as I've been making it out to be.

A thought crosses my mind, and I reach for my phone on the nightstand. "Hey, how about we send Jake a picture to say goodbye?"

Meadow's eyes light up, and she immediately pulls a silly face. "Like this, Mama?"

"Exactly like that," I laugh, adjusting the camera to capture all three of us. "Come on, Noah, let's make Jake smile."

Noah breaks into a grin, before the three of us pull our most ridiculous faces: Noah sticking out his tongue, Meadow with her bunny ears, and me puckering up with an exaggerated kissy face. We look ridiculous with hair mussed, still in pajamas, and completely unfiltered.

But we also look happy. Really happy.

I send the picture to Jake with a quick message.

> **Me:** Good luck, Captain Thunder! We're thinking of you

As soon as I hit send, a pang hits me, missing him already. But the thought of him seeing that picture, knowing we're thinking of him, brings a smile to my face.

It doesn't take long for my phone to buzz. I open the message to see a photo of Jake on the plane, sticking his tongue out and his eyes twinkling with mischief. He's holding the phone close, his expression playful, but there's something tender in the way he's looking at the camera.

> **Jake:** You three just made my whole damn morning Missing you like crazy already. And now I get to flash my new screensaver at anyone who tries to sit next to me.

I laugh, imagining him with our silly picture as his screensaver. I show the kids the photo, and they both giggle at Jake's silly face. It's so Jake, and even with miles between us, it makes me feel close to him.

As the kids and I get ready to head out for the day, I take one last look at the picture on my phone. The three of us, messy and carefree, captured in a moment of pure joy. It's a reminder that no matter how far away Jake is, no matter how complicated things might get, we're building something special together.

Something worth holding on to.

CHAPTER THIRTY

YOU'RE SO STRONG, JUST LIKE MAMA

———◆———

Charlotte - 12 years ago

The muffled sounds of laughter and singing drift through the infirmary window. It's late, and while everyone else is probably roasting marshmallows or sneaking in one last game of capture the flag, I'm sitting here beside Tommy's cot, trying to keep him calm as he dozes off to sleep.

"Shh, it's okay," I whisper, offering him a comforting smile as I tuck the blanket around him. "You're safe. Try to get some rest."

Tommy, the smallest in our group, finally closes his eyes and starts to drift off. Sick all day, his fever has only worsened his homesickness. My heart aches for him. I know how it feels to be away from home, even if this camp is just a summer adventure.

The door creaks open, and I glance up to see Jake standing there, looking rumpled and a little out of breath. His hair's a mess, and he's still in his camp leader uniform.

"Hey," he says softly, walking over to where I'm sitting. "How's the little guy doing?"

"Better," I reply, keeping my voice low. "Finally asleep, but he's still really homesick."

Jake nods, concern crossing his face as he watches Tommy. "Yeah, it's tough being away from home, especially when you're not feeling well."

I smile a little, appreciating that he gets it. "He just needs someone to be here with him. I don't want him to feel like he's alone."

Jake glances at the clock on the wall and then back at me. "You've been here for hours. Why don't you take a break? I can keep an eye on him."

I shake my head, though I'm exhausted. "I'm fine. Besides, I don't mind being here. It's kind of nice, actually."

He chuckles, settling into the chair beside me. "You're too good, you know that? Most people would be out there having fun, but you're in here playing nurse."

I shrug. "It's not that big of a deal. I just... I know what it's like to be sick and scared."

"What do you mean?"

I take a deep breath, toying with the hem of my hoodie. "When I was eight, my older brother got really sick. It started with a fever, just like this. My parents thought it was the flu, but it kept climbing. They didn't realize how serious it was until it was almost too late."

Jake's brows knit together. "What was it?"

"Pneumonia. It hit him hard and fast. He pulled through, but it was close. Ever since then, fevers... they just put me on edge. Even when I know it's probably nothing, I can't help but worry."

Jake nods, his gaze dropping to a sleeping Tommy. "That kinda thing sticks with you."

"It does," I murmur. The memory is still sharp, like it's etched into my bones.

After a moment, Jake leans back in his chair. "You're pretty amazing with these kids, you know? They love you."

There's a pause, and I can feel my heart beating faster at the way he's looking at me. It's a look that makes me feel special. Like maybe there's more to me than just being the girl who's good at taking care of everyone.

"Well, thanks," I say, keeping my voice light. "But don't go getting all sappy on me, okay?"

He laughs, the sound soft and warm. "No promises."

***

Charlie – Present Day

The morning starts like any other. Rushed, chaotic, but manageable. I'm in the middle of reviewing a campaign proposal for an onboarding meeting when my phone buzzes.

"Hey, Nina, what's up?" I ask, balancing the phone between my ear and shoulder while typing a quick email.

"Charlotte, I think you should come home," Nina says, her voice tinged with concern. "Meadow's not feeling well. She's running a fever, and she's really lethargic."

My fingers freeze over the keyboard. Meadow was fine this morning, just a little tired.

"Okay," I reply, my voice steady despite the sudden surge of worry. "I'll be there soon. Can you keep her comfortable until I get home?"

"Of course. Do you want me to call a doctor?"

"No thanks, I'll handle that. Just... keep her comfortable."

I hang up, and take a breath. I'm used to handling things on my own, being the one everyone relies on. But the thought of Meadow being really sick sends a spike of fear through me. I grab my bag and rush out of the office, my mind racing.

As I drive home, the logical part of my brain tries to take over. It's probably just a bug. Kids get sick all the time. But the what-ifs start creeping in. What if it's something serious? What if I can't manage this on my own?

By the time I pull into the driveway, my nerves are frayed. I rush inside, finding Nina in the living room with Meadow curled up on the couch, her little face pale and flushed.

"Mama," Meadow whispers, reaching out for me.

I kneel beside her, pressing a kiss to her forehead. She's burning up. "Hey, baby. Mama's here. How are you feeling?"

"Not good," she whimpers, and my heart breaks a little more.

I turn to Nina, her brow furrowed and lips pressed into a tight line. "Thank you for calling me. Will you be okay to pick up Noah from school later? That way I can stay with Meadow."

"Of course, no problem," she replies. "Do you need anything before I go?"

"No thank you, I've got it," I say, more to myself than to her.

Nina gives Meadow a gentle pat on the head before heading out, leaving me alone with my daughter and my rising panic. I check Meadow's temperature—it's high, way too high. I give her some Tylenol, but it doesn't seem to help.

I pace the room, my mind cycling through options. I could take her to the doctor, but the thought of sitting in a waiting room with a feverish child makes my skin crawl. I consider calling Jake, but I hesitate. He's in a different city, likely in the middle of training. What would I even say? That I'm scared? That I feel like I'm failing?

I pull out my phone, my thumb hovering over Zoe's number. But she's out of town for work, and I don't want to worry her. The weight of the situation presses down on me, the familiar burden of being the one in charge, holding everything together.

My phone buzzes, breaking through my thoughts, and I realize how tightly I've been gripping it.

Jake: Hey Lady Lightning, just checking in. How's your day going?

I stare at the screen, my eyes flicking to Meadow. Jake's been gone for over a week, and I miss him more than I'd thought possible. But I don't want to burden him with this. He has enough on his plate.

Me: It's been okay x

He replies quickly, and I can feel his concern radiating through the screen.

Jake: Everything alright?

I take a deep breath, my resolve crumbling.

Me: Meadow's sick. High fever. Just trying to get it down, but it's not working

Before I can set my phone down, it starts buzzing in my hand, and Jake's name pops up. I swipe to answer, pressing the phone to my ear. "Hey."

"Charlie, what's going on?" His voice is calm but tinged with concern.

"I don't know," I admit, my voice wobbling. "She's burning up. The Tylenol isn't working, yet. I think I should probably take her to the ER, but I'm trying not to panic."

"You're doing the right thing," he says, reassuring me. "If it doesn't break soon, take her in." He pauses, and then murmurs, "I wish I was there."

"I do, too," I whisper, my throat tightening. "But don't worry—I've got this."

"You're such a good mom, Charlie girl. You know that, right?"

I swallow hard, trying to hold it together. That was not what I expected him to say, but suddenly, it's everything I needed to hear.

"I'll check in with you later, okay? Call me if you need anything. I mean it."

"I will," I say, forcing myself to stay calm. "Thanks, Jake."

We hang up, and I take a deep breath, steadying myself. But as the morning drags on and Meadow's fever doesn't break, the panic I've been holding back starts to creep in. When Nina returns with Noah, I make a decision.

"I'm going to take Meadow to the ER. Can you please stay with Noah until I'm back?" I ask Nina, trying to keep my voice even.

"Of course," she says without hesitation. "I'll take care of him."

239

I nod, trying to muster a smile, but it feels like my world is teetering on the edge of something I can't control. I bundle Meadow into the car, her small body limp against mine, and as I pull out of the driveway, I send Jake a quick message.

Me: Taking her to the ER. I'll keep you posted x

I don't wait for a reply. My focus is on Meadow, on getting her the help she needs. But as I drive, the fear I've been holding back starts to break through, and I feel tears prickling at the corners of my eyes.

The ER waiting room is packed, a swirling mess of noise and anxiety. I cradle Meadow in my arms, her feverish body feeling too heavy, like she's melting into me. Each minute drags, the pounding worry in my chest growing sharper with every passing second. We sit and sit, watching critical cases go before us, and it's all I can do to keep myself from crying. I've handled plenty alone, but this—her tiny body so hot against mine—pushes every nerve to its edge.

For a fleeting moment, I'm eight years old again, watching helplessly as my brother lay in a hospital bed, his fever raging out of control. The memory sharpens, as vivid as if it happened yesterday. My parents' hushed tones, the beeping machines, the cold, sterile smell that clung to everything. The fear back then had been a suffocating thing, something I didn't understand fully until now.

I murmur soft reassurances, but the fear eats away at my composure. I shoot Alex a quick update, hating that I have to involve him. I feel so raw, so exposed in this cold, impersonal place, alone in a new city with strangers passing by.

Finally, they take us back to a room. My phone buzzes with Jake's name lighting the screen, but I silence it, my focus on Meadow as I settle her onto the bed.

When the doctor finally arrives, relief mingles with a persistent worry. I'm afraid I'm overreacting, but more afraid I'm not. He examines her, administers medication, then tells me to take her home—she'll recover better in her own bed.

I clutch the bottle of water the nurse hands me, noting that I need to coax Meadow to drink. It sounds so simple, but I feel like I'm holding us together by sheer willpower alone.

By the time I bundle her back into the car, exhaustion hits me like a wave. Meadow is quiet, barely stirring, and it takes everything I have not to break on the drive home. *Not yet, Charlie.* As I pull into the driveway, my mind spins through tasks: get Meadow to bed, monitor her, stock up on meds, call in tomorrow if needed. One thing at a time.

I'm so focused on holding it all together that when the front door opens, I almost don't register who's standing there.

Jake.

Disheveled but real, his eyes search mine with an intensity that breaks through my exhaustion.

"What..." I barely manage to find the words.

"I caught an earlier flight." He steps forward, reaching out for Meadow. "I couldn't just sit back and let you handle this alone."

The relief that hits me is overwhelming, breaking through every wall I've spent years building. Tears I've been holding back threaten to fall, and I can barely breathe, let alone speak. "You... didn't have to."

"Yes, I did," he says simply, wrapping an arm around me. "I didn't want you to be alone in this, Charlie."

The words sink in, both a balm and a reminder of how much I've been carrying by myself. I lean into him, feeling his warmth, his strength—things I never thought I'd need this much. He holds me, and for the first time in hours, I can breathe. Finally, I can breathe.

Jake presses a firm kiss to my forehead, then guides me inside. "Let's see how she's doing."

I nod, willing back the tears as I move into the house. He lays Meadow on the sofa, his big hands gentle as he checks her temperature. "She's still hot," he says calmly. "Let's try to cool her down."

A mix of awe and relief washes over me as Jake scoops Meadow up, holding her close as he heads to the bathroom. He doesn't hesitate, simply rolls up his sleeves and turns on the shower to a lukewarm spray. Then, without a second thought, he steps under the water fully clothed, cradling Meadow to his chest.

Something in me stills as I watch him, every doubt dissolving as his low, steady voice fills the bathroom. His words are soothing, a constant voice that draws me in. "It's okay, Princess. I've got you," he whispers close to her ear. "We're going to make you all better, okay? You're so brave. I'm right here, and I'm not going anywhere."

Meadow's small body shivers against him, but I see her gradually relax as the water cools her down. Jake continues speaking, his tone gentle. "You're doing great, Meadow. Just a little longer and you'll start feeling better. I'm so proud of you."

I hover in the doorway, the cool tile pressing against my bare feet. I've never seen anyone do something so simple and naturally loving for my children. Jake holds her like she's always been his, loving her like she's his. Like he's been doing this his whole life. And it pulls every fragile part of me into focus. He's here. He came for us.

"I know it's scary, sweet girl, but you're safe." His voice feels like an anchor in this storm of emotions. "You're so strong, just like Mama. We're going to make sure you're okay."

His gaze flicks to me. "I remember what you told me, Charlie," he says quietly. "I get why this is hitting you so hard."

The words stop me in my tracks, the memory rising unbidden. How I told Jake all those years ago about how helpless I'd felt watching my brother's fever climb and not knowing if he'd be okay. It's something I rarely shared, yet Jake remembers.

"You're not alone in this, I'm here. I've got you."

Tears blur my vision, his quiet reassurance unravelling the knot of fear in my chest. Of course he remembers. Even back then, Jake didn't just hear things—he kept them. *He kept me.*

My phone suddenly buzzes from the hall, and Jake glances over with a nod. "Check your phone, it'll be Dr. Hayes."

I blink, exhaustion making everything feel slow as I grab my phone, confirming Dr. Hayes, Jake's private doctor, is en route. It dawns on me that he organized for him to come, making sure we'd have the best care. Every small thing he's done in the past few hours stitches a part of me back together. I have someone here, someone who steps in when things go sideways. *I'm not alone.*

Jake steps out of the shower, his clothes soaked but his face calm. Meadow is still cradled in his arms, her small body now relaxed, fever finally easing.

"She'll be okay, Charlie," he murmurs.

The tears I've held back start falling as I take Meadow from him, wrapping her in a towel and holding her close. My heart finally slows. Relief floods in, quieting every last fear.

"Thank you," I whisper, voice breaking. "For being here."

Jake reaches out, his hand warm as he cups my cheek, brushing away a tear with his thumb. "There's nowhere else I'd rather be, Charlie girl."

I look up at him, and everything I need to know is right there in his eyes. He's my rock, my steady place to fall. For so long, I've convinced myself I could handle it all on my own. But this moment—this quiet, steady presence of his—undoes that. He's here.

I think I love you.

CHAPTER THIRTY-ONE

DON'T GO GETTING ALL SAPPY ON ME, OKAY?

———————◆———————

Jake

I've spent my whole life balancing on a tightrope, trying to be everything for everyone. Teammate, leader, star player. But this is different, this is real. It's not about winning games or making the right play; it's about showing up, being the man they need me to be. The man *I* need to be.

Dr. Hayes arrives, and his calm presence steadies the house instantly. "Let's get her checked out," he says.

Charlotte's eyes flick to mine, her surprise still evident. She hadn't expected me to call my own doctor. But I couldn't leave this to chance. Not with Meadow.

I stay by their side, my hand on Charlie's shoulder, grounding her as Dr. Hayes examines Meadow. His methodical approach helps settle her, but I can still see how tightly wound she is, still holding onto the day's tension, struggling to keep it together.

"It's a viral bug," Dr. Hayes says after a thorough check. "She'll need rest, fluids, and some meds, but she'll be fine."

Relief floods Charlie's face, the tightness in her expression loosening. I squeeze her shoulder gently. "Thank you," she whispers, her voice thick with emotion.

She looks at me, and for a moment I see every unspoken word.

I love you, too.

After Dr. Hayes leaves, we settle Meadow into bed. She's still groggy, but the worst of it seems to be over. Holding Meadow's small weight against me as I carry her, I realize just how much this little girl—and her mother and brother—mean to me.

We tuck Meadow in, Charlotte brushing a gentle kiss across her forehead, pulling the covers up. I stand back, giving her space but ready to step in if she needs me. Noah's fast asleep, thanks to Nina, so Charlie peeks her head in to check on him before we head downstairs.

In the kitchen, the day's exhaustion hangs between us. I make her a tea, needing to get something into her, realizing she's barely even had water all day.

She leans against the counter, her gaze distant, as if she's replaying the events of the day over and over. I want to reach through that haze, ground her in something real.

"You did everything right today," I say, watching her carefully.

She doesn't respond right away, just lets out a slow breath, her eyes falling to the floor. "I don't know," she mumbles, almost to herself. "It didn't feel like I did."

There's a vulnerability in her voice that makes my heart ache. I step closer, placing a gentle hand on her arm. "Charlie, you did everything you could. Meadow's okay."

She finally looks up at me, eyes glazed with doubt. "I've always managed on my own. But today, I felt like I was failing her. Like I didn't know what I was doing."

Hearing that, protectiveness rushes through me. "You weren't failing her. You were being a mom, doing everything you could to keep her safe. That's not failing."

She sucks her lower lip into her mouth, shoulders still tight with tension. "You showed up, and... I didn't even know you were coming. Why did you come back, Jake?"

Because I love you more than anything.

I take her hands in mine, pulling her close. "I couldn't stay away. I didn't want you to feel like you were alone, not for this situation. I knew it'd be stressful for you."

Her eyes search mine, and I see the realization settling—the moment she feels this is connection for what it is. That what we have is real, rare. That she might love me just as much as I love her.

A tear slips down her cheek, and I gently kiss it away. "You have no idea how much that means to me," she whispers.

I lean in further, pressing a lingering kiss to her lips. When we pull apart, I catch the faintest hint of a smile on her face and rest my forehead against hers. "I'm here for you, Charlie girl."

She looks up, a tired smile ghosting over her lips. "Don't get all sappy on me though, okay?"

The corner of my mouth lifts. "No promises."

***

We're curled up on the sofa, the house finally quiet around us. Charlie's head rests on my chest, and I hold her close, feeling the tension from today slowly dissolve. She's drained, worn to the bone, and all I want is to keep her in this calm bubble.

I'm about to suggest heading to bed when her phone buzzes. She glances at the screen, fatigue clouding her face. "It's Alex," she says, almost to herself.

My gut tightens. I know she texted him earlier about Meadow, keeping him updated despite it being the middle of the night in New Zealand. He hadn't replied, and it's clear to me that he's the type to ignore his own kids unless he's looking for control.

I swallow back the brewing anger, but I know he's about to push every button I have.

"Do you want me to leave?" I ask, but she shakes her head.

Good. I tighten my hold on her, brushing my thumb along her arm.

She takes a steadying breath, then answers. "Alex."

Even before he speaks, I sense the tension. His tone is sharp, cutting through the calm we've built. "What the hell is going on, Lottie? Why didn't you contact me sooner?"

Charlotte's body stiffens at the nickname—*Lottie*. I know she hates it, but she keeps her voice steady, holding back her frustration.

"I did, Alex. I texted you as soon as we headed to the ER. It was late there, I didn't want to wake you unless it was urgent."

A pause on his end. I know his type, the kind of man who's always twisting the knife, always needling for control.

"You should have called," he snaps. "I'm her father, Lottie. I deserve to know what's happening with her."

I see her inhale slowly, keeping her composure. I slide my hand up her back, hoping she can draw strength from me.

"I handled it, Alex. Her fever spiked, then Dr. Hayes checked her over and she's fine now. Asleep in bed."

"Dr. Hayes?" he spits. "Who the hell is Dr. Hayes?"

"Jake's doctor," she replies, glancing at me. She's drained but steady. "He made a house call to ensure Meadow was okay."

There's a loaded silence, and I feel the simmering anger from his end, an anger he clearly thinks he can unload on her, like he probably has a hundred times before.

"Who's Jake?" he demands.

Charlie hesitates. She opens her mouth to downplay it, but something shifts. Instead, she squares her shoulders.

"Jake's my boyfriend."

I feel a surge of pride and love, and an urge to let Alex know exactly what kind of man she's with now. She's standing her ground, claiming us, and it makes me want to pull her in and never let her go.

"Your *boyfriend*?" Alex sneers. "Jake who?"

"Jake Brooks. He's a hockey player I met through Zoe."

I already know from Zoe that the two of them despise each other, and the thought that this connection will rile him up even more satisfies me immensely.

"A *hockey player*?" His laugh is sharp, dripping with disdain. "You seriously think you can just replace me with some overpaid meathead Zoe shoved at you? God, Lottie, you're pathetic. Chasing after some jock like a desperate little girl."

Her hands tighten, knuckles turning white. I want nothing more than to rip the phone from her and tell him exactly what I think. The realization that he's likely treated her like this for years, the thought of her ending up with this guy after everything we shared at camp—it *burns*. This should have been us from the beginning. It should have been me from the start.

Every word he spits is like poison, a calculated attempt to unravel her confidence, to manipulate her into feeling unworthy of anything real. I hold her closer, watching her breathe through the barrage. She doesn't flinch, just meets his cruelty with a strength he doesn't deserve to witness.

"This isn't about you, Alex. It's about Meadow. Jake was there when we needed him, and he actually cares about our kids. That's what matters."

"Oh, I *bet* he cares," he says with a venomous scoff. "Wake up, Lottie. You really think this hockey hotshot's going to stick around for you and two kids? You're nothing but a convenience for him, a little ego boost for the road."

I can barely keep my hands from balling into fists. He's fucking deluded if he thinks he can belittle her and plant some twisted doubt in her mind. I hold her tighter, letting her know I'm right here and ready to fight back if she needs me.

"I'm not asking for your permission, Alex," she says. "Jake's here because he chooses to be. That's something *you'll* never understand."

The line goes silent, his shock almost tangible before he finally snarls, "You don't get to just cut me out, Lottie. I'm still their father, and you'd better remember that."

Her hand trembles slightly, but she doesn't retreat. "I know you're their father. But I'm not apologizing for moving on. *My* life isn't your business anymore."

The line goes dead, but her hand is still shaking as she slowly lowers the phone. I don't hesitate. I pull her onto my lap, wrapping my arms around her, a protectiveness radiating through me.

"You were incredible, Charlie," I murmur into her hair, my voice a blend of pride and fury. "You didn't put up with his bullshit, and I'm so damn proud."

She buries her face against my shoulder, her breath uneven. "I hate how he makes me feel so small. Like I'm some failure, never good enough."

I tip her chin up, meeting her eyes, feeling something fierce and unshakeable rising inside me. Every part of me aches to tell her, to show her, just how wrong he is.

"He doesn't get to control that anymore. You're stronger than that, and I swear to you Charlie girl, you're so damn worth it. I'll remind you every day. No one's ever making you feel that way again."

She stares at me, eyes shining. I lean down, capturing her lips in a kiss that's soft but filled with everything I feel—pride, love, and a fierce need to protect her from anyone who tries to hurt her.

She wraps her arms around my neck, holding me close. "Thank you," she whispers, her voice laced with something that goes beyond words.

"For what?"

"For being here, for being you."

A surge of resolve rises in me as I stroke a tear from her cheek. This woman in my arms deserves the world and everything I have to give.

"If being me means I get to be here with you, then I'm all in."

Her eyes glisten as she gives me a soft smile, and her next words—simple but so profound—bring me right back to a moment under starlit skies, to the words I'll never forget.

"I'm glad you exist," she whispers.

And just like that, she's turned my world upside down again. But unlike last time, when we were too young to understand the magnitude of this connection, I pull her in and kiss her. Slow and tender, a promise, a vow. I know I'll have to tell her soon.

She's it for me, and I'll be damned if anyone lets her doubt it.

CHAPTER THIRTY-TWO

WHAT'S THE POINT OF HALF-ASSING IT?

───────────✦───────────

Jake - 12 Years Ago

The kitchen is quieter than usual, the chaos of meal prep finally winding down. I'm scrounging around, hunting for a snack, when I hear it. A soft, melodic voice drifting from around the corner.

Curious, I follow the sound, slowing my steps as I near the dishwashing station. And there she is. Charlotte, sleeves rolled up, hair tied back, belting out a song like she's on stage at Madison Square Garden.

It takes me a second to recognize it: "Iris" by the Goo Goo Dolls. Not exactly my go-to, a bit too sappy for my taste. But the way she's singing it, I'm captivated.

Charlotte's completely in her own world, voice growing stronger as she hits the chorus, a dish brush in one hand like it's her microphone, hips swaying slightly to the rhythm.

I lean against the doorframe to watch. She's always been a mystery, this mix of strength and softness, and right now she's showing a side I haven't seen before.

The song swells, and she turns, spotting me standing here. But instead of stopping or looking embarrassed, she grins and doubles down on her performance, raising her imaginary mic and belting out the lyrics with even more passion.

I let out a laugh, shaking my head. "You're really going for it, huh?"

"Of course!" She grins, eyes bright with mischief. "What's the point of half-assing it?"

I chuckle, moving closer until I'm leaning against the counter beside her. "Not a fan of half-measures, are you?"

"Nope." She keeps singing but gives me a wink. "Especially not when it comes to this song. You've got to really *feel* it."

I watch her, a strange mix of admiration and amusement bubbling up. "I dunno, Charlie. It's a bit... I don't know... sappy?"

She pauses mid-lyric, narrowing her eyes at me in mock offense. "Sappy? Jake Brooks, you just don't get it."

I raise an eyebrow and cross my arms. "What exactly am I not getting?"

"The lyrics, obviously. It's about being so in love with someone that you never want to leave them, about wanting them to truly *see* you."

I blink, caught a little off guard. I'd never given the song a second thought—just another radio hit. But hearing her say it, I wonder if I've missed something.

"Okay, I'll bite," I say, keeping my tone light. "Maybe it's not so bad. But I think I like it better when *you're* singing it."

Her laugh is bright and genuine, then she goes back to scrubbing the pot. "That's because I've got *soul*, Captain Thunder."

"You've definitely got *something*, Lady Lightning."

We both laugh, her voice filling the kitchen as she finishes the song. And as I stand there watching her, I realize there might be more to this song than I gave credit for. Or maybe there's just more to Charlotte than I ever expected.

***

Jake – Present Day

The bar is packed, buzzing with the electric energy of holiday cheer and drunken karaoke performances. It's the 22nd of December and we've just had our last home game before the break, so the whole team's making the most of it.

It's been over a week since Meadow's illness, and life's finally starting to settle again. Meadow's back to her playful self, and I'm with Charlie every chance I get.

Most nights when I'm in Denver, I'm at her place. Things between us are shifting and getting deeper. Normally, this is when I'd start feeling that itch to pull back. But not with her.

With Charlie, the old rules don't apply. The kids, too. Telling them about us had been nerve-wracking as hell. Charlie and I sat on the couch like two awkward teenagers, overthinking every word, while Noah and Meadow watched us like we'd grown three heads. We were braced for a million questions or maybe even tears. Instead, Noah had just looked at us with this deadpan expression and said, "Yeah, I figured. You kiss all the time."

I'd choked on my water and Charlie had gone bright red, but before she could say anything, Meadow climbed right into my lap and declared, "Good. 'Cause you're my Jake."

It was so simple for them, like they'd already decided I belonged there long before we did. And damn, if that didn't knock me flat.

Those kids mean the world to me, just as much as their mom does. Every moment of the past twelve years feels like it was leading me back to this life with them, to Charlie. And the way she's looking tonight? I'm ready to set the whole place on fire.

I scan the crowd, drink in hand, looking for her. Zoe and Charlie came here earlier with some of the WAGs, while I stayed behind to wrap things up at the arena.

Nothing could have prepared me for the outfit she wore to the game. She looks fucking incredible. When I saw her from the ice in those leather pants, my brain short-circuited.

Every time I glanced up at her, I lost focus. She'd thrown a blazer casually over her shoulders, but it did little to hide the skimpy camisole underneath. She knew exactly what she was doing, and I've been a ticking time bomb ever since.

I catch sight of her now at the bar with Zoe. Her legs are crossed, that damn blazer draped over the back of her chair, the casual vibe she had at the arena replaced with a sultry confidence that's driving me out of my mind. She's glowing, her auburn hair tumbling over her shoulders, cheeks flushed from the heat of the room or maybe the espresso martini she's holding. Every teasing glance she throws me is a playful dare, and I'm more than ready to collect.

I weave through the crowd, feeling the eyes of far too many guys lingering on her, and I'm about two steps away when I hear Logan calling out behind me.

"There she is, Brooks! Damn man, you sure you've got that locked down?" He's a few drinks in so I forgive this rookie for being so bold.

I smirk, pushing past him. "Trust me, Pooks, it's locked down."

When I finally reach them, Zoe has her sass turned up to eleven, clearly enjoying the show. "Well, well, look who finally decided to show up."

Charlie turns, her gaze locking on mine. That familiar pull hits me, the one that clears everything else from my mind. Her smile quirks, like she's letting me in on a secret only I'm worthy of. It takes every ounce of restraint not to grab her and haul her home immediately.

"Hey, you," she says playfully. There's a spark in her eyes—a mix of challenge and quiet certainty, like she's been waiting for this moment as much as I have.

I slide a hand around her waist, fingers grazing the bare skin under her top. "Distracting me with this outfit?" I murmur, lips brushing her ear. "You think you can just walk out of the arena after that and not expect payback?"

She laughs, the sound traveling straight to my cock. "Payback, huh? What did you have in mind?"

I don't answer. Tugging her off the barstool, I guide her to a dim corridor, away from prying eyes. The second we're alone, I press her against the wall, crashing my mouth onto hers the way I've been dying to all night. Her hands tangle in my hair, nails scraping lightly against my scalp, and I grip her hips, fingers digging into the smooth leather.

She moans softly into my mouth as I press my body closer, letting her feel exactly what she's doing to me. "You've been driving me crazy all night," I growl against her lips.

"Good. That was the point."

My hands slide to her ass, grabbing a handful. "These pants... no VPL, huh?"

She bites back a grin, eyes glittering with mischief. "Wouldn't you like to know?"

I'm about to lose all control when Zoe's voice cuts through from around the corner. "Jake! Charlie! If you two don't get your asses back here, I'm sending a search party in with a bucket of bleach!"

Charlie giggles, burying her face in my chest. "We should probably get back."

I force myself to take a steadying breath, adjusting myself before stepping back. "This isn't over," I warn, stealing one last kiss before letting her go.

"Counting on that." She straightens her top and saunters back out to Zoe. I follow her, though I'm two seconds from dragging her back into that corner.

Zoe's standing there with her arms crossed and a smirk plastered across her face. "You two are disgusting," she says, shaking her head. "But damn, Charlie, you're gonna give this poor guy a heart attack in this outfit."

Charlie throws her head back in a laugh, and I have to stop myself from leaning in to suck the curve of her throat. "You're the one who convinced me to buy it!"

Zoe nods proudly. "Best purchase you ever made."

"Not sure if I should be grateful or pissed," I mutter.

"Oh, shut up, Brooks," Zoe says with a playful shove. "Just enjoy the fact that every guy here wishes they were you right now."

Charlie glances over her shoulder, throwing me a wink as she starts to rejoin the group. "They can keep wishing."

I playfully smack her on the ass as she steps into the booth. *Damn right they can.*

Zoe scrunches her nose. "God, you two are nauseating."

We settle into our booth, but the tension between us hasn't cooled, the heat from earlier simmering beneath the surface.

Chase slides in beside us. "You two ready to sing your hearts out tonight?"

Charlie shakes her head, laughing as she takes a sip of her drink. "Don't count on it."

I smirk. "She's just being modest."

"Traitor," she mutters with a ghost of a smile on her lips.

254

"Come on, Charlie! You've got to do it." Zoe's voice rises through the noise, tugging on her hand.

Charlie laughs, shaking her head. "No way, you're not getting me up there."

"You promised!"

With an exasperated laugh, Charlie lets Zoe lead her to the stage, and I sit back watching as the opening chords of "I Will Survive" start playing. I can't help but grin as Charlie reluctantly grabs the mic. Her eyes meet mine across the bar.

I raise my drink in a mock toast, mouthing, "You got this."

As she starts singing, her voice cuts through the bar, commanding everyone's attention. I can't look away. By the time she hits the chorus, the entire place is singing along, and I'm grinning like a fool. Knowing she's mine, that I get to be the one holding her at the end of the night, fills me with a rare kind of contentment.

"She's killin' it," Chase says, taking a sip of his beer. "Didn't know your girl had pipes."

I chuckle. "I did."

When the song ends, the bar erupts in applause. I'm on my feet before I realize, making my way to her through the crowd.

"You were incredible," I say, pulling her into me.

"Yeah?" She looks up at me, catching her breath.

Instead of answering, I kiss her, letting her know exactly how I feel without saying a word. But before things get too heated, Zoe's voice interrupts.

"Hey, lovebirds! Don't leave me out here on my own!"

We turn to see Zoe on the dance floor, waving us over. But she's not alone for long.

Charlie laughs, leaning into me as Chase sidles up to Zoe. "Looks like Chase might make a move."

"About time," I say, tightening my arm on her waist.

We join them on the dance floor, but I can't shake the eyes on us. I feel a burn to stake my claim. There's an energy between us tonight, something heavier than just the fun we've been having. It's like we're standing on the edge of something, and neither of us knows what comes next.

"Hey, you were amazing up there," a guy says, eyeing Charlie in a way that sets my teeth on edge.

"Thanks," Charlie replies, giving him a polite smile. "My boyfriend thinks so, too."

The guy's smile falters a little, and I don't miss the way his eyes flick to me before he nods and steps back. I tighten my arm around her waist, pulling her closer as we sway to the music.

"You're mine, Lady Lightning," I murmur in her ear.

The night continues, laughter and music blurring around us. Zoe and Charlie buddy up to do that dramatic sing-dance thing girls do together on the dance floor while Chase and I watch from a distance. We're talking hockey until I see some asshole move in behind Charlie, his hands on her waist, pulling her back against him. My blood boils, and before I know it, I'm over there shoving him off her.

"Back off," I growl, voice lethal. The guy stumbles back, eyes wide with surprise, muttering an apology before he disappears. Smart move.

I turn to Charlie. "You okay?"

She nods, a mix of relief and gratitude in her eyes. "Yeah, I'm fine."

I don't say anything, my jaw ticking as I scan the crowd for any more idiots.

"Jealous much?" she says, a glint in her eyes as she steps into me, but I'm not ready to joke.

"You're damn right I'm jealous. That guy had his hands on you, Charlie."

She laughs, her eyes twinkling. "That's what happens on a dance floor, Brooks. You don't have to go full caveman."

I pull her closer, my voice lowering. "I protect what's mine. No apologies."

She smiles, leaning up close. "Keep dancing, and maybe I'll let you keep me."

I can't help the laugh that rumbles through my chest, pressing my lips to her ear. "You're pushing it, you know that?"

"Yep. But you love me for it."

Oh baby, you have no idea.

I don't respond, just lean down to kiss her, sucking her lower lip into my mouth. The truth is, she has me completely, in every way possible. There's no question, no room for doubt.

As the night winds down, I can tell the drinks are catching up to her. She's more than a little tipsy, her steps slower and more deliberate. I wrap an arm around her waist to steady her, guiding her back to the booth.

When we finally sink into our seats, the noise of the bar fades around us, like we're in our own little world. I'm grateful that the rest of our group is still on the dance floor or at the bar. She leans into me, quietly resting her head on my shoulder, as if something's weighing on her mind. I run my hand gently along her arm, waiting for her to speak.

After a long pause, she lifts her head and her eyes meet mine. There's a vulnerability there I don't see often, and it pulls at something deep inside me.

"Jake..." She bites her lip, like she's debating whether or not to continue.

"Yeah, Charlie girl?"

She takes a deep breath, her fingers fidgeting with the hem of her top. "I've been thinking... about us."

The words hang, and a knot tightens in my chest. I have no idea where she's going with this, but I know it's important.

"About us?" I repeat.

She nods, looking down for a moment before meeting my eyes again. "Yeah. I mean, we've been spending so much time together, and it feels... serious."

I nod slowly, trying to keep my tone even. "It does."

She pauses, her gaze searching mine, almost as if she's looking for reassurance. "It's just... sometimes I wonder..."

I can see the struggle in her eyes, like she's wrestling with whether or not to say what's on her mind.

I don't push her, letting her take her time, but praying to God she's not about to tell me she wants to cool things down. After a moment, she sighs, her shoulders relaxing slightly, and she leans into me a little more.

"Wonder what?" I prompt.

"Wonder if..." She trails off, her voice barely above a whisper, as if she's scared to say it out loud. "... if you feel the same way. Like, do you... you know..."

My heart pounds as her words sink in and I realize what she's asking for. She's practically confessing, and I know she wants me to bridge the gap, to make this clear.

I reach out, tucking a strand of hair behind her ear. "Charlie..." I start, my voice as gentle as I can make it, feeling the weight of this moment.

But before I can say more, she shakes her head, an embarrassed laugh escaping her. "God, listen to me. I shouldn't be asking you this."

But I can see the vulnerability in her eyes, the hope she's trying to downplay. She wants to know, even if she won't ask again.

"Charlie." I take her hand in mine and hold it between us. "You're a little drunk..." *You're the love of my life.*

She lets out a frustrated laugh, rolling her eyes. "Dutch courage."

I chuckle, squeezing her hand. "I know. But when I tell you how I feel, I want you to remember it. I want it to be clear. I want you to remember every word."

She pouts, looking more like Meadow than she probably realizes. "Fine," she mumbles, tilting her head towards the ceiling. "But you will tell me?"

I run my thumb along her cheek. "Yeah, Charlie girl. I'll tell you. I promise."

She holds my gaze for a long moment, then finally nods, her body relaxing as she leans into me again.

I hold her close, my mind racing with everything she's said. The truth is, I'm absolutely, without a shadow of a fucking doubt, in love with her. It's a fact that feels as undeniable as gravity.

I think I've known since that night under the stars. I've spent twelve years chasing my dream. The dream we promised each other we'd chase. I didn't realize until recently, the dream was always her.

But she deserves more than a confession while she's half-asleep on my shoulder, tipsy from a night out. She deserves to hear it when we're both fully present, fully aware of what we're saying. I want her to soak in every damn word I tell her. Because once I say it, that's it. *She's it.*

I catch a glimpse of Chase out of the corner of my eye. He's guiding Zoe away from the dance floor, his arm around her shoulders. They're laughing, and she's completely unaware of the way he's subtly steering her away from the crowd, away from any potential trouble. I've never seen Chase laugh like that, and it suits him.

As the night winds down, I help Charlie outside, her steps unsteady. I guide her into my car, and as we drive back to her place, she's quiet, her head resting against the window.

When we pull up, I turn to help her out of the car, but she surprises me by leaning in and crushing her lips to mine in a kiss that's anything but innocent.

"I want you," she says, hand trailing up my chest.

I groan, pulling back slightly. "Charlie, you're drunk."

"So?" Her fingers play with the fabric of my shirt.

I gently cup her face. "*So*, I'm not taking advantage of you when you're like this."

She stares at me for a long moment, then huffs and crosses her arms. "You're too good, you know that?"

"Just trying to do the right thing," I murmur, pressing a kiss to her forehead.

Leaning back in her seat with a sigh, her eyes droop with exhaustion. "But you'll stay, right?"

"Of course," I say, getting out to help her inside.

Once upstairs, I tuck her into bed, stripping down to my boxers and sliding in beside her. She immediately curls up against me, her head on my chest, arm draped over my stomach.

"I *do* know you love me, you know," she mutters groggily, her breath warm against my skin.

I smile, resting my lips against her hair. "Get some sleep, Lady Lightning." *I'm fucking obsessed with you.*

Humming softly, her body sinks deeper into my hold. Within moments, her breathing evens out, and she's fast asleep.

Holding her close, I replay her words in my mind, letting them settle deep inside me. This is where I'm meant to be, right here with her. And when she's ready, when she's sober, I'll be here to tell her exactly how much I love her.

CHAPTER THIRTY-THREE

YOU'RE STUCK WITH ME NOW

———————— ✦ ————————

Charlie

T he muted daylight sneaks through the curtains, stabbing at my skull like a personal attack. I groan, burying my face deeper into the pillow, trying to escape the brightness and the tiny hammers pounding in my head.

I shift to find a more comfortable position, when I realize there's a warm, solid body beside me. Memories of last night trickle back, and with them comes a rush of embarrassment.

Shit. I sang karaoke. Not just sang, but belted out "I'm a Survivor" like it was my final audition for *The Voice*. And then... fuck. I tried to ask him if he loved me.

But then other memories filter through: the way Jake held me close, steady and grounded, refusing to say those three words while I was drunk. Because he wanted it to be real. For me to remember them. That thought alone makes me realize how certain I am about him.

I crack one eye open, hoping Jake's still asleep so I can slip away to wallow in my humiliation alone.

But no. Of course he's awake. Propped up on one elbow, grinning down at me with that devilish look in his eyes, like he's been waiting for me to wake up just to torment me.

"Morning, Lady Lightning," he says, his voice annoyingly chipper.

I pull the blanket over my head. "Don't talk so loud."

He chuckles, the sound vibrating through the mattress. "Feeling rough?"

"Like death," I mumble, voice muffled by the covers. "Tell me I didn't embarrass myself too much."

"Hmm..." His hand slides up my side, warm and gentle. "Shall I start with your stellar karaoke performance or the part where you loudly declared I'm your boyfriend to half the bar?"

I peek out from under the covers, shooting him a glare. "I did not."

"Oh, you absolutely did. And then you asked me if I loved you."

My face flushes, and I immediately hide under the blanket again. "Can we just pretend last night didn't happen?"

Jake laughs, pulling the covers back down. "No way. Highlight of my week."

I groan dramatically, covering my face with my hands.

His teasing fades into something softer as he takes my hands away, his touch tender. "Hey, it wasn't that bad. You were just enthusiastic."

I squint up at him. "You didn't... record the singing, did you?"

"Nope," he pauses with a grin. "But Zoe might have."

I close my eyes. "Kill me now."

Jake leans in, pressing a kiss to my forehead. "Can't. We've got a cabin to get to."

I blink, trying to remember what day it is. "Right. The cabin..."

Christmas at Jake's cabin with the kids is the only thing motivating me to crawl out of this nest of self-pity. But right now, the idea of moving feels impossible.

"I brought you water and Tylenol." He nods toward the nightstand.

"You're a saint." I reach for the water, gulping it down with the pills.

Jake's about to say something when the door bursts open, and two little whirlwinds come charging into the room.

"Mama! Jake!" Meadow launches herself onto the bed with all the grace of a small elephant.

Noah follows, a little more composed, but just as eager. "Are we going to the cabin today?"

I sit up slowly, trying not to aggravate the throbbing in my head. "Yes, we're going to the cabin today."

Meadow notices Jake beside me and tilts her head curiously. "Did you have a sleepover, Jake?"

Jake chuckles, sliding his hand to rest on my back. "Yeah, Princess. I stayed over to make sure your mama was okay."

Noah looks between us, then at me, concern in his eyes. "Are you okay, Mum?"

I wince, but Jake jumps in smoothly. "Your mom's just tired from singing karaoke."

Noah's eyes go wide. "You sang?"

"Not just sang," Jake adds, shooting me a playful grin. "She *rocked* the place."

Noah and Meadow both giggle, and I groan, leaning into Jake's side. "You're never letting me live this down, are you?"

"Not a chance," Jake replies, pressing a kiss to the top of my head.

Meadow climbs into my lap, her little face full of concern. "Are you okay, Mama?"

I smile down at her, smoothing her hair. "I'm fine, honey bee. Just need some more sleep."

"No more sleep!" Noah protests. "We have to go to the cabin!"

Jake chuckles, standing and offering me a hand. "Come on, Charlie. Let's get you fed and packed up. Then we can hit the road."

I let him pull me to my feet, wobbling slightly as the kids run off, already chattering about the cabin.

Jake keeps his hand on my back as we head downstairs. "You know, if you wanna rest longer, I can handle the packing."

I shake my head, fighting off the lingering hangover. "I'll be fine. Just need caffeine and something to eat."

"Greasy food and coffee, coming right up."

The smell of bacon fills the air not long after, and the sound of the kids running around lifts my spirits. With a giant mug of coffee in hand, I slowly start to feel human again.

Jake keeps an eye on me, making sure I'm eating and drinking water, and every time our eyes meet, I see that warmth, that tenderness in his gaze that makes my heart thunder.

"I'm never drinking again," I announce, popping a piece of bacon into my mouth.

Jake chuckles, leaning over the counter. "You say that now..."

I swat at him playfully, but let my hand rest on his head as my fingers tangle in his hair. "Thanks for looking after me last night."

"Always," he says, kissing my palm.

Despite the embarrassment, despite the hangover, I feel lucky. I have Jake, my kids, and we're about to spend Christmas together in a beautiful setting. Everything feels right.

***

The road stretches ahead, winding through snow-covered forests and towering pines. The kids are fast asleep in the backseat, their small heads bobbing with each gentle movement of the car. Jake's hands are steady on the wheel, his focus on the road as we drive deeper into the mountains.

It's been about an hour since we left Denver, and the landscape has transformed into something breathtaking. Snow blankets everything, making the world feel still and quiet, like we're driving through a postcard. I glance over at Jake, noting the way his jaw is set, his brow furrowed slightly as he navigates the turns.

"You really love it up here, don't you?" I ask, watching as his expression softens, gaze briefly flicking to me before returning to the road.

"Yeah," he says, a small smile tugging at his lips. "It's my haven. I've been coming here for years, bought it early in my career. It's the one place where I can just be me."

I rest my hand on his thigh, offering a silent connection. "Everyone needs a place like that."

He's quiet for a moment, eyes still focused ahead. "I've never brought anyone here before," he admits. "It's always been mine. But I wanted to share it with you. And the kids."

A warmth spreads through me, settling deep in my chest. "That means every-thing. To all of us."

He nods, but there's a weight in his silence, something unspoken still hanging between us. The road winds higher, the mountains rising around us like giants. I can feel him retreating into his thoughts, so I squeeze his knee gently.

"Wanna talk about it?"

He exhales slowly. "I've been thinking about my mom."

The sadness in his voice tugs at me, and I give him space to continue. He's men-tioned her struggles with depression before, but I know it's a sensitive subject.

"She's better now, but it's still there, you know? That weight. She's never come to a game, never feels up to it. Too many people, too much pressure."

My heart aches for him. I know how much he's wanted her to be part of his life, to share in his successes. "That's hard. But she knows how much you love her, how much you've done for her."

He shrugs, the gesture small but heavy. "I hope so. Sometimes, I feel like no matter what I do, I could do more. I've offered to bring her to games, to have her in the WAGs box with Claire and Tamara, but she's never felt brave enough. I just want her to know she's not alone."

"You're a good son, Jake. Don't doubt that."

He nods, the tension in his shoulders easing slightly. "I'm trying. And I guess that's all I can do."

I squeeze his knee again and he reaches down to run his thumb in circles over my knuckles. We fall into silence, but it's a comfortable one this time. The cabin is getting closer, and with it, the promise of a few days away from the world.

As the road flattens out, we turn onto a private driveway, and I spot the cabin nestled at the foot of the mountains. Snow blankets everything in sight, untouched except for the road we're carving through. The cabin looks like some-thing out of a storybook—warm, inviting, with smoke curling from the chimney.

I unbuckle my seatbelt and turn to check on the kids, who are now wide-eyed and staring out at the snow as we pull up.

Meadow's little hands press against the window, her breath fogging the glass as she whispers, "Mama, look! It's *snowing*! Can we play?"

Noah leans forward, taking in the view with wide eyes. "It's so *white*. I've never seen snow like this before." He reaches for the door handle, unable to hold back any longer.

"Hold up, bud," Jake says with a chuckle, glancing at him in the rearview mirror. "Let's make sure we've got all our snow gear on. Don't want you turning into ice cubes before we've even unloaded the car."

Both kids groan, but the excitement in their faces is contagious. Christmas in New Zealand was always warm—beach days, barbecues. This snowy wonderland is new for them, and seeing their joy makes my heart happy.

As we step out of the car, the cold mountain air bites my cheeks. I wrap my arms around myself for a moment, letting my breath cloud in front of me as I take it all in.

The landscape is breathtaking, the snow-glittered hills leading up to towering peaks under the fading light. There's something about it that tugs at a memory, a familiarity in the way the mountains cradle the valley.

The smell of pine and the crispness of the air brings me back to the camp where Jake and I first met. It's a little like that—vast and full of possibility—and for a moment, I feel like we're those kids again, staring out at the world with our whole lives ahead of us.

Jake wraps an arm around me, pulling me close as we look out over the snow-covered valley.

"It's beautiful, isn't it?" I murmur, looking out.

He glances down at me, eyes scanning my face. "It is..."

I lean into him, my cheek grazing his shoulder. "It reminds me of camp. The mountains, the quiet."

Jake's lips brush against my temple. "That's what I thought when I bought it. It reminded me of camp."

"And now you're sharing it with us."

Before Jake can respond, the kids come barreling out of the car, bundled up and racing toward the nearest pile of snow. Meadow immediately flops down, kicking her legs to make a snow angel, while Noah forms a perfect snowball and aims it directly at Jake.

Jake dodges, laughing. "Hey, easy there, buddy! You wanna start a snowball fight already?"

Noah giggles, scooping up another handful of snow, and before long both kids are shrieking and running through the snow, their laughter echoing through the valley. I watch them, my heart full at the simple joy of the moment.

Jake turns to me, his eyes sparkling with mischief. "What do you say we leave them out here for a bit? I'll show you around the cabin."

"Trying to get me alone, Brooks?"

"Maybe." He holds out his hand. "But I did promise you a grand tour."

Inside, the warmth envelops me instantly—the smell of cedar and pine, the crackling of the fire. The cabin is stunning. It feels lived-in, not like some flashy vacation rental, but it still has all the perks.

The large stone fireplace dominates one wall, and plush furniture is arranged around it in a way that invites you to curl up with a blanket and never leave. The wooden beams overhead give the space a rustic, homey feel, and there's a Christmas tree, still undecorated, standing tall in the corner.

Jake steps behind me, wrapping his arms around my waist, his breath warm against my neck. "The housekeeper came by earlier, so everything's set. We've got food, drinks... and I figured we could all decorate the tree together."

My heart melts at the thoughtfulness. "That sounds perfect."

We stand there holding each other, the soft glow of the fire casting a warm light over the room. There's a peace here, a sense of belonging.

Jake pulls back slightly, his lips brushing my ear. "Think we should go rescue the kids before they turn into snowmen?"

I laugh, turning in his arms to face him. "We probably should."

He leans down, pressing a soft kiss to my lips, and I feel lit—the warmth, the love, the quiet promise of everything that's still to come.

CHAPTER THIRTY-FOUR

BEST CHRISTMAS EVE, EVER

---------------- :✦ ----------------

Charlie

The night air is cold, the kind that bites at your skin and turns your breath to mist, but the hot tub is warm and inviting, steam curling up into the dark sky. Snow falls lightly, dusting everything in white, and the cabin's twinkling lights cast a soft glow over the deck.

The kids are finally asleep, and it's just Jake and me now. I pull my robe a little tighter around me as I step outside, my bare feet darting over the frosty decking until I reach the hot tub. Jake's already in, leaning back, his strong arms stretched along the sides as he watches me approach. His gaze is smoldering, tracking every move I make.

He doesn't speak, just lets his eyes travel over me as I drop my robe. The ridiculous bikini I packed for this exact moment has his lips curling into a slow grin, his stare hot and possessive.

"Stop staring," I say, stepping up to the edge. The steam swirls around me, warm and soft against my skin.

"Can't help it," he murmurs. "Get in here."

I smirk, taking my time as I slip into the water, feeling the heat slide up my body. His eyes never leave me, dark with desire, as I sink down until the water bubbles around my shoulders.

"Tease," he mutters, reaching for me and pulling me against his chest.

"Maybe a little." I lean back into him, feeling the steady rhythm of his heartbeat against my spine. His quiet laugh vibrates through me, making me feel more at home than I ever have before.

We sit with the quiet night wrapping around us, the only sounds the occasional crackle of the fire inside and the soft hiss of snow falling around us. I close my eyes, letting the tension of the past few months melt away.

Jake shifts behind me, and I hear the soft click of his phone as he starts a playlist. Music drifts into the air, the kind of background noise that lets the quiet feel even more intimate. I'm about to say something when the first few notes of a familiar song play, and my eyes fly open.

Iris.

I freeze, instantly transported back to a different time. My cheeks heat as a flood of memories rush back—singing this very song in the camp kitchen, scrubbing pots and thinking I was alone. Of course, I wasn't. Jake had been watching.

"Oh God," I groan, sliding deeper into the water. "You remember this?"

Jake chuckles, his mouth brushing my ear. "How could I forget? You were giving the performance of a lifetime, scrubbing those pots like a rockstar."

"I was *so* off-key," I mutter, but he squeezes my hips.

"You were perfect," he says, pulling me closer. "You got so caught up in it, like nothing else existed. I couldn't take my eyes off you."

I laugh despite myself, the warmth in his words melting away my embarrassment. "I just really loved that song. It always got to me, you know?"

Jake's fingers trail up my arm, his touch steady and reverent. "You told me that you loved it because the lyrics meant something real to you. About loving someone so much you'd let them see you, flaws and all."

I swallow, feeling the weight of his gaze on me, the playful tension shifting into something deeper.

"Yeah," I say. "I guess I did."

He leans closer, his voice a low murmur in my ear. "Charlie, you're the only one who's ever seen me like that. You saw past the bravado, that hockey swagger and all the crap I hid behind. You just saw me—the kid who didn't have a damn clue who he was."

My throat tightens, and I turn in his arms, wanting to see his face. The look in his eyes is unguarded. He's not just saying this, he means every word.

"I should've kissed you that summer," he says softly. "I should've told you how I felt under those stars."

"We were just kids," I whisper, fingers trailing along his jaw. "We didn't know what we were doing."

"I did." His hands cup my face, thumbs brushing my cheeks. "I knew even back then that you were it for me. I thought time and distance would make it easier, but seeing you again has just made me more sure of what I lost. And this time, I'm not letting you go."

A fierce protectiveness blooms in his eyes, and my heart pounds in my chest as I realize he's been waiting for me. Waiting for me to understand what we've been dancing around for months, maybe even years.

"Do you remember karaoke the other night?" he asks suddenly.

I cringe, recalling my drunken attempt to pry out his feelings. "I was out of my mind, Jake. Don't make me relive that."

He chuckles, eyes twinkling. "You were trying to get me to say something."

"Yeah... I wasn't thinking straight."

"I was," he says, voice dropping. "I wanted to tell you then, but I didn't want it to be like that. Couldn't risk that you might not remember every word."

My eyes move to his and I try to respond, but no words come out. It's hard to believe someone could love me like this, so wholly and completely. I'm frozen, overwhelmed by the weight of this moment as he speaks.

"Twelve years, Lady Lightning. That's 4,514 sunsets since the last one we had on that hill. Countless games... A lifetime of moments without you." His voice catches, head shaking slightly like he still can't quite believe how much time has passed.

And all I can do is stare back.

"I love you, Charlie. I think I've loved you all along, even before I knew how to say it. You're the reason nothing else ever felt right, the reason I waited without realizing I was even waiting. And I swear to you," his voice pauses, wavering slightly, "you'll never doubt this. You'll *never* wonder how much I love you, because I'll make sure you feel it. Every damn day."

I'm speechless as his words wrap around me, floating up between us in the steam and sinking deep into the spaces within me. He doesn't just love me now—he loves every part of me, every version of who I've been and who I am.

For the first time in so long, I feel whole in a way I never thought was possible. My heart pounds as I meet his gaze, his emotions wide open, waiting.

"I love you, too," I whisper, the words trembling but certain. "So much, Jake. More than I ever thought I could."

A slow, breathtaking smile breaks across his face, his hands cradling my cheeks as he pulls me into a tender kiss.

"Say it again," he whispers against my lips.

I laugh softly, feeling the emotion bubbling inside me. "I love you."

"Again."

"I love you."

His kiss deepens, consuming me, and the last of the tension between us dissolves. There's nothing left but us, wrapped in the quiet of falling snow and the overwhelming sense of rightness.

"God, I love hearing you say that."

"Well, get used to it. I plan on saying it a lot."

"You better." He pulls me onto his lap, the water sloshing around us. His lips skim along my neck, breath warm against my skin. "I never thought it'd feel this good, knowing you love me too."

My hands slide up to cup his face, capturing his mouth in another deep, needy kiss. I feel him press up towards me, and we move together, the water lapping around us as the kiss intensifies.

"Show me how much you love me," I murmur, gripping his shoulders.

His hands glide down my back, unclipping my bikini top in one fluid motion. With equal ease, he slips off my bottoms and his shorts, leaving nothing between us.

A wicked grin spreads across his face as he hooks his hands under my thighs and lifts me to the edge of the hot tub, the cold air biting my skin. His possessive gaze roves over me, as if I'm the only thing in his world.

Maybe I am. Maybe I always have been.

"You're stunning," he rasps, reverence in his voice. "Mine. Every single part of you."

"Jake," I whisper, trying to reach for him.

"Spread your legs," he orders. I can feel the intensity dripping beneath his words as I let my legs fall open.

Kissing a trail up my inner thigh, he reaches my center and takes a long, languid stroke with his tongue. I let out a soft moan, gripping the edge of the tub as my body arches toward him.

"I love you," he mutters against me, lips teasing my clit. "And I love this fucking pussy." He latches on again, his tongue moving in tandem with his fingers like I'm some kind of sacred ritual he's unwilling to rush. "I'm gonna worship you every day for the rest of my life."

Pulling back again, he floats over to rest against the other side of the tub. His eyes lock on mine, and his lips curl. "Now come sit."

"What?"

"You heard me. Come sit. Right here." He taps his lips with his fingers, making damn sure I know exactly what he means.

I stare at him, my thoughts scattering.

"Charlie, I said come sit on my face. I want you on my tongue—*now.*"

I hesitate, letting out a nervous laugh. "I can't—"

"Yes, you can." His hands slide up to my thighs, tugging me gently. "Don't be a brat. Sit. I wanna taste you."

I scoff. "I'm not killing you on Christmas Eve."

"If that's how I go, it'll be the best damn Christmas present I've ever received." His tone softens, a trace of humor in it. "Now, get over here."

I take a deep breath, then move toward him. He guides me into place, and I hover, nerves alight. But his hands grip my thighs, pulling me down toward him with no hesitation.

"You're gonna tell me how much you love me while you ride my face."

Before I can respond, he's on me, his tongue finding its rhythm, dragging desperate, unfiltered sounds from my lips.

"Holy shit," I moan, fingers tangling in his hair. His tongue darts in and out, swirling around my clit as my eyes roll back.

"You're mine," he mumbles between each stroke. "Every. Single. Part of you. Now, tell me."

My body rocks against him, the waves of pleasure mounting. "I love you."

"That's right, baby," he rasps. "Tell me again."

"I love you," I pant, my voice breaking on the last word. His grip tightens as he devours me, his tongue relentless.

But before I can come undone, he pulls back, lips glistening and eyes dark with desire. His hands wrap around my waist as he lifts me back into the water, straddling me over his lap.

"Jake," I whisper, capturing his mouth in a searing kiss, tasting myself on his lips. His cock nudges against me, and I sink down onto him, his low groan echoing into my mouth.

"Fuck, Charlie, I love you so much." His voice is wrecked, rough with restraint. "You're so tight, so perfect... made for me."

A needy noise escapes me, feeling him fill me completely, the warmth of the water bubbling around us, the cold night air licking at my skin.

His mouth finds my nipple, teeth grazing as he sucks it into his mouth, his tongue flicking against it. I arch against him, helpless to do anything but cling to him.

"Don't fucking stop—oh, *god*..."

My head tilts back toward the sky, snowflakes melting on my flushed skin as steam rises around us. Every sensation blurs together, every sensation but him. The grip of his hands tightens, one sliding up to fist in my hair, pulling my head back to expose my throat.

"You're making me fucking feral, Charlie," he husks against my throat, tongue dragging a slow path up the column of my neck where a snowflake melts on my skin. "Say it. Tell me again while I make you come."

"I love you," I whimper. "You're it for me, Jake."

The tension inside me coils tighter, every thrust pushing me closer to the edge. His hands slide back to my ass, squeezing and spreading me, controlling the rhythm as his cock hits every spot that makes me gasp.

"That's it," he growls, voice dark and filthy. "Feel how deep I am? You're mine, baby. Every inch of you to fuck, every sound of you to claim, every damn heartbeat to love. I'm never letting you go."

"Jake," I gasp. "I'm gonna—"

"Not yet," he rasps, his thumb sliding between my cheeks, pressing lightly and teasing as his cock drives deeper. "You're gonna come when I say. You trust me?"

"Yes," I pant, every nerve on fire. "I trust you."

"Good girl," he praises, breath heavy.

His thumb presses more firmly, and the new sensation sends a jolt of pleasure through me. I cry out, clenching tighter around him, and his groan is primal as his control frays.

"Now, baby," he orders, circling my clit with his free hand. "Come for me. Come all over my cock."

The coil inside me snaps, and I cry out as the orgasm tears through me, my body shuddering around him. His hand tightens on my ass, pulling me down hard as he buries himself deep one last time, moaning my name like a vow as he comes.

For a long moment, we're motionless, the water sloshing softly around us as the world comes back into focus. His lips find mine, pressing soft, slow kisses along my jaw, my temple, my cheek.

"I love you," I whisper again, letting the words settle in the quiet around us.

Jake's smile is slow and content, arms wrapping tighter around me as if he'll never let go.

"Goddamn, Charlie girl," he murmurs. "You're my everything."

"Best Christmas Eve ever."

CHAPTER THIRTY-FIVE

YEAH PRINCESS, I HEARD YOU...

————————— ✦ —————————

Jake

I've always liked waking up early. Hockey drilled it into me. Early morning practices, ice time before the sun's even up.

But this morning feels different.

This isn't waking up for the grind, or the game. This is waking up to something I didn't even know I was allowed to want.

Before I even open my eyes, I can feel Charlie next to me. Her body soft and warm, tangled up with mine. My arm's draped over her waist, holding her close. I lie here for a moment, remembering how many more times I made her moan my name last night. I savor the way her hair tickles my chin, the sound of her slow breathing. Everything about this feels like home.

Yeah, this is different.

She shifts beside me, the subtle movement enough to pull me out of my dozing. I keep my eyes closed, soaking up the moment. But an unmistakable feeling of being watched prickles at me. She's staring at me. I know it.

"Mmm... caught you staring, Lady Lightning," I mumble, eyes still closed.

She huffs out a quiet laugh. "You were sleeping. I was admiring."

"Admiring the view?" I finally crack an eye open to find her watching me with that half-amused, half-in-awe look.

She still doesn't get it. She looks at me like I'm everything, when really, it's the other way around.

"Stalker's privilege," she teases. "You looked so peaceful. It's rare."

"More than just peaceful, judging by the way you're staring." I run my thumb lazily along her side. "But I get it. I'm a pretty good Christmas gift to wake up to."

She scoffs, but I see the smile tugging at her lips.

"What? You don't like this gift?" My hand drifts lower, tickling her side just enough to make her squirm.

"Jake, stop!" she laughs, trying to wriggle out of my grasp.

"Say it." I trap her under my arm, fingers tormenting her in just the right spots. "Admit I'm the best Christmas gift you've ever had."

She tries to escape, but I'm stronger and she knows it. Her giggles fill the room, breathless and free. "Okay, okay! You're the best gift ever!"

I pull back, grinning like I've won something big. "Damn right."

Her eyes roll, but I can see it—the way her whole face lights up, that warmth that she brings out for me. Every second with her reminds me how lucky I am, how right this all feels.

She's bright enough to rival the sun itself, like I've been orbiting nothing until her. All I want to do is be close to her, to bask in her light for as long as she'll let me.

We settle back into the pillows, my arm still wrapped around her. For a moment, everything's quiet. It's just us in this little bubble we've built together, and I can't imagine being anywhere else.

Then, out of nowhere, her voice cuts through the stillness.

"I love you."

Something shifts inside me every time she says it, like a part of me that's always been missing just clicks into place. I've heard those words before, sure—but never like this. Not from someone who sees me the way she does, who gets me down to my bones.

"Say it again," I say, my hands roaming up her back.

Charlie lets out a soft chuckle. "You're ridiculous."

"Come on," I coax, tilting my head to look at her. "It's Christmas."

"I love you, Jake Brooks."

"You have no idea how much I love hearing that," I whisper, brushing a strand of hair behind her ear. "It's my favorite thing you've ever said."

She quirks a brow, unconvinced. "I dunno. What if I said, '*hey Jake, here's a never-ending pile of brownies I made just for you?*'"

I snort and nuzzle into her neck. "That's basically the same thing."

"Hmm..."

"It is. But I still prefer hearing the words straight from your lips." I lean up and dot a kiss onto her nose, letting my eyes roam her face for a moment.

"Well, I'll keep saying it if you keep looking at me like that," she says, running her fingers lightly through my hair.

I close my eyes, savoring this moment, committing it to memory forever. Her touch grounds me, her words settling deep in my chest like they were always meant to be there.

"I love you, too."

"Merry Christmas, Captain Thunder," she whispers against me.

I can't help it. I kiss her slowly, like I'm trying to pour every ounce of how I feel into it. When we finally pull back, my forehead rests against hers, and I can barely breathe, my chest so full of love for this woman.

"Merry Christmas, Lady Lightning."

Then I kiss her again, just because I can.

***

I've never had a Christmas like this.

My childhood ones were a blur of tension, silence, and gifts that felt more like obligations than anything special. But this is different.

"Alright, who's first?" I ask, grabbing a brightly wrapped box and handing it to Noah. His face lights up as he tears into it, a wide smile spreading when he sees the LEGO set he's been wanting for weeks.

"Thanks, Jake!" Noah beams at me before diving straight into the box, ready to sort out the pieces.

I chuckle, ruffling his hair. "You're welcome, buddy."

Meadow's practically bouncing while waiting her turn, and I glance over at Charlie. She's on the couch, hair a mess, cradling a coffee, but she's smiling like she's never been happier. And hell, knowing I'm part of that is the best thing I've ever felt.

"Your turn, Little Lightning," I say, passing Meadow her present. She tears into it before I even let go, squealing when she sees the stuffed unicorn.

"Unicorn!" she yells, holding it up like treasure.

Charlie's laughing, shaking her head at the excitement, and my heart feels like it might explode with how much I love this. How much I love her. *Them.*

I grab the last set of gifts, three boxes wrapped in the same navy paper. Charlie frowns at me, curiosity piquing. I shrug, trying to play it cool.

"Last gifts," I announce, handing one to each of them. I grin, waiting for the reactions as they pull out matching Colorado Storm jerseys. With my name and number on the back.

"Brooks?" Charlie lifts a brow, but I see the smile she's holding back.

"Gotta start 'em young," I say. "Plus, we've gotta match for games."

Noah's already pulling his on, beaming from ear to ear. "I'm gonna wear this every day!"

"Don't encourage him," Charlie laughs, pretending to scold, but I know she loves it. She stands up, holding the jersey against her and tilting her head. "So, we're officially part of Team Brooks now, huh?"

"Damn right." I stand and pull her into my arms. "You've been part of the team for a while now."

She leans up and kisses me softly, and for a second everything fades into the background—just me and her, wrapped up in this perfect little bubble. But then Meadow's voice breaks through, tugging at my arm.

"Dada, look!" she says, her voice innocent and full of joy. She's put her jersey on back-to-front, 'Brooks' emblazoned across her front. "We're on the same team!"

I don't register it to start with. It's just Meadow, talking a mile a minute like she always does. But then it hits me, knocking the air from my lungs.

For a moment I can't move. Can't breathe. All I can do is see that one word echoing in my mind.

Dada.

The ground is shifting beneath my feet, the whole world tilting on its axis.

Charlie catches my eye, her soft smile brimming with a love that says everything without a word. She knows—she always knows. And she's giving me the space to feel this.

Meadow, oblivious to the impact of her words, tugs at my arm again, this time with more insistence. "Dada? *Did you hear me?*"

My throat bobs, and I blink, trying to push back the burn in my eyes as I crouch down in front of her. "Yeah, Princess," I say, my voice hoarse, fighting to keep it together. "I heard you."

A knot forms in my chest, tightening with every beat. Overwhelmed, thrilled, terrified. And damn if it's not breaking me in the best way possible.

"We're all on the same team," I repeat softly, the weight of the moment settling over me.

Meadow beams, blissfully unaware that she's just flipped my entire world upside down with that one word. She goes back to playing, her little world unchanged.

Noah glances up from his LEGO, his eyes flicking to mine for just a second before he goes back to his building. Like he's registering what just happened but doesn't know what to do with it. He doesn't say anything, but I can feel the shift in the air, a new kind of bond quietly taking root.

We'll figure it all out in time. Right now, I just want to let this sink in, let it fill up parts of me I didn't even realize were hollow.

I stand slowly, my mind still racing, and I catch Charlie's eye again. She's not freaking out. If anything, there's a knowing smile on her lips, like she's been waiting for this moment.

I clear my throat, trying to shake off the intensity of it all.

Charlie steps closer, lacing her fingers with mine and squeezing gently, grounding me in a way only she can. I look at her, and the smile we share is full of understanding, of unspoken promises we'll unpack later.

We let the moment settle, pretending it's as ordinary as any other day, even though I can feel its weight sinking into my chest.

"Guess I've got some big shoes to fill," I say, just loud enough for her to hear, a mix of pride and awe thickening my voice.

She leans in, her lips brushing my cheek. "You're doing just fine, Captain Thunder," she whispers, love woven into every word.

I wrap my arm around her waist, pulling her closer as we watch the kids continue playing, blissfully unaware of how much they've just changed my life.

In the back of my mind, that one word keeps replaying on a loop.

Dada.

It's not something I ever expected to hear, but now that I have, I can't imagine wanting to be called anything else.

This is what home feels like. To belong. To have a family. To be *Dada.*

And I wouldn't trade it for anything.

***

The cabin is alive with the sound of laughter and Christmas music, Mariah Carey belting out "All I Want For Christmas" for what feels like the hundredth time.

Charlie's been dancing around the living room like a woman possessed, singing at the top of her lungs, twirling Meadow in her arms, belting out the high notes with exaggerated theatricality. The kids are still hyped up on sugar from the chocolate Santas they've devoured, and the chaos of the morning hasn't slowed down much since.

I can't help but grin as I watch her, completely caught up in her own ridiculous performance, making goofy faces and spinning around like a kid herself. Every now and then she shoots me a look, daring me to join in, but I stay planted on the couch, chuckling at her antics.

She's had a glass or two of bubbly, and I'm pretty sure that's fueling this Christmas karaoke spree.

"I know you want to join me, Brooks!" she shouts over the music, her face flushed and her hair bouncing around her shoulders as she wiggles her hips.

"You're doing just fine without me, Lady Lightning."

She rolls her eyes dramatically, grabbing Meadow's hand again and twirling her in a circle as the song hits its big crescendo. Noah's dancing around the tree, trying to copy Charlie's ridiculous moves, and the whole scene is such a mess of happiness and chaos that I just sit back and soak up.

Later, when the kids are distracted with their new toys and Charlie's in the kitchen, I find myself staring out the window at the snow-covered landscape. The Rockies are majestic in the distance, towering over the cabin, with the sun starting to dip behind the peaks.

It's breathtakingly beautiful here. Quiet. Peaceful. And as I sit watching the snowfall softly outside, I feel the weight of the morning settling into my bones.

The kids, this cabin, Charlie—it's more than I ever thought I'd have. Being settled or having a family should terrify me. I always thought I'd mess it up, that I wasn't the kind of man who could make this work. My dad sure as hell didn't show me how to be a father.

But sitting here, watching this life grow with Charlie and the kids, I know one thing: I'm not going to be like him. I'm going to be better, show up every damn day, no matter what it takes.

I hear footsteps behind me, and a second later, Charlie's voice breaks through my thoughts.

"Hey, you," she says softly, settling down right on my lap.

I pull her close as she hands me a mug. Taking a sip, I realize it's cocoa with a splash of something stronger mixed in. "Eggnog?"

She smirks, leaning in to kiss my cheek. "You caught me."

I laugh softly, tightening my arm around her waist. She's still flushed from all the dancing, her cheeks pink and her hair a mess, but she's beautiful. She always is.

With her on my lap, we both look out at the snowy landscape in comfortable silence. The kids are quiet in the next room; everything feels still.

After a moment, I clear my throat. "I was thinking earlier... how different this all feels from when I was little."

Charlie shifts slightly, resting her head against my shoulder. "Yeah?"

I nod, staring out at the snow-covered trees, running my fingers absently through her hair. "Christmas was always tense. There were presents, a tree, the whole setup. But it never felt like this—like warmth," I say, my voice soft, feeling for the right words. "I guess I never really knew what Christmas was supposed to feel like until now."

Charlie tilts her head up. "You deserve all of this, Jake. Every bit of it."

I swallow, a need to get this out before I clam up. "I'm not gonna be like him," I say quietly, my voice rough. "I won't check out the way he did. I'm going to be there for them. For you. All of it."

Her hand moves to my cheek, thumb tracing a soft line against my skin. "You already are, Jake."

I take a deep breath, letting her words sink in. The weight of everything—my past, my fears, my hopes—it all feels so heavy sometimes. But sitting here with her, feeling her warmth against me, I start to believe it's possible. That I can have this and not screw it up.

Charlie shifts in my lap, grinning at me, knowing I need a mood lightener. "By the way, nice touch with the jerseys. Subtle, Brooks. Real subtle."

I chuckle, setting the mug down and pulling her closer. "What? We all need to match. It's about team spirit."

"Uh-huh." She rolls her eyes. "No one's ever accused you of being humble, huh?"

"Not when it comes to hockey," I admit, brushing my lips against hers. "But when it comes to this," I say softly, kissing her, "I'm the luckiest guy in the world."

She smiles against me, and for a moment it's just us, the snow falling softly outside, the warmth of the cabin wrapping us in a cocoon of quiet happiness.

Before I can say anything more, Charlie shifts slightly. "I um, wanted to talk to you about earlier..."

I tense for a moment, my heart stuttering as I remember that moment when Meadow flipped my world upside down. It hit me hard, but I wasn't sure if I should address it or let it slide.

"Yeah?"

Charlie pulls back just enough to watch me. "I just want to make sure you're okay with it. I know it was unexpected…"

I let out a breath, running a hand through my hair. I'm caught off guard, half expecting her to tell me how she doesn't think it's right, or it's too soon. But this is so quintessentially Charlie. To be checking *I'm* okay with it, instead of telling me how she feels. She's always in mom mode, always checking in on others first.

"Honestly? At first, I didn't know how to react. But…" I pause, throat tight. "It meant *everything*, Charlie."

Her eyes crinkle, and she reaches up to brush my hair back. "She loves you, Jake. You've been there for her in ways others haven't. It's natural for her to see you as that figure."

I nod. "I just… didn't want to overstep. I mean, I know I'm not her actual dad, and I wasn't sure how you'd feel about it."

Charlie's smile is warm. "You're *her Jake*. She sees you as someone who loves and protects her. That's what matters."

A wave of emotion hits me again. "You sure you're okay with it?" I ask quietly, needing to hear it again.

"I'm more than okay with it," she whispers. "I'm grateful for it."

I swallow, letting her words sink in.

Charlie cups my cheek, bringing my gaze back to hers. "You're their family, Jake… Just like you're mine."

I can't reply; I know I'll crack. So instead I lean in to kiss her deeply, hoping she feels everything I don't say.

CHAPTER THIRTY-SIX

I'LL WEAR THAT TITLE WITH PRIDE

———————— ✦ ————————

Charlie

I knew this Christmas would be special, but nothing prepared me for Meadow's innocent slip of the tongue. *Dada.* The word echoes in my head, stirring emotions I haven't fully unpacked yet.

It's been a short time since Jake entered our lives, yet he's woven into our fabric in a way that feels like he's always been here. The kids adore him. And I love him. *I love him.*

The memory of telling him last night ripples through me. I meant it with every cell in my body, even though they trembled while I said it. But hearing Meadow call him *Dada*? That's different. It's as if she's voiced a future I barely dared to imagine—a future I haven't let myself fully dream about until now.

I glance at Jake, sitting across from me on the opposite sofa. He's relaxed but weighted, still processing everything. I've seen all the emotions flicker on his face today. Surprise, pride, and something deeper, a quiet resolution that fills my heart in the best way.

Meanwhile, the kids are oblivious, sprawled by the fire and surrounded by wrapping paper and toys. I want to freeze this moment—just us, tucked in this winter wonderland, safe and happy. But I can't avoid the inevitable any longer.

I glance at the clock, and that familiar knot tightens in my stomach.

It's time to call Alex.

"Alright, guys," I say, trying to sound upbeat. "Time to call Dad."

Noah groans, resting his head on the fluffy rug where he's building a spaceship. "Do we have to?"

Meadow, on the other hand, bounces around with her doll. "We call Dada?"

"Yeah, honey bee," I say, reaching for my phone. "Just for a few minutes, okay?"

I glance at Jake, who's moved to an armchair out of camera view, his expression carefully neutral. But I know the signs: the tight jaw, restless fingers drumming his leg.

He hates this. And I hate it, too. I hate how it shifts the mood, how Alex still claims part of this day. But I also know Alex—possessive, controlling, always needing the upper hand. The last thing I want is unnecessary drama, especially on Christmas.

So Jake holds it in for me. For the kids. And I have to make the effort too, for their sake.

"I'm sorry," I say quietly, meant only for Jake's ears. "This won't take long."

He nods, frustration simmering beneath the surface. "It's fine. Do what you need to do."

Giving an apologetic smile, I turn back to the kids, open the video app and hit dial. The call connects, and Alex's face fills the screen, smile wide and overly enthusiastic.

I know that smile. The practiced kind, the one he uses for business calls when he's not really paying attention.

"Merry Christmas, Dada!" Meadow chirps, waving excitedly.

Alex's face lights up, but there's a hollowness only I can see. "Merry Christmas, Princess," he says smoothly. "And hey there, Noah."

"Hey, Dad," Noah replies, a little less enthusiastic than his sister, but still polite.

"Did Santa bring you everything you wanted?" Alex asks, using that overly cheerful tone—the one he uses when he's just going through the motions. The one that says, 'I'm checking the box.'

"Yeah!" Meadow holds up her doll. "Look! A dolly!" Her excitement is so innocent, so pure.

"Very nice," Alex says, but his eyes are already distant, checking out of the conversation. He glances at me briefly, his smile fading. "Where are you guys? That's not your place."

I stiffen slightly, forcing a smile. "We're at Jake's cabin."

There's a beat of silence, and I see his eyes narrow just a touch, though his smile stays plastered on. "Jake's *cabin*, huh? Must be nice."

There it is—the condescension. It's always there, bubbling beneath the surface. He hates it when I'm happy.

I catch Jake's expression flicker with annoyance, but I keep my voice neutral. "Yeah, it's been really nice. The kids are loving the snow."

Before he can respond, Meadow jumps up. "Oh, my shirt!" She runs off, little feet pattering. Noah barely looks up from his LEGOs. I nudge him gently, but he shrugs, not in the mood to talk to his dad.

Noah's quiet detachment from these calls has become a pattern. The further Alex drifts, the more Noah shuts down.

Alex's eyes linger on Noah before shifting back to me, as if he's about to comment further on our location. But Meadow returns, clutching the Storm jersey Jake got her.

"Look! Jake got me this!"

I glance at Jake, who's watching silently from the armchair, a small smile tugging at his lips. Meadow's holding up the jersey with Jake's name and number on the back.

Alex's eyes narrow, and I see the irritation he's trying to hide. "A *hockey* jersey, huh? Cool, Meadow. I hope you said thank you."

"Yeah, Dada!" Meadow says, her enthusiasm bubbling over. "It's just like his one!"

I brace myself for it—the moment he'll deflate her, like he always does.

There's a pause, and I see Alex's eyes flash. "Meadow, you're not a baby anymore. It's *Dad,* not Dada. Okay?"

Meadow frowns, little brows knitting together. She doesn't understand. She's three, and she loves him—the version of him she gets, when she gets it.

My eyes flick to Jake, who's gone deathly still, knuckles white as he grips the armrests. His body is coiled, as if ready to jump up and shield her from every sharp word. I know what he's thinking—that he'd never correct Meadow like that, never take the joy out of her words.

Heart sinking, I bite my tongue and force a smile, trying to keep things calm. "It's okay, honey bee," I say softly to Meadow. "Daddy just means you're a big girl now."

Noah glances between Meadow, the phone, and Jake. He doesn't say anything, but the tension feels palpable.

The conversation drags on for a few more minutes, with Alex making small talk. Each question feels like meaningless static, filling the space but meaning nothing.

"Alright, guys," I say finally. "Let's say goodbye to Daddy, okay? Time to wind down."

Noah gives a noncommittal wave, still barely looking up. "Bye."

"Bye, Dad," Meadow chirps, her earlier excitement now slightly dulled.

"Bye, kids," Alex says, eyes already drifting away from the screen. "And Merry Christmas, *Lottie*," he adds with a smug smirk.

I end the call before I have to respond, letting out a long, slow breath.

Jake's already standing, fists clenched, jaw tight, muscles straining.

"I'll be in the kitchen," he mutters, walking away before I can say anything.

The tension radiating from his body is undeniable. The kids are blissfully unaware, already back to playing with their toys, so I push myself off the sofa and follow him. My feet feel heavy, weighed down by what's coming.

I find him by the counter, hands gripping the edge of the sink, staring out into the snowy landscape. His shoulders are tense, whole body taut with barely contained anger.

"Jake..."

"I hate that guy."

His words are sharp, too controlled.

I step up behind him, resting a hand on his back. "You okay?"

He lets out a slow breath, shoulders still rigid. "He told her not to call him Dada," Jake says. "What kind of asshole says that to his own kid?"

"I know," I whisper, rubbing his back. "It's awful."

Jake shakes his head, turning to face me, his eyes clouded with frustration and something deeper: pain. "No, Charlie. She called *me* Dada today. And then he... he brushes her off like it's nothing. Like he doesn't even *want* it."

I can see the unresolved emotions of his own childhood swirling beneath the surface. He's holding it together, but this moment has pushed him over the edge.

"Jake..." I pause again. I don't know how to make this better for him.

He runs a hand through his hair, jaw tight. "I love those kids, Charlie. And hearing him dismiss her like that, like he doesn't even care..." His voice is raw and vulnerable in a way he doesn't often show.

"I know. I hate how he talks to them too, like it's a chore."

Jake's eyes flash with anger, tempered by determination. "He doesn't deserve them if that's how he treats them. He never deserved you, either."

"I know," I whisper, feeling the weight of his words. "But he's still their father, and they love him, even if he doesn't always deserve it."

He looks at me, expression softening as he takes my hand, grounding himself in our connection. "You know I'd never—"

"I know," I cut in, squeezing his hand. "You love them, Jake. They know that. And Meadow calling you Dada is because you've been there for her. She trusts you."

He studies me, then brushes his lips to my forehead. "But what if it confuses her? What if she thinks—"

"Jake," I say gently. "Meadow is three. She's figuring it all out in her own way. And you're becoming a constant. What Alex said doesn't change that."

His breath comes out shaky, like he's releasing some of the tension. "I just... I don't want to screw this up."

"You won't. You're not him, Jake. You're everything he isn't."

His fingertips trace my cheekbones, searching my face for reassurance. For a moment, he just looks at me, his eyes filled with a mixture of quiet fear and unshakable resolve.

"I'll never correct her," he says firmly. "If she wants to call me Dada for the rest of her life, I'll wear that title with pride."

A lump forms in my throat, and I nod, blinking back tears. "Thank you," I whisper, pressing a soft kiss to his lips.

He kisses me back, lips lingering on mine, and when we pull away, a new determination fills his eyes. "You've got me, Charlie. Them, too. Always."

I let the truth of his words seep into me. This is what I've wanted. A partner who will stand by me, who will love my kids as his own, who will fight for us even when things get tough.

He studies my face like he's reading every single thought running through my head, then pulls me into his arms, holding me tightly. Like he needs to anchor himself to something solid just as much as I do.

And I let him. Because if there's one thing I know for sure, it's that Jake is nothing like Alex.

CHAPTER THIRTY-SEVEN

IT'S NOT THAT KIND OF JEWELRY BOX

————————:✦————————

Jake

The house is peaceful now. The kids are asleep after a sugar-fueled, joy-packed day. I'm sprawled on the sofa, legs stretched out and Charlie curled up against my chest. We've got glasses of wine on the coffee table, and the only sounds are the crackling fire and the distant hum of the wind outside.

"You're gonna have to peel me off this sofa," I say, pressing a kiss to the top of her head. "I think I've consumed more sugar today than the kids."

"I saw you sneaking Christmas cookies earlier," Charlie chuckles, her fingers tracing patterns over my chest. "Don't think I won't use that to blackmail you with the Storm's nutritionist."

I squeeze her closer. "Can't prove anything. Besides, I wasn't the one belting out Mariah Carey like it was my last concert on earth."

She groans, hiding her face in my chest. "Stupid champagne. I must've looked ridiculous."

"You did," I agree with a chuckle. "But I love seeing you like that. So happy, not caring that you definitely weren't hitting those high notes."

She swats me, but there's a softness in her smile. These quiet moments, so completely easy and real, make me realize how much I love her.

After a while, I glance at the gifts on the coffee table that haven't been opened yet.

"Hey," I say softly, reaching for one. "We've got one last Christmas tradition to get to."

She sits up as I pull the small jewellery box over. Her eyes widen a little, and I see a flicker of surprise, maybe a hint of nerves. I know what she's thinking.

"Whoa there, tiger," I say with a wink. "It's not *that* kinda box."

She smirks, nudging me with her elbow. "I wasn't thinking... that."

"Sure you weren't." I hand her the box. "Open it."

Her fingers brush against mine as she takes it, and for a moment I just watch her—soak in everything I feel for this woman, this family we're creating.

Charlie lifts the lid carefully, revealing a delicate gold lightning bolt necklace with tiny diamonds embedded in the design.

"Jake..."

"I thought it suited you," I say. "Strong. Electric. Lady Lightning."

She stares at it for a moment, then back at me, a soft smile curving her lips. "It's perfect."

"You are," I murmur back.

I lift the necklace from the box, moving her hair aside to clasp it around her neck, grazing a soft kiss to her jaw. It rests just below her collarbone, catching the firelight.

"Thank you," she whispers, her eyes glistening.

I lean down and kiss her, tasting the faint sweetness of the wine on her lips. It's a soft kiss, the kind that settles deep in my chest. "Merry Christmas, Charlie girl."

"Best Christmas ever," she says, touching her new necklace as it sparkles. "Thank God it's not a ring."

I smirk, leaning in to nuzzle her neck. "Easy, Lady Lightning. Let me enjoy the moment."

She laughs, relaxing into me, and new feeling rushes over me. A sense of belonging; of permanence. Something I never had growing up.

As she turns in my arms, our eyes meet, and I feel it again—like every wall I've ever put up has crumbled. I'm giving her every ounce of my heart, hoping she'll protect it as fiercely as I do hers. It's vulnerable as fuck, but instead of turning to run, I'm thanking her for the privilege.

"So you thought it was a ring, huh?" I tease, brushing her hair from her face.

Charlie rolls her eyes, her lips twitching. "Maybe just for a second."

I laugh, but inside, the thought lingers. A ring, a future. Kids—more kids. That used to scare the hell out of me, but now it's something I want more than anything. Only with her.

"Well, Mr. NHL Superstar, it's your turn." She grabs her own gift from the coffee table and hands it to me.

I tear the paper carefully, revealing a leather-bound notebook. It's sleek and polished, the leather soft under my fingers. I flip through the blank pages, imagining the thoughts and ideas I'll jot down in the months to come.

"I've noticed you always have one around," she says quietly. "Thought you might need a fresh one for the new year."

She doesn't know it, but my notebook is more than just a place for hockey plays and strategy. It's where I've written every thought I've had about her since she crashed back into my life.

It's where I've drawn little stars for every fleeting moment I've thought about her, the kids, about this life we're building. The fact that she noticed this, and didn't push me to share it—it's everything.

I look up at her. "You have no idea how much this means to me."

She just smiles softly, fingertips running over my jaw.

I set the notebook aside and pull her onto my lap, holding her close. The warmth of her against me, the way she fits perfectly in my arms—I'm home. For a moment, neither of us says anything. We just sit there, the fire crackling softly, the warmth of the room wrapping around us.

"You're it for me, Charlie," I whisper against her ear. "I hope you know that."

She presses a kiss to the corner of my mouth, her lips trailing across my skin. "You're it for me, too," she whispers back.

The kiss that follows starts slow, but it doesn't stay that way for long. Her hands slide up my chest, and I feel her body pressing closer, everything in me lighting up.

"Think you've had enough Christmas spirit for the day?"

"Enough? Sweetheart, I've got enough Christmas spirit to last all night."

Before she can respond, I scoop her up and toss her over my shoulder. She yelps, laughing as I give her ass a playful smack.

"Jake!"

I carry her toward the stairs, her body wriggling in my arms. Every step feels like I'm walking toward something more permanent, something I want to hold onto for the rest of my life.

"Let's go, Lady Lightning." I playfully bite her side as we head upstairs. "Time for bed."

CHAPTER THIRTY-EIGHT

BEAR JAKE DOESN'T PLAY NICE WHEN HIS TERRITORY'S THREATENED

---◆---

Jake - 12 Years Ago

The campfire sparks into the night sky as the kids huddle closer, their eyes wide with a mix of fear and curiosity.

"Are there bears out here?" Tommy asks, voice trembling a little.

A couple of kids shift nervously, and I catch Charlie's eyes flick toward me. She sits up straighter, her eyes darting around the kids and out to the woods, like she's scanning the shadows.

"Nah, no bears around here," I say, keeping my voice calm. "You're safe."

Tommy exhales with relief, but tension lingers in the group. I can feel it—even Charlie's trying to play it cool, but her shoulders are a little tighter than usual.

"But... what if we were somewhere with bears?" Annie pipes up.

I chuckle, hoping to ease the mood. "If we were, you'd be fine. Bears don't mess with people unless they feel threatened. They're mostly protective of their territory and their young, so as long as you give them space, they'll leave you alone."

Charlie's watching me now, her eyes steady but with a flicker of unease. It's subtle, but I catch it. And I don't like it.

Without thinking, I add, "And if you ever ran into one, I'd be right there to make sure it didn't come close. You wouldn't have to worry about a thing."

The kids relax, a few leaning back on their logs with reassurance. But it's Charlie's reaction I'm watching for. Her lips curve into a small smile, and the tension in her shoulders eases. It's like she needed to hear that as much as they did.

A warmth settles in my chest, knowing I made her feel safe.

"You got a lot of bear facts, huh?"

I shrug, smirking. "Guess I just know how to deal with danger when I see it."

***

Jake - Present Day

Noah and Meadow's laughter fills the living room as I chase them, pretending to be a bear. It's chaos—the kind I've come to love. Meadow tumbles over the rug, landing in a pile of cushions, her laughter infectious as she clutches her teddy bear.

A month's passed since Christmas at the cabin, and every time I hear Charlie say she loves me, I feel it just as strong as the first time. Whenever I'm back from an away game, I'm here with Charlie and the kids. Every time I see her, I'm reminded of how much I love her, and I make sure she knows it.

I'm playing better than ever, and Coach has noticed. But when he asked me what's changed, I just smirked. Can't exactly tell him it's because I'm head over heels for a woman who I get to rail every chance I get. Who makes every day a win.

"Gotcha!" I scoop Meadow up, growling playfully. Noah jumps onto the couch, dodging me as I pretend to swipe at him.

"Bear needs a snack," I rumble, carrying Meadow around as Noah squeals.

Across the room, Charlie leans against the kitchen counter, watching us with a smile. There's something about the way she looks at me, that familiar pull always wanting her closer. Her hair's piled in a messy bun, cheeks flushed from the heat of the stove. She's cooking, glancing over every now and then to make sure no one gets hurt. But I know she trusts me. We've built that trust over these past few months.

"You're too good at that," Charlie teases, shaking her head as she slices vegetables. "Bear Jake might need to retire soon."

I chuckle, setting Meadow down and kissing her forehead. "Bear Jake's got a few good years left."

Moving to the kitchen, I brush my fingertips on the small of her back. The warmth of her skin through her shirt sends that familiar jolt through me. I've just got back from a string of away games and I'm desperate to get her alone.

She glances up at me, eyes glimmering with a playful challenge. "Careful, or I'll add you to the dinner menu. Bears might not like that."

"Depends what's on the menu," I murmur just for her, leaning in. "Could be worth it."

Her lips curl into a smile, and our eyes lock. My grin slips for a second as I let my gaze coast over her face, drinking her in. I'm about to pull her closer when the doorbell rings.

Charlie steps back, frowning. "Who could that be? It's almost bedtime." She wipes her hands on a dish towel and heads for the door.

I follow on instinct. We weren't expecting anyone, and an unannounced visitor at this hour is never a good sign.

When she opens the door, every bit of the evening's warmth is sucked out instantly.

Because standing there, all smug like he owns the place, is Alex.

"Surprise," he says, his voice laced with fake enthusiasm. "Thought I'd swing."

Charlie's hand tightens on the door and her body goes rigid. "Alex? Wh-what are you doing here?"

Alex shrugs, glancing past her into the house. His eyes land on me, and his smile falters before snapping back. "I'm in town for business, so I figured I'd drop by. Spend some quality time with *my* kids."

I stay back, leaning against the wall with my arms crossed, but every muscle in me is coiled tight. The memory of him telling Meadow she was too old to call him Dada still burns, let alone the way he speaks to Charlie. My hand flexes at the thought, but I force myself to stay calm. This isn't about me. It's about the kids, and I won't let him rile me up in front of them.

"It's late, Alex," Charlie says, her voice taut. "The kids are getting ready for bed."

He smiles, but it's all teeth. "Perfect timing then. I can read them a bedtime story." He steps forward like he's going to push past her, but I move instinctively, closing in behind Charlie.

"Bedtime's usually a family thing," I say, keeping my voice calm but eyes locked on his. "And right now, that's us." There's no mistaking my possessiveness, but I don't care. He needs to understand that it's not just about him.

Alex's eyes narrow at me, just for a second. He's not used to being challenged, especially not by me. But I don't back down.

Charlie glances between us as the tension builds. She knows I'm holding it together, but she's worried how this could go.

I look at her, giving a small nod. *I've got this, Charlie girl.*

"Look," I say, turning to Alex, "it's great you want to see the kids, but next time, give us a heads-up."

His jaw ticks, but instead of pushing back, his voice softens, dripping with faux sincerity. "I'm just trying to be a good dad, Lottie. You know I miss them."

I see the flicker of frustration in Charlie's eyes. She hates that nickname. I know it, and he damn well knows it too. But he continues to call her that, just to needle her.

"Fine," she says, stepping back and opening the door wider. "But you don't have long. They need to go to bed."

Alex smirks, strolling in. He brushes past me, his chest puffed out like he's the king of the damn castle. "I won't take long."

Meadow spots him first and bolts toward him, squealing. "Daddy!" She's too young to remember the broken promises.

"Hey, sweetheart!" he says, all smiles and his voice sickly sweet.

As this nightmare unfolds before me, I bite down hard on the inside of my cheek, watching as Alex scoops her up and spins her around. It's the perfect father act. He's all smiles and sweet words, lavishing her with attention.

Noah doesn't move from the sofa. He watches, assessing and unsure. And I know that look. The uncertainty, the wariness. He doesn't trust it. Doesn't trust *him*.

That protectiveness flares in me, stronger than ever. I know what it's like to be that kid, watching someone play the role of a parent but never really being one. He looks at me, his expression asking a question he's too young to verbalize: *Is this okay?*

I cross the room, placing a hand on Noah's shoulder, crouching to meet his eye. "Hey, buddy. You can go say hi to your dad if you want."

He hesitates, glancing at me before looking back at Alex. I squeeze his shoulder gently, letting him know I'm here, whatever he decides. It's his choice, and I want him to know he doesn't have to if he's not comfortable.

Finally, he nods and takes a few steps forward. But he doesn't rush in like Meadow. He's cautious. Observing. And Alex doesn't even notice.

He's too busy putting on his show for Meadow, his voice dripping with compliments. Noah stands there, uncertain. He watches as Alex sits on the sofa with Meadow on his lap, lavishing attention on her. I've been there before—watching my father dote on someone else, feeling invisible. Wondering why you're not as special or needed.

"You're getting so big, Princess," Alex coos, still ignoring Noah, who stands there like he's lining up to wait his turn for some sort of reward.

My fists clench. Charlie stands beside me, her arms crossed tightly, frustration mirroring mine. She's torn, it's obvious. She's fighting the urge to pull the kids away.

"You know, Lottie," Alex says, glancing back with a smirk, "you could've invited me to stay. Might do the kids some good to have both parents under one roof again."

Fuck this.

I step forward before I can stop myself, but Charlie's hand on my arm stills me. The longer this goes on, the more I want to throw Alex out on his ass. And the fact that he keeps calling her *Lottie*? It's just making me want to punch him harder.

"We agreed on boundaries, Alex," she says firmly. "This isn't the time."

"Right, *boundaries*," he chuckles, ruffling Noah's hair as he flinches slightly.

I watch as Alex continues to give Noah the bare minimum and lavish his faux adoration on Meadow. It's like he's making the kid pay a price for his uncertainty. I can't take it anymore. Noah clearly doesn't want to be there.

"Noah," I say softly. "How about we get your PJs on, bud? I'll help you brush your teeth before bed."

Noah's eyes flick to mine, and the relief in them is almost immediate. He doesn't say a word, but I can tell he's ready to get out of here. I give him a small nod, a quiet reassurance. *I've got you, bud.*

Alex watches, his smirk fading. "You don't even want to say hi to your dad, Noah?" His voice is soft but manipulative. Playing the victim.

Noah freezes. His eyes bounce between me and Alex, like he's waiting for someone to tell him what the right answer is. It tears me up inside.

I crouch down, hand on Noah's back. "It's okay, buddy," I say gently. "*You* can decide. You don't have to do anything you're not comfortable with."

There's no hesitation this time. Noah moves fully into my side, and I place a hand on his shoulder as we turn toward the stairs.

I catch Charlie's eye over my shoulder, seeing the gratitude in her expression. She's thankful I stepped in, but all I can think about is getting Noah out of this shit show.

As we climb the stairs, I feel Alex's eyes burn into my back, but I couldn't give two shits. My job right now is to protect Noah, not use him as some pawn.

Once upstairs, I kneel to Noah's level. "You okay, buddy?"

His head dips, and he shrugs. "I don't think Dad likes me much."

The words of his small voice hit hard, pulling me back to my own past. I see myself in him—in the way his voice wavers, in the way he shrinks under the weight of what he just said. That hollow ache of wondering why you're not enough. The memory is visceral, clawing its way back from a part of me I'd thought I'd buried. I won't let him feel like that. Not ever.

"Hey," I say. "Look at me."

He hesitates but eventually lifts his tear-filled eyes to mine, so heartbreakingly small and unsure.

"You're important, Noah. You matter so much more than you ever know. And if anyone makes you feel different, they're wrong. Okay? They're dead wrong." My voice wavers, and I take a breath, willing myself to stay steady for him. "You're smart, and kind, and brave. Anyone would be lucky to know you. And I'm *so* glad I get to be someone who does."

He looks at me, uncertain for a moment. Then his lip quivers, eyes flicking between mine, searching for something—hope, reassurance, anything to cling to. And then he breaks. His little face crumples as he stumbles forward, wrapping his arms around me like I might disappear.

I freeze as the force of his trust seeps into me, but then I pull him in, holding him close. My hand moves to the back of his head, smoothing his hair as he buries his face in my chest, his small body trembling against mine. I close my eyes and just breathe, the weight of his body solidifying something in me. A protectiveness like no other.

I've always known I cared about these kids, but this is different. This feeling is embedded into the very bones of who I am. Who I want to be for them. I don't know what I've done to deserve this kid's trust, but I know one thing with absolute certainty: I'll never break it.

"I've got you, buddy," my voice cracks a little. "Always." I clear my throat, hoping he doesn't notice. But he squeezes me tighter, like he knows exactly how important this is.

When he pulls back, I ruffle his hair, trying to ease the mood. "Let's get those teeth brushed."

He nods, and as we head toward the bathroom, I make a silent vow. I will *never* let this kid down. I'll be there for him, for Charlie, for Meadow. No matter what Alex does, no matter what happens.

I'll protect them.

***

We've all said goodnight to the kids, and I'm the last to come downstairs. I close Noah's door quietly. He fell asleep fast, curled up with his stuffed shark, safe and sound.

As I head down the stairs, the tension hits me like a wall. It prickles at the back of my neck and sets my jaw tight. When I step into the living room, Alex is sprawled out on the sofa, one arm draped lazily over the backrest, that smug grin plastered across his face.

It's the kind of look that makes me want to knock him out cold. Charlie stands by the kitchen counter, arms crossed, her face tight with frustration.

I walk up beside her, my palm instantly finding the flat of her back. holding back the urge to tear into him. I need to stay calm for Charlie—this isn't about me.

"You don't have to act so defensive, Lottie," Alex sighs, his tone dripping with condescension. "I'm just trying to be here for my kids."

Charlie closes her eyes slowly like she's holding back a storm. Another deliberate dig. He knows exactly how to push her buttons, and it's infuriating.

"Still calling her Lottie?" I say. "Cut the crap."

Alex barely acknowledges me, but the corner of his mouth twitches like he's pleased he got under my skin. He keeps his eyes on Charlie, ignoring me like I'm just background noise.

"I'm in town for business, Lottie. It makes sense that I'd see my kids. That a crime?"

Inhaling a slow breath, her voice is measured when she replies. "A heads-up would've been nice, Alex. You can't just show up whenever it suits you. We agreed."

He shrugs, leaning further back into the couch. "I don't see the problem. I'm their father, it's not like I'm some stranger."

I push off the counter, stepping closer, my eyes locked on him. "Maybe not, but you sure act like one."

His eyes finally flick to mine with a flash of irritation, but he doesn't bite. Not yet. Instead, his voice turns softer, smoother—more manipulative.

"Listen, I just want to spend time with them. What's the harm?"

Charlie's voice tightens. "The harm is you don't communicate, Alex. It's 9 p.m. on a school night. The kids need stability. You agreed to that."

He leans forward, smirking. "They seemed pretty happy to see me, especially Meadow."

That smirk nearly does me in. The urge to knock him out is growing, but I force myself to stay quiet. Charlie's in charge here.

"That's not the point," Charlie says, her voice firmer. "They need consistency. You can't just drop in and expect everything to be fine. If you want to be part of their lives, show up in ways that matter."

Alex hesitates, his bravado slipping for just a second. But he shrugs it off. "I don't need to check in every time I want to see *my* kids. Last I checked, I'm still their dad."

I can't hold back. "You sure? Because it looks like you breeze in when it suits you. That's not being a dad—that's being a visitor."

His stare sharpens, locking onto mine. "And what do *you* know about being a dad, huh? You think playing house with my wife for a few months makes you an expert?"

"Ex-wife," I bite back.

The air shifts. But I catch Charlie's gaze—pleading for calm—and I take a breath. "I know enough to show up. Every day. That's what they deserve."

Alex stands, finally facing me. "You think you can replace me, Jake? Think *you're* their father now?"

He's good-looking in that polished, too-perfect Ken doll kind of way—lean, six feet tall, blond hair combed back like he's just come from a business meeting. I could easily pummel him. The way he's sizing me up tells me he knows it too, so I stand my ground, glaring down at him.

"I'm not replacing anyone. But I'm sure as shit not gonna let you screw them up."

Charlie steps between us, her voice sharp. "Enough. The kids need us to be adults about this, Alex."

He glances at her, then smugly back at me. "Well, isn't this cozy? The perfect little family playing house, huh? But let's not forget, I've got more of a right to be here than he does."

Charlie's voice is cold as ice. "We talked about this. You don't get to come and go whenever you want. Communicate or don't come at all."

Alex's smirk falters, just for a second. But he recovers quickly, sliding his mask back on. "Alright, I'll play by your rules, Lottie."

"Her name is *Charlie*."

Charlie crosses her arms tighter, but I can see how drained she is. This whole thing is taking a toll on her, and it pisses me off how easily Alex plays the victim. "You don't care about them, Alex," she says. "If you did, you'd stick to the plan. Not just pop in on the off chance."

Good girl.

Alex shrugs nonchalantly, but there's an edge to his voice now. "You know Lottie, maybe we should rethink visitation, then. If you're going to be strict about this, maybe it's time to revisit that custody agreement."

My fists clench. It's bullshit, but the way Charlie stiffens tells me she's taking him seriously. He's a snake, throwing out empty threats just to get a rise out of her.

"Don't, Alex." Her voice is steady despite the tremble. "This isn't about you or me. It's about what's best for the kids."

"Oh, I'm sure you think so. But it's funny—just when I thought you couldn't do any worse, you bring *him* into their lives." He flicks his gaze toward me like I'm dirt on his shoe. "Must be nice, though. Handing off your responsibilities to someone who doesn't know better."

I'm done.

I step in front of Charlie, shielding her from the venom spouting from this asshole.

"You don't get to waltz in and act like you give a damn. You don't get to threaten custody like you're some devoted father when you're anything but. And you sure as fuck don't get to stand here insulting Charlie because your ego can't handle the life she's built *without you*."

He stiffens, like he knows I'm two seconds away from putting his face through the wall. But he doesn't back down completely. Instead, he throws on that fake smile, like he's won.

Charlie steps up to the front door, opening it with steel in her voice. "If you can't stick to the boundaries we agreed on, then we'll *definitely* revisit custody. And trust me Alex, you won't like how that turns out."

Silence. I can see the wheels turning in his head. Then he sighs, grabbing his coat. "Fine. Have it your way. But I'll be back to see them. I'm here for the next week."

He throws one last look my way as he heads out the door. "I'll be in touch, *Lottie*."

It takes everything in me not to kick him down the stoop.

When the door clicks shut behind him, the room feels like it's still buzzing with tension. Charlie's still facing the door, her shoulders sagging with the exhaustion of it all.

I'm across the hall in two strides, wrapping my arms around her waist, pulling her against me. "Hey," I whisper, pressing a kiss to her temple. "You okay?"

She leans into me, but I feel the weight on her shoulders. "Yeah, I'm fine," she says, but her voice trembles.

I turn her to face me, tipping her chin up. "You handled that so well."

Her smile is tired. "I just hate that it always feels like a fight. Like we're always in a battle."

"That's because he's a manipulative asshole," I spit. "But I've got you, Charlie girl. We're in this together. He doesn't get to control this."

She looks up, her eyes a little glassy under the stress and pressure. I rest my forehead against hers, protective instincts flaring. She's mine. Those kids are mine too, even if they don't have my DNA. And I'll be damned if Alex thinks he can mess with their emotions like this.

I press a slow kiss to her forehead, then her nose, then to her lips.

"Come on, let me take you to bed... I've got a way to help with all that stress."

She scoffs softly. "Jake Brooks, are you seriously using this moment to get me naked?"

I brush my lips against her ear. "Stress relief is important, y'know."

She rolls her eyes but links her hands behind my neck. "Fine. But if this is your idea of therapy, you'd better be good at it."

"Oh, Lady Lightning," I whisper, pulling her toward the stairs. "I'm the *best* at this kind of therapy."

CHAPTER THIRTY-NINE

I'LL MAKE YOU FORGET EVERYTHING BUT ME

―――――・✦・―――――

Charlie

As we climb the stairs, Jake's hand grips mine, grounding me with his presence. Reminding me he's here. His eyes are on me, scanning for cracks, like he's bracing himself to catch any piece that might shatter. I try to smile, but it doesn't reach my eyes. Not after tonight.

At the top of the stairs, I glance at him. His brow is furrowed, watching me carefully. He lets go of my hand, his fingers trailing up my arm as we step into the bedroom. I sink down onto the edge of the bed, the weight of Alex's visit settling over me like a heavy fog. I can handle him—I've done it for years. But every time he shows up, it's me left picking up the pieces.

It's exhausting.

I run a hand through my hair with a sigh. I hate how much space Alex still occupies. Hate how he shows up when it suits him, pushing his way in with that smug smirk. *Hate* how he calls me Lottie like he still has a claim on it. On me.

Jake steps in front of me, his eyes soft but cautious. He's waiting for me to say something, to let him in. But the words are stuck. My skin feels too tight, my muscles tense, and all I want is for this night to be over.

"He's always like this," I finally murmur. "Shows up, throws everything off balance, then disappears again. I'm always left to fix it."

He crouches down, hands gently covering mine. "You're not alone in this, Charlie girl," he says quietly. "I've got you."

I swallow. "I want the kids to have their dad. I really do. But they deserve better."

Squeezing my hands gently, something protective flickers in his eyes. His reaction to my words could have been jealous or bitter, but it's not. He hasn't tried to push Alex out, even though I know he wants to. He knows how much I want the kids to have their father, no matter how hard things are between us.

Tonight, he didn't come barreling in like some knight in shining armor. Jake stood beside me, letting me handle Alex. But I felt his presence, his eyes on me the whole time. *You're not alone in this.* He keeps saying it, and his actions keep proving it.

"You're doing right by the kids, Charlie," he says. "Don't let him twist that."

Another sigh escapes me, and I nod. Jake's right. Alex is the inconsistent one, not me. But that doesn't make it any easier to navigate.

I feel the burn behind my eyes and clench them shut. I refuse to give Alex one more tear. Jake's silent support is everything Alex never was. When things got tough, Alex bailed. When the kids needed consistency, he was onto the next business trip. Onto another affair.

But Jake—despite his own crazy schedule, training, media commitments—is here. Never hesitates. My throat tightens as I think about tonight, about how he stood quietly beside me for Noah, giving him the space to choose without pressure. It's the kind of support that makes my heart ache.

"What you did for Noah tonight... You have no idea what that meant to me."

Jake stands and pulls me up with him, wrapping his arms around me. I feel the weight of his chin on top of my head, breath warm against my hair as I melt into him. "You don't need to thank me," he whispers.

"I need a shower," I say, exhaustion clinging to me like a second skin. "Need to wash tonight off."

Jake nods, stepping back. "Want me to leave you to it?"

I consider telling him yes, that I need a few minutes alone. But I feel the pull—the need to be close to him.

"No," I say softly. "I want you with me."

Jake's eyes flash, a slow smirk forming. "Yeah?"

"Yeah... I missed you."

Without another word, Jake pulls off his t-shirt, and my pulse quickens. He's just back from a stretch of away games, and I haven't had a chance to really feel him yet. To remind myself that he's home.

We step into the ensuite and turn the shower on, letting the steam rise around us. I strip out of my clothes, each piece falling away like the weight of the day. The heat of Jake's body is immediate as he steps in behind me, his arms circling around my waist. His lips gently brush my shoulder, sending warmth through me that's entirely different from the water.

"Missed you, too," he murmurs, hands gliding up to my ribs, fingers tracing lazy patterns that make my breath hitch.

I lean back into him, tilting my head onto his chest. The hot spray hits my skin, and I sigh as the tension starts to melt. His lips move to my neck, pressing soft kisses that ground me in the moment. With Jake, I don't have to think about anything else. It's just us.

He kisses up to my ear, his breath hot. "Let me take care of you tonight."

"I hate that Alex can still get to me like this," I whisper before I can stop myself.

Jake's grip tightens, his voice possessive. "Don't mention his name right now. He doesn't belong here, not with us."

A shiver runs down my spine at the tone of his voice. "I'm sorry," I say, turning in his arms. "I just hate that he's still part of our lives."

Thumbs brush over my cheeks as he cups my face. "He might be part of the kids' lives," he says, leaning in. "But he's not part of yours. Not anymore."

My hands slide around his neck, and his grip tightens around me.

"I don't want to think about him," I say. "Wanna forget everything but you."

"I'll make you forget," he whispers.

The water washes over us, but it's Jake's warmth that grounds me, his touch that makes everything else fade. My mind whirs, and I try to silence it. I don't want to hold it all together. But the tension clings to me, stubborn.

"Jake..." I lift my head to meet his eyes. I know he sees it—sees how worn down I am, how badly I need to let go.

His fingers brush my cheek, wiping away droplets of water. "Tell me, Charlie," he says softly. "What do you need?"

I swallow, hands sliding down to rest against his chest. Strong, solid, hot as hell. Jake. I want to lose myself in him. To stop thinking, to stop holding it all together.

"Take control," I whisper, barely audible above the hiss of the shower.

A flicker of heat passes through his eyes as he registers. His grip tightens, pulling me closer. There's no space left between us, just the feel of him growing harder against me.

"You sure?" His voice is low and gravelly.

"Yes." My voice trembles, but not from fear. From need. From the overwhelming desire to let go. "Tell me what to do."

His lips curl into a wicked smile, and he makes a noise low in his throat as his hands glide up to stroke my nipples.

"Good. Get on your knees."

My legs almost buckle from the command alone, but I sink to the ground, keeping my gaze on his. He adjusts the shower head, water pulsing in rhythm with the heat building between us.

His cock sways hard and demanding in front of me, and I hold my breath waiting for his next instruction.

"Grab it," he orders, his eyes dark.

Without breaking eye contact, I wrap my hand around him.

"Mmm, harder."

"Like this?" My breath skates over the tip of him as I tighten my grip, working him up and down.

"Just like that," he husks. "Now open that pretty mouth."

I tease him with a flick of my tongue as I part my lips. His hand tangles in my hair, fingers curling with authority. "Eyes on me, baby."

I look up, loving the way his muscles ripple through his forearms as he fights for control. He presses forward, the tip of him brushing my lips. I swirl my tongue around him, drawing a guttural moan.

"God, your fucking mouth," he groans, pushing his hips forward. "I think about this every day. Sinking into you, fucking you like this."

The vibrations of my moan pull another deep sound from him. His hand slides to my jaw, thumb pressing against my bottom lip.

"You're mine, Charlie. Only I get you like this. On your knees, moaning around my cock like your mouth was made for it."

I hum at his words, and he thrusts harder, a hand flying out to brace against the tile, his body trembling with restraint.

"You like that, baby? You like my cock down your throat?"

I nod, bobbing my head faster, eager to please. I've never wanted anyone like this before—never been so desperate to draw out those sounds of pleasure from him. To know that I can unravel him like this. I sink down further, my hands gripping his thighs for leverage.

"Such a good fucking girl, taking me so deep." His voice drops lower, almost feral. "But I know you can take more."

He presses deeper until I feel him slide down my throat. My nose presses against his pelvis, and for a second I can't breathe. The intensity only makes me want more, to be consumed by him.

"Fuck, Charlie." He pulls back to let me breathe, but he doesn't stop, fingers gripping my jaw. "You look so good like this. So fucking perfect."

My hand moves to stroke his balls as I hollow my cheeks, taking him deeper. I pull back briefly, licking up the underside of him, keeping my eyes locked on his. His hand tightens in my hair, guiding the pace.

"I want you to remember this," he rasps, his voice molten with lust. "Whenever you're questioning yourself, whenever you're overwhelmed. Remember this moment—my cock down your throat, reminding you how incredible you are. Got it?"

A shiver runs through me as I nod at his words, my body igniting with a need that goes beyond desire. I slip a hand between my thighs, a wave of heat rolling over me as I touch myself, desperate to feel every inch of him.

"That's my good girl." His lips curve as he watches me obey, my mouth still working him.

Then, with a sudden motion, he pulls me up. His hands grasp my hips as he lifts me off the ground, and his eyes meet mine with the sexiest, dirtiest grin I've ever seen.

His mouth is on mine in an instant, like he's trying to leave his mark on me. The cool tiles on my back contrast deliciously with the heat between us, his cock pressing against my entrance as he holds me there, suspended.

"Jake..." I whisper, barely able to catch my breath as his mouth moves lower, sucking my nipple into his mouth, teeth grazing.

"Fuck, you're so wet," he murmurs against my skin, holding me open and thrusting up, filling me completely in one hard stroke. "You loved sucking my cock, didn't you?"

"Yes," I moan, my hands gripping his shoulders as he drives into me again, his rhythm frantic. My head falls back against the tiles, giving him access to nip my throat, leaving a trail of heated kisses.

Jake's voice rumbles against my skin. "You're mine, baby," he rasps, breath hot on my throat. "This body? This sweet, greedy pussy? All fucking mine."

"Don't stop," I gasp, my body rising and falling in rhythm with his. "I love everything you do to me."

His hands tighten on my thighs, his pace becoming more urgent. The sound of the water hitting the tiles blends with the slap of our bodies, creating a rhythm that makes my head spin. My hands slide down to grip his biceps, feeling the strength in every thrust like he's determined to own every part of me.

"That's my girl," he whispers, nipping at my earlobe. "You're doing so good, taking all of me like this."

I moan loudly, my eyes rolling back as the intensity builds between us. He smiles against my neck, teeth scraping my skin in a way that drives me wild.

"You ready to come for me, Charlie?" he growls. "You gonna come with me buried deep inside you?"

"God, yes," I breathe, my body trembling as I feel the tension coiling tight.

"My good fucking girl," he grunts, his thrusts becoming harder. "Come for me. Let me feel it, baby. I've got you."

His words are all I need. The orgasm crashes over me, consuming me whole. My body trembles, the tension snapping as I come so hard I cry out, my entire world narrowing to the feel of him buried deep inside me.

"Fuck, Charlie," he pants, his pace faltering as he thrusts one last time. His grip on me tightens as his own release follows, and he comes buried deep inside me with a hoarse moan.

For a moment, there's nothing but the sound of our ragged breathing and the water still raining down around us. Slowly he lowers me, our bodies untangling as he pulls me close, pressing soft kisses to my forehead, my cheeks, my lips, each one a silent promise.

"You're incredible," he says, his voice softer now but still laced with intensity as his thumb brushes my cheek. "And I'll remind you every damn day how strong you are, how perfect you are. My Charlie girl."

I smile breathlessly, feeling his unwavering presence, the way he's carved a space for himself in my heart.

"I love you," I whisper, tracing the edge of his jaw with my fingertip.

His dimple deepens as he presses one last lingering kiss to my lips. "I love you too, and I'll never let you forget it."

CHAPTER FORTY

HE'S TASTED MY WOUNDS AND LOVES ME ANYWAY

---·✦·---

Charlie

The warmth of Jake beside me is the first thing I notice as I blink awake. His arm is slung loosely over my waist, chest rising and falling in that steady rhythm that always seems to soothe me. For a moment, everything feels calm. Safe.

I close my eyes again, soaking up the security of his presence. The way he held me last night, like he was shielding me from the weight of the world... I don't know what I'd do without him. But the peace doesn't last long. The anxiety over Alex still lingers, curling through my mind.

Last night was a mess. Alex showing up unannounced, throwing around those veiled threats. I hate this—the uncertainty, not knowing if he'll show up or if he'll let the kids down again. The thought clings to me, heavy and suffocating.

I shift slightly, trying to push it down, but Jake stirs and his arm tightens around me. "Mm, stay," he murmurs, voice heavy with sleep. "You're warm."

A soft chuckle escapes me, and I snuggle back into him as he presses a lazy kiss to the back of my neck.

"Morning."

"Morning," I reply softly, turning in his arms.

He's barely awake, hair a mess and a sleepy smile tugging at his lips. I press my forehead to his chest, breathing him in. For a moment, the knot in my chest loosens, the tension dissolving in his steady presence. His fingers thread through my hair, a gentle rhythm that quiets my mind.

"You good?"

I nod, even though I'm not entirely sure it's true. "Yeah, I'm fine."

Jake cups my cheek, tilting my face up to his. Sleepy hazel eyes search mine, watching for any sign I'm slipping back into my thoughts. His thumb strokes my cheek, quiet worry evident even though he's trying to hide it.

"You're thinking about him. Don't let him take up space here."

I nod again, but the weight of everything still presses down on me. "It's hard to shake the feeling that he's going to push things further. Last night felt like the beginning of something."

Jake's jaw tightens slightly, his arm pulling me closer. "If he pushes, we push back. He doesn't get to walk in and disrupt your life, their lives." His voice softens when he adds, "Our lives."

I sigh, leaning into him, letting his warmth surround me. "I just don't want to lose any of this." My voice is barely above a whisper.

Jake pulls back slightly, his eyes locking onto mine. "You won't. I meant what I said last night, Charlie. You're mine. We'll figure this out."

His words are a balm, even as the worry still gnaws at the edges of my mind. "I know. I love you."

His smile widens, and he brushes my hair back, admiring me like he's memorizing the moment. "I love you, too." Then he leans in and kisses me like he's trying to erase the tension with every touch. And for a moment, it works.

We lay there for a few more minutes, wrapped up in each other. Jake's fingers trace light patterns on my skin, his presence grounding me, reminding me that the world outside can wait.

"You know," Jake hums, his lips grazing my temple, "we could always stay in bed. Skip the day altogether."

I let out a soft laugh. "Tempting, but I think the kids might notice if we never come out."

"They'll survive."

Before I can respond, a soft knock on the door makes us both freeze.

"Mum?"

Noah's voice is quiet. Jake moves beside me, reaching for a t-shirt and pulling it on.

I roll over and adjust my tank top, offering Jake a reassuring smile before calling out, "Come in, buddy."

Noah pushes the door open, his small face peeking around the corner. He clambers onto the bed, crawling between us. I smooth a hand over his hair as he curls up next to me.

"You okay?" I ask gently.

Noah nods but doesn't speak right away. After a moment, he whispers, "Are we seeing Dad today?"

My stomach twists, that familiar dread rising up in my chest. I hate this—hate how Alex holds the reins. Hate that I don't know how to answer Noah because his father hasn't bothered to give me any information.

"I'm not sure, honey," I say softly. "Your dad hasn't told me yet."

Noah's face falls, and he burrows into my side, quiet and still. "I don't want to see him," he whispers, and my heart aches.

I glance at Jake, who's watching us with that protective look, his jaw ticking slightly.

"You don't have to if you don't want to, Noah," I reassure him, stroking his hair. "It's your choice, okay?"

Noah nods, but the tension in his small body doesn't ease. Jake leans over, brushing a kiss against my shoulder before murmuring, "I'll go check on Meadow."

He ruffles Noah's hair gently before slipping out of the room, leaving the two of us cocooned in the warmth of the blankets.

A few moments later, I hear Meadow's happy shrieks echoing down the hallway, and then Jake walks by with her perched on his shoulder.

She spots us through the doorway as they stroll by. "Mama! Pancakes!"

I chuckle, pressing a kiss to Noah's head as I watch them disappear down the hallway. My heart feels full despite the lingering stress from last night. Jake's presence, the way he handles everything with such steady confidence, makes me feel like we can get through anything. Even Alex. Even custody threats.

"Come on, bud. Let's get some breakfast."

***

Downstairs, the smell of coffee fills the air, mingling with the sound of Meadow's giggles as she runs circles around the kitchen island. Jake's busy at the stove flipping pancakes, but he throws me a playful wink as I step into the room.

I scoop Meadow up, kissing her chubby cheeks. "Good morning, sweet girl."

She beams, snuggling into me. "Jake's making pancakes!"

I raise an eyebrow at him. "You're spoiling them."

Jake just grins, flipping another pancake. "Nothing's too good for *my* family."

There's a pointedness to his words, a quiet possessiveness that makes my heart swell. He's doing everything he can to show me he's here—that he's not going anywhere. That he's ready to be whatever I need him to be. The gratitude I feel for him, it's overwhelming.

He loves me and my kids fiercely. Even though I still house heartache, even though I have deep battle wounds. He's tasted them, and he loves me anyway. Despite them. Like I was always meant to be his.

Meadow darts over to Jake, immediately attaching herself to his leg. He laughs, lifting her up easily with one rippling forearm, reaching for his coffee with the other.

"You're clingy today," he jokes, kissing her head.

My throat burns. This man. If I focus for too long on the sheer love he showers us with, I'll lose it. So instead, I grab the coffee he poured for me, sipping it as I watch them.

For a moment, everything feels normal. Like this is just an ordinary morning. Jake with the kids, the rush of breakfast before the day begins. It's easy to forget the shadow of last night, the weight of Alex's sudden appearance looming over us.

I take a breath and remind myself I need to shift gears. I have a big client onboarding meeting next week, and my mind is already spinning with everything I need to do. This is a make-or-break moment for me at work, and it demands all of my focus.

Jake has practice today, and then he's off for another week of away games tomorrow. I know he's feeling the pressure too. The playoffs are looming, and the pressure is ramping up for him as much as it is for me.

Nina arrives a moment later, her energy filling the room as she helps get the kids ready for the day. "Morning, team! Ready to conquer the world?"

"Nearly," I mutter, but she catches it.

"Long night?" she asks quietly.

I nod, not elaborating. She doesn't press, but I can tell she's reading the tension hanging in the air. Nina has been with us long enough to know when something's off.

Jake moves beside me, his hand sliding to the back of my neck, a silent reassurance. I smile up at him, the tension easing ever so slightly under his touch.

The moment shatters as my phone buzzes on the counter and Alex's name flashes across the screen.

I pick up the phone, stepping out of the kitchen as I open the message.

> Alex: Meeting tonight to discuss the kids. 7 p.m. My hotel bar.

I stand there for a second, staring at the screen. Of course this isn't over. Alex wouldn't let it be that easy. And naturally, he schedules the meeting at a time that suits only him. Not even considering that 7 p.m. is dinner, bath, and bed time for his own children.

"Everything okay?" Jake's voice pulls me out of my thoughts.

He's leaning against the doorway, eyes steady but filled with concern. I hold up the phone, letting him read the message.

His expression hardens. "You're not going alone."

I shake my head, frowning slightly. "You've got away games starting tomorrow."

He steps closer, his eyes locking on mine with that unyielding intensity I've come to love. "I don't care, I'm coming with you. He's not pulling this shit again."

Jake wraps his arms around me, holding me close. "I'll stay here tonight, then head to the airport in the morning. We'll deal with Alex together."

I lean into him, grateful for his unwavering support. "I hate this. What if this custody thing is real? What if he actually follows through?"

His arms tighten around me. "Then we fight, and we win. You're an amazing mom, Charlie. You've built a beautiful life for your kids. Alex is just trying to rattle you. He won't follow through."

I close my eyes, letting his words sink in, but the anxiety still simmers. "I hate that he can still get to me. After everything, he can still get in my head."

"That's because he's a prick who hates he's lost control of you," Jake mumbles. "He's all talk. But you've got me. And we've got this."

I breathe him in, some of the tension loosening. "I love you."

"I love you, too." Jake's hands skate up to my shoulders and squeeze lightly. "Go get ready, I'll make sure Nina has everything she needs with the kids."

I close my eyes, shaking my head with a smile. Moments like this show me just how deeply Jake cares, how he's always two steps ahead, thinking of me. He loves me enough to know all the little things as much as the big ones.

"You're too good to me," I say, pressing a soft kiss to his cheek.

"Trust me, Lady Lightning," he says, pulling me in, voice dipping into that possessive timbre. "You make it easy. And it's not about being too good, I want to be the man you deserve."

I nod, swallowing the lump in my throat. "Okay, I'll go get ready."

"Good," he says, his hands sliding down to give me a light tap on the ass as I head for the stairs.

I laugh, already feeling a little lighter. Like he's injected his own brand of sunshine into my veins, and I'm ready to take on the day.

CHAPTER FORTY-ONE

PUSH ME, ASSHOLE. SEE WHAT HAPPENS

———————— ·✦· ————————

Jake – 12 Years Ago

The sun's setting, casting a golden glow across the field, but something's off. Charlie sits alone in the bleachers, her head bent low, fingers twisting in her lap. The usual spark in her is dim. She's closed off, and it sends a ripple of unease through me.

The rest of the group is still goofing around on the field, but I can't focus on anything except her. Something's wrong. I feel it, a heavy shift in the air that sinks into me. And I don't like it one bit.

I move toward her, an instinct kicking in. I don't know what's wrong, but it doesn't matter. She's not okay, and that's all I need to know.

I make it to the bleachers and slide in next to her, close enough to feel the tension. "Hey. What's going on?"

She glances at me, her eyes rimmed red. My chest tightens—she's holding back tears. "Nothing," she whispers, voice small. "It's stupid."

I shake my head, jaw tight. "If it's got you like this, it's not stupid."

She sighs, running a hand through her hair. "I don't know... Everything's just messy. I don't know what I'm supposed to do when this is over."

Her shoulders sag, and it's like watching the strongest person I know crumble. Something inside me twists—hard.

"You're not stuck, Charlie," I say, voice rougher than I intend. "You'll figure it out, you always do."

She forces a smile, but it doesn't reach her eyes. It's hollow. "Sometimes it feels like I'm just pretending I've got it together."

Anger stirs in me. Not at her, but at whatever or whoever has made her feel like this. Like she's not enough. The need to shield her from it flares in me, fierce and possessive. I've never felt this surge to protect before. Without thinking, I reach out and place my hand on her knee.

"You don't have to have it all together. Not with me."

Her wide eyes snap to mine, startled. Something passes between us, unsaid but undeniable. I hold her gaze like I'm daring her to look away, but she doesn't.

Her hand slides over mine, sending a jolt through me, solidifying this unspoken connection. It's a move that's too much for just friends. Too close. Too familiar. It's something more, something deeper than either of us will openly acknowledge.

"Thanks," she whispers.

I tighten my grip on her knee as I lean closer. "And if anyone ever makes you feel less than what you are, they'll answer to me."

The words come out fierce and low, more promise than threat. They hang between us, heavier than I intended. But I mean every damn word. The thought of someone hurting her, of making her feel any less than the magic she is... It sets something raw and primal alight in me. Something that says she's mine to protect.

She laughs softly, but there's a weight to it, like she knows exactly what I'm saying. Like she knows I'd go to war for her if I had to.

We sit there in the dusky light, my hand on her knee, hers on mine. The world around us fades, like it always does when it's just the two of us. But this time, it's different. It's not just comfort in her presence—it's the weight of something deeper. It's the weight of realizing I'd do anything for her.

Always.

***

Jake - Present Day

I pull up outside Charlie's office, the SUV humming as I wait. The building looms, reflecting the fading light, and I feel the weight of everything settling on me.

The custody threats, the away games coming up, playoffs looming, and Charlie's big client meeting next week which she's been working on non-stop.

When I see her walking out of the building, her usual confidence seems a little dimmed. Her sharp blazer and sleek hair could fool anyone else into thinking she's in control, but I see the heaviness in her eyes.

She slides into the passenger seat, offering me a tired smile. "Hey."

"Hey." I lean over to kiss her. "How'd work go?"

She sighs, sinking back into the seat. "Busy. Lots of prep for this onboarding meeting next week. If it goes well, it'll really prove I'm capable here."

I glance at her as I pull back into traffic, watching her fingers fidget with the hem of her sleeve. She's stressed, and I don't blame her. "You're gonna kill it, Charlie. No one can handle this stuff like you do."

She tries to smile, but it doesn't quite reach her eyes. "Thanks. It just feels like there's so much at stake, and I can't shake the feeling that something's gotta give.

I take her hand, my thumb brushing her skin. "Nothing's gonna give. You're amazing at your job, and we'll deal with Alex together."

Her gaze shifts to the window, tension creeping back into her shoulders at the mention of him. "It's not that simple, Jake," she says quietly. "You don't know him like I do."

Something in her tone catches me off guard, and I glance at her. "Tell me."

For a long moment she's quiet, like she's weighing whether or not to open up. Then she lets out a soft sigh. "I was always a bit of a trophy wife in his eyes, my career never really mattered to him."

I keep my eyes on the road. "He tried to make you quit?"

"All the time, but especially once I was pregnant with Meadow. He thought I should just stay home, focus on the kids. He never got how much my work meant to me."

There's a tightness in my throat as I hear the frustration in her voice. How could anyone—especially someone who claimed to love her—try to diminish what she loves? The thought pisses me off.

She swallows, avoiding my eyes as she continues. "He was so manipulative, so obsessed with his own job. And he'd use his size to intimidate me when things didn't go his way. He never hit me, but he always made me feel like he could."

A hot and sharp protectiveness surges in me. Just thinking about that asshole looming over her makes my fists clench on instinct.

"He's a fucking coward."

She nods, but her eyes are distant, haunted by memories I can't erase. "I kept telling myself it would get better, that I could make it work. But I was miserable. He was never there for the kids, he let them down every time. And that's what broke me the most. I didn't care if he hurt me, but the kids..."

Her words echo my own memories of growing up in a house where my mom was always miserable, stuck in a marriage she didn't have the strength to leave.

I take a deep breath, trying to keep my anger in check, but I can't stand hearing her talk like that.

"You did the right thing, Charlie."

She nods, but there's still a shadow of something dark in her expression. "I know, but I stayed for the kids. I thought I could hold it together for them. But then, a week into our trial separation, he slept with someone else."

"He *what*?"

She shrugs, expression pained. "And then I found out there had been others. Affairs on his business trips. He said they didn't mean anything, that he just needed to scratch an itch when he wasn't with me."

Nausea twists in my gut. "He said that to you?"

"Yeah," she says quietly. "Like it was nothing."

I can't even put into words the rage I feel at this moment. The idea of him treating her like some accessory—when she's the whole damn world—makes me want to drive straight to his hotel and rip him apart.

"Charlie..."

"I know." She laughs, but it's humorless. "That was when I knew it was really over. He didn't care about me or the kids. It was always just about him."

Hearing the way he hurt her makes my chest burn with fury. I already hate the guy, but now I want to break his neck. It's like he's tried to erase the best parts of her, piece by piece. And I can feel every protective instinct in me flare, demanding I shield her from this kind of hurt forever.

"He's disgusting," I spit. "And he thinks he can stroll back into your life and pull rank? Screw that. He's fucking delusional."

She doesn't say anything, just stares out the window as we drive. Finally, she speaks, but her voice is small and uncertain. "I don't know what he's planning, and that's what scares me. He's never cared much before, but now... There's nothing in writing, no legal documents proving I have custody. It was all verbal. He could try to take them back."

"He won't," I say firmly, but underneath, I'm rattled. I don't like that there's nothing in writing, no formal custody agreement. That bastard could use that to tear her life apart. "We'll fight him if we have to. You're a great mom, Charlie. No court is going to take those kids away from you."

She nods, but I can see the doubt still lingering in her eyes. And honestly, I can't blame her. Alex isn't just some asshole we can brush off—he's a real threat, and I hate that he still has this hold over her.

We pull into the hotel parking lot, and I cut the engine, letting the silence wrap around us. I can feel the anger still bubbling under my skin, but I force myself to focus on her. On Charlie.

She's staring out the window, her shoulders stiff, bracing herself for whatever bullshit Alex is about to throw at her. And I realise it's not just anger simmering in me anymore, it's fear.

Fear that despite everything, Alex might still have some hold on her. Fear that he'll manipulate her, and she'll cave. Because she's got such a big heart and always tries to do what's best for the kids—even if it means giving in to him. Giving another piece of herself. I can't let that happen.

I turn to her, grabbing her hand. "Charlie girl, look at me."

She blinks, her eyes finding mine, and I don't soften the way I usually do. I need her to see how serious I am. How much I mean every word that's about to come out of my mouth.

"I love you," I say, my voice full of conviction. "You and the kids, you're everything to me. I don't care what he says—he's not controlling this. Got it?"

Her eyes widen slightly, and I can see the doubt still lurking there, the worry she's still carrying. The part of her that thinks maybe she needs to give Alex some kind of power to keep the peace. But I need her to get this. To really hear me.

I grip her hand tighter, leaning closer. "He's done, Charlie. You've been so strong, but I'm here now, too. I'm gonna fight for you, for the kids. And I'll rip him apart before I let him mess with you again."

She exhales shakily, her lips parting like she wants to say something, but I keep going. I'm not leaving any room for doubt. Not when it comes to this.

"And I'm not saying this because I think you need saving," I continue. "But I'll be damned if he thinks he's gonna use his words, his size or the past to control you. I'm not letting him pull you back into his web."

That's what's driving me mad—the thought that Alex could still find a way to get to her, through the kids or through his threats. And worse, that Charlie still might give in, thinking she has to.

"You're mine, and he doesn't have any power over you." The words coming out harder than I intend. "Or the kids, or what we have. You're safe with me. "

Her lips tremble as she leans into me, her forehead pressing against my shoulder. "Jake..."

I cup her face, tilting her head back up to look at me. "You don't deserve this, Charlie. Not him, not his bullshit. You deserve someone who's going to stand with you. Someone who'll fight with you. And that's exactly what I'm going to do."

For a moment, it's just us, the intensity of what I'm saying crashing between us. Her eyes are full of so much emotion but I see the shift in her, like she's finally letting herself believe me.

"I love you," I whisper, but it's not soft. It's a promise. "And I'm not going anywhere."

She leans into my touch, her eyes closing for a second as she exhales shakily. I kiss her slowly, like I'm sealing my promise into it.

When we pull back, I brush a thumb over her cheek and nod toward the hotel. "Ready?"

She takes a breath, straightening in her seat. "Yeah. Let's do this."

As we step out of the car and walk toward the hotel bar, that possessiveness claws its way up inside me. I've kept it in check for her sake, but every time I think about Alex—what he did to her, how he treated her, how he let those kids down—I feel it pushing me closer to the edge.

He can try all he wants to mess with Charlie, but he's not getting near her again.

Not with me standing right here.

***

It doesn't take long to spot him. He's sitting at a table in the corner, that smug look already plastered in place. I fight the urge to wipe it straight off him.

He rises when we approach, but I catch the flicker of surprise when he spots me with Charlie. It's subtle, just a quick clench of his jaw. Good. Let him be pissed.

"Jake," he says smoothly, his voice dripping with mock surprise. "I thought you'd be off... what is it, hitting pucks or fighting on the ice by now?"

"Funny, I'm real good at both. You wanna find out which one I feel like doing today?"

Alex's smirk falters for a split second before he turns his attention to Charlie. "Hi, Lottie."

His voice is soft, trying to play the caring ex-husband, but I see right through him. He's sizing her up, already playing the game. I grit my teeth, but I keep quiet—for now.

We take a seat across from him, and I position myself so Charlie's tucked against my side, my arm draped casually over the back of her chair. Alex's eyes flick between us, a flash of irritation crossing his face.

"Nice of you to bring an escort," he says, his tone dripping with condescension. "But I thought this meeting was about the kids."

"It is," Charlie says, her voice steady, though I can hear the strain underneath. "Jake's here because we're in this together."

"*Together*," Alex repeats, leaning back in his chair with a smirk. "Must be nice to have a... distraction." His eyes dart to me and I resist the urge to nail his hand to the table. "Although I do wonder how stable that is for the kids. You know, them being dragged around while you're playing house."

I can see what he's doing—trying to rattle her, trying to plant those seeds of doubt. She's strong. But I also know this is a pressure point for her because she's always thinking about the kids, about their stability. And he's weaponizing that against her.

Charlie doesn't bite. "The kids are fine, Alex. They're happy."

"Are they?" He leans forward, resting his elbows on the table like he's trying to be reasonable. "Lottie, I know we haven't always seen eye to eye, but I'm genuinely concerned. I don't think this move was the right decision. Uprooting them like that... It's a lot for them to process. And now you're throwing a new relationship in the mix? That's a lot of instability for two young children."

I feel Charlie stiffen beside me, see her knuckles turning white as she grips the edge of the table. My hand moves instinctively to her knee, a steadying touch. But internally I'm seeing red. I can't believe this asshole has the nerve to talk about stability after everything he's done.

"You're worried about stability?" I snap. "That's a joke, coming from someone who only shows up when it suits him."

Alex's gaze lands on mine, and I see the flash of irritation again. Good. Push me, asshole. See what happens.

"Look, Jake," he says, charm slipping. "I know you think you're swooping in here being the hero, but this is between me and Lottie. It's about what's best for *our* kids."

"Exactly," I spit back. "Which is why they're here with *her*. Because she's the one who's been there for them. Not you."

The smirk falls away, his face hardening as he shifts his focus to Charlie. "You know what? I'm done playing nice. I want the kids back in New Zealand, and I'm taking this to court."

Charlie inhales sharply. I tighten my grip on her knee, a silent anchor, but I can see it—the fear creeping over her face.

Alex leans in, his voice dripping with faux concern. "It'll be easier for you to just agree now. You could find another job back home. Save the kids the trauma of a legal proceeding. Don't you want to avoid all that stress for them? For you?"

And there it is. The manipulation. He's laying it on thick, trying to guilt her into agreeing, pretending like he's doing it for the kids. I can see her struggling, trying to hold strong, but the doubt is creeping in. And that's when I lose it.

I stand abruptly, the chair scraping against the floor. "We're done here."

Alex looks up at me startled, but his lips curl into a mocking smile. "What's the matter, Jake? Can't handle a real adult conversation?"

I brace my hands flat on the table, leaning in just enough to let Alex know I'd like an excuse to throw him over it. "You don't give a shit about those kids. So you don't get to sit here, manipulating her and pretending you do."

His jaw twitches, but he stays silent. He knows exactly how close he is to crossing a line.

I straighten up, turning to Charlie. "We're leaving."

She looks up at me conflicted, wanting to fight, but the weight of it all is pulling her down. I'm not letting him twist the knife any further.

"Charlie," I say softly, holding out my hand. "Let's go."

She swallows and takes my hand, standing slowly. Alex watches us, his smirk returning, but I don't give him the satisfaction of reacting.

As we turn to leave, his voice follows us, smug and sharp. "This isn't over, Lottie. It'll be easier for everyone if you just come home."

I turn, ice in my voice. "She *is* home."

With that, I place my hand on the small of Charlie's back, guiding her out of the bar. She leans into me as we walk, the weight of it all pressing down.

She's strong, but even strength has limits. And I'll be damned if I let Alex touch it.

CHAPTER FORTY-TWO

I CAN'T BE THE ONLY ONE STANDING IN THE RING

————— ✦ —————

Jake

T he house is too quiet when we walk in. Nina says goodnight, leaving the silence echoing around us. Charlie paces the living room, arms crossed tightly, barely holding it together. I can see the cracks, her panic creeping in, and all I want is to fix it.

"I can't believe him," she mutters. "How does he still have this hold over me?"

Her words twist like a knife, because that's exactly what's happening. Alex still has some kind of fucking grip on her. Despite everything we've talked about, he's still in her head, twisting her emotions. It makes me feel powerless.

"Charlie, don't let him get to you like this," I say, fighting to keep my voice calm. "You know exactly what he's doing—manipulating you, again."

She stops pacing, eyes flashing as they meet mine. "I know that, Jake! But what am I supposed to do? He's threatening to take my kids back to New Zealand!"

"He won't," I say firmly, taking a step toward her. "He's a bluffing asshole. He's trying to scare you into giving in."

Her arms drop to her sides and she stares at me. "But what if he's not bluffing? What if he actually tries to take them? He's got the money, the resources... I have no legal documentation, no agreements, no paper trail. It's all been verbal."

I reach for her, but she steps back, and the distance between us suddenly feels like a chasm.

"Then we'll fight him," I say, my voice sharper than I intend. "We'll fight like hell and we won't back down."

She shakes her head and starts pacing again, and then she mutters the one thing that makes the floor drop out from under me. "Maybe it'd just be easier if I went back to New Zealand."

I stop dead, the room suddenly too quiet, too still.

"*What*?"

She shrinks slightly, looking down. "It'd save the kids from all this. Might be easier."

"You're kidding, right?" The hurt leaks through despite me trying to hold it back. "You're seriously telling me that after everything you've built here, you'd give up because it's *easier*?"

Her eyes fly up, blazing with guilt and frustration. "I'm not *giving up*, Jake! I'm trying to think about what's best for my kids. What am I supposed to do?"

"You don't run," I snap, the frustration boiling over. "You *fight*. You think giving in to Alex is what's best? Running back to New Zealand, away from the life we're building? From a place where the kids are safe and loved by someone who actually gives a shit?"

She flinches, her lips tightening. "It's not about running away. It's about protecting my kids. Going back might be better for them."

The hurt flares hot in my chest. "Better for them—or easier for you?"

"That's not fair," she whispers.

"No, what's not fair is even *considering* leaving what we have here. Do you really think I'm going to just stand here and let you walk away from all of this? From *us*?"

"You don't have kids Jake, you don't get it!"

And there it is. The gut punch.

The words hang between us as I step back, feeling the air leave the room. Her eyes widen as she realizes the words she just threw at me, and she stands there, staring.

It's not that she's wrong—I don't have kids of my own. But fuck, that doesn't mean I don't understand. I love her kids like they're mine. I'm here fighting for them, for her—and she's telling me I don't get it. Like I can't relate. Like it wouldn't completely break me.

"You think I don't understand because I don't have kids?" My voice wavers. "Maybe I don't get every part of it, but I know I'd do anything for them. I *love* Noah and Meadow, and I love *you*. I'd lay down every single thing for you and the kids. And if you don't see that, if you don't trust me to stand beside you... then what the hell are we even doing?"

"Jake," she breathes, guilt written all over her face.

I walk to my bag and pull out my leather-bound notebook. I hesitate, running my thumb over the worn edges, then hold it out to her.

"What..."

"Open it."

She takes the notebook, her hands trembling. As she flips through the pages, her eyes gloss over as she realizes what's inside. Page after page, star after star, each one different, each one meaningful.

"I started drawing these every time I thought about you," I explain. "Every time I missed you. When I missed the kids. When I thought about what our future could look like."

Her fingers brush over a page where Meadow's name is written, surrounded by tiny, delicate stars. Another with Noah's, bold and bright, shining like a constellation. Her breath hitches when she finds one with her name in the center, a cluster of stars around it, like they're orbiting her.

"You're the stars, Charlie. You and the kids... You're my whole fucking night sky."

Tears spill down her cheeks, and she closes the notebook, clutching it to her chest. "Jake..."

"I've been in this from the start," I say, stepping closer. "But if you're willing to run the second things get hard—"

"I'm not *running*!" she shouts, eyes frantic with tears. "I'm trying to protect them!"

"By doing exactly what Alex wants? I've never had anything like this, Charlie. Never had anyone in the stands, never had anyone love me the way you and the kids do. *You're my family*. And you're telling me you're willing to walk away—like this was nothing?"

She goes quiet, and I can see her crumbling in front of me. But instead of reaching out to comfort her, I'm frozen. Hurt. Shocked.

"I'm not walking away from you," she chokes out. "But I don't know how to fight Alex. I don't know how to keep everything from falling apart."

The hurt tightens in my chest. It's like she hasn't heard a single word I've said. "You don't have to. I'm here, Charlie. *I'm right fucking here*, fighting for you and the kids. But now I'm wondering if you even want that... Or if this is just an excuse to bail."

Her face crumples, and I instantly regret those words. But I can't take them back. The truth is, I need to know. I need to know if she really wants this. Because right now, it feels like I'm the only one fighting for it.

"I'm not trying to bail, I... I'm not giving up on us, I just don't know what else to do."

I close my eyes, trying to keep it together. "I get it. But you don't just walk away because it's hard. I love you so much it scares the hell out of me. And I've been all in with you, *always*. But I need to know you're all in, too. I need to know you're not gonna give up."

She wipes at her cheeks with the back of her hand, but the tears keep coming. "I just... I don't want to lose my kids. And I don't want to lose you either, but I feel like I'm gambling. I don't know how to fix it!"

I can't breathe watching her like this. Broken. Panicking. I hate it. I hate that Alex has driven her to this point, that she feels like there's no way out. And it kills me that no matter how much I keep telling her, it's not enough to make her believe she's safe, that we can fight this together.

"Charlie, listen to me." I step closer, my hands gripping her shoulders. "You won't lose the kids. You won't lose me. But I need you to *fight with me*. I can't be the only one standing in the ring."

She lets out a sob and my heart clenches. For a moment, all the frustration and hurt fades. I can't stand it anymore.

I pull her into my arms and hold her tight against me. Pressing my lips to the top of her head, I close my eyes as I try to ground myself in the feel of her. "I know you're scared, baby. I know."

She clings to me, her face buried in my chest. "This is what I was scared of from the beginning. This mess, Jake. *My* mess... And now you're dragged into it." Her voice is tight, words spilling out like she's admitting something painful she can't hold back. "I warned you. I'm too broken, too complicated."

I pull back just enough to cup her face in my hands, forcing her to look at me. "Don't say that." My voice is rough, breaking with emotion. "You're not broken, baby. And you sure as hell aren't dragging me into anything. I *chose* this. I chose you." I exhale sharply, my grip tightening like I'm trying to hold her together. *Hold us together.*

"But fuck, Charlie." The words come out thick and tangled in frustration. "You have to stop pushing me away."

My voice is sharp, but I can't help it. The thought of her thinking she's too broken, too messy for me—it cuts me to the core. *She's all I want.*

Her tears keep falling, hands gripping my shirt as if she's afraid to let go. We stand there wrapped in each other's pain, until I can't take it anymore. I love her too much to see her so torn apart. But I also can't ignore that she's wavering, that she's thinking about running.

I pull back again, my thumbs brushing away her tears. "I love you, Charlie," I husk, trying to keep myself together. "But I can't be the only one in this. I need you to want it, too. I need to... I need to go."

Her face crumples, gutting me. "You're leaving me?"

"I'm not breaking up with you," I clarify quickly. "I promise you. I just need time to cool down. You're still mine, got it?"

Hands loosen on my shirt, and I see the devastation in her eyes. It's fear, deep and raw. The fear of losing everything. Of losing me.

And fuck, it's nearly enough to break me.

Her throat works as she swallows. "I'm sorry," she whispers, barely getting the words out.

I press my lips to hers, tasting the salt of her tears. I kiss her like I'm trying to brand something into her, to make sure she knows I'm still here. That I still love her.

When I pull back, my own throat burns, my own voice cracking at the edges. "I've told you from the beginning, I'm *all in*. And when I get back, I need to know that you are, too. Or this won't work."

Her tears fall faster, her body shaking, but I force myself to step back, heart in tatters. I can't give her the comfort she needs right now—I need her to understand what's at stake.

I need to know she loves this enough to fight for it.

"I love you." My voice is rough, scraping against the wreckage of this moment. "So fucking much."

Then I turn and walk toward the door, every step killing me, every part of me screaming to stay.

***

I've been staring at the ceiling for hours, trying to calm the fuck down. Night's fading into morning, but all I see is her face when she said going back to New Zealand might be easier.

Easier. Like this isn't worth fighting for.

I glance at my keys on my dresser. She gave me a key weeks ago. That key means something. *We* mean something.

I could've grabbed that key and gone back to her hours ago, crawled into bed, wrapped her in my arms, and told her it's going to be okay. But I didn't. Not after the way we left things. We both need space to breathe.

From the second we reconnected, something clicked into place, like I'd found what was missing in my life. And now, hearing her suggest leaving? Packing up the kids and *going*?

It hurts. Hell, it fucking kills me.

I thought we were solid. That she was in this as much as I am. And now I'm not sure.

But there's a part of me that gets it. *Fuck*, I get it. I don't have kids. I've never had to be terrified of losing them. But I've lost people. I know what it's like to stand on the edge of something good, only for it to be ripped away.

I close my eyes, trying to reel it all in, but my mind spins. Alex, that *asshole*. He knows exactly how to get in her head. Knows how to make her question everything, and it's working.

But I remember her face as I left. How her voice cracked when she admitted she was scared. She's not walking away because she *wants* to. She's walking away because she's scared. And hell, deep down I'm scared, too.

I bet she's lying in bed right now, thinking it's all falling apart. But it's not. She's my family. The only family I want. And there's no way I'm letting Alex, or fear, or anything else take them away from me.

The sun's starting to creep up, and it's taking everything in me not to drive back to her.

I grab my phone, the time glaring up at me, thumb hovering over her name. There's enough time to talk before I head to the airport. So I hit call before I can second-guess myself.

It rings. Once. Twice. My gut twists. Finally, a click on the other end, but she doesn't say anything. I can hear her breathing—shallow, ragged.

"Hey," I say softly, trying to keep my voice steady.

"Hey," she whispers, sounding wrecked. *Shit.* My chest clenches and I run a hand over my face, wishing I could be there to hold her.

Silence stretches between us, heavy and raw.

"You okay?" I ask, already knowing the answer.

"I've been better. Didn't really sleep."

"Me either."

More silence. I can't take it. My fingers twitch with the need to pull her close.

"I'm sorry, Jake," she croaks. "I didn't mean it. Any of it. I was scared, and I... I didn't mean what I was saying."

I close my eyes, swallowing the lump in my throat. "I know," I say quietly. "But it still hurt. Hearing you say that, it felt like you were giving up on us. And I can't—" My voice catches. "I can't lose you, Charlie."

"You're not going to lose me," she says, her voice desperate. "I love you. I *love* us. I was just scared."

"I know," I whisper again, hating that this conversation is happening over the phone instead of with her in my arms. "I love you, too. More than anything."

We both fall silent again, the weight of everything still hanging between us. I can tell she's struggling, and I want to fix it, but I'm not sure how.

"I'm heading to the airport soon," I say. "But I'll be back before you know it."

"Okay," she says softly.

I hesitate, but I need to say it. "Just... be careful with Alex. I don't trust him."

She sighs, and I can practically see her rubbing her temples. "I'll be fine, Jake. I'll handle it."

"I know you will," I say, but it doesn't make me feel any better. "I'll call when I land. And Charlie, we'll figure this out together. Okay?"

She's quiet for a moment. Then finally, "Okay. I love you."

"I love you, too. And tell—" I pause, my voice catching again. "Tell Noah and Meadow I love them, too."

"I will," she manages to say, and I can hear her tears.

My heart aches as I end the call, scrubbing a hand over my face. I stare at my phone for a long moment. I don't want to leave things like this, but I don't have a choice. Not right now.

This couldn't be happening at a worse time. Every game right now is critical. We're fighting to make the playoffs, and I can't afford to let my focus slip. If we lose a couple of games, our shot at the postseason is done. But if I lose *her*... God, I don't think I could come back from that.

Before I head out the door, I shoot Zoe a quick text.

> **Me:** Hey, keep an eye on Charlie while I'm gone. Alex is still here and I fucking hate him.

Zoe: Don't worry, big guy. I got her. That asshole tries anything, he'll regret it. Focus on winning—I'll keep her safe. ☒

I smirk at my phone, then pocket it. I have no doubt Alex would regret messing with Zoe. As I step into the cold morning air, my heart feels split. But I shove it down. Compartmentalize.

I just hope Charlie can do the same.

CHAPTER FORTY-THREE

GUESS WHO'S COMING TO DINNER?

---·✦·---

Charlie

I stare into my coffee, stirring it in slow circles, but it does nothing to ease the mess in my head. Guilt sits heavy in my stomach, each sip of caffeine only adding to the jitters since last night.

Zoe's perched on the edge of her seat across from me, coffee in hand, one eyebrow arched like she's ready to pounce. There's a smirk on her lips, but her eyes are sharp and too perceptive.

"Charlie, stop," she says, leaning forward. "You've been stirring that coffee like a cauldron for five minutes. I'm about to go find you a black cat and broomstick, but you're way too pretty for a wart."

I try to smile, but it doesn't quite land. No energy for a comeback. I drop the spoon, my fingers tightening around the cup instead.

Her eyes narrow as she takes a slow sip of her own coffee. "Alright, what's going on? You've been stuck in your head since you walked through the door."

I sigh, glancing out the window like it might hold answers. The coffee's warm scent fills the air, but all I can taste is the guilt lodged in my throat.

"Jake left this morning," I mutter.

Zoe nods. "Yeah, I know that. It's a week. You two are disgustingly obsessed with each other, but you'll survive. You've gone longer without seeing him."

I shake my head, biting my lip. "It's not that. We had a huge fight last night... and I said something really stupid."

She leans back, surveying me closely. "Define stupid. Like '*I don't like your hair*' stupid or '*I made out with my ex*' stupid?"

I frown. "Why would a comment about hair cause a massive fight?"

"They're all obsessed with their hair."

I laugh weakly, but it's hollow, and the weight in my chest doesn't lift. "Well, thank God it wasn't that."

She grins, but she doesn't continue the joke. Instead, she tilts her head, studying me. "What happened?"

I hesitate, my fingers tightening around my cup. "I told him maybe I should go back to New Zealand. For good. Because I'm scared of what Alex might pull with the custody stuff." I feel the shame creep up my neck. "And then when he protested that, I told him he didn't understand because he doesn't have kids."

Zoe's eyes widen. "Jesus. You really went for the jugular, huh?"

The guilt presses down again. "Yeah."

She's quiet for a second, then leans in, her elbows resting on the table. "Why would you say that?"

"I don't know. I panicked," I admit, rubbing my temples as the tension knots tighter. "I didn't mean it, Zoe. It just... came out."

Zoe's gaze softens, but there's a seriousness in her tone when she speaks. "I get it. Alex has you on edge, and you feel cornered. But Jake's *crazy* about you. Don't spiral over one fight."

"I know," I say quietly, "but Alex is such a nightmare to deal with. The idea of a custody battle, of losing the kids, it feels like too much. Like maybe leaving would be easier than—"

"Easier for who?" Zoe cuts in. "You? The kids? Jake?"

I pause, running a hand through my hair. "I didn't mean it like that. But now I think Jake believes I'm not serious about staying. Or about him."

Zoe stays quiet for a moment, letting the words hang between us. Then she asks, "*Are* you?"

I swallow hard, blinking back the sting in my eyes. The emotions have been flooding through me in waves—fear, guilt, regret—they're all tangled together and I can't separate one from the other. But there's no doubt when it comes to my love for Jake.

He's never wavered, never given me a reason to doubt him. And I've let fear take over, let Alex and my insecurities twist everything until I couldn't see straight. But running isn't the answer. It never was.

My voice is husky when I nod my reply. "I love him so much it hurts."

Zoe's expression softens, and she leans back again, nodding like she's waiting for me to finish.

I think back to the night under the stars all those years ago—when we promised to chase our dreams, to follow our paths. Back then, it seemed like the universe was pulling us in different directions. But now I realize that *Jake* is my path. He's my home. And I was stupid enough to let fear almost pull me off course.

What if he doesn't want me anymore?

The thought sends a fresh wave of panic through me. Deep down, I know Jake. I know how much he loves me. But what I said last night—it's a wound, and it'll take time to heal. He needs space, and I need to figure out how to show him that I'm all in, too.

I can't lose Jake. Not because of fear, and *definitely* not because of Alex.

"I panicked," I say again, the words heavy. "What if Jake doesn't want me after this?"

Zoe snorts, setting down her cup with a clink. "Girl, you've got to be kidding me. Jake's not walking away because of one stupid argument."

"I told him I might leave," I remind her. "I threw New Zealand in his face, Zoe."

She purses her lips and nods. "Okay, so you freaked out. You're human! And we all know Alex is an A-grade asshole, the custody stuff is no joke. But Jake? He's been obsessed with you since the second you two reconnected."

I glance out my office window again, watching a couple stroll by below, bundled up against the cold. Their easy laughter feels like a world away from the mess I've made.

"That's the thing," I say. "Jake's been perfect. He's patient, supportive, and he loves the kids like they're his own. And then I go and drop the '*I might leave*' bomb on him like an idiot."

Zoe narrows her eyes, but there's no judgment. "You didn't drop a bomb, you just showed him you're scared. And honestly? Jake's not Alex. He's not going to punish you for freaking out. If anything, he'll get it."

"He's gone for a whole fucking week. I don't think I can cope with not speaking to him for that long."

She scoffs, giving me a knowing look. "You two can't go five hours without texting each other. He'll probably FaceTime you between every damn period just to mark his territory."

I let out a small laugh. She's right. Jake always checks in, no matter where he is. He makes me feel like I'm never far from his mind.

"I hope so."

Zoe stands, hands on her hips. "Here's what's going to happen. Get through the day, make your pre-planning your bitch. And when Jake calls, which he will, you'll talk to him like a normal person. No overthinking every damn thing. Okay?"

My shoulders rise as I take in a deep breath, the tension loosening just a fraction. "Okay."

She smirks, leaning down to grab her cup, eyes twinkling mischievously. "And hey, look on the bright side—makeup sex is the universe's way of rewarding all that tension. Might as well make the most of it."

I can't help the laugh that bursts out of me. "You're incorrigible."

Zoe gives me a wink before turning toward the door. "That's why you love me, babe."

***

The office buzzes, but I can't focus. My eyes keep drifting to the notes for Friday's client meeting, but the words blur. All I can think about is last night's fight, the tension lingering like a shadow.

My phone buzzes beside me, the screen lighting up with a new message. I grab it, hoping it's him.

Jake: How's your day?

A familiar tightness twists in me. He's checking in, but the words feel heavy. Measured. He's still hurt, and even though we're both pretending, everything's not fine.

Me: Busy. Trying to stay focused for the meeting on Friday.

I set the phone down, but the guilt lingers. This meeting is supposed to be my moment, my chance to prove myself. But all I can think about is Jake—the hurt in his eyes when I threw leaving Denver in his face. The silence that followed.

Jake: You've got this. I know it.

Tears burn the back of my eyes. His belief in me is so certain, but I can't shake the fear gnawing at me—that I might lose him because of my own panic.

Me: Thanks. How's practice?

Jake: Good. Missing you.

I stare at the screen, heart sinking. I miss him too, but I don't know how to bridge this gap between us. Our fight hangs unresolved, and every text feels like we're dancing around it.

> **Me:** Miss you, too. Wish we could talk.

The dots appear, then disappear again. The tension builds as I wait for his reply.

> **Jake:** We will. Once I'm back.

I close my eyes. He doesn't want to talk about it over the phone. He's holding off, waiting until we're face-to-face. I understand, but it doesn't make the weight any easier to carry.

My phone buzzes again, but this time it's not Jake. Alex's name flashes on the screen, and my stomach clenches.

> **Alex:** I'll come for dinner Thursday. Need to see the kids.

Of course. Alex, swoops in and invites himself over, like having a family dinner with him doesn't sound like the worst fucking thing in the world right now. I grit my teeth. Jake's halfway across the country, and I'm just trying to hold everything together.

> **Me:** Thursday works.

I send the message before I can overthink it, knowing it's going to be a disaster. Alex always manages to insert himself when things feel too fragile to handle. But

I have no choice. I need to show I'm being reasonable about letting him see the kids.

The stress gnaws at me as I pick up my coffee, the warmth doing little to settle my nerves. I'm stretched too thin. Between Jake, Alex, and the kids, I feel like I'm trying to balance a hundred spinning plates, and I'm terrified they're all going to crash down around me.

A thought hits me: I need backup for Thursday. If I do this solo, Alex will pull his usual bullshit. I quickly pull up a new message to Zoe.

> **Me:** Mayday. Alex invited himself over for dinner on Thursday. Can you come? Please?

I hit send and stare at the screen, tapping my fingers against the desk. It only takes Zoe a few seconds to reply.

> **Zoe:** Mayday? Babe, I'm offended you think I wouldn't be there to run interference. I'll be there with bells on. Wine too. And a tranquilizer gun for Alex.

A laugh escapes me before I even realize it, and I type back quickly.

> **Me:** If you have one, bring it. You'll need it more than I do.

> **Zoe:** I'm booking in for a fresh set of claws just for him. Thursday it is.

I exhale, feeling a tiny bit lighter knowing that Zoe will be there. She lives for any opportunity to knock him down a peg, stripping his ego to shreds with a smile on her face.

I roll my shoulders, focusing back on my computer screen. This day can't end soon enough.

***

I'm exhausted. It's been the longest day, and all I want to do is sleep for a hundred years—or at least until Friday when Jake gets home. As I settle into bed, my phone buzzes. This time, it's not a text. It's Jake, video calling me.

I hesitate for a second, my heart racing as I swipe to answer. His face fills the screen, and even through a phone, seeing him makes my chest ache.

"Hey," he says, his voice carrying a familiar longing, like he's been thinking about me all day.

"Hey." I try to smile, but my throat's dry. His hair's still damp from a shower, and the sight of him looking so good makes the distance between us feel vast.

"You okay?" he asks, eyes scanning my face like he's studying a battle report.

I nod, but it's weak. "Yeah. Just... work stuff. Kids stuff. You know."

"Uh-huh." He doesn't buy it. "And Alex? He sniffing around?"

I sigh, shifting under the covers. "He's coming Thursday for dinner."

He pauses, like he's collecting himself. "Why?"

"The kids need to see him, I can't just block him from seeing them..." I shrug. It's a tough position, but I can't not let him see his own kids. Especially when he's throwing custody threats around.

Jake sucks his bottom lip into his mouth, like he wants to say more but is holding back. "Make sure Zoe's there."

I snort. "Yeah, already organized. She's sharpening her claws as we speak."

A small smile tugs at his lips. "Good. She'll keep him in line."

"I hope so." My voice is softer than I intend, and I see the way his expression tightens. He knows there are things I want to say, but he doesn't push. Not tonight.

"I miss you," he says. "Wish I was there *with* you right now."

I nod, blinking back the tears that threaten. "Me too."

There's a pause, and for a second I wonder if he's going to bring up the fight. But he doesn't. Instead he watches me, his gaze steady and warm, and even though we're miles apart it feels like he's right here with me.

"Get some sleep, Charlie girl," he says gently. "We'll talk when I'm back."

I nod again, my heart twisting with the weight of everything I want to say. "I love you."

"Love you too, always." His expression softens, lips curving into that crooked smile.

The words wrap around the hollow ache, soothing it just enough to make it bearable.

"Night," I whisper, my voice barely steady.

"Night, beautiful."

***

Thursday arrives too quickly, and tension hits the second Alex walks in. Meadow bounces on the couch, clutching her unicorn, while Noah watches us all, gauging the mood.

"Hey, Lottie," Alex says with a cocky grin, strolling in like he has some claim on this place. My spine stiffens at the nickname, but I force myself to smile for the kids' sake.

Behind me, Zoe steps into the foyer at the perfect moment. Alex's face shifts, irritation flashing. She's the one person who's always seen through his bullshit.

"Well, if it isn't Mr Biannual Visits himself!" Zoe coos, all teeth. "How's the world's most involved father doing?"

Alex's smile tightens as he steps into the kitchen, smugness flickering under Zoe's sharp tongue. "Zoe," he says with forced politeness. "Always *such* a pleasure."

"Oh, the pleasure is mine," Zoe replies, her eyes flicking to the kids, who are oblivious to the daggers being exchanged. She gives Meadow a wink. "Excited for dinner with your dad, sweetie? Such a rare treat!"

"Yeah!" Meadow beams, clutching her unicorn. "Daddy's staying for dinner!"

"Of course," Alex replies, but his eyes spear Zoe as he straightens his cuffs. "So what brings you to dinner? Thought this was just a *family* thing."

Zoe settles into a dining chair like it's her throne. "Oh, you know me. I'm like the aunt you never wanted but got anyway. Couldn't resist the chance to see *you* again."

I bite back a smile. Alex expected me to struggle through this dinner, but Zoe's presence makes him visibly uncomfortable, and it's glorious.

We all sit, and Alex slides right into his routine, acting like he's been here all along. The kids chatter about the party Meadow's been invited to, oblivious to the tension beneath the surface. Meanwhile, Zoe sips her wine like it's ammunition, trading barbs with Alex whenever the kids aren't watching.

"So, how's the presentation prep going?" Zoe asks me, pointedly ignoring Alex.

"It's getting there," I say, pushing food around my plate. "Trying not to let everything else distract me."

Alex smirks, catching the dig. "Feeling the pressure, Lottie? Kids, work, all on your own—must be a lot."

Before I can reply, Zoe cuts in. "Oh please, Charlie doesn't drop the ball with her kids. Work's never been an excuse for *her*. Besides, she has Jake."

The name drops like a bomb. Alex's smirk falters for a split second before he recovers, his tone dripping with mock disinterest. "Ah yes, the *hockey player*. Such a stable choice."

"Funny," Zoe drawls, swirling her wine. "That's what we all said about you."

Alex exchanges a glare with her. "Still, even Lottie has her limits."

Her glass pauses mid-sip. "It's *Charlie* now," she says, tone sharp as a blade.

"Oh, did I miss the rebrand? Old habits die hard, I suppose." He shrugs.

Zoe leans toward me as she stage-whispers, "Some things need to die harder than others."

I stifle a laugh, but Noah looks up, curious. Zoe quickly redirects, "Noah, how's that new LEGO set *Jake* got you?"

Noah lights up, launching into an excited description. I shoot Zoe a grateful look while Alex seethes silently.

My phone buzzes, and my heart lifts at Jake's name. I answer, and his face fills the screen, tired but smiling warmly.

"Hey, babe." He grins and the flutter in my stomach is immediate.

Babe. He's never called me that before, and I don't need to guess why he's chosen now. Even with tension between us, he's staking his claim in earshot of Alex.

I smile back. "Hey. We're just finishing dinner."

Jake's grin widens when I tilt my phone toward the kids. "Hey, munchkins! How's dinner?"

Meadow waves excitedly. "Hi, Jake! We had chicken and potatoes!"

Noah tugs at his Storm jersey. "Jake! Look! I'm wearing the jersey you got me!"

Jake chuckles. "Looks awesome, buddy."

Out of the corner of my eye, I catch Alex's jaw tightening. The tension creeps back in.

"I'll be right back," I say quickly, standing up. "Zoe, can you—?"

Zoe waves me off. "Go, have your lovey-dovey moment." She winks, turning her attention back to Alex, her eyes gleaming with mischief.

I step into the hallway, pulling the door behind me. Jake's face fills the screen again, eyes roaming my face like he's searching for cracks.

"How's everything going?" he asks. "How's *he* being?"

I glance back toward the dining room. "He's being Alex," I reply, trying to keep it light.

His jaw ticks. "I hate that he's there."

"I know," I murmur, feeling the weight of his absence. "I hate it, too."

Before Jake can respond, Zoe's voice floats through from the dining room, dripping sarcasm. "So, Alex, what are your plans for the rest of the week? More *disappearing acts*?"

Jake's lips twitch with amusement. "Zoe giving him hell?"

"Just a little."

"Good. He deserves it."

"I should get back," I say reluctantly.

"Okay," he pauses, eyes sliding down my face. "I miss you. I miss the kids."

"We miss you, too," I whisper, blinking back the emotions rising up.

"We'll talk more when I'm back," Jake says. "Gonna figure this out together, okay?"

I nod, holding it together. There's another pause, the weight of our unresolved argument lingering.

"I love you," he adds, voice soft—a reminder of what we still have.

My voice barely holds steady. "Love you, too."

When I return to the table, Alex looks like a storm cloud, and Zoe looks smug, lounging back in her chair like a queen.

"Everything good?" I ask, slipping back into my seat.

"*Peachy*," Zoe says sweetly, her eyes glinting. "Just catching Alex up on all the time he's missed."

"How's Jake?" Alex asks with thinly veiled sarcasm.

"He's great," I reply, my tone clipped.

Zoe doesn't miss a beat. "Jake's always great."

Alex glowers, but doesn't rise to the bait. He ignores Zoe and turns to me. "So I'll pick Noah up from school tomorrow, since you haven't organized anyone else."

I freeze, caught off guard. I glance at Zoe, who's already eyeing Alex like she's about to pounce, but she says nothing. I realize I haven't arranged any other option. Between my meeting, Nina taking Meadow to her party, Jake out of town and Zoe away on business tomorrow, there's no-one else.

I want to say no. I want to tell Alex to fuck off and stop playing *pretend dad*. Stop trying to catch me out for this twisted custody case he's trying to build. But I have no choice. I swallow the anger, forcing a calm.

"Fine," I say, swallowing my anger. "But don't be late. I've got my presentation, and I don't need any more stress."

"Relax, Lottie," he says, smirking like he's already won. "I've got it under control."

Zoe's eyes nearly roll out of her head, but she bites her tongue, taking a deliberate sip of wine.

Once the kids are excused, Zoe helps me clear the table while Alex leans back in his chair, scrolling through his phone like he owns the place.

"So, Alex," Zoe continues to stack plates as she speaks. "What's it like pretending to care? Exhausting, or does it come naturally now?"

Alex lowers his phone, his smirk icy. "You've always had such a way with words, Zoe."

She shrugs, unbothered. "Oh, I try. But you know me—I'm all about the truth. And the truth is it must be tough to keep up appearances when you're barely in the picture. Lucky for you, Jake's here to pick up the slack."

Alex's fingers grip his glass like he's picturing hurling it at her. His nostrils flare, but he keeps his voice smooth. "I'm their father. No one is *holding it together* for me."

"Right," Zoe says, voice dripping with mock sympathy. "You're their father... when it's convenient."

"Zoe," I interject softly, but she's already locked in.

"Relax, Charlie," she says, not taking her eyes off Alex. "Just clearing up a few things. Like how dropping by now and then doesn't magically make you dad of the year. Turns out, parenting is a full-time gig."

Alex rises slowly, shoulders squaring as he steps toward her, deliberately invading her space. "This isn't any of your business."

"Oh, it absolutely is," Zoe shoots back, unfazed. She tilts her head, voice almost sweet. "See, Charlie's my best friend. Which means when you waltz in here with your fake concern and manipulative bullshit, it becomes my business. And spoiler alert—I'm really good at calling it out."

His jaw ticks, but the smirk remains. "You're such a bitch, you know that?"

She takes a slow sip of her wine, savoring it like she has all the time in the world. Her smile is slow and dangerous as she takes another deliberate step closer.

Daring him.

"Oh honey, if I'm a bitch, it's because men like you have made me one. And guess what? I've gotten really fucking good at that, too."

"You're unbelievable," he sneers.

"And you're predictable," Zoe sighs, casting an unimpressed glance at her freshly manicured nails. Like he's barely worth the effort. "But hey, don't worry—the kids are *thriving*. Jake's a fantastic role model. They're lucky to have someone who actually shows up."

Alex's grip on his glass tightens, and with a loud clink, he sets it down harder than necessary.

I step between them, my hands raised. "Alright, that's enough."

Alex mutters something under his breath and storms out to say goodbye to the kids.

Zoe snorts, watching him leave. "He's such a bag of dicks."

I nod, but my thoughts are already miles away—on Jake, and how he'll react when I tell him Alex is picking Noah up. I hate this.

CHAPTER FORTY-FOUR
YOU HAD ONE JOB

———————— ✦ ————————

Charlie

I stand at the head of the boardroom table, eyes on the slides. The room is filled with our new potential clients, people who could change the course of my career.

"... and with this approach, we can increase engagement by thirty percent next quarter."

There's a murmur of approval, a few nodding heads, but I can't focus. My mind keeps drifting back to Noah. Back to Alex picking him up from school today.

You shouldn't have agreed to this. It was a mistake.

My throat tightens as I glance at the clock. Jake's back in Denver today, probably at the rink right now. I can't wait to see him. Can't wait to wrap my arms around him, kiss him, tell him I'm sorry.

I take a breath and click to the next slide. There's been no message from Alex since he said he was en route to school. My gut churns, because I should've heard back from him by now.

"...and that concludes our presentation," I finish, forcing a smile.

As Marcus takes over with closing remarks, I barely hear him. The sharpness inside of me continues to rise. I want to grab my phone and text Alex to check he got Noah, but I force myself to stay professional. It's the longest ten minutes of my life.

HAILEY RODGER

When the meeting finally winds down, I make my way out of the room and check my phone again. That's when it lights up with Alex's name flashing on the screen.

I frown as I start walking towards my office. He never calls.

"Alex?"

There's a pause, and when he speaks, his tone is tight. "Uh... we've got a bit of a situation."

My stomach drops. "What do you mean? What kind of situation?"

"I stepped into a business meeting for a minute," he says in a rush. "When I came back out... Noah wasn't there."

Everything inside me screeches to a halt. The air feels thin, like I'm choking on it, and I reach out to grip my desk, trying to keep steady. "He wasn't... What do you mean, he wasn't there?"

"I looked everywhere," Alex continues. "He didn't listen, like always. Maybe if you taught him to follow instructions, we wouldn't be in this mess."

My mouth opens and closes like a goldfish. *What the fuck?*

Before I can scream at him, he continues. "I've checked the café, the lobby, the streets nearby—he's just gone. I don't know where he is."

A wave of dizziness crashes over me. My knees weaken, and I clutch the desk harder. Noah, my baby, is somewhere alone in downtown Denver. And the one person I trusted him with has *lost* him.

"Alex, how could you be so—" My voice breaks, and I press my lips together. Yelling at him won't bring Noah back. Panicking won't help. "Where are you?" I manage, the words like acid. "Where was the last place you saw him?"

"LoDo. Near Union Station. That's where I last saw him before my meeting."

My heart races, brain mapping the area. LoDo. Crowded, chaotic, full of places where a six-year-old could disappear. *Did he wander off? Is someone with him? Is he safe?*

"I'm heading there now," I choke out, barely holding my voice steady. "Stay there, Alex. Don't move."

352

I hang up, my hands trembling as I throw my phone in my bag, worst-case scenarios spinning through my mind. Noah could be anywhere. Hurt. Lost. What if he's...

No. I have to stay calm. I shove the fear down and pull out my phone again. There's only one person I want to call.

***

Jake

My skates cut across the ice as I push through practice drills, but my head's not fully in it. All I can think about is seeing Charlie and wrapping my arms around her. She probably nailed her client meeting today—I can't wait to tell her how proud I am.

I've got it all planned out. As soon as practice ends, I'll drive straight to her place. We still need to talk about what happened, but I know we'll get through it.

As I circle back for a quick drink, my phone buzzes on the bench. It's Charlie. She wouldn't usually call during practice. I skate off the ice, pulling my gloves off as I answer.

"Hey, you okay?"

She's so hysterical I can barely understand her. "He's gone. Noah—he's gone! Alex lost him!"

My heart stops. "*What*?" I'm already yanking off my helmet, waving off Coach as I rush toward the locker room. "Charlie, slow down. What happened?"

"I don't know!" Her voice cracks, her raw terror slicing through me. "Alex took him to some meeting, and now he's gone. I don't—he's not answering my calls anymore. Jake, my baby, he's just gone—"

Fury blazes inside me. That asshole couldn't even keep an eye on his own kid for an hour. I feel my pulse spike, my protective instinct roaring.

Alex, you son of a bitch.

353

"I'm on my way," I say, already ripping off my gear, fingers shaking with rage. "Stay calm, Charlie. We'll find him."

My blood thrums through me, but I can't lose it now. Not yet. I need to stay steady for her and Noah.

"Where's the last place he saw him?" I ask, trying to sound calm, but the anger is a storm inside me.

"L-LoDo," she stammers, barely able to get the words out. "Some business meeting, I don't know where—Jake, I wasn't there! I should've been there, I—"

"Charlotte, stop," I interrupt, voice sharp. "Where in LoDo? Have you called the police?"

"I... No, I haven't," she breathes. "I just—"

"Call them. I'm five minutes away in my car. I'll meet you in LoDo. We'll find him, Charlie."

"I can't—I can't—" She's breaking down, and my chest feels like it's splitting open. *I need to get to her.*

"Charlie girl, breathe. Do it with me, okay? One breath in, then out." I throw on my clothes, grab my keys, and sprint for the exit.

My mind is racing, adrenaline surging. I can hear the fear in her voice, and every second that passes feels like a countdown. I'm trying to keep my voice steady, but my hands are shaking as I tear open my car door.

I swear to God, if anything happens to Noah because of that piece of shit...

I shove that thought aside. I need to focus and stay calm for Charlie, because she's unraveling a mile a minute. Her fear is a wildfire, and even through the phone I can feel it consuming her.

She doesn't respond, but I hear the muffled sounds of traffic and that's when it hits me. *She's driving.* She's falling apart behind the wheel.

"Charlie, pull over. Right now."

"I'm not—"

"Charlotte, listen to me. Pull over. You're no good to Noah if you're not safe. Do it for him, okay?" My voice stays calm, even though my heart's hammering. "Breathe, baby. Give yourself a minute."

There's a beat of silence, and I hear her breathing, shaky but slowing. "O-Okay. I'm pulling over."

"Good girl," I murmur, my chest loosening just a fraction. "We'll find him. You're doing great."

"Jake, I can't lose him—I can't—" Her voice shatters into sobs, and it takes everything in me not to tear my steering wheel straight off my dash.

"You won't, sweetheart. I'm on my way." My voice is calm, even though inside I'm on fire, just like her. "We'll find him, I promise."

I don't care what Alex's excuses are. He's lost Noah.

Stay focused. Find Noah first. Then deal with Alex.

My SUV roars to life as I peel out of the parking lot. Charlie's voice echoes in my head, her fear clawing at me. All I want is to hold her, make sure Noah is safe, then tear Alex apart for letting this happen.

He had *one* job.

***

Charlie

The streets of LoDo blur as I pull up to the building Alex mentioned, my heart pounding so fast it feels like it might burst. My hands are shaking as I rush out of the car, stumbling onto the sidewalk.

I can barely think, can barely breathe. Noah. My baby. The words Alex said on the phone keep repeating in my head. *He's gone. I lost him.*

People move around me as I scan the bustling streets. They're all going about their day as if my entire world isn't falling apart right in front of me. Panic squeezes my throat, suffocating me. I need to find Noah.

I turn toward the entrance of the building, my phone clutched in my hand, but I can't think. I can't function. My mind is a haze of what ifs.

Then I see Alex. Leaning against his car, scrolling through his phone, looking like he's barely inconvenienced. He looks up as I approach, but before he can say a word, my anger flares.

"How could you lose him?" My voice is sharp, cutting through the noise of the street. "He's six years old, Alex! How could you just leave him?"

Alex straightens, a flicker of irritation crossing his face. "He wandered off, Lottie." His tone drips with impatience, like I'm the one being unreasonable.

"*Wandered off*?" I echo, my voice trembling with fury. "He's a little boy, not a dog you can let wander while you have a meeting!"

Alex's expression hardens, his lips curling in disdain. "He didn't listen, like always. Maybe if you taught him some discipline, we wouldn't be in this mess."

I feel my pulse spike, my vision blurring with rage. "Don't you dare blame this on me or Noah," I seethe, stepping closer. "You were supposed to watch him, Alex! You—"

"Lottie, calm down," he interrupts, his voice low and patronizing, his hand waving me off like I'm being hysterical. "I've already called the police."

Calm down?

I take another step forward, my hands shaking. My voice drops to a dangerous whisper. "Don't you *dare* tell me to calm down. This is your fault, and if anything happens to Noah—" My voice breaks, and I can't finish the sentence.

"He's my son, too," Alex snaps, his eyes flashing with irritation. "I'll deal with this. You need to stop overreacting."

I jerk back as if he's slapped me, disbelief swirling with fury in my chest. How can he be this detached when our child is missing? He reaches for my arm, but I yank it away.

"Don't fucking touch me," I spit, my voice shaking as much as my body. I'm unraveling, the panic tightening around my chest like a vise. My mind is spinning with all the terrible possibilities.

I dart my eyes around, searching the streets, hoping to see a flash of Noah's blond hair. But it's just a sea of strangers. I feel sick.

I wish Jake was here.

The tears spill over, hot and uncontrollable. I sink onto a bench and bury my face in my hands. I can't hold it in anymore. My body shakes with sobs, the fear, and the helplessness breaking me from the inside out.

"Charlie!"

I look up, blinking through the tears, and there he is. Jake. Running toward me, his eyes locked on mine, face etched with concern.

Relief crashes over me like a wave as I stumble to my feet, rushing toward him. A sob escapes me as he catches me in his arms, holding me so tightly I can barely breathe—but I don't care. His arms are the only thing keeping me from falling apart completely.

"I'm here," he whispers into my hair. "I'm here. We're gonna find him."

I cling to him, fingers digging into his jacket, tears flowing freely now. "Jake. I can't— I can't lose him…"

He pulls back just enough to cup my face, his eyes fierce. "You won't," he says, voice protective and certain. "We'll find him, Charlie. I promise."

With Jake holding me, the difference between him and Alex is so clear. Jake, who's all in. Fighting for me and the kids, loving us down to his very bones. And Alex—the man who never cared enough to stay. The man who couldn't take care of his own son.

I lean into Jake, heart pounding, allowing myself a moment to rein in some of the crazy since this nightmare began. He's here.

And I know that if Jake says he'll find Noah, he means it.

***

Jake

She's barely holding it together. Trembling in my arms, her fear so thick I can taste it. It's clawing down my throat, tightening my chest.

357

For a moment we just stand there, her body shaking against mine. Everything we've been through this week—the argument, the tension—none of it matters now. All that matters is Noah.

"I don't know what to do," she whispers, her voice breaking. "I trusted him. I didn't have a choice, but I trusted him..."

Her voice cracks, and I feel a surge of fury again. That someone could hurt her this much, disregard her trust like it was nothing. Cut her so deep she's barely hanging on.

My eyes slowly trace over her face, trying to find the right words, when they catch something over her shoulder.

Alex.

Something snaps inside me and I see red. This motherfucker is the reason for all of this. Everything that's been hurting her, everything we're dealing with this week.

I pull away from Charlie, my hands tightening into fists as I storm toward him, rage blazing in me like a wildfire. He's leaning against his car, arms crossed like this is just some minor issue. His face is a mask of frustration, and when his eyes meet mine, there's defensiveness there. He straightens like he's ready for a fight.

Good. He fucking should be.

"You lost my kid," I snarl, shoving him hard against his car before I can think twice. "We trusted you with him for one goddamn hour, and you couldn't even handle that!"

Alex stumbles back but recovers quickly, anger flashing in his eyes as he shoves me off. "He's not *your* kid, Jake. I'm his father, not you."

The words land like a slap, but they don't weaken me—they just piss me off more. My chest heaves as I step closer, practically nose-to-nose with him. "A father doesn't lose his kid. A father doesn't use his kid as a pawn in some power game. I'm here cleaning up *your* fucking mess."

Alex scoffs, rolling his eyes, but I see the flicker of guilt behind the arrogance. "It was a mistake. I stepped away for two minutes—"

"That's all it takes." My hands fist in the collar of his jacket, yanking him close. "Two minutes. You had *one job.*"

"Let go," Alex spits, shoving me harder, squaring up like this is some kind of pissing contest. "I just stepped into my meeting for a minute. Noah wandered off. This isn't my fault."

"The hell it isn't," I reply, voice lethal. "You threaten to take them back to New Zealand, thinking you can handle it. Then you pull this shit?"

Alex shoves back against me, his voice rising. "He didn't listen to me! What was I supposed to do?"

"What were you supposed to do?" I repeat, incredulous. My grip tightens on his jacket as he struggles. "You were supposed to *watch him*, you son of a bitch. He's six!"

He shoves back again, but this time I slam him harder against the car, my breath coming in short, furious bursts. "I don't care what excuses you have, you lost Noah. He could be anywhere, scared out of his mind, because *you* weren't paying attention."

"Stop it!" Charlie's voice cuts through the tension, sharp and desperate. She's between us, pushing against me, tears streaking her face. "Jake, please."

I breathe hard, staring Alex down for a moment longer before I force myself to let go. He glares at me while he straightens his jacket, but there's no fight in him. He knows I'll fucking pummel him given half the chance.

"Where's the last place you saw him?" I snap, my voice cold.

Alex rubs at his collar, scowling, then points down the street. "I went into that building near Confluence Park for five minutes, came out, and he was gone." He turns his sneer on Charlie, venom dripping from his voice. "And if you weren't so busy playing house with your *hockey boyfriend*, maybe you'd remember to teach your son some damn listening skills."

I watch his words hit Charlie like a slap, her face crumbling under the weight of the nightmare we're in. The pain in her eyes sends my fury into overdrive.

My jaw clenches, every muscle in my body tensing as I take a step forward. "Say that again."

"Jake—" Charlie starts, but I cut her off by holding up my hand. Not this time.

"You want to repeat that, big man?" I ask, tone dangerous. "Because you might think you can say whatever you want to her, but one more word and you'll wish *you* were the one lost."

"She's still the mother of my kids," Alex snaps, his voice dripping like he thinks that's his trump card.

"And that's the only thing saving your ass right now," I bite back. "So here's what you're gonna do—you're gonna shut your fucking mouth, and you're gonna focus on finding Noah, or I swear to God you'll never come near them again."

The tension crackles between us, but I see him falter, his sneer flickering as reality sinks in.

I turn away from him, the fury still burning in my veins, but Charlie's right. We don't have time for this. Pounding him into the ground won't help Noah. I need to pull myself together for her, for Noah. We need to find him.

Charlie's pacing again, her phone pressed to her ear talking to the police. I want to hold her, tell her it'll be okay, but I can barely keep it together myself.

I scan the area, my heart pounding in my chest. LoDo is busy: people walking, cars moving, noise everywhere. I jog down the street toward Confluence Park, thinking about where a scared six-year-old might go.

My mind is racing, every second that passes only adding to the weight of the situation. People pass me by, maybe recognizing me and unaware of the hell we're in, and I have to fight the rising panic clawing at my throat.

Then, through the chaos, I spot him.

Noah.

My heart slams into my ribs. He's huddled on a bench near the river, knees pulled to his chest, his face streaked with tears. But he's safe.

"Charlie!" I shout over my shoulder, sprinting across the street, dodging traffic. I hear her shriek and start running behind me, but all I can focus on is Noah.

Relief floods through me as I reach the bench and drop to my knees in front of him, pulling him into my arms. "Noah," I breathe, holding him tight, feeling the weight of him in my arms. "You okay, buddy? You scared us."

He clings to me, sniffling against my shoulder. "I'm sorry," he whispers, his little voice shaking. "I wanted to see the little boats on the river…"

I hold him closer, kissing the top of his head. "It's okay. We're here. You're okay."

Charlie catches up, tears streaming down her face as she throws her arms around us both. "Oh my God, Noah…"

Her voice breaks as she presses her lips to his forehead, holding him fiercely, her shaking hands skating over his face, his hair and his shoulders. Like she's feeling every cell of him to ensure he's okay. Like she might be right back in a moment when he was a newborn, cradling him close, absorbing every bit of him.

The sight knocks the air out of my lungs. The sheer, overwhelming love she has for him, the way she holds onto him like he's her whole world—it radiates from her. And I feel it stronger than ever: that being part of this, part of *her*, would make me happy forever.

I hold them both tighter, my eyes closing as I fight to regulate the flood of emotions swirling around us. We found him. He's safe. They're safe.

For a brief moment, the nightmare feels over.

But then Alex finally catches up, slowly jogging over like he he doesn't want to crumple his suit, voice sharp and grating. "Noah, why the hell did you wander off like that?"

The shift in the air is instant. I feel Charlie stiffen beside me, her whole body tensing with anger as she turns to him.

"Don't you *dare*," she spits. "Don't you dare blame him. This is on you, Alex."

Alex scoffs. "I didn't—"

"Shut the hell up." I step forward, my voice dangerous, every cell in my body screaming to put his body six feet under. "You don't get to blame a kid for your own fucking negligence. You left him. *You*."

No one moves. The tension hums like ozone in the air.

Charlie's between us, holding Noah protectively, her disgust written all over her face.

Finally, Alex sighs, holding up his hands in fake surrender. "Fine. Whatever."

But I'm not finished.

"You're done." My pulse pounds as I stare him down. "Stay the hell away from them."

Charlie's arms tighten around Noah, her eyes meeting mine. A silent understanding passes between us. She knows. I won't let this happen again.

With one last glare at Alex, my body still wired with anger and adrenaline, I force myself to turn away from him. He's not what matters.

I step back to where Charlie holds Noah, wrapping them both in my arms, grounding myself in their warmth. I need to feel them, to know they're safe.

I press a hand to the back of Noah's head, my voice gentler now.

"Let's go home, buddy."

CHAPTER FORTY-FIVE

THAT? UH... IT'S AN APOLOGY BROWNIE

———————✦———————

Charlotte - 12 Years Ago

The bus engine hums beneath me, a low vibration matching the mix of excitement and sadness swirling in my chest. I press my forehead against the cool glass of the window, watching as the camp fades from view. Summer's over. Soon, I'll be on a plane back to New Zealand. Back to reality.

As we pull away, part of me lingers, still lying under the stars with Jake. Sharing jokes and dreams, feeling like anything was possible. I close my eyes, trying to hold onto the memory for just a few more seconds.

Suddenly, the bus lurches to a stop. I glance up, confused, and that's when I see him.

Jake.

He's sprinting up the road, bag slung over his shoulder, hair a mess like he didn't think before taking off. My heart skips, and before I know it, I'm pushing through the aisle to the front.

The bus door swings open and there he is, breathless and grinning like he's just pulled off the greatest stunt of his life.

"What are you doing?" I laugh, stepping down onto the gravel.

"I couldn't let you leave without a proper goodbye," he says, catching his breath. "And to remind you... you sealed the deal, remember?"

I tilt my head, smiling. "The pinky promise?"

He nods, smiling wider. "Exactly. You promised you'd follow your dreams, no matter what. So don't let anyone stop you, okay?"

I roll my eyes but his words feel warm and sure. "You're serious about this, huh?"

"Of course I am. You're gonna do amazing things, Charlie. I know it."

I smile, touched by his confidence. "Thanks, Jake. But remember, you promised, too."

He laughs, nodding like he's satisfied, then reaches into his bag. "Before you go…" He pulls out a small, folded piece of paper and hands it to me.

"What's this?"

Jake's smile softens, and for the first time I see a hint of shyness. "It's my gran's brownie recipe. You asked for it, and you're special enough to have it."

I unfold the paper, revealing the handwritten recipe. Simple and neat, yet priceless. I look up at him, my throat tightening.

"Jake… thank you."

He shrugs, playing it cool, but I see the pride in his eyes. "Just promise you'll think of me whenever you make 'em."

I nod. "I promise. And I'll seal the deal." I extend my pinky, and he hooks his around mine.

"Deal," he says, voice rough as he kisses his thumb to seal it.

For a moment we just stand there, grinning awkwardly at each other. Before I can overthink, I step forward and hug him tight. He's warm, solid, and feels like home.

"Don't forget about me," I whisper into his shoulder.

"Not a chance."

I pull away, just enough to meet his eyes. There's something earnest there, something that makes my heart stumble.

"I'll miss you," I admit.

"Same here," he says, his expression soft. "But hey, if we ever meet again we'll make more Mega S'mores."

I smile, blinking away the burn in my eyes. "See ya, Jake."

As I turn to climb back onto the bus, he calls after me in a mock superhero voice, "Remember, Lady Lightning—chase your dreams!"

I laugh, waving as I step up. "You too, Captain Thunder!"

The bus pulls away, and I watch him through the window until he's just a speck in the distance. My heart feels full and heavy all at once, but there's a new resolve in me. A promise to keep that spark alive. To chase my dreams, just like we promised under the stars.

***

Charlie – Present Day

I sit on the couch, Noah nestled under my arm, his small body warm and safe against mine. The day's events have drained me, but all I can focus on now is the steady rhythm of his breathing. He's here. He's safe. For the first time in hours, my lungs feel like they can fill again.

Jake sits on Noah's other side, his eyes following him warmly as he chats away. He's relaxed, but there's a tension beneath his steady exterior, like a rope pulled too tight. We haven't had time to talk yet, not since everything today.

Noah squirms beside me, his energy fading into something quieter. He glances up at Jake, his voice soft. "You didn't say goodbye before you left last week, Jake."

The words slice through the room, unexpected. I glance at Jake, feeling the flicker of guilt pass between us. Neither of us was ready for that.

Jake shifts, running a hand through his hair. "I know, buddy," he says gently, meeting my eyes for a beat before looking back at Noah. "I wanted to. But... I'm sorry. It won't happen again, I promise."

Noah studies him, his brow furrowing as if weighing the apology. Finally, he nods and leans closer, fingers reaching out to brush Jake's knee, like he needs the connection.

The tightness in my chest loosens a little more. Jake's become so much to all of us. Watching him with Noah, it's clear how much we've all missed him.

But the fight—the things I said—they're still there, waiting to be acknowledged. I owe Jake more than a quick sorry. He deserves better than the fear I threw at him, the doubts I let control me. But I'm not sure where to start.

My eyes flick toward the kitchen counter, where the brownie I made this morning sits under a cake stand. The one I planned to give him after my meeting, after I told him I was sorry. It feels small now, insignificant after today. But the words I iced on top are still true.

You're the dream.

Noah's voice pulls me back. "Jake, did you know the biggest volcano in space is on Mars?"

Jake grins, that familiar warmth lighting in his eyes. "I didn't know that, but now I do. Thanks to you, buddy."

Noah beams, sinking deeper into my side as he rambles about space. Jake listens, his soft laughter matching Noah's energy, but his gaze keeps drifting to me, unspoken words pressing into the space between us.

The front door opens, and Meadow's giggles suddenly fill the air before she's even in sight. She bursts into the room, her face lighting up when she spots Jake.

"Dada!" she squeals, sprinting toward him. It's a title that still tugs at my heart. Jake's expression falters for a fraction of a second, but he quickly recovers, catching her in his arms.

"Hey, Little Lightning," he says, pressing a kiss to her head. "Did you have fun at the party?"

Meadow nods, proudly flashing her goodie bag like a prized possession. "We had cake! And games! I got this!"

Jake settles her into his arms. "Sounds like a blast. I missed you."

She snuggles closer, clutching his shirt. "I missed you, too."

Nina enters, pulling off her jacket and giving me a sympathetic smile. She knows what happened with Noah today—knows how shaken I've been.

"How's our brave boy doing?" she asks, ruffling Noah's hair. He leans into her touch but stays quiet, still a little lost in thought. Nina's brows furrow, but she turns back to me, offering a soft smile. "You okay?"

I force one back. "Getting there."

She nods, then glances between Jake and me with understanding before clapping her hands. "Alright, time for bubbles! Who's ready for bath time?"

Meadow squeals and wriggles out of Jake's arms, racing up the stairs. Noah perks up, following Nina out, leaving Jake and me alone.

The room feels suddenly too big, too quiet. The silence between us fills every corner, brimming with everything unsaid.

I glance toward the kitchen again, at the brownie on the cake stand. It feels almost ridiculous now, but it's something. And God knows I need to start somewhere.

Jake follows my gaze, raising an eyebrow as he walks to the counter. "What's this?"

"That? Uh... it's an apology brownie."

He lifts the glass dome, his face softening as he reads the message I'd iced on top. There's something something vulnerable in his eyes as he studies it.

I shift awkwardly, suddenly feeling exposed. "I made it this morning, before everything went to shit. I was going to give it to you after work, to say sorry." I let out a nervous laugh. "It felt like a good idea then, but now it seems..."

"Silly?" he finishes for me, though there's no mockery in his tone. He's waiting, watching me.

"Yeah," I breathe. "Compared to everything else."

Jake's eyes trace the words I iced on top. *You're the dream*. He's absorbing the message slowly, piece by piece. When he looks up, his eyes are softer, almost encouraging.

"An apology brownie, huh?" There's an edge to his voice, like he's waiting for more.

I shrug, throat tight. "It's a start."

He sets the brownie down with deliberate care and turns to me. His presence pulls me in, and I search for the words, the courage.

"Charlie," he says, voice wavering just enough to make my heart crack. "You don't have to apologize. We both said things, but that doesn't mean I'm walking away."

I shake my head. "But I *do*. I said things that weren't true. I hurt you, and I regret every word."

Jake steps closer, and I make myself to look up at him, even as my hands tremble. He doesn't interrupt. He just listens, eyes searching mine like he's afraid to miss a single word.

"I've been thinking about that night at camp," I whisper, forcing the words. "We promised to chase our dreams. And I thought coming to Denver was doing that. But then we reconnected, and I realized..." My voice breaks, but I push on.

"The dream I've been chasing my whole life is to feel the way you made me feel back then. Happy, safe. Cherished."

Jake's breath shudders, his jaw tightening as if he's physically holding himself together. He reaches out, his thumb brushing my cheek like he needs the contact to believe this is real.

"I love you, Jake. And when I said I should go back to New Zealand... that was fear talking. Not doubt in you, or us. I don't want to lose us because it means *everything* to me."

His forehead drops to mine, hands flexing against my waist to ground himself in the moment. I feel the warmth of his breath as he speaks. "You're not losing me, Charlie. I've been a goner for you since we were eighteen."

Tears blur my vision, but I press forward. I have to say this. I need him to hear it.

"I know I hurt you when I said you don't have kids, because you do, Jake..."

His whole body trembles, waiting for me to continue.

"Alex may be their father, but *you know them*. You know what they love, what makes them smile. You know Noah loves his action figures and hates when they don't stand up right, you know his favorite space facts. You know Meadow still needs '*Goodnight Moon*' every night, even though she pretends she's too big for it. You know how Noah's face lights up building those complicated models and how Meadow only eats pancakes with pink sprinkles."

Jake chokes on a breath, his eyes blinking rapidly as a tear slides down his cheek.

"Alex doesn't know those things because he's not here," I whisper. "But you are. You're here every day thinking about us, loving us out loud with your whole chest." My voice fractures, but I don't stop. "And we love you right back."

Tears spill down his face now, but he doesn't wipe them away. Instead, he yanks me into him, crushing me against his chest like he's terrified to let go.

"I love them, too." His lips tremble against my forehead. "And I love you, Charlie. *So fucking much.*"

His lips tilt to mine before I can say anything more, and we kiss with all the things we've been holding back. Desperation, love, fear.

I lean back to look at him, fingers gripping his shirt. "I'm all in, Jake. I promise."

Jake's eyes shine with a mix of relief and love as he slowly lifts his hand, wiggling his pinky finger at me. "Seal the deal?"

A watery laugh escapes me as I lift my own hand, linking my pinky with his. "Seal the deal," I whisper, kissing our joined thumbs like we did that night under the stars.

His lips find mine again, kissing me slowly like he's committing this moment to memory. Like he's reclaiming every year, every second we've spent apart. Gathering every fleeting thought, every quiet wish we ever made for each other, and pouring them into this moment. An invisible string pulls us tight and sighs *finally,* like in every universe, every lifetime, it was always meant to be us. Together.

The world blurs in our shared breaths, the soft press of his mouth, the way he holds me close like I might float away. With each soft exhale I let go of everything that came before him, all the doubt, every wall crumbling into the quiet between us.

He pulls back slightly, his breath mingling with mine. "You're my dream too, Charlie. I'm convinced I was always made to love you."

We stay like that, neither of us moving, just breathing each other in. The weight of everything slowly eases, each breath a little lighter than the last.

Jake's grin curves, breaking the quiet as he glances back at the cake stand. "So, about that apology brownie..."

A breathy laugh escapes me as I wipe at me cheeks. "You want it now?"

"Hell yeah," he says, eyes still glassy but full of warmth. "I'm starving."

I watch as he walks to the counter, cutting a piece and popping it into his mouth. He closes his eyes, groaning low in his throat like it's the best thing he's ever tasted.

"Damn, it's always so good."

I chuckle, a mixture of shy fondness stirring in me. The same feeling I felt on that bus all those years ago. "I hope you remember I've had this recipe all along..."

Jake's gaze darkens, the playful edge giving way to something deeper. He sets the brownie down and reaches for my hand, pulling me into him.

"I never forgot anything about that summer, Lady Lightning," he murmurs, his thumb tracing slow circles over my knuckles. "Especially you."

The charge between us shifts, more intense and tangled in the longing after our week apart. I meet his eyes and feel the pull—something hungrier, something that's been waiting to surface to let me know exactly how this night will end.

Before I can respond, the creak of footsteps on the stairs make us spring apart.

Nina appears, smiling. "Both kids are out cold," she says, her eyes flicking between us with sharp amusement. "I'll head out. Enjoy your night!"

I barely manage to keep my face neutral as I mumble a quick thank you. The second the door clicks shut, I barely have time to turn before—

Jake's hands are on me.

He presses me back, his body caging me against the counter.

"You know," he whispers, breath hot against my jaw. "I think it's time we seal the deal properly."

"Oh yeah?" I manage shakily, body already reacting to him.

He nods, and then his lips crash onto mine.

CHAPTER FORTY-SIX

I THINK WE'RE GONNA NEED MORE BROWNIE

———————— ✦ ————————

Jake

Her breath catches as I drag slow, open-mouthed kisses down her neck, skimming her delicate skin as her fingers tangle in my hair. They flex, like she's trying to say everything she can't with words. The apology, the need, the fire simmering between us.

And fuck, I'm ready to burn for her.

"I missed you so much," she whispers, her voice shaky as her hands slip under my t-shirt, fingertips like fire on my skin.

A low rumble rolls through me as I kiss my way down her throat, breathing her in.

"You have no idea how much I missed you, Charlie girl." I nip at her pulse point, pulling a soft moan from her lips.

My hands grip her hips, lifting her onto the counter. Her legs wrap around me, pulling me in, and I press against her, groaning at the feel of her body against mine.

Pushing her top up, my mouth finds her skin warm and soft beneath me. "You don't know how hard it's been," I tug her bra down to suck a nipple into my mouth, "hearing your voice but not being able to touch you."

She lets out a shaky laugh, her body arching into me. "Oh, I know it's been *hard*," she teases, slipping her hands under my shirt, pulling it over my head

371

I chuckle darkly as I drag my teeth over her, letting my hands map her body like I need to memorize it all over again. But it's not enough. It's never enough with her.

"Turn around."

She shivers, but obeys—her feet hitting the floor. I spin her gently and press her over the counter, my hands gliding down her arms before covering her hands on the cool surface. She looks back at me with her wide eyes and parted lips, and fuck, the sight of her so vulnerable and willing has me rock hard in an instant.

I drag my hand down the curve of her spine, reveling in how she arches beneath me, her body begging without words. My hips press into her, letting her feel how hard I am already through the denim between us.

"Jake..." Her voice trembles with anticipation.

I undo her jeans, tugging them down just enough to bare her. My hand slides over the soft swell of her ass, squeezing gently before pulling her back against me.

"God, you're perfect," I growl, breath hot against her ear. "Walking around like you own me."

She lets out a soft, sultry laugh. "Don't I?"

Her boldness shoots straight to my cock. "Brat," I murmur, gripping her hips harder. "But yeah, baby. You fucking do."

She shivers, and I drink in the sharp inhale, the way her thighs clench like she's barely holding herself together.

Not happening.

Tonight, I'm going to wreck her. Every inch, every sound, every second of her surrender is mine. I kiss down the column of her throat, lips grazing her shoulder, sucking softly as she melts into me.

"Stay still," I whisper, pressing her back down to the counter. "I'm gonna ruin you for anyone else."

"You already have," she breathes, fingers gripping the counter tighter.

Sliding a hand between her legs, I groan when I find her soaked, already dripping for me. She gasps, pressing back against my fingers, her hips rolling instinctively.

"Jesus, Charlie," I breathe, my free hand tightening on her waist, holding her still as I slide my fingers in.

She moans, and the sound drives me wild as I curl my fingers slowly, reveling in the way she clenches around me.

"Jake..."

I smile against her shoulder, my fingers slowly teasing. "You're soaked," I murmur, letting the filth drip into my voice. "So ready. You missed me, didn't you? Been waiting for this all week."

"Yes... fuck, yes."

My eyes catch on the apology brownie, a wicked grin curling across my lips as an idea takes root. I swipe a bit of frosting and bring it to her lips.

"Taste."

She glances back, her eyes wide. "What?"

I chuckle, dragging the frosting across her lips. "You heard me. Taste it while I fuck you."

Her lips part around my fingers, and I watch her tongue slowly flick out to take the chocolate, her lips shiny, eyes hazy with pleasure. It undoes me.

Groaning, I yank her jeans down further, my other hand sliding back between her legs. She's so ready, so wet, and the thought of fucking her right here right now pounds through me like a war drum.

"Good girl," I say, sliding my fingers deeper into her, drawing another moan from her lips. "Taste good?"

She nods frantically. "So good."

I lean in, letting my lips ghost over ear. "You want more?"

"Please..."

My fingers circle her clit, the movement deliberately slow as I swipe another bit of brownie. "Taste again."

She takes it, her eyes meeting mine as she sucks it clean off my finger.

Fuck.

"You're so close already, aren't you?" My fingers move deeper, making her tremble. "My needy girl, ready to come all over my fingers."

Her moan is desperate as her hips buck against me, searching for more. "Jake, I—"

"Say it," I demand, curling my fingers and pulling a cry from her lips. "Tell me how much you missed me."

"I missed you," she says with a desperate breath. "God, I missed you so much. Please, I need to—"

"Not yet." I ease back just enough to make her whine. She's so close, but she's not coming yet. Not until I say.

"Please, Jake..."

"Tell me again," I growl, unbuckling my jeans, my cock already aching for her. "Tell me how much you need me."

"I need you so fucking much," she gasps as I slide my fingers back through her, teasing her clit mercilessly. "*Please*, Jake."

That's it. The sound of her begging, the tremor in her voice—it snaps my last thread of control.

I line myself up behind her, gripping her hips. "Fuck, I missed this," I rasp, slowly pushing into her, taking her deep. "Feeling you wet and gripping me like you never wanna let go."

Her body stretches around me, a breathy cry escaping as I fill her. I thrust slowly, my hands sliding to her ass, pulling her hard against me.

"So damn greedy" I husk, reaching for another swipe of brownie and smearing it across her lips. "Taking every inch like you're welcoming me home. Like you've been waiting all week for me to remind you who you belong to."

"Shit, God, don't stop," she moans as I bottom out, feeling her tighten around me.

"Fuck—" My grip tightens as I pull her back onto me harder, faster. "Every damn time, baby. Nothing even comes close to fucking this pussy."

She's trembling, so close, her body barely holding on.

"Jake, please—"

"You don't come 'til I say," I murmur, slowing my movements just enough to make her squirm beneath me. I dip my fingers into the brownie again, slipping them into her mouth. "Taste."

Her breath hitches, body shaking, held right on the edge. I'm the only one who can give her what she needs, and it makes me feral for her.

I thrust deep again, my hand sliding up her back to grip the base of her neck, controlling every damn movement.

"Fuuuck!" She's desperate now, bowing her back and grinding against me.

"God yes, just like that. Stay with me."

My fingers dig into her as I pick up my pace, hands clutching her ass as I pound into her relentlessly, relishing the sound of our skin slapping together.

"Fuck, Charlie," I grit out, barely holding it together as she clenches around me.

Her breath comes in short, desperate bursts, and I feel the tension coiling in her. Her body tightens, and I feel the shift—the edge of control slipping.

"Now," I growl, thrusting deep again, my hand finding her clit and slapping it against the wetness. "Come for me."

Crying out, her body convulses, falling apart beneath me as I keep driving into her, milking every last wave of her release. Her head drops to the counter, her body trembling as she collapses, spent.

I follow her, groaning loud as I come, pressing kisses to her back as my body shudders against hers.

"You're fucking mine," I murmur against her damp skin, chest heaving as I catch my breath. "Forever."

A shaky laugh tumbles from her. "Jesus, Jake..."

I chuckle, kissing up the curve of her neck. "That apology brownie hit the spot."

She turns in my arms, cheeks flushed, a lazy smirk on her face. "I think we're gonna need more brownies."

My snicker rumbles through me as I scoop her up, her own laughter soft against my chest, body still trembling in the aftermath. There's frosting smeared at the corner of her lips, and when I lick it off, her eyes sparkle.

"Let's get you upstairs," I murmur.

Her arms loop around my neck, breath easing into a gentle rhythm as she melts against me. The wildness from earlier fades with every step I take up to her room, each beat of her breath against my chest anchoring me in something quieter. Softer. Like the world's taking a breath and leaving just us behind.

I lower her to the bed, my hands lingering at her waist, watching her sink into the pillows. Her eyes search mine, and I see the same thing I've been feeling all night. Certainty.

"Come here," she whispers, reaching out for me.

I climb in beside her, pulling her close. My lips brush slowly over her shoulder, up her neck, over her jaw. Downstairs was desperate and raw. But here in this space, it's just us. No rush. Just me and her.

There's a tenderness now, the kind that only comes after you've seen someone bare their soul. And fuck, she's done that tonight. She let me in—completely.

"I love you, Charlie," I whisper against her skin, my hands gliding down her sides. "I've loved you for so long, even before I knew it."

Her fingers find mine, threading together. She doesn't hesitate, doesn't overthink. Just looks up at me with that kind of trust that wrecks me.

"Then show me," she breathes.

So I do.

This time is different. I take my time, exploring every inch of her like it's the first time all over again. I kiss her slowly and deliberately, like I'm sealing the night's confessions into her.

She presses closer, her body so warm and plaint under me, breath catching as I sink inside her, but there's no rush. No frenzy. It's something deeper, almost sacred. Like worship, like prayer. I'm cherishing every second, every inch of her, revering the feel of her skin under my hands. Like every touch is a vow.

My hand cradles her cheek, and I watch—her parted lips, the way her eyes soften and turn dreamy as she pulls me close. She's the one who sees the parts of me I've kept hidden, the dark spaces where I thought nothing good could grow.

And she fills them all.

Her fingers tighten in mine, our hands tangled above her head as I dot featherlight kisses over her throat, my breath catching as the weight of it all settles in.

She's everything.

I love her in the cracks of time, in the pauses, in the places people forget to look. Even in the dark spaces where nothing else exists, she's there. Filling everything.

The thought crashes over me, and I kiss her again, letting it sink deep into my bones. She's not just a part of my life, she's the best part.

She always was.

Her breath hitches, and she whispers my name as her body trembles beneath mine. I watch her let go, and it undoes me. The moment is infinite and quiet, stretching as I hold her tight, anchored in her as we fall apart together.

For a while we just lie there tangled in each other, breathing in sync with the soft rhythm of the night around us. My hand trails up her arm, brushing a stray strand of hair from her forehead.

She shifts beside me, turning to face me fully, her fingers drawing lazy circles on my chest. "I think I love you in every universe," she whispers.

Her words thrum through me, and I press a hard kiss to her temple, lingering there, trying to gather myself. All I can manage is a hoarse, "Me too," before I bury my face in her hair, holding her close.

We fall asleep like that, wrapped up in each other. No noise, no chaos. Just us and the quiet hum of the night, steady and sure.

CHAPTER FORTY-SEVEN

OH, DON'T WORRY BUD—I'VE GOT PLANS

———————— ⋆ ————————

Charlie

The soft hum of cartoons drifts from the living room, mingling with the rich scent of coffee. Noah and Meadow sit curled up on the couch, their eyes glued to *Paw Patrol*, yesterday's drama already forgotten.

Jake hands me a coffee, pressing a kiss to my temple, his fingers lingering just enough to make my skin spark. He slides onto the stool beside me, the warmth of his knee brushing mine.

Before I can speak, a sharp knock at the door breaks the peace. My stomach knots. There's only one person who would show up unannounced this early. I glance at Jake, who's already put down his cup, his body rigid.

"Stay here," I say, but he shakes his head, following me to the door.

I open it cautiously, and there he is—Alex, dressed in a suit despite it being barely 7 a.m. on a Saturday. His gaze flicks over me in my robe, then to Jake, standing just behind.

"Lottie," he says, voice dripping with condescension as he greets me.

Before I can even respond, Jake steps forward. "Call her that again, and I swear to God, we're gonna have a real problem."

Alex's smirk falters for a second, but he quickly recovers. "Alright, alright. No need to get all *hockey player* on me. I'm just here to see my kids."

I cross my arms. "Now's not a good time. We haven't discussed what happened yesterday."

Alex waves his hand, dismissing me. "We found him in the end, didn't we? Shit happens. He was fine."

Jake's fists tighten, anger simmering close to the surface, but before he can speak, Meadow's voice breaks the tension.

"Jake, guess what!"

She bounds into the hallway, her face lighting up when she sees him. He immediately softens, scooping her into his arms as she giggles.

Alex watches, his lips pressing into a straight line. "Meadow," he calls, forcing a smile. "How about coming back to New Zealand with me? Wanna see Granny and Grandpa again?"

Meadow's eyes brighten at the mention of her grandparents. "Granny!" she squeals. "Yes!" But then she shifts to Jake, and her little brow furrows. "Jake... are you coming too?"

Jake holds her a bit tighter, glaring at Alex. "No, Princess. But you're staying right here with me and Mama."

Noah, overhearing, appears in the hallway, his expression cautious. "You mean... like for a holiday?"

Alex, smug and unbothered, shrugs. "Not just for a holiday, for good! Wouldn't you like to come back home?"

Noah's face falls, glancing between Jake and Alex. "No. I like it here. I wanna stay with Mum and Jake."

Meadow's small hands cling tighter to Jake's shirt. "I don't wanna go," she whimpers, her bottom lip trembling. "I wanna stay with Jake!" Tears spill over, and my heart shatters for her.

Jake's face darkens, and he holds her close, rubbing her back soothingly. "You're not leaving, Princess. I promise," he murmurs, his voice a protective rumble.

Alex takes a step forward, but I've had enough.

"No." The word is sharp and final as it snaps from my throat. "You don't get to mess with my kids' heads. You can't just throw out the idea of taking them to New Zealand and walk away like there are no consequences. You have *no idea* how to be a real parent."

He has the audacity to shrug, still trying to play it cool.

"I'm just giving them options, Lott—"

"If you call me Lottie one more time," I cut him off, "I will rip your balls off and shove them down your throat."

Jake lets out a low chuckle beside me, pride flashing in his eyes. "Listen to her," he adds, his voice dark. "She's not joking."

He places Meadow down, kissing her forehead and gently sending her back toward the living room. I nod, encouraging both kids to go back. They don't need to see this.

"Well, isn't this a cute little family," Alex sneers, flicking his eyes to Jake. "How's playing house treating you?"

Jake doesn't take the bait, but I can see the tension, feel the restraint barely holding him together. I take a slow breath, keeping myself calm for the kids' sake, now oblivious back in the living room.

"Don't get too comfortable," Alex continues, smirk growing. "They're *my* kids, not yours."

Before I can respond, he turns to me like a snake ready to strike. "And you really think this guy's going to stick around, *Charlie*?" He twists my name, making it sound like an insult. "You're just a convenient distraction between games. Once the novelty wears off, you'll be back to square one—with two kids and no help."

The words slice through me, but Jake steps forward, his voice lethal.

"You think this is about *convenience*, Alex? I'm not going anywhere. And it kills you, doesn't it? That someone's *actually* here for them. Because you never were."

Alex scoffs, rolling his eyes, but Jake doesn't stop.

"And as for Charlie being some *distraction*?" Jake's lips twitch, though there's no humor. "We're great together. In *every* way. But it's so much more than that, and you know it."

Mask slipping, Alex's voice drops into something uglier. "Well, I'm sure we can both agree she's a good lay, but—"

CRACK

380

Jake's fist slams into the doorframe beside Alex's head so hard the wood splinters. I jump, but it's Alex who flinches, his smirk wiped clean off his face.

"You don't talk about her like that. *Ever.*"

Alex tries to sneer, but the flicker of uncertainty in his eyes betrays him. He's scrambling for control, but Jake's already stepped closer.

"Here's the thing, Alex—you lost your shot. I'm with her now. *Every* part of her, and none of it has to do with you. It's about how she lights up when *I* walk in the door. The way she melts into me when *I* hold her. You wanna talk about what happens between us? How about the fact that she feels *safe* with me."

Jake's gaze doesn't waver as Alex tries to scoff again.

"She trusts me, with everything. Because I *show up*, I listen. And I love her the way she's always deserved to be loved. And you? You couldn't even watch your own kid for an hour."

He lets the words hang between them, watching as Alex's cocky facade begins to crumble. My eyes drop to his hands, watching his fingers clench like he wants to throw a punch, but knowing he won't stand a chance against Jake.

Jake tilts his head, studying him like he's already dismissed him as any kind of opponent. "So yeah, we're good together. We fit in every way you never could. Because she's *always* been mine."

He steps back, lip curling in his signature sneer. "You really think you're going to replace me, Jake?"

Before Jake can answer, I step forward. "Stop it, Alex. You lost Noah yesterday. The only reason he's safe is because Jake was there to clean up your mess. Again."

Alex's face twists into something ugly, his glare sharpening on me. But before he can retort, Jake's right there, voice eerily calm.

"You think this is about replacing you?" Jake's words slice through the air. "I'm not trying to be their father. They already have one—he's just never around when it matters. But here's the difference: what we have isn't temporary. It's real, and I'm not going anywhere. So next time you wanna compare notes? Remember you lost them. And I'll be keeping them forever."

"Well then," he mutters darkly, face pale. "We'll see how this goes in court. I've got lawyers lined up—"

"You wanna talk lawyers?" Jake steps takes one step closer, nearly nose to nose. "I've already spoken to mine. Trust me, you won't win this. You've got *nothing* on me. Waste your time and money if you want."

Alex stiffens, realizing he's in over his head. He's not just up against me, he's up against Jake, too. And Jake doesn't lose.

"This isn't over, Jake."

Jake's eyes don't leave his. "It is for you."

Alex's gaze flicks between us before he mutters, "See you in court."

"Get out," Jake says, his voice carrying an edge he means every word. "Before I forget the kids are in the next room."

As soon as the door closes, I release a long breath, my body trembling with adrenaline. I turn to look at Jake, who's already moving toward the living room, his anger fading into something softer as he kneels to scoop Meadow into his arms.

"You're not going anywhere, Little Lightning," he says, brushing a tear from her cheek. "You're stuck with me forever, okay?"

Meadow snuggles into his chest, her fingers gripping his shirt. "Jake," she sniffles, "you stay forever?"

Jake smiles, kissing her head. "Forever and ever."

Noah, who's been watching quietly, suddenly speaks up. "You should just marry Mum, Jake." He says it so matter-of-factly, like it's the simplest solution in the world.

I freeze, eyes widening as the air shifts, tension dissolving into amusement. Noah looks completely oblivious to the weight of his words, but I feel them settle deep, pressing into my ribs like a truth I wasn't ready to hear out loud.

Jake's slow grin spreads across his face as he meets my eyes. There's a teasing glint, but beneath it, something steadier. Like a promise.

"Oh, don't worry bud, I've got plans."

A breathy laugh escapes me, shaking loose some of the pressure still gripping my chest. I make my way back to the kitchen, leaning against the counter, calming the aftershocks of adrenaline in my veins.

Less than a minute later, Jake's hands find me. One sliding to the small of my back, the other curling around my hip. His touch is grounding, like reassurance wrapped in warmth.

"You okay?"

"More than okay." I let him see the mischief flicker in my eyes. "That was hot as hell."

Jake raises an eyebrow. "Yeah? The doorframe, or me telling him off?"

I press my lips together, tilting my head. "All of it," I whisper. "But I think the doorframe's going to need some attention."

His grin turns wicked, lips brushing my ear. "I don't think that's the only thing that needs some attention..."

I glance toward the living room, where the kids are still engrossed in cartoons. "Jake, the kids are right there."

He hums against my neck, lips teasing against my skin. "Cartoons are on. We've got a good ten minutes."

Before I can respond, his mouth is on mine, claiming me with a hunger that's been burning below the surface since Alex arrived at the door. The kiss is rougher than usual, laced with everything he's been holding back—the frustration, the protectiveness, the need to remind exactly where I belong.

He fists a hand in my hair, tilting my head back as the kiss deepens. My pulse pounds as he presses into me like he's trying to erase the last hour, replace it with something better that belongs to just us.

"I'm thinking," he murmurs against my lips, "we lock the door, turn up the cartoons, and see if we can break another door frame."

I huff out a laugh, tipping my head back as his mouth trails along my collarbone. "You're impossible."

"And you love it." His hands slide lower, curving possessively around my hip and sending a delicious ache right through me.

Brushing my lips against his, my voice is barely a whisper. "Nah... I love *you*."

CHAPTER FORTY-EIGHT

LOVING HIM IS THE EASIEST THING I'VE EVER DONE

———————✦———————

Charlie - 3 Months Later

Glenwood Springs lies quiet, nestled between the towering Rockies and the steady rush of the Colorado River, its streets framed by the fresh green of spring. It feels worlds away from Denver, from the whirlwind of our busy city lives.

As we pull up to the house, a flutter of nerves settles in my chest. Meeting Jake's mom isn't just about saying hello, it's about stepping into a part of his world he keeps carefully guarded. It feels like a privilege to visit this small town that holds pieces of Jake I've yet to know.

This is a gamble, but it's something I haven't been able to stop thinking about since the Storm made the postseason. Now, with the team heading into the final game of the championship series, I have to give this a try—surprising him with his mom at the game. After everything we've been through, he deserves this moment, surrounded by everyone who matters.

Noah's been asking a million questions, and even Meadow is bouncing in her seat, clutching her stuffed unicorn.

I turn to them before we get out of the car, raising an eyebrow. "Remember, best behavior, okay?"

Noah nods seriously, while Meadow just giggles. "Okay, Mama!"

As we approach the door, I take a deep breath and knock gently. Noah and Meadow chatter excitedly behind me. Noah's been telling Meadow all about the Stanley Cup, trying to explain how big it is.

"It's the biggest thing in hockey," he says, eyes wide. "Jake could win it all."

Meadow however, is more focused on her new sparkly shoes. "Jake's gonna win, and I'm gonna show him my shoes when he does."

I can't help but smile at their excitement, but a pang of gratitude hits me, one I've been carrying for months. It's been quiet since Alex's last stunt. True to form, he never followed through on his custody threats. Once he realized Jake and I were united and that Noah's incident had been documented, he must have seen it for what it was: a losing battle.

Since then, he's only made sporadic efforts to see the kids when he's in town, and while I've kept the door open for him, he's done little more than keep it cracked. I'll never stop wanting more for them, but I can't force him to step up. What matters is that we're finally free to live our lives without Alex's shadow darkening our happiness.

The door opens, and Alison Brooks stands there, her mouth forming a perfect 'o' of surprise. She's smaller than I expected, with a quiet, understated elegance. Jake's always said she keeps to herself, but her eyes soften the moment they land on the kids.

"Mrs. Brooks?" I offer her a warm smile. "I'm Charlie, and this is Noah and Meadow. I hope it's okay that we've come to visit."

For a second, she just stands there, then her eyes soften further. "Jake's Charlie," she says quietly.

"I know it's probably a surprise," I say. "But I've heard a lot about you, and I thought... maybe it's time we met."

There's a brief pause, then she opens the door a little wider.

"Please, call me Alison," she says, stepping aside. "Jake's told me about you. All of you." Her eyes flick to the kids again with a faint smile. "I've been hearing a lot about you two, especially."

The kids bound inside, eager to explore, while I follow more slowly, watching Alison closely. She leads us into a warm, tastefully decorated living room. It's not what I expected based on Jake's stories. He's clearly been taking care of her—the space feels like him in some ways: calm, tidy, everything in its place. But there are added comforts, the kind of room that invites you to sink in and stay a while.

"Can I get you something to drink?" she asks hesitantly, unsure of what to do with the sudden energy filling her quiet home.

"Water's fine, thanks," I say, sitting on the couch.

Alison brings over a tray with water, tea, and juice boxes for the kids. Noah and Meadow settle in quickly, pulling out their toys. Within minutes, Meadow takes a seat at Alison's feet, gazing up at her with wide eyes.

"Do you like unicorns?" She holds up her stuffed animal.

Alison's lips quirk into a small smile. "I think they're magical."

Meadow beams. "Jake got her for me. She's my favorite."

Her eyes soften further, and I see the emotion beneath them. She watches Meadow for a long moment, then glances at Noah, quietly fiddling with his action figures.

"You have beautiful children," she says softly, her voice tinged with wistfulness. "They remind me of Jake when he was little."

"They adore Jake," I reply, smiling.

Alison nods. "He's always been good with kids," she says. "I always thought if things had been different... maybe I'd have done better with him when he was their age."

I blink, surprised by the vulnerability in her words. There's a quiet weight she's carried for a long time.

"You raised a good man, Alison," I say firmly. "He's one of the best."

Alison's eyes remain distant as she watches the kids. "He's always had a big heart, even when he didn't show it. When he came back from camp all those years ago, I could tell something had changed. He mentioned you... briefly, of course. He was always careful about his feelings."

The memory catches me off guard, and I smile softly. "That summer meant a lot to both of us."

She looks at me, her eyes so reminiscent of Jake's as they roam over my face. "Jake's told me all about you," she says quietly. "He speaks about you often. He clearly loves you very much, Charlie."

My throat bobs. It's one thing to feel Jake's love; it's another to hear it from someone else, especially his mom.

"Jake's brought us together," I say softly. "We've built a life with him, and he's made us whole."

Alison smiles, but there's a hint of sadness. "He deserves that. He's always deserved that." Her gaze drifts to Noah, flipping through a book on the table. "When he came back from camp, there was something different about him. For a while, he seemed calmer. Sadder, but in a thoughtful way. Like he'd met someone who made him see things differently."

My heart skips at her words. It's strange to think Jake was changed by that summer as much as I was.

"Of course, it didn't last," Alison continues with a soft sigh. "He was drafted not long after, and everything swallowed him up—the fame, the pressure. I watched him get caught in it all, and I... I wasn't there for him like I should have been."

I reach out, gently placing my hand over hers. "You're here now. That's what matters."

Alison looks at me, her eyes watery, and she nods. "I suppose so. I just wish I could go back and fix things."

Before I can respond, Meadow climbs onto the couch, snuggling into my side. Alison watches her, a wistful smile tugging at her lips.

"She's got Jake wrapped around her little finger, doesn't she?" Alison's voice is lighter now, almost amused.

I laugh. "Completely. He can't say no to her, even when he tries."

Alison chuckles warmly. "I can imagine. Jake's always been a softie, deep down."

There's a pause, filled only with the kids' noises as they play. I glance at Alison, sensing an opening.

"I know it's a lot to ask," I begin gently, "but Jake's about to play in the Stanley Cup Final, and I know he'd love to have you there."

Alison's eyes widen slightly, and she shifts in her seat. "The Stanley Cup..."

"It's a big deal," I continue, my voice calm. "It could be Jake's last shot. I know it would mean the world to him if you were there."

She remains quiet. I can see the hesitation, but also the resolve slowly forming. "I don't know if I'd be any good at a big event like that," she says with uncertainty.

"You wouldn't be alone," I reassure her. "You could stay with us. The kids would love to spend time with their grandma."

Alison's eyes widen at that name, but she doesn't protest. And I have no doubt she deserves that title.

"And," I smile, "I've got your mother's brownie recipe—I'll make some while you're with us."

She blinks. "Jake gave you that recipe?"

I nod. "On the last day of camp. He said it was the best thing his grandma ever made."

She lets out a soft laugh, her eyes misting over. "I always thought he'd forgotten those little things."

"No." I shake my head, squeezing her hand. "He hasn't forgotten. He's proud of you, Alison. He talks about the things that matter to him. *You* matter to him."

Her eyes brim with tears as she nods, her decision made. "I'll come," she whispers. "I'll be there."

I squeeze her hand again, relief and joy swelling in my chest. "He's going to be so happy. And I'll take care of everything. You won't have to worry."

Alison smiles through her tears and reaches out to embrace me. "Thank you," she whispers. "Thank you for loving my boy."

I hug her back, feeling the warmth of her words wrap around me. "Loving him is the easiest thing I've ever done."

When we pull back, the kids are watching us, wide-eyed. Meadow leans into Alison for a cuddle, and Noah sits down next to her, eager to hear what Jake was like at his age.

Alison's face lights up as she starts telling them stories, her voice soft but filled with affection. I sit back, watching them, my heart full. I know this moment will mean everything to Jake.

He'll have his mom there. For the first time in his career, he'll have everyone he loves cheering him on.

CHAPTER FORTY-NINE
BEST DEAL I'VE EVER MADE

———————— ✦ ————————

Jake

I'm staring at the ceiling of my condo, trying to force myself to sleep, but my mind's racing. Charlie. It's always her. Even tonight, the night before the biggest game of my life, she's the one thing I can't stop thinking about.

She's at home with the kids, probably getting them ready for bed, while I'm here trying to do the 'focus on the game' routine that's been drilled into me since day one. Usually I can tune everything else out, but tonight, nothing works.

This isn't just any game—it's the Stanley Cup Final. The thing I've been chasing my entire career. I should be dialed in, laser-focused. Instead, all I want is to be with them.

I spent years in this place chasing nothing but wins, nothing but the next high of a game. But now, there's more on the line. It's not just for me anymore. I'm not skating for some contract extension, some headline. I'm skating for them, for my family.

My phone buzzes on the nightstand, and the second I see her name light up the screen, my whole body relaxes. I grab it, not even trying to hide the smile in my voice.

"Hey, Lady Lightning."

Her soft laugh is all it takes to ease some of the tension clawing at me. "Hey, Captain Thunder. How's the pre-game routine going?"

I exhale, rolling onto my side. "I wanna be with you. This shit's driving me crazy."

"I know," she says, her voice a gentle balm. "But you've got this. Tomorrow's *everything* you've worked for. I'm so proud of you."

"I don't care about that," I mutter, half-joking. "I just wanna come home."

She scoffs, and I can almost see her shaking her head. "Now I *know* you've lost it. You care, Jake. You've poured your whole life into this. And we'll all be there tomorrow, cheering you on."

"I know. It's just hard not having you next to me." I pause, my voice dropping. "I miss you."

"I miss you too," she whispers. "But just think, after you win we'll celebrate properly."

The idea of celebrating with her... yeah, that's something I can focus on. "How are we celebrating, exactly?"

Her soft laugh has me beaming in the dark. "Focus on the game, Brooks. Then we'll discuss."

I smile, imagining her sitting on the couch, a grin tugging at her lips. "Fine. Tell Noah and Meadow I love them, okay?"

"Already have. And Jake... we'll be there, right behind you."

"I love you," I say, wishing more than anything I could reach through the phone and pull her close.

"Love you, too," she whispers before hanging up.

I stare at the phone in my hand for a long moment before setting it back on the nightstand. Somehow just hearing her voice has calmed me, like she's the one thing keeping me grounded in all this chaos.

***

Game day is a blur. The energy in the rink is a living thing, crackling through the air. Everything—the crowd, the noise, the weight of what's on the line—it's all turned up to eleven. This is the biggest game of my life, and everyone knows it.

We're up against New Jersey, and they're not going to make it easy. They never do. We've been battling them through the Stanley Cup Final series, going toe to toe. Tonight will be no different.

As we skate out for warm-ups, the place is packed, the roar of the crowd vibrating through my bones. Normally, I can block it all out. Focus on the ice. But tonight feels different. Something's pulling at me. Something huge. Everything's on the line.

I go through my routine, stretching, skating, firing a few shots at the net, but my mind drifts back to Charlie, to the kids. To that quiet phone call the night before when all I wanted was to be with her.

Every time I hit the ice, I tell myself it's just another game. Just another battle. But I can't fool myself anymore. This isn't just another win. This is everything. Every inch I skate, every hit I take, it's not for the Cup—it's for them. For Charlie, for Noah, for Meadow, for the family that made me whole again.

Focus, Brooks.

When the anthem starts, I do what I always do—sweep the crowd, looking for Charlie, Noah, and Meadow. I expect to see them up in the WAGs box with Zoe, Claire, Tamara, and the rest of the crew.

But when I look up, my heart stops.

My mom.

She's never been to one of my games. All these years, she's stayed away. Too anxious. Too fragile. The excuses were always there, always lingering in the background, a weight I carried with me through every game, every season.

She's sitting *right there.*

I blink, convinced I'm imagining it. But there she is—my mom, holding Meadow on her lap, with Noah sitting right next to them in his Storm jersey. And Charlie's sitting close, holding my mom's hand like they've been family for years.

I can't breathe.

My throat goes dry, and I fight the heat behind my eyes. My *mom.* Who's never watched me play in person, is sitting with the people I love most, holding my little princess on her knee. The sight knocks the breath out of me.

I'm fucking wrecked.

392

I swallow down the emotion threatening to spill over. There's no time for this. Not now. I need to focus. One last game. One last win. And then I'll have them all in my arms.

The game starts, and it's a dogfight. New Jersey comes at us hard, crashing the net, throwing hits like they've got nothing to lose. Every shift feels like a war. The hits are harder, the plays faster, and the pressure heavier than anything I've ever felt before.

First period—it's a bloodbath. They're in our faces every time we touch the puck. I take a hard hit into the boards, the impact rattling my teeth, but I shake it off and keep skating. I give as good as I get, dropping my shoulder into one of their defensemen, sending him sprawling into the boards. The crowd roars, and adrenaline surges through me.

But New Jersey isn't backing down. They play dirty, and before long, tensions boil over.

Midway through the second period, I'm digging in deep behind the net, fighting for control when one of their enforcers slams into me from behind. My face hits the ice, and a sharp sting shoots through my jaw. I see red.

I push up, swing around, and drop gloves without a second thought. The crowd is on its feet, screaming. I'm in his face, fists flying before I even register the pain in my knuckles. He takes a couple of swings, but I don't stop. I can hear the boys banging their sticks on the boards, the arena vibrating with the noise.

A punch lands on my cheek, but it only fuels me. I grab his jersey, yank him in and throw another right hook. He stumbles, and I take him down to the ice with me. The ref blows the whistle, breaking it up, but by then the damage is done. I feel the blood dripping from a cut over my eyebrow, my chest heaving as I skate to the penalty box.

The crowd's going wild. Even through the haze of adrenaline, I can see my teammates grinning at me from the bench. My blood's still pumping, my heart racing like I'm in a damn war zone. But this is our game. I can feel it.

By the third period, we're tied 2-2. Every muscle in my body is screaming, but I'm not stopping. We're so close. New Jersey is playing like they've got nothing left to lose, and I'm grinding it out on every shift, battling for every puck like it's the last one I'll ever touch. We're running on fumes, but no one's backing down.

Five minutes left. We get a power play, and I can feel the momentum shifting. The puck slides to me, and without thinking, I fire it. Top corner. Net.

The horn blares. 3-2. The arena erupts, the noise deafening. My teammates pile on me, shouting, banging helmets, but I know it's not over yet. There's still time on the clock and New Jersey's not done fighting.

They pull their goalie with two minutes left. The pressure is suffocating. Every second drags out like an eternity. My legs are burning, my body screaming for rest, but I block another shot, throwing myself in front of the puck like it's all I know how to do. Desperation is fueling me now. Desperation to hold the line. Desperation to win.

Fifty seconds. Forty. Thirty. The puck's flying everywhere, ricocheting off the boards, the net, bodies. Everything's a blur.

Then, with ten seconds left, New Jersey gets one last rush. One of their forwards breaks free and comes flying toward our net. I'm already moving, my legs on fire, heart pounding in my chest. I get in front of him just as he winds up for a shot, and I throw myself in the way. The puck hits my shin pad, and pain explodes up my leg. I don't even feel the ice as I hit it, my body going numb from the collision.

But the final horn pierces the air, and everything stops. For a second, there's just ringing in my ears, and then—mayhem. We've done it.

We've won.

We've fucking won the Stanley Cup.

The arena explodes around us, my teammates screaming, throwing their gloves and sticks into the air. I barely register the chaos as they pile on top of me, all of us crashing to the ice in a heap of relief and triumph. All I can feel is the weight of it. The years, the sacrifices, the endless nights, all leading to this moment. We've fucking done it.

It's chaos—beautiful, euphoric chaos.

But even in the middle of all the madness, there's only one thing I'm thinking about.

I need to get to them.

I barely wait for the cup to be handed off to Ryan before I'm peeling away from the crowd, my skates carving into the ice as I head straight for the WAGs box. I don't care about the cameras, the media, or the fans.

When I reach it, skates sliding on the polished floor, the first thing I see is her. My mom. She's standing now, holding onto the rail as Charlie helps her, and I'm there in two strides, pulling her into the tightest hug of my life.

I lose it.

"Mom," I choke out, face buried in her shoulder. "You're here."

She holds me tight, her voice full of love. "I'm here, Jake. I didn't want to miss this."

I pull back, staring at her, and the weight of all those years she wasn't there lifts in an instant. "I can't believe you're here."

She smiles, her own eyes wet. "Charlie made sure of it. She wanted to make this moment perfect for you."

Charlie. I turn to her, and I'm wrecked all over again. She's watching us, her eyes full of love, and I can barely hold myself together.

"You did this," I say, my voice a rasp of emotion. "You brought her here."

Charlie nods, swiping away a tear. "Surprise."

I don't even think. I pull her in, cradling her face and pressing hard kisses all over it. Not caring about who's watching, not caring about anything but her.

I pour everything into the kiss—all the love, the gratitude, the sheer disbelief that this woman, who I almost lost years ago, is now the reason my life feels complete.

"You have no idea how much I love you," I whisper against her lips.

"Brooks! You planning on missing your own Stanley Cup celebration?" Coach's voice cuts through the moment.

I grin, holding Charlie close. "Gimme a minute, Coach. Just making sure my number one fans are looked after."

Coach shakes his head in exasperation but I can see the amusement in his eyes. "You've got thirty seconds, Brooks. Then I want you back on the ice. You've got a Cup to lift."

I pull Charlie in for one last kiss, murmuring against her lips, "You coming down later?"

"Of course. We'll be right behind you."

Coach clears his throat again, louder this time. "Tick-tock, Brooks."

I smirk and ignore him, lost in the warmth of the moment.

"You don't need to stay up here with me," my mom says gently. "Go with Jake, Charlie. Take the kids."

Charlie hesitates, but Meadow tugs her hand. "Yeah, I wanna go with Dada!"

"I'll be just fine." My mom waves a hand, her eyes twinkling with amusement. "Besides, this is his moment. He wants his family down there with him."

I glance over at my mom, feeling a surge of emotion at her words. Family. My family.

"Can we go, pleeease?" Noah pipes up.

Charlie looks from the kids to me, then back at my mom. "Alright. Let's go."

I can't wipe the grin off my face as I scoop up Meadow, Noah trailing behind, Charlie's hand in mine.

As we reach the rink, the chaos of the celebration swallows us—but all I can focus on is the fact that my family is with me. The love of my life and the kids I love like my own. This is what matters.

I let Meadow down to join Noah, and they immediately run toward the boards, wide-eyed with excitement.

Before Charlie can say anything, I pull her in close. "I love you, Charlie. You and the kids—you're everything."

She smiles back with that teasing glint in her eyes. "We know. Now go lift that Cup, Brooks."

I skate back out to the ice, and everything's a blur. The guys are hugging, shouting, celebrating like crazy. Then the Cup is in my hands. The weight of it is nothing compared to the way my heart feels, full and alive. I lift it high above my head, the roar of the crowd deafening.

As I skate back over to Charlie, I pull her into my arms and kiss her, still trying to wrap my head around the fact that she did this for me. She brought my mom here. She's given me everything I've ever wanted.

"You brought my mom," I whisper in between kisses. "And we won the damn Cup."

Charlie laughs, her eyes shining with tears. "You deserve it all, Jake."

I rest my forehead against hers, everything in me raw and vulnerable. "You know I'm gonna marry the shit out of you, right?"

"You better," she teases. "But maybe when you're a bit less stinky."

I chuckle, lifting my hand to curl my pinky around hers. "Let's seal the deal then."

She laughs softly. "Deal."

We lean in at the same time, our thumbs pressed together, and I kiss mine lightly, feeling her lips graze the other side. My heart skips a beat, just like it did all those years ago, but this time I don't hesitate.

I capture her lips with mine, cupping the back of her neck and dipping her low. She's the girl I let slip through my fingers all those years ago, and now she's the woman I'll spend the rest of my life with.

When I pull back, her eyes are a little misty. "That's one hell of a deal, Captain Thunder."

"Best deal I've ever made, Lady Lightning."

Before I can even take a breath, I hear Chase's voice booming from behind me. "Zoe, baby! You gonna kiss me like that, too?"

She rolls her eyes but her grin is wide from celebrating. "In your dreams, Walton!" she calls back, but before she can step away, Chase skates up and sweeps her into his arms, spinning her around as she yelps in surprise.

Zoe shoves him, laughing despite herself. "Put me down, you sweaty idiot!"

Chase smirks, not budging an inch. "Will you let me take you on a date now that I'm a Stanley Cup champion?" He leans in, waggling his eyebrows. "I'll even let you touch it."

Zoe snorts, catching his double meaning, still squirming in his arms. "Not a chance in hell."

He finally sets her down, smile widening as she straightens her clothes and turns on her heel. "The offer's still on the table, you know!" he calls after her, voice still teasing as she flicks her hair.

Zoe shoots him a look over her shoulder, but the curl of her lips deceives her. "Keep dreaming, bud!"

Chase watches her walk off, grinning like a fool, like he's just won something bigger than the Cup.

The world continues to spin around us with the cheers of my teammates, the flashing of cameras, but none of it matters. I stand there with my arms wrapped around the love of my life, surrounded by our family as the world celebrates around us. And in this moment, I know—this is the real win.

Not the Cup, not the fame.

This. Them. Us.

It's everything.

EPILOGUE

---·✦·---

I'M GLAD YOU SAID YES

Jake – 6 months later

"You ready?" I ask, crouching beside the kids. We're perched behind a tree, and their excitement is vibrating through the air.

Charlie's down by the lake, collecting flat stones Noah asked her to help find for stone skipping. She's oblivious, completely caught up in the moment of being back at this place.

Noah nods, his little face serious. "You think she'll cry?"

"Probably," I chuckle, ruffling his hair.

"Good," he says firmly, like he's decided this is the appropriate response. "But happy tears only, right?"

"Only the happiest," I promise.

Meadow, clutching her unicorn, looks up at me with wide eyes. "Do I say the pinky thing now or later?"

"Later." I brush a kiss to the top of her head. "When I kneel, you kneel. Just like we practiced."

Her little feet bounce, too much excitement to hold still. "Mama's gonna love this!"

"She will," I say, the words catching in my throat. "Because we're showing her just how much we all love her."

I glance back at the hill, the blanket spread out right at the top where we stayed up all night talking thirteen years ago. The candles flicker in the dusk, and the peach-hued sunset stretches out over the horizon, painting everything in a golden light. It's perfect.

"Should we go get her now?" Noah's all business.

"Give me a five-minute head start, then I'll meet you guys at the top."

They nod excitedly and rush off toward the lake, their laughter trailing behind them.

As I make my way back up the hill, heart hammering, my foot catches on a rock. "Shit," I yelp, stumbling but managing to catch myself.

I pause at the top, taking a deep breath, letting the view wash over me. The camp hasn't changed much, but the weight of time feels heavy. This is it. This is everything I've ever wanted, everything I didn't think I'd get to have. Charlie, the kids, this messy, chaotic, beautiful life we've built. It's not just that I love her—it's that I can't imagine a life without her.

The crunch of footsteps on the trail pulls me from my thoughts. Meadow skips ahead, twirling as she reaches the top, while Noah drags Charlie along, her voice floating up in protest.

"Noah, slow down! What's the rush?"

"Come on, Mum!" Noah says, his hand tugging hers insistently.

Charlie looks up, her steps faltering as her eyes land on me. I'm standing at the edge of the blanket, hands shoved in my pockets to keep from reaching for her too soon.

"What..." she whispers, her voice barely carrying across the space.

"Hey, Charlie girl," I reply, swallowing hard. "Come here."

Her lips part, confusion giving way to something softer, like she knows what's coming but doesn't quite believe it. She takes a hesitant step closer, caught between disbelief and quiet knowing.

"What's all this?" Her gaze sweeps over the kids, the candles, the blanket, and finally lands back on me.

"It's us," I reply, stepping toward her. "It's where we started. And it's where I want to start the rest of my life with you."

I hear the faintest intake of breath, her lips moving as though she wants to speak, but nothing comes out.

Dropping to one knee, Noah and Meadow rush to join me as I pull out the ring box. I can see the realization dawning in her eyes as she takes it all in, her hand trembling as she brings it to her chest.

"And just in case you're thinking of saying no," I add with a nod to the kids now kneeling beside me, "I have reinforcements."

A breathy noise escapes her, somewhere between a laugh and a sob, and I'm a goner. I've got to get the words out before she completely wrecks me.

"I've been waiting for this moment for a long time," I begin, voice husky. "Thirteen years ago, under this same sky, you changed my life." I pause, willing myself to keep it together as I look into her tear-filled eyes. "Charlie, you're everything. You're my home, my best friend, my family. My whole night sky. You've shown me what it means to truly be loved, the best bits and the messy bits, and I'll spend every day loving this beautiful life you've given me."

I glance down at Noah, giving him a small nod. I'd asked both the kids if they'd help me with this, but I have no idea what they're planning on saying. His little face is serious as he steps forward, but his voice trembles with emotion.

"Mum," he says, his gaze flicking between us. "Jake's... Jake's the best. He takes care of us and makes us laugh and happy. And I... I really want him to be our dad. He told me he promises to love us forever."

The words slam into me, and I barely manage to hold it together. Noah's never said anything like this before, and it's a wrecking ball to my chest. Nothing in my life compares to this moment, to hearing him say he wants me as his dad. That he's choosing me, believes in me. Trusts me to prove it. And I fucking will, every single day.

Charlie's expression shatters like glass, her hand moving to cover her mouth. Tears streak down her face, and I'm right there with her, floored by this seven-year-old who's taken my heart and smashed it to pieces in the best way. I'd die for this kid, for all of them.

"And me too!" Meadow chirps, jumping up from beside me.

She steps forward, clutching her little hand into a tight fist before holding up her pinky finger. She looks at her mom with such fierce sincerity, her voice clear but tender as she says, "Will you promise, too?"

Charlie stares at Meadow's outstretched little pinky like it holds the weight of everything we've been through, everything we've become. When her gaze lifts back to mine, it's filled with all-encompassing love, the kind of look I'd chase through every lifetime.

Choking out a laugh-sob, she kneels down to hook her pinky with Meadow's, tears falling freely. "Yes, honey bee. I promise."

Meadow grins, beaming at Charlie before pressing her thumb firmly against her mom's, sealing the deal in the way only she can. Charlie pulls Meadow into a tight hug, her eyes darting between me and Noah over her shoulder. The tears keep rolling, and a soft laugh escapes her.

I reach out, tilting her chin up gently, catching her gaze. Her eyes are shining, cheeks streaked with tears, and my breath hitches for a moment as I collect myself.

"Say yes, Charlie girl," I whisper. "Marry me, and let me love you all forever."

I open the ring box, the delicate gold band and large solitaire diamond glinting in the candlelight. The inscription inside reads: *You're the dream.*

Her gaze moves from the ring to the kids, to me, and back again. Her lips tremble, and for a second, my heart stops.

"Yes," she breathes, voice cracking. "Of course."

I try to hold back my own sob as I slip the ring onto her finger, my hands shaking as I do. The kids cheer, and I barely have time to react before Charlie throws her arms around me, her lips crashing against mine.

When I pull back, I cup her face, brushing away her tears with my thumbs. "You're gonna be my wife, Lady Lightning."

"About time, Captain Thunder," she replies, a smile breaking through the tears.

I kiss her again, my lips slowly moving over hers as I clasp her face, committing this moment to memory.

"Ewww," Noah mutters, making Meadow giggle.

Charlie laughs against my lips, pulling back to glance down at the ring. Her eyes widen as she holds up her hand, blinking at the diamond.

"Jake," she says, her voice filled with mock disbelief. "This... this is—" She lets out a breathless laugh. "You're pushin' it, Brooks."

I grin unapologetically, secretly loving I have a huge adornment on her that makes her mine. "Blame Zoe. She said, 'go big or go home.'"

"Of course she did. This thing's gonna need its own security detail!"

I reach for her hand to link our pinkies together before bringing our joined hands to my lips. "Then it's in good hands."

Her eyes soften as they lock onto mine, and in that single look I see every laugh, every tear, every moment that has led us here. All the love we've built together.

"I love you," she whispers, pulling me close again.

"Forever."

GRANDMA BROOKS' BROWNIES

Perfectly fudgy brownies with a little kick of coffee, just the way Jake likes them.

Ingredients:

1 cup (230g) unsalted butter
1 cup (200g) granulated sugar
1 cup (200g) brown sugar
1/3 cup (80ml) strong brewed coffee (cooled)
3 large eggs
1 tsp vanilla extract
2/3 cup (80g) unsweetened cocoa powder
3/4 cup (95g) all-purpose flour
1/2 tsp salt
3/4 cup (135g) chocolate chips (optional, but Jake insists they're not)

Method:

Preheat oven to 350°F (175°C) and grease an 8x8-inch baking pan.

Melt butter in a saucepan or microwave. Stir in both sugars and coffee until smooth, then whisk in eggs and vanilla.

Sift in cocoa powder, flour, and salt. Gently fold (IYKYK) until just combined. Stir in chocolate chips if using (Jake will complain if you don't!).

Pour batter into the prepared pan and bake for 25-30 minutes, or until a toothpick comes out with moist crumbs (not wet batter).

Cool, slice, and enjoy—preferably with someone who thinks you're the eighth wonder of the world.

ACKNOWLEDGEMENTS
INSERT OSCAR SPEECH HERE

Writing a book turned out to be much more than typing out an idea—who knew? (Not me.) It's been a journey of diabolical hours, endless rewrites, and extra admin I knew nothing about. But I've been lucky to have the love and support of so many incredible people.

To my husband: thank you for putting up with my late nights, long days, and for letting me dream big. The patience, love, and joy that you have held for me means I've not only done something I never thought I'd be able to, but in the process have shown our babies it's okay to have big and unique dreams. You're my favorite person in the world to raise our two favorite people in the world with. Love you forever.

To my besties: Nomi, Michelle, and Becky—thank you for being my alpha readers, cheerleaders, and reality-checkers. You told me I could, and I would, and here I am because of you. I love you all so much.

To my beta readers & editor, Gabby: thank you for helping me hone this story to what it is today. Your insight and enthusiasm has been invaluable.

To my author pals: Brit, Landyn, Rachae and The Diamond Dolls—you were dropped into my life by the universe itself. I'm endlessly thankful for you. You've made this journey so much brighter, and I love you all.

To Marge at Caravelle Creates: thank you for designing a cover I absolutely adore. You took my endless list of notes and made my vision a reality.

To my incredible street team: your excitement and hype have meant everything to me. Thank you for always being ready to scream about Seal The Deal!

And to every single person who picks up this book: thank you for taking a chance on Jake and Charlie's story. You've made this dream come true.

About Hailey Rodger

The page where I write about myself in third person

Hailey Rodger writes swoony, spicy romances filled with heart, heat, and humor for readers who love protective heroes, fun banter, and the kind of love that lingers long after the last page. With her Colorado Storm series, she's found herself firmly in the world of sports romance, and she's having way too much fun to leave anytime soon.

A lifelong lover of words, Hailey has been crafting stories since she wrote fanfic novels for her friends during math class many moons ago. Storytelling isn't just something she does, it's something she can't imagine living without.

When she's not writing, you'll find her drinking unreasonable amounts of coffee, stress-Googling absurd things for her books (or watching hockey for "research purposes"), and side-eyeing her TBR pile as it threatens to topple over. She firmly believes fictional men make the best emotional support characters and will absolutely die on this hill.

Visit www.haileyrodger.com
or find her on Instagram and Threads: @haileyrodgerwrites